Praise for John Mackie
and
Manhattan North

"Fans of Mackie's debut, *Manhattan South*, will be pleased to note that NYPD Det. Sgt. Thornton Savage, the larger-than-life protagonist of this high-intensity police procedural, hasn't lost his hard edge or his renegade impulses. . . . [The] relentless pacing and spine-chilling suspense will keep readers on their toes." —*Publishers Weekly*

Manhattan South

"Retired NYPD Detective Mackie captures the character of Manhattan in his gripping debut novel, the first in a series featuring Detective Thornton Savage and his homicide task force. . . . Mackie writes with authority and presents a street-wise protagonist that readers will welcome." —*Publishers Weekly*

"*Manhattan South* is not only a terrific read, it's the real deal. Mackie was a cop's cop; now he's a writer's writer."
—Bernard Kerik, former NYPD Commissioner and *New York Times* bestselling author of *The Lost Sons*

continued . . .

ALSO BY JOHN MACKIE

East Side
Manhattan North
Manhattan South

Published by Onyx

For Bonnie

ACKNOWLEDGMENTS

My thanks to Suzanne Mather and Sharon Townley for their tireless efforts in easing the arduous, sometimes painful, processes of writing. They continue to be so generous with their time, knowledge, and encouragement. For his invaluable assistance on technical matters—and his great insights into the investigative function—a very special thanks to my good friend Lieutenant Jon R. Perkins of the Glendale (California) Police Department, truly a cop's cop. I would also like to thank Brent Howard, my enthusiastic and skillful editor at New American Library, for his steadfast belief in my work.

ONE

R. Charles Janus, M.D., magna cum laude graduate of Dartmouth Medical, fellow of the American Academy of Neurology—and longtime closet homosexual—had spent the waning minutes of Memorial Day slowly cruising his pearlescent gray Jag past the doors of the remaining gay bars that still dotted the dimly lit side streets and avenues of West Chelsea.

With longtime associate George Granger occupying the passenger seat beside him, Janus was in search of a single solitary gay man. Not just any gay man, but a very special gay man, one who would be perfect for the all-important role he would have to play tonight. But they were having little luck; the pickings were unusually slim. It dawned on Janus that a lot of the action had probably gone off to Fire Island this weekend, to welcome the start of a new season at summer places and beach houses in the gay enclaves of the Pines or Cherry Grove. Stopping the XJ8 for a red light on Fourteenth Street at Tenth Avenue, he thought about how the epicenter of gay nightlife on the West Side of New York City had shifted around in the last twenty years.

Time was when the whole waterfront area just below Chelsea—on the far western edge of Greenwich Village—used to be teeming with gay sex clubs. He remembered being able to step out of one and turn immediately into another. It had been, as he had always called it, a cornucopia of copulation. But, one by one, all of those buildings had been gobbled up by the wealthy and converted into million-dollar luxury loft residences. The blue bloods who invested that kind of money didn't want to step out of their front door to find a naughty S&M club across the street, or a raunchy bar full of flaming faggots down the block, so they all had to go. He also thought how most people would think that it was the AIDS thing that drew the curtain on all those hot places along the waterfront, but he knew different. There'd been lots of new construction south of Thirteenth Street, gentrification, to say nothing of the incredible political pressure from the old Giuliani administration.

When the light finally switched to green, he steered the Jaguar uptown on Tenth and resumed the search. Passing Sixteenth Street, Janus slowed almost to a stop to carefully eyeball a pair of broad-chested, tight-jeaned cowboy types making their way from bar to bar on the warm spring holiday night.

"What do you think?" he said.

Exhaling a plume of cigarette smoke, Granger replied simply, "Nah."

Normally Janus would have ignored the cowboy type. His taste ran more to the intimidating leatherboys—preferably threesomes, foursomes, and moresomes. Their ranks contained a far greater ratio of souls who shared his fundamental association of pleasure with pain. But tonight's needs were different, tonight it was business, *all business,* and a leather-boy type would not fill the bill. Tonight they needed something . . . softer.

George Granger, a slender, almost bony man whose gray-streaked brown hair was giving way to male-pattern baldness, again brought the burning cigarette to his narrow lips and sucked in another deep drag.

"I can't believe the waterfront clubs have all been wiped out," he said, allowing the smoke to exhale in staggered bursts. "The Hellfire, the Glory Hole, the Ramrod . . ."

"Long gone, my friend," Janus responded, shaking

his head. "You've been away from our fair city far too long." He lowered the window to let Granger's annoying smoke vent.

Janus had met George Granger ten years ago when Granger was claiming all kinds of back injuries sustained in a minor traffic accident. A classic insurance flimflam. He needed a corroborating neurological diagnosis, and for a share of the settlement, Janus had obliged. They'd been friendly ever since, had run a few more insurance scams, and had been casually intimate many times down through the years.

"Unbelievable," Granger said, sucking in yet another heavy drag of his filtered coffin nail. "This is all that's left, some low-key queen places and a few midnight cowboy joints in freakin' Chelsea?"

"That's about it, Georgie. If you want Levi's-leather-motorcycle action, there's nothing anymore from Houston all the way up to Twenty-third."

"Shit."

Janus had no delusions about George Granger. He never lost sight of the fact that Granger was surely psychotic and truly paranoid; the man saw bogeymen everywhere, and Janus strongly suspected that sometimes he probably killed them.

"It's still a damn sight better than Hicktown, USA," Janus chided, flicking on his high beams as the Jag loped along the avenue. "I know that you and John Boy both loved living here in New York, and then in San Francisco, but why did you relocate to Columbus, Ohio, of all places?"

"The whole thing was John's idea," Granger said unhappily. "He was born and raised in that jerkwater town, *and* his suffocating *mother* still lives there. Need I say more?"

Janus grimaced. *"Dear Mother Holloway,* I've spoken to her on the phone. Tough bitch. John always was a mama's boy, but why would he go back there? More importantly, how did he ever talk you into going there with him?"

"John Boy can be very charming," Granger said in

a suddenly defensive snarl, "and extremely persuasive."

"I know that," Janus replied cautiously. "Please don't take this as any disrespect to your relationship with John," he added, "but I know the man pretty well myself, and when thinking of him, several adjectives do come quickly to mind."

"Such as?"

"The man is coldly *cal-cu-la-ting,* and a *com-men-su-rate* liar," Janus said, splitting the syllables for emphasis. "And we're both putting a whole lot of faith in him on this gig."

"As if you're not capable of bending the truth," Granger said haughtily.

"I'll tell you this," Janus replied. "If John Boy intends to tell you a lie next September, he begins laying the groundwork for that goddamned lie in January. However, you're absolutely right; he's also charming and extremely persuasive. But, *Columbus*?"

"He'd gotten word from his mother about this terrific 'business opportunity' that would make both of us *very* rich. So we packed up and left San Francisco thinking that when we became fabulously wealthy we'd simply move back. Hell, I still have my California driver's license. Instead, the goddamned business has put us both in the poorhouse. We're stone broke; we owe out a damn fortune."

Janus knew all about the pair's failed athletic-clothing business, and their dire financial straits. After all, it was that, along with *his* personal money problems, that had brought them here tonight. But the pressure was on. If the plan was going to work they had to move fast; they were running out of time.

"If things go the way we've planned," Granger continued, "John Boy and I will be able to simply walk away from Columbus and that miserable damn business and all of our fucking debts . . . *and* be very rich." His tone morphing to one of mild regret, he added, "The only downside is, we will be forced to go our separate ways—for a little while at least."

"What have you both got in mind?"

"John plans to travel, sail, do his hiking and rock-climbing bit to keep his buns nice and tight, and live like the hot-blooded playboy he's always fancied himself to be."

"You?" Janus asked. "You gonna make Miami permanent?"

"I really like California," Granger said ruefully.

"You can't be thinking of going back to San Francisco," Janus said in disbelief. "There are people who know you there."

"I know that!" Granger replied, annoyed. "Right from the get-go we all knew that I would have to go someplace and start all over again. That's why I've been creating that identity down in Miami for the past few months."

"You going to stay there?"

"No," Granger said flat out. "Don't really like Miami . . . too crowded. I'm thinking I'm going to buy myself a nice place down in Key West. It's warm there year-round, and there's plenty of . . . stuff."

"I'll come and visit," Janus announced, half in jest. He turned to Granger with a lascivious glance. "You'll put me up, right?"

"I won't be putting anybody *up* if we don't find what we're looking for," Granger replied. "It's getting late. What about that Cowpokes place that we passed a few minutes ago? It seemed to be really mobbed. So did the other place, Jock's." He crushed out the bitter end of his cigarette in the dashboard ashtray, and in almost the same motion reached into his shirt pocket for the pack of Merits. He immediately lit another.

Janus smiled. "Cowpokes is the watering hole for midnight cowboys out prowling for stray . . . long-horns."

Granger laughed. "You always did have a way with words, Charles."

"Jock's, on the other hand," Janus went on, "caters to all types looking for wanton whoopee—from butchers, bakers, and candlestick makers to very well-heeled Wall Street execs."

"Isn't Jock's where you picked up that guy a few weeks ago?" Granger asked. "The one who almost had your ass arrested?"

"No," Janus snapped. He didn't need to be reminded of the clumsy failure. "Him I met in a private S&M club down off Houston. We're not likely to run into him up here."

"So what happened with him? When you got back to your office and socked it to him, why didn't the son of a bitch go down and out?"

"He wasn't drunk enough, dammit, and despite being very slight he was just a little too strong for me to handle all by myself. That's why *you're* here tonight, Georgie Boy. If you had been there, we'd already have the damn ball rolling. I'm not wrestling any more alligators all by myself. This time, with two of us, we'll get the job done."

"You know we dodged a bullet there, right?" Granger said. "If that dummy had talked the cops into arresting you for assaulting him right in your damn office, this whole project would have gone right down the dumper. All this planning would have been for nothing. And I don't have to tell you that our illustrious third partner, Mr. John Boyer Holloway, would have gone absolutely ballistic."

"I'm well aware of that," Janus again snapped, further annoyed by the second reminder. "Fortunately, when the cops found out we'd met in an S&M parlor, they simply wrote the whole thing off as a lovers' quarrel and went back to their coffee and donuts. It wasn't a problem, and it's not going to be."

"Yeah, well, this time we can't afford another fuckup. That term policy expires in five more days, and then it's all over—we're finished."

"You're sure there's absolutely no chance that they'll renew you?"

"Not a chance in hell." Granger took another long,

deep drag and slowly exhaled. "They found out I'm HIV positive."

As Janus slowly turned onto Eighteenth Street for the third time that night, a slightly built man with thinning, tousled hair, in his mid- to late thirties, suddenly staggered right into the headlights of the slow moving Jaguar.

"Look out!" Granger blurted as Janus lurched the rakish sedan to a panic stop. He missed plowing into the man by mere inches.

"Goddamned idiot," Janus snarled. "That's all I need, to run over some stupid son of a bitch. As if I don't already have enough goddamned problems."

The near miss jolted all his legal and financial worries to the front burner. His mega-successful world that had once known Rolls-Royce automobiles and huge estates was gone, completely reversed from what it had once been. Terrible investments, an incredibly expensive divorce, and several financial broadsides from malpractice-suit awards had put him on the balls of his ass and taken everything he'd ever worked for. Only a month ago, he had lost his privileges at St. Vincent's. Within the last week, the same had happened at the Hospital for Joint Diseases.

He was in debt up to his ears and had been reduced to living in a rented studio with a roommate who doubled as his office assistant. If something good didn't happen soon, if he couldn't come up with a pile of money within the next few weeks, even his leased Jag was going to get repossessed. He sighed deeply.

"Jesus," Granger muttered, firmly tapping Janus on the right forearm to get his attention. "Am I wrong, or did that guy look like a real prospect?"

"Huh?"

"I think that guy you almost hit could pass for me," Granger went on excitedly. He spun in his seat to keep an eye on the man. "Hell, he's the same general height and weight, same color hair, albeit a bit more. I'd even bet he's right around my age. What do you think?"

Janus pulled over and focused his attention on the booze-soaked fool he had almost run down. Dressed in a long-sleeved striped western shirt, well-worn jeans, and cowboy boots—and apparently oblivious to how close he'd just come to being seriously injured or killed—the man slowly negotiated the wide sidewalk and stumbled haplessly into the busy Cowpokes Saloon.

"Talk to me, already. . . . What do you think?" Granger said. His words were followed by three rapid smoky puffs. "I'm thinking he's our mark. And he certainly seems drunk enough. Jerk'd be a piece a cake."

"My, my. I think you just might be right, Georgie," Janus purred agreeably.

He smiled, accelerated the Jag through the block, and parked it off the corner of Ninth. "Put out that goddamned cigarette and let's go have us a drinkee-poo in Cowpokes. Maybe we can interest our new cowboy friend in a little one-way trip to Pleasure Island."

"With a follow-up stay at Boot Hill," Granger quipped coldly.

After paying the cover charges to the unshaven and burly would-be saddle tramp at Cowpokes' front door, R. Charles Janus and George Granger worked their way to the noisy, crowded bar. Janus ordered an extra-creamy Brandy Alexander and Granger a large Diet Coke. Taking his first sip on the smooth cocktail, Janus looked around to get his bearings, hoping to spot Mr. Right, but the blue-and-white-striped western shirt was nowhere in sight. A funky rap song with heavy bass blared from the almost overpowering sound system. He grimaced. For him, the rap crap was noise . . . static . . . aural torture, created by pseudo street thugs with a flair for sophomoric antisocial rhyme, whose audience was mostly those with IQs hovering somewhere around the moron range and below.

"Well, at least they've got a back room," Granger said, nodding toward several heavily draped portals near the rear of the bar.

"Cowpokes has several back rooms," Janus replied, whispering directly into Granger's ear. "It's where the lonesome hombres, the ones who haven't met someone interesting at the bar, can wander when they hear the call of the wild."

Granger grinned in understanding.

"In Cowpokes it's casually referred to as the Arena," Janus went on. "Inside, it's a virtual rodeo. A *dude* can try his hand at a variety of . . . events."

Granger's grin morphed to a wide smile, then he took a long pull on his soda.

"There's an open table way over there," Janus said, pointing to a four-top in the far corner of the main bar. "Why don't you go hold it down for us while I do some prospecting?"

For a long second, Granger glared back at Janus through heavily hooded, searching eyes, dissecting the innocent suggestion as if trying to discern some hidden meaning or duplicity.

"Just go," Janus directed with an annoyed sigh. *Fucking nut,* he thought.

After scanning the entire room, Granger took another pull on his Diet Coke, nodded slowly, and slipped off into the crowd.

"Hi, big guy. I'm Robert. Come here often?"

Janus turned to see that the trite query came from a short, droopy-eyed, aging screamer who had edged furtively alongside him. Dressed in skintight jeans, tan snakeskin boots, and a red neckerchief, the pale, slight man sported a brown tooled leather vest over his hairless, sunken chest. The intended roughrider image was hardly enhanced by the strawberry daiquiri held in a frail, almost feminine hand, the small 24K hoops dangling ridiculously from his nipples, or the large gold Rolex that accentuated his broomstick wrist.

"Not really," Janus replied, using his best dismissive tone.

"That's strange," Robert said, speaking loudly enough to be heard over the alleged music. "Seems I've seen you here many times before. Just last Friday night, as a matter of fact." With his manicured free hand, he fingered the sleeve of Janus' jacket. "I love your suit . . . *Valentino*?"

There was more Dale Evans than Roy Rogers to this cowboy, Janus thought. Besides, the droopy eyes were blue . . . no good. His man would be twenty years younger, have eyes of green or hazel and a thinning head of graying brown hair. Like Granger, he would be in his early to mid-forties, at least five nine but no more than six one. Unlike the aggressively amoral Granger, who had absolutely no compunction, at all, about doing ungodly things for profit, he would be the passive type, or quite drunk . . . preferably both.

Janus glared down at the ersatz drover and flashed an ugly, angry, go-away look. The little putz shrugged, rolled his eyes in a mild snit, and slipped back into the lively crowd massed at the bar. In only seconds, the little fruit fly was reengaged in conversation and fingering someone else's sleeve.

Janus leaned against a steel column in the middle of the lounge area, sipped casually at his drink, and watched the never-ending ebb and flow of horny dudes circulating, some zombielike, into and out of the busy Arena. Where the hell was Western Shirt?

Janus didn't do grope rooms anymore. Within their almost total darkness, one could never quite tell who was doing what to whom. Hell, one could wind up swapping bodily fluids with that Dale Evans creep. He shuddered at the thought.

The annoying, offensive, and pulsing rap song that seemed to go on forever finally ended. Immediately, and mercifully, it was followed with an old Judy Garland rendition of Gershwin's "The Man I Love." At that very instant Western Shirt reappeared.

Still zipping up his fly as he emerged from the restroom just off the jukebox, the man moved unsteadily through the lounge, right past Janus. His eyes were watery and blinking for focus as he searched for an open spot in the crowd, a place where he might get the bartender's attention. Reaching into his pocket, he came out with a few crumpled one-dollar bills. He wobbled and swayed while trying to count them.

Remembering the old opening chess gambit in which a player seeks to obtain some advantage by sacrificing a pawn, Janus tugged on the sleeve of the man's shirt and held out a ten-dollar bill he'd plucked from his own pocket. "I believe you just dropped this," he said.

"I did?" the man replied in a gentle voice, clearly confused.

"You sure did," Janus assured him, slowly and suggestively tucking the bill into the left front pocket of the man's faded jeans. The cowpoke did not pull away.

"Well, that's real good of you, mister," Western Shirt finally drawled. He smiled, and through a fog of liquor-laced breath, added, "Real honest of you. Let me buy you a drink."

Janus couldn't place the accent, but the man was clearly not from the Northeast . . . or the Deep South. Texas, maybe, he thought.

"Come here often, big boy?" Janus inquired, intentionally playing on the stereotype while studying the man's receding hairline and greenish-brown eyes. He couldn't get over how much the drunken hick's overall look and build approximated that of Georgie Granger. The two men were not clones of each other—Western Shirt was younger, no question—but they were close enough. And with only five days remaining to pull off the gig, he would simply have to do.

"Never been here before in my whole life."

"*Never?*"

"Never. Heck, I just blew into town last Tuesday. Came in on one of them there Greyhound *Scene-O-Cruisers*. Don't ever travel by bus . . ." The man's expression suddenly changed, and he hiccupped and swallowed a belch. "Lordy," he then continued, as if not missing a beat, "buses are nasty."

"Friends in New York?"

"Got me an old aunt and uncle up in the Bronx; they're puttin' me up till I get myself situated. Other than that, I don't know me a damn soul. This is the first time I've ever been east of the Mississippi. I'm what you might call a country boy."

"Is *that* right?" Janus blurted too happily. He quickly reminded himself not to sound overanxious. "What part of the country?" he asked more calmly. "Texas?"

"Oklahoma"

"How interesting. What part of Oklahoma?"

"Tribbey, Oklahoma. Population six." Western Shirt flashed a warm, friendly grin, giggled at his joke, and turned his attention back to the bar. Getting a drink was clearly his priority at the moment.

"I bet you've got a lot of family back there in Tribbey?" Janus inquired obliquely. "Most country people do."

"Nah. They're mostly all gone now. Got me an old uncle on my mother's side livin' just outside Tulsa. But ain't seen him since I was 'bout twelve."

"My," Janus muttered sadly, "you must be so lonely. Is there no other family? No wife or children, brothers, sisters?"

"Nope. I was hitched once—a long time ago—but I sure ain't got me no damn kids, thank God."

Janus held out his hand. "My name is Charlie Janus, Mr. Country Boy. What's yours?"

"Elvin. Elvin Welch."

"Well, Elvin, now you can say you know at least one more person in New York City."

Elvin Welch smiled that broad, homey smile again and nodded. Still weaving and unsteady, he suddenly braced himself on the support column Janus was leaning against.

"You look like you might be a little under the

weather, Elvin. Why don't you join me and my friend over at our table and get off your feet for a while?"

"I have to get me a drink first," Welch slurred, looking around for a waiter.

"Allow me to get it for you," Janus said, giving a friendly and gentle squeeze to Welch's unmuscular, if not skinny, arm. "It's on me. What are you drinking?"

"Jack Daniel's," he burped. "Neat."

"Good choice, Elvin. I truly do appreciate a man who likes the *good* things in life," Janus said with a sly wink. "A man who doesn't like those good things, shall we say, watered down, or in any way diluted . . . if you get my drift?"

"So, you're not here alone?" Welch inquired.

"No, I'm with a friend," Janus said, pointing toward Granger. "See that fellow seated at that table over there—"

Welch squinted and blinked his eyes for focus. "You mean that balding guy with the big Adam's apple?"

"Right," Janus said with a slight chuckle. "Anyway, that's our table. Why don't you go on over and make yourself comfortable, Elvin? I'll bring your drink right along. My friend's name is George; he's very nice. I'm sure he's going to like you."

"Gotta tell ya," Welch said, his look and voice suddenly hangdog. "I've got the bug."

"Is that a fact?" Janus said softly, then added reassuringly, "Well, we're no strangers to that problem in these parts, Elvin. It just so happens that my friend George is HIV positive also. Now, like I said, you go on over there, sit down, and make yourself comfortable. I'll only be a minute."

Still blinking for focus, Welch smiled lightly and shrugged passively. He nodded, turned, and stumbled off in the direction of the table.

Janus intercepted one of the fast-moving cocktail waiters and quickly ordered another Brandy Alexander, another large Diet Coke, and a triple Jack Daniel's with no ice for the country boy.

He had found the perfect match, and this was defi-

nitely going to be the night. All those horrendous
money problems would soon be over, he could just
feel it. He was so weary of being broke and living
virtually hand to mouth—like some pathetic lowlife.

Charlie Janus was meant for far better things, and
this drunken hick, this moron . . . this insignificant
piece of humanity from Piss Ass, Oklahoma, would
be his express ticket back to the top. Besides which,
he rationalized, the poor bastard had the bug. Hell,
he was living on borrowed time anyhow.

He had to give John Boy Holloway all the credit;
this was easily the greatest scam that he had ever con-
cocted. If it worked—as he knew it would—it would
be the greatest scam that he, Granger, and Holloway
had ever pulled off. It would be, perhaps, the greatest
scam ever.

As he moved through the vigorous and upbeat
crowd toward the table, the soft Judy Garland song
that had been playing in the background came to a
gentle end. In only seconds, the massive speakers
again came to pulsing life with the down-and-dirty
bass and snare intro of Queen's "Another One Bites
the Dust."

Almost giddy with anticipation and thinking how
apropos the choice of music, Janus whistled along. He
also made a mental note not to forget the ten-dollar
bill he'd slipped into Country Boy's front pocket.

TWO

The all-too-short Memorial Day weekend was over. The three-day impromptu vacation with Maureen Gallo out on the east end of Long Island had been great, but Detective Sergeant Thornton Savage was ready to get back to the city. Truth be known, he was even looking forward to getting back to The Job, Manhattan South Homicide, doing what he'd done now for decades—that which he did best: tracking down people who killed other people within the city of New York.

It can be said that there are some people who actually *look* like their jobs. Priests who exude that undeniably firm yet gentle aura of reverence associated with the clergy, whether attired in a Roman collar or relaxing in a bathing suit at Jones Beach; doctors who possess the clinical, detached—if not godlike—authoritarian qualities that fit the stereotype of a physician, whether wearing surgical scrubs in the OR or plus fours on the eighteenth hole.

Thornton Savage would never be mistaken for a priest. Neither would he be mistaken for a doctor, lawyer, or for that matter an Indian chief. He was a cop who just flat out looked like a cop. He had that indefinable yet unmistakable cop bearing.

As far back as his basketball and track days at Cardinal Hayes High, and his running-back years at Fordham, he had the look, the attitude, a grace-under-fire composure that was hardwired into his DNA. His father, his uncles, his brother, cousins, and nephews all were—or had been—New York City cops. So it was understandable that he possessed a genetic predisposition for The Job.

Now, after more than three decades in the NYPD, that image and carriage had fully coalesced. His streetwise savvy, poise, and self-assurance were set in stone, as permanent and undeniable as the spectacles Borglum had jackhammered onto the face of Mount Rushmore's TR.

Savage downshifted the Thunderbird into second gear, then carefully guided the gleaming classic through the winding slalom of dented orange barrels, flashing-yellow caution lights, and battered road cones that delineated the temporary path between the westbound Long Island Expressway and the approach to the Kosciusko Bridge and the BQE.

Road construction never ended in this town, he thought. It seemed that this stretch of highway, in particular, had been under some sort of continuous construction now for thirty years or more, yet it never seemed to get any better. From this point on, until he crossed the Williamsburg Bridge into Lower Manhattan, he would be on hyper road-surface alert. The elevated Brooklyn-Queens Expressway, with its notoriously bad potholes—which had been known to swallow entire Volkswagens—had already cost him two very expensive and rare Kelsey-Hayes wire wheels. It wasn't going to happen again.

"Well, we had a wonderful time," Maureen Gallo said, her baby-fine deep-red hair blowing wildly in the wind as they cruised, top down, beneath the iron framework of the ancient Kosciusko.

"Sure did," Savage agreed firmly. With the downbeat of Willie Nelson's rendition of "Always on My Mind" suddenly filtering through the radio, he turned up the volume a notch. The simple but poignant tune was one of his favorites. Reaching across, he gently squeezed Maureen's left knee. Along with her many other physical attributes, she had great legs.

In the distance, beyond the tapering church spires and tenement rooftops of Greenpoint, Brooklyn, silhouetted in black against the glow of Manhattan's eastern skyline, he glimpsed the Art Deco beauty of the Chrysler Building's pinnacle and saw that the upper reaches of the Empire State Building were aglow in holiday red, white, and blue. God bless America.

"There's something I haven't told you yet," Maureen said, speaking loudly over the nasal Willie and the roar of the T-bird's throaty exhaust. "I've been sort of saving it."

Savage looked at her.

"Doreen and Randy offered us the place again for the middle weekend of August, Friday night till Sunday, the sixteenth to the eighteenth. They can't use it; they're going to be away. Interested?"

"Sure," Savage replied. He kept his eyes glued to the road while drifting left to pass a banged-up taxicab stopped in the far right lane with its hood open.

The small beach cottage that belonged to Maureen's oldest and closest friends, Doreen and Randy Heimgartner, was a great place to relax and unwind. Perfectly situated on the dunes of Southampton, it was comfortable, well furnished, and spotlessly clean. Who wouldn't want to spend time there, he thought, especially when it was gratis. Similar places in that area supposedly rented for five grand and more a week during season. Who the hell could afford that?

"All right," Maureen said. "I'll tell them we'll take it. It's only that . . ."

"Only that what?"

"Only," Maureen hedged, "if I tell them we're going to take it that weekend, thereby preventing them from offering it to some of their other friends—or renting it out for a bunch of dough—and then at the last minute something happens on your job that causes us to have to cancel . . ."

Here we go, Savage thought. After three fantastic days of sun, surf, and terrific sex, things were about to go negative. But this was typical Maureen, and typical of the tenuous relationship they'd always had.

"You know I have absolutely no control over things like that," Savage offered, turning down the radio volume and taking his eyes momentarily off the road to look at her again.

"I know," Maureen said resignedly. "It's just that I sometimes get tired of having my plans turned to garbage every time some jerk decides to kill some other jerk somewhere south of Fifty-ninth Street."

"It's not *every* time," Savage calmly protested. "In fact, most of the homicides are actually handled by the precinct detective squads. It doesn't even come over to our office unless we're requested . . . or it's a heavy . . . or particularly high profile in some way."

They'd known each other for more than ten years, and all during that time Maureen had disliked his job—hated it, actually—and seemed to never cease looking for ways, no matter how oblique or subtle, to let him know. That thorny issue alone was probably the key reason why they'd never gotten around to tying the knot. Well, one of the key reasons at least.

"Hey, we had a nice time this weekend," Savage said, again turning to face her and stare momentarily into her amazing blue-gray-greens. "Let's not spoil it at the last minute worrying about something that will probably never happen. Besides, the middle of August is almost three months away."

"If we go ahead and make plans," Maureen said flatly, "and I give Doreen my word that we'll take the place that weekend, then something *will* invariably happen. You *know* that. Something always happens whenever we make plans. It's only these impromptu spur-of-the-moment escapes that ever seem to work out for us."

Now he really couldn't wait to get back to work. He gave the dual-carbureted 312 a tad more gas and watched the needle climb to sixty.

"Well, then, I guess I'll just go ahead and tell Doreen we'll take it," Maureen said, following her terse words with a resigned sigh. Savage never actually *heard* the sigh through the maelstrom of late-evening air, but he knew it was there nonetheless—it had to be.

"And I'll just have to hope for the best," she tagged on. He watched her turn away and gaze off into the starlit distance.

Despite the warmth of the night, Savage felt the frost. Turning back to face the roadway, he instantly spotted the mega-pothole, but it was too late. He felt the expensive *whack* all the way up into his already tight jaw.

For the rest of the ride to Maureen's place down in SoHo, where he quickly dropped her, her bags, and her attitude, the two-seater '57 Thunderbird vibrated as if it had a square wheel and pulled strongly to the right. Savage had managed to bite his lip in silence, but he knew his blood pressure was as bent as the spokes in the six-hundred-dollar right front wire rim.

After tucking the injured T-Bird away in the secure private garage he rented over on Thompson Street, he quick-walked the three short blocks to his Greenwich Village digs at 184 Sullivan. Weary from the long weekend, the drive home—and Maureen's last-minute ball grinding—he climbed the stairs and let himself into apartment 2. He set his overnighter on the dinette table, went to the kitchen for a glass of cold water, and found Ray curled up into a fetal ball atop the Kelvinator. It was one of the smoky gray cat's favorite napping spots; he seemed to like the way the relic refrigerator vibrated.

"You're in early," he said, rubbing Ray's battle-scarred head. "What's the matter, you have a bad night too?"

Ray barely opened one yellow eye. He swished his tail in annoyance and went right back to dreamland.

"You're looking a little washed out there, big guy," Savage said, expecting a somewhat better greeting from his roommate after a three-day absence. "You feeling okay?"

Aside from a wide-mouthed yawn, Ray did not bother to respond.

Savage opened a new bag of Meow Mix and filled Ray's food dish. He would have to stop by that Ukrainian bakery over in the Ninth Precinct and get Mrs. Potamkin some of that expensive baklava that she loved—and couldn't afford—for cat-sitting the independent, if not downright unsociable, Ray. Mrs. P was a Holocaust survivor who lived above him in the third-floor apartment, and despite her prickly personality and phony complaints about his violin playing, they were fond of each other. Mutual respect and a certain toughness to withstand desperate loss had formed an interesting bond between them. Like him, she understood how it felt to lose someone you loved more than life—and have to move on. He had learned from her that you had to live in the present and hope for the best. A half smile crept across his face—those were Maureen's words.

In an unusual act of detente on his part, he considered putting in a quick call to Maureen to help ease the tension between them after the night's spat. He plucked the phone from its cradle and, after punching in part of her number, changed his mind. It was too soon; it would only resurrect the argument. Better to let it rest awhile.

He wondered why and how their relationship, one that had been on and off a dozen times, had managed to last all these years. He leaned against the frame of the kitchen window, gazed out at the darkened city, and pondered the intricate dynamics of his seemingly self-defeating taste in women.

It wasn't that Maureen wasn't a good woman—she was certainly better than good. It wasn't that she didn't possess many, if not most, of the qualities he needed in a woman—she did. It was just that she also possessed a few that made him nuts.

He had known since the first time he ran a razor across his teenage face that his eye and attention seemed always taken by slim, small-breasted, intelligent redheads, preferably ones with bedroom eyes of green and a sultry smile—Maureen Gallo to a damn T. However, he had only recently come to accept that his masculine excite-o-meter must also become additionally charged when the green-eyed redhead was a strong-willed, opinionated, worldly type A—again Maureen Gallo.

What the hell was it about the aggressive female personality that attracted him so? He decided that it must be the stimulation of constant turmoil that appealed to him. Maybe he was a low-grade masochist who derived subconscious gratification from aggravation. Life for him, he knew, would be so much easier if only he could swim in romantic waters with easier-going, laid-back type Bs, like his late wife, Joanne, had been. Or like Gina McCormick had been . . . but Gina was dead now too.

He left the night-light on in the kitchen for Ray and went to bed.

THREE

Sixth Precinct police officer Billy Cox placed the dinged, chipped, and varnish-bare nightstick—the old-fashioned wooden type with the leather thong that cops of yore would unconsciously twirl while walking their street posts—into the narrow space alongside the driver's seat. The hickory had been handed down to him from his favorite uncle, Will, who'd retired from The Job way back in the early eighties. Uncle Willie could really twirl the damn thing; Cox had never quite gotten the hang of it. After whacking himself in the knees a few dozen times, he'd given up trying.

Along with the corner call box, and a lot of other old and endearing images and ways, baton twirling was rapidly becoming a dying art in the police world. In his time in The Job, Billy Cox had seen too many things become high tech. So much of the human element to policing was gone. He wondered if it would ever come back. The friendly cop on the walking beat, who knew most everybody's name, good and bad, had become a faceless figure behind tinted glass, rolling by in an air-conditioned Crown Victoria at thirty-five miles an hour.

Even some of the rookies today were different, he thought, just too damn . . . inflexible, or out of touch. They were coming out of the academy unwilling, or unable, to use discretion. They were, to some extent, taught to be automatons. Everything was always by the damn book. He swore that some of them would give their own mothers a ticket, or worse. The Job he'd loved so when he came in was changing, and Cox couldn't wait to retire. A little more than two years from now—758 days—and he was out—not that anybody was counting.

He tossed a clipboard crammed with the usual department forms onto the dash. Then, careful not to aggravate the sciatic condition that had been flaring in his right hip for the past week, he slowly slid in behind the radio car's steering wheel. It was the start of the last tour of the set, and at 1530 hours—3:30 P.M.—he would begin his long-awaited vacation. Fifteen consecutive days off—they were all his and he was going to enjoy them; he hoped the beautiful spring weather would continue. Peace, quiet, and maybe a little fishing with his brother-in-law were his plans.

Two minutes later, his radio-car partner for the last ten months, Officer Harry Maxwell, climbed into the passenger side. The overgrown kid—twenty-some years Cox's junior—dropped his modern side-handled polycarbonate baton next to his seat, set his rechargeable halogen Mag-Lite into the dash bracket that he'd personally custom-fashioned, and, as always, slammed the damn door.

"Let's do it," Maxwell announced. He said the same damn thing at the start of every damn tour. Harry Maxwell was not a multifaceted personality.

Cox pulled the gearshift lever into DRIVE and idled slowly from the Sixth Precinct's tight parking lot into Charles Street. It was shift change, and the narrow block was choked by the overlap of cops' personal cars squeezed in and double-parked along both sides. Once the midnight shift had changed into civvies and headed home, the block wouldn't be so cramped—until the four-to-twelve troops began arriving and looking for spots. At Hudson Street, he turned the cruiser uptown toward Abingdon Square, the virtual center of their patrol sector.

"Coffee?" Cox asked, as if he had to. The Alex Ajente of the Sixth Precinct, Harry Maxwell could consume more coffee than any human who had ever lived. And there hadn't been a day on patrol with him in the last ten months that hadn't begun with an immediate search for a stiff cup of java—and a heavily buttered bagel.

"But of course," Maxwell replied, without looking up. He was busy scratching the day's opening heading into his memo book.

"This is my last one, you know," Cox advised. "Vacation."

"I know," Maxwell said. "Spoke to Roll Call. Joe Granos is gonna fill your seat for the next two sets."

"Joe's good."

"A May-June pick, hah?" Maxwell drawled in a curious tone. "Why didn't you pick something in July or August? You've got the seniority. You must have a hundred years in the job. Who was the mayor when you came on, anyway? John Lindsay? Wagner? . . . Jimmy Walker?"

Cox gave his partner a cold stare. "When I came in The Job, you were still wearing diapers, buster. I've *forgotten* more about police work than you will ever *know*."

Maxwell sneered. "Know what I got for vacation picks?" he asked with an edge.

"Let me guess. Based on your knowledge of The Job, your competence, your overall performance, and your lack of seniority . . . I would say you got the first five minutes of February and the last five minutes of November."

"Pretty close."

Cox steered the car to the curb in front of the Gristedes on Abingdon Square, and Maxwell hopped out.

"Want anything with it?" Maxwell asked. "Buttered roll . . . bagel?"

"Nah, been putting on a few pounds lately," Cox replied, tapping his stomach. "But see if they've got a *Post*."

Cox offered a friendly wave to Mrs. Olivia Mc-

Manus. The sprightly widow was dragging her rickety tagalong grocery cart past the radio car to do her weekly shopping. She had lived in a third-floor walk-up on Jane Street since the early fifties and was a very familiar face around the square. The long-winded octogenarian smiled warmly and waved back. She too disappeared into Gristedes. Cox figured she'd get Harry's ear in there, and by the time he could possibly escape, the morning coffees would probably be lukewarm.

"Central to Six-Boy, K." The department radio came alive.

"Go ahead, Central," Cox replied through the handset.

"Investigate a male with difficulty breathing, possible cardiac arrest, at Four-twenty West Thirteenth, K. The aided is inside the medical office of a Dr. R. Charles Janus at that location. Ground floor."

"Ten-four," Cox replied, tapping the yelp siren for just a second to alert Maxwell.

"Be advised further, unit," Central added. "An EMT bus is already on the scene and having difficulty gaining entrance to the building."

"Ten-four, Central," Cox acknowledged, as his partner reappeared and climbed back into the passenger seat.

"Where are the coffees?" Cox asked.

"Javier's making a fresh pot; we'll have to come back."

"No *Post*?"

"Dammit." Maxwell grimaced at his forgetfulness.

Cox rolled his cycs, then flipped the roof lights on, goosed the gas, and headed for the West Thirteenth Street location, only four blocks away.

Upon arrival at the six-story brick building that housed offices for doctors, lawyers, and other professionals, they found an orange and white City of New York ambulance parked directly in front. Exiting the radio car, they crossed paths with emergency medical technician Stu Stanowicz, who was leaving the building through the street-level glass doors. He was toting a portable EKG machine.

"I see you managed to get in," Cox said.

"Finally," Stanowicz replied. "We waited at least five minutes for the damn doctor to come out and unlock the place."

"All's well that ends well," Maxwell uttered.

"I'm going to the bus to get rid of this," Stanowicz growled, holding up the EKG machine. "Ain't gonna need it." Then, stepping closer and speaking ominously out of the side of his mouth, he added, "Something's wrong here, boys. Something is really weird. . . ."

"How do you mean?" Maxwell asked.

"This ain't no difficulty breathing . . . or possible cardiac," Stanowicz explained, still whispering. "This son of a bitch is DOA, and," he added, flashing his eyebrows cryptically, "he's been dead for a while."

"How do you know he's been dead for a *while*?" Maxwell pressed.

"He ain't breathing, he's got no pulse, he's got early signs of lividity in the lower extremities. He's got stiffening in the back of the neck, which I believe to be the beginnings of rigor. He's already cold, for God's sake."

"He's supposed to be in a doctor's office," Cox said. "Is that right?"

"Yeah," Stanowicz mumbled derisively, throwing his thumb over his shoulder. "Ground floor. The office is at the end of the hall. Dr. *Janus*—a *neurologist*; he's in there now." As the EMT moved toward his parked ambulance, he added, "Good luck, fellas."

Cox and Maxwell exchanged quizzical glances and continued into the building. At the end of the first-floor hall was a wide-open glass-paneled and gilt-lettered door: DR. R. CHARLES JANUS M.D.— NEUROLOGY. They let themselves into the office, passed through a small waiting room permeated with that typical antiseptic aroma, and followed the sound of voices emanating from an examination room at the rear.

Supine on the tile floor was a male, his face a ghostly purple. He appeared to be in his mid- to late thirties. The man was dressed in a long-sleeved white-and-blue-striped western shirt that was unbuttoned and pulled up to his armpits, faded jeans that were buttoned and zipped, and a pair of well-worn and scuffed cowboy boots. His feet were elevated on a pillow. Also in the room were Stanowicz' EMT partner, Maritza Flores—a dark, curvy looker for whom Cox had always had a bad case of the happy hots—and a well-dressed, fatigued-looking man in his mid- to late fifties, who he assumed was Dr. R. Charles Janus.

"How long has he been dead, Maritza?" Cox asked, bending over to stare closely at the body. He noticed several pale red marks—like tiny hickeys—spaced randomly on the man's chest and sides. Beneath the purple cast of the DOA's face, he noticed some blotchiness and what appeared to be some broken capillaries or veins.

The Hispanic looker offered a queer look, shrugged, and replied, "Not really sure, Billy. But I'd say an hour or more at the very least. He's got purplish discoloring in his fingertips, neck, and face."

"It was a heart attack," Janus commented in an angry monotone. "And it took you people forever to get here."

"What are you talking about?" Maxwell piped up, affronted. "We just got the call two minutes ago."

"Well, I've been calling and calling," Janus said with a snarl. "And I got nowhere."

Cox looked over at Maritza Flores. With a palms-out shrug, the EMT said, "I don't know. We got here almost immediately after getting the assignment. Which couldn't be more than seven or eight minutes ago."

"When did this all start?" Cox asked Janus.

Nodding down at the body, the doctor began,

"George called me around three thirty, complaining of severe chest pains. Asked if I'd meet him here at the office. Said he thought an elephant was sitting on his chest."

"George?" Cox inquired, intrigued by the obvious implied familiarity.

"We were old friends," Janus said offhandedly.

"What's his last name, Doc?" Cox then asked, all the while wondering what his own doctor's response would be if called by him at that hour—even if he was a friend. *Take two aspirins and call me in the morning,* no doubt—if he would even answer the damn phone.

"Granger," Janus answered. "George Granger. So happens Mr. Granger actually lives—lived—in Columbus, Ohio, but his business frequently brought him to New York."

The doctor handed Cox a small square of lime green paper. "I've written down his home address and phone number. I've also included the name and phone number of the person he had on file to be notified in case of emergency, a Mr. John B. Holloway."

Cox glanced quickly at the information, slipped the note onto his clipboard, and inquired, "Have you contacted this Mr. Holloway as yet?"

"Surely you jest, Officer," Janus said, rearing back, annoyed. "Just where do you think I would have found the time to go telephoning Ohio this morning, for God's sake? But to answer your question: No, I have not notified Mr. Holloway. But then, notification in a matter such as this is a police job, is it not?"

Beginning to dislike the pasty-faced doctor, Cox squinted in disbelief and said, "Let me get this straight, Doc. This guy called you at three thirty *in the morning,* to have you meet him at your office because he was having chest pains?"

"That's right."

"When he told you he felt like there was an elephant sitting on his chest, what exactly did that mean to you as a physician?" Cox inquired.

Janus did not answer immediately. When he spoke, he seemed to measure his words cautiously. "I thought it possible that he was having a heart problem."

"A heart *problem*?" Cox asked incredulously. "Don't you mean *heart attack*?"

"Why didn't you direct him to an emergency room?" Maxwell inserted. "Hell, St. Vinnie's is right around the corner."

"Mr. Granger was desperately fearful—neurotically so—of emergency rooms and hospitals." The doctor frowned. "God almighty, I had no choice. George begged me to come in. It was my duty; the man had been my patient for many years . . . and my friend."

"Just how good a friend *was* he?" Maxwell asked, his unsubtle innuendo sounding a little like Dana Carvey's priggish *SNL* Church Lady. Cox knew what his partner was implying. Apparently so did Janus.

Janus glared coldly at Maxwell for many seconds, but did not respond.

"What time was it when you first saw Mr. Granger this morning?" Cox asked, breaking the silence.

"I got to the office here around four, maybe four fifteen," Janus replied, glancing at his gaudy Rolex. "George . . . Mr. Granger . . . arrived a few minutes later. He'd taken a taxicab over."

"From where?" Cox inquired.

"Don't know," the tired-looking man replied. "Don't know where he was staying this trip. He never said. All he told me was he'd come to town for the holiday weekend."

"How was he when you first saw him?" Maxwell asked.

"When?" the doctor said, cupping a hand behind his ear.

"Whenever he got here," Maxwell followed up with a mildly impatient snap, gnarly from not yet having his required caffeine fix.

"He was in distress," Janus replied evenly. "I assisted him in getting out of the cab; he was very weak. I had to support him all the way into the building. I helped him in here and gave him a general examination. His blood pressure was one-forty over one-oh-two. His pulse was high . . . one-twenty-four. I had him lie down on the examining table, then ran an EKG." Janus waved his arm halfheartedly at an EKG machine in the corner of the room.

"His boots are on," Cox said. "Didn't you have to take them off?"

"No," Janus answered flatly.

"What did the test show?" Cox inquired.

"The EKG wasn't bad," Janus responded, making strong eye contact. "Looked normal. Would you like to see it?"

"I wouldn't know how to interpret it, Doc," Cox replied. "But someone may wish to see it."

"I have it here," Maritza Flores said, handing Cox the narrow strip with the staggered peaks and valleys.

Cox glanced at it quickly, noting that the time printed along its border was 00:01. On the reverse side it bore the handwritten date "May 28th." Cox stepped immediately to the EKG machine in the corner of the room and noted the time on the machine to be 07:22.

"Is this the actual machine that you used to perform the EKG?" Cox inquired.

"It is," Janus said condescendingly.

"Big discrepancy in the times here, Doc," Cox announced, returning the physician's intense eye contact. "If the time printed on this strip is correct, according to the present time on the EKG machine, this strip was taken over seven hours ago. How do you explain that?"

During an extended pause, Janus slowly ran his tongue between his teeth and lower lip, then swallowed nervously. His gears were turning. "I must have inadvertently reset the clock," he finally said.

You are so-o-o fulla shit, Cox thought. He handed the EKG strip back to Maritza Flores. "How would you interpret the test, Maritza?" he asked.

"Well, it's a twelve-lead strip," she replied. "It doesn't show anything unusual—nothing significant about it to show signs of an imminent heart attack, that's for sure."

"Should there be?" Cox asked.

Flores offered a pondering grimace and a slight shrug. "I would say so."

"That is not at all true in every case," Janus blurted out defensively.

"A *twelve*-lead strip?" Cox mused. "That means that some of the EKG leads would get attached to the patient's lower calf. . . . Is that right, Doctor?"

"That's right," Janus replied.

"In the area, say . . . just above the boot line?"

"That's correct," Janus snapped, appearing bored.

Cox consulted his notes. "You said you didn't remove his boots."

"That's correct," Janus snapped again. "I helped him pull down his pants to attach the leads."

"Would it not have been considerably easier to simply remove the boots and slide the pants legs up, say to just below the knee, in order to attach the leads?"

"What's your point, Officer?" Janus snarled.

"My point is this. Surely those heavy jeans would have gathered well above the calf if you lowered them—as you said you did—because of those boots, the boots you said you never took off. How then was it possible for you to have attached the lower leads?"

Janus' jaw tightened visibly. "Well, they didn't gather," he shot back angrily. "And if you keep up this line of questioning, as if I'm some kind of suspect, I'm going into the next room to call my lawyer."

"Hey, Doc," Cox said, making a blasé face, "don't get bent. We do have an obligation to fully understand what happened here, okay?"

Janus snorted and turned away.

Harry Maxwell squatted beside the body, carefully rolled it, and removed a brown leather wallet from the man's back pocket. He handed it up to Cox, then rolled the body back to its original position.

The skinny and timeworn wallet contained only three credit cards, all in the name of George Granger,

and a folded-up copy of his New York State birth
certificate. A quick calculation, based on the recorded
date of birth, put the DOA at forty-five years—
somewhat older than he appeared. Oddly, all three
credit cards—a Visa, an American Express, and a Din-
ers Club—had expired long ago. Odder still, the wallet
contained no photographs of Granger or possible kin,
no driver's license or any other documentation.

"Anything in the shirt pockets?" Cox asked Maxwell.

The rookie undid the mother-of-pearl snaps on the
western shirt's two pocket flaps; the one over the left
breast contained a single brass Kwikset house key, the
other was empty. He then searched the front pants
pockets.

"What else we got?" Cox asked.

"Basically, all we got here is a crappy old Benrus
on his wrist," his partner replied. He stood, casually
unwadded a loosely crumpled ball of bills he'd removed from the DOA's left front pants pocket, and
counted. "And six bucks. All singles. The freakin' guy
was broke."

"Any other money in the right front pocket?"
Cox asked.

Maxwell shook his head.

Cox heard Janus self-consciously clear his throat.
"After the EKG, what happened next, Doc?"

"Well, at around six a.m., George . . . Mr. Granger . . .
complained that he was feeling tired and wanted to
rest. I closed the door and left him alone in here while
I completed some paperwork in my private office.
About ten minutes later I heard a thud, came back
in, and found him lying unconscious just where he
is now."

Janus raked his slender, manicured fingers through
thinning silver-edged hair. "I immediately started
doing CPR."

"What took you so long to call us, Doc?" Harry
Maxwell inquired.

"I tried calling," Janus replied, glaring again at the
younger cop. "All I got was a busy signal."

"You called 911, and got a *busy*?" Maxwell followed up in disbelief.

"Well, not initially," the doctor responded with a hedging head bob. "At first I was dialing the Sixth Precinct station house." He pointed to a typewritten list of telephone numbers taped to a cabinet door alongside the wall phone in the examining room. The first number on the list was that of the Sixth Precinct.

"And you're saying that the precinct line was busy?" Cox asked, thinking that the bullshit he'd been listening to was beginning to collect, getting deeper and deeper by the moment.

The doctor nodded vigorously. "That's what I'm saying. Someone must have had the phone off the hook. Are you saying that you doubt me?"

"There's a switchboard there with a dozen rollover lines, Doc," Cox advised. He picked up the wall-phone receiver and got a dial tone. He hung it back up. "What time were you doing this calling?"

"I'm not sure . . . I can't recall."

"Why would you dial the precinct in an emergency?" Maxwell interjected. "Surely you know to dial 911."

"I did, with the same result," Janus said, with a mildly annoyed dismissive laugh. "I was too busy performing CPR in order to keep a friend alive to keep trying to get through on the damn telephone."

The police officers exchanged another quizzical glance. "How long did you do CPR?" Cox inquired.

"Forty . . . forty-five minutes maybe," Janus responded, his annoyance clearly escalating again. "I don't know for sure. Hell, I wasn't watching the clock."

"Got a lot of inconsistencies here, Doc," Cox said, shaking his head.

Jutting his chin full out in anger, Janus snapped, "Are you going to continue to grill me all morning as if I were some kind of a criminal? Must I remind you that I am a highly respected physician? I graduated magna cum laude from Dartmouth Medical School, for God's sake. I've published in *JAMA* six times." Janus' voice began to rise, the caustic edge now fully sharpened. "Do you really think I would risk my reputation, or my practice—not to mention maltreat a friend?"

Cox fully understood Stu Stanowicz' sense that something was wrong, weird . . . not right. He had performed CPR countless times, and he knew how grueling an exercise it could be. Ten minutes would exhaust most guys, but at the very least they'd break out in a sweat and their clothes would be in disarray. Though Janus appeared to be tired, his hair was neatly combed, his shirt and tie were perfect, his thousand-dollar suit looked crisp. No sweat, no wrinkles—and he wasn't a damn bit out of breath. This guy is full of shit, Cox again concluded.

"Did you start an IV?" Cox asked flatly, ignoring the man's protests.

"No! There was no time. I had no assistance here."

"Do you maintain a crash tray?" Maxwell asked.

"Huh?"

"You know, Doc," Cox said, allowing a hint of sarcasm to ride on his words. "Syringes preloaded with medications, like lidocaine, for treating emergency cardiac patients. That kind of stuff."

Janus, appearing suddenly nervous, shook his head.

"You got paddles here to help with resuscitation?" Maxwell pressed.

Again Janus shook his head.

"Oxygen?" Maxwell pressed harder. Janus remained silent.

"All right," Cox said calmingly, in an attempt to reduce the mounting tension in the room. He placed a fresh piece of unlined paper at the top of the clipboard and clicked his ballpoint. "What more can you tell us about this man?" he asked Janus, deciding to finish collecting the preliminary information before taking his next step, a step that he had already decided upon.

"Just that he's had a long history of heart problems," Janus replied.

"What patient with a long history of heart problems goes seeking treatment from a *neurologist* at three thirty in the morning?" Maxwell asked.

"I have urged Mr. Granger, on any number of occasions, to see a cardiologist," Janus shrugged. "Unfortunately, I was the only doctor he trusted. He just never listened."

"Have you maintained a medical file on Mr. Granger over that period of time?" Cox asked.

"Certainly," Janus responded. "That is privileged information, but under the circumstances you are more than welcome to peruse it. You'll find a long history of chest pain complaints, earlier EKG strips, and referrals to heart specialists. This death is not unexpected, Officer. It is my opinion that Mr. Granger has for some years been living on borrowed time."

"Yes, I'd like to see that medical file, Doctor," Cox replied. "Would you mind getting it for me?"

As Janus left the room and headed for his private office, Cox motioned Harry Maxwell to join him in the waiting room. When Maxwell followed, Cox led him into the outer hall before speaking.

"This guy didn't die in the way this jerkoff quack would like us to think," Cox said quietly. "What's your guess?"

"I'm betting that both these guys are fags," Maxwell whispered back, raising his eyebrows. "This all came out of some *romantic* situation."

Cox nodded his head and bit his lip pensively, considering Maxwell's opinion.

"Well?" Maxwell said. "What are *you* thinking?"

"I think you might be right. But if not that, then drug related, maybe," Cox replied, unsurely.

"Where to from here?" Maxwell asked. Then he added cautiously, "You know, the guy *is* a damn doctor. Are we gonna go up against *his* word?"

"Go outside, get on the radio, and notify the sergeant on patrol," Cox said flatly. "Then notify the ME and get our detective squad up here ASAP. Have them all respond: 'Suspicious death.'"

"What are you gonna do?" Maxwell asked.

Cox slipped the small piece of lime green paper from his clipboard and scanned it. "I'm going to use the good doctor's nickel to make a long-distance call to Columbus, Ohio. I've got to make the notification to Mr. John B. Holloway that his friend Mr. George Granger has gone off to begin taking harp lessons."

Later that day . . .

The Delta MD-88 was fifteen minutes behind schedule when it pulled up to the gate at Miami International. The long day of travel and slow connections had begun at noon when George Granger boarded Delta flight 1089 at New York's LaGuardia. There had been an hour and a half layover in Atlanta, where he changed to flight 1255. In need of a shower and shave, a good meal, and a comfortable bed, he boarded a taxicab and went directly to the posh Delano Hotel in Miami Beach. A handsome young Hispanic bellman, Ramon, took his one bag and guided him through the elaborate peach marble lobby to the registration desk.

"May I help you, sir?" a familiar-looking woman in wire-rimmed glasses behind the gleaming counter asked. The name tag pinned to her starched white blouse identified the freckle-faced redhead as DAPHNE DEMPSEY, RESERVATIONS MANAGER. He decided Daphne was a prime candidate for breast augmentation surgery.

"My name is Eric Von Deutsch," Granger said. "I would like a nice suite. A smoker."

"Certainly, Mr. Von Deutsch," the woman replied with a smile. She turned to face a monitor screen as her manicured fingers raced across the reservation desk keyboard. "Our one-bedroom suites come with king bed, balcony with ocean view, and marble soaking tub. The rate is six-fifty per night."

"Six-fifty?" Granger queried, both pleased and dismayed. "I stayed here two weeks ago. How come I had to pay a thousand per night then?"

"Yes," the clerk acknowledged with an even broader smile, "I do recall your stay with us, sir. That would have been our midseason rate. During *high* season the rate for that suite is as much as two thousand."

"Lucky me," Granger quipped.

"How long will you be staying with us this time, Mr. Von Deutsch?"

"That's indefinite just now," he replied. "However, I would say ten days at the very least."

Surely within that time he could find suitable short-term living quarters here in Miami—an apartment, a rental condo perhaps. It would give him a good home base while he looked into permanent property investment down in Key West.

Daphne Dempsey placed a registration card and ballpoint atop the counter. The exhausted George Granger again registered at the Delano as Mr. Eric Von Deutsch.

"Ramon," Daphne Dempsey said to the bellman, "show Mr. Von Deutsch to suite fourteen-twenty."

As they rode the burl-lined elevator to the fourteenth floor, Granger made sure that Ramon, the good-looking bellman, realized that he was being ogled. Once inside the suite, Ramon drew back the pastel floral-print drapes, revealing a magnificent view of the sunny beach below and the inviting blue-green of the Atlantic for as far as the eye could see.

"Will there be anything else, *Mr. . . .* ?" Ramon asked.

"Granger . . ." he started, then, catching himself, cleared his throat and quickly recovered. "Von Deutsch. *Eric* Von Deutsch. Do please call me Eric, though." He overtipped the man with a ten spot and, winking coyly at him, added, "Perhaps later . . . Ramon."

He suspected that the slender Hispanic—probably Cuban—was a player, and probably very well hung.

He decided that before the week was out, he would know the answer to both those questions.

Ramon smiled back, bowed slightly, and left the room.

I've got to get used to using my new name, he thought, upset at his near slip. Whenever asked, I've got to be able to make my response one of total second nature, a knee-jerk reaction, a reflex. He lit up a Merit, reached for the phone, and dialed the Columbus, Ohio, residence phone number of John Boyer Holloway. He got Holloway's answering machine but, knowing not to leave the voice of George Granger on Holloway's tape, he hung up. He then dialed the New York City number of Dr. R. Charles Janus.

"What's the word?" he said directly when the doctor answered.

"There's been a slight snag," Janus replied. The doctor's voice was even but contained a hint of concern.

"What do you mean, there's been a slight *snag*?" Granger snarled back.

"The police are playing Sherlock Holmes. They've ordered an autopsy."

"Now just how in the fuck is that possible?" Granger asked, feeling a category-five twister beginning to form in his head. "You told us that would never happen," he raged. "You assured us the body would go straight to a funeral home and a quick cremation. Ashes dumped right away into the sea . . . no goddamned DNA . . . *no nothing*! Now you're talking about a fucking . . . *slight snag*?"

"Generally it doesn't happen this way," Janus answered smoothly.

"Fuck *generally*. Why is it happening this time?" Granger sucked as hard as he could on the Merit.

"They think they smell something."

"Oh, you're pissing me off, Doc," Granger snarled again. "Let's get down to the bottom line here. Give me the worst possible scenario."

•

"I really believe that the worst possible scenario would be cause of death: undetermined."

"Which means?"

"It means just that, for crissakes. *Undetermined*. It means they can't say that there *was* foul play or that there *wasn't* foul play. In either event, it doesn't make a damn bit of difference. We ride free."

"You telling me they can't determine a fucking strangulation at a goddamned autopsy?"

"I've already told you," Janus replied in a low, controlled, but impatient tone. "It wasn't strangulation, it was asphyxiation. There is a difference."

"Because of the method we used?" Granger said. "*Burking,* isn't that what you called it?"

"Right. I'm telling you, the method is virtually impossible to determine. It's so easy to miss. If they don't know precisely what they're looking for, they'll never find it."

"Well, maybe they *do* know what it is they're looking for, Doc. Have you ever considered that?"

"They don't. Trust me, they don't."

"All right. *If* they don't find it, then what happens?"

"Best possible scenario. Then the cause of death will be natural. Period."

"You damn well better be right, Doc."

Eric Von Deutsch slammed the phone down and took a final heavy drag on the Merit. He crushed what little remained of the cigarette in the ashtray on the nightstand, stepped onto the east-facing fourteenth-floor balcony, and concentrated on calming himself.

Standing in the gentle breeze, gazing out at the endless ocean, he realized that the payout from the insurance company to Holloway—and the subsequent divvying up of the proceeds—might well take several weeks. During that time, he was determined to get used to some of the creature comforts that his new-found wealth would bring.

After dining on a rare rib eye, a twice-baked potato, and two one-liter bottles of Diet Coke from room service, he lit up another Merit, dug out the business card of Dr. Herbert Koremvokis from his luggage, and set it by the phone. It was too late in the day to call the plastic surgeon's office now. He would contact the office first thing in the morning and schedule the procedures that they'd already discussed.

This problem would pass. Life would be good. His thoughts wandered to kinky fantasies of swarthy Ramon.

FOUR

Dressed in running shorts, a washed-out Yankees T-shirt, and a pair of scuffed-up Nikes, Savage made his fifth lap around Washington Square Park. Instinctively, he read the subtle feedback on the faces of the street mopes with whom he made eye contact.

At first glance, they knew he was a cop. Savage knew that they knew, and they knew he knew they knew. A sharp cop could spot a lone bad guy in a circus crowd a hundred yards away, needing only a split-second eyeball. Conversely, sharp bad guys—the really savvy ones who knew the system and had a strong aversion to bunking at Rikers Island and dining on baloney sandwiches—knew a cop right off the bat as well. Such was life in the Big Apple. It was a place for survivors, both good and bad. Savage had no illusions about the realities of the street; it was a simple code: Sometimes you get the bear . . . and sometimes the bear gets you.

It was hot, the late-morning sun unrelenting. The glaring yellow ball hovered mercilessly over Lower Manhattan like a broiler chef's salamander Pittsburghing a New York strip to medium well. Visible, the heat radiated in griddle-like waves from the sidewalks, easily penetrating the soles of pumps, brogues . . . and scuffed-up Nikes. Savage opted to make this his last lap around the park, after which he would sprint over to Curley's kiosk to pick up a late-edition *Post* and some Wint-O-Greens, then do a quick wind-down walk back to his apartment for a much-needed shower and shave. He and his three-member team of detectives were scheduled for a four-to-midnight at Manhattan South Homicide. He knew, too well, how the searing summer heat always seemed to spur on the business of man kills man. Tonight might just be a busy one.

At West Fourth Street, he headed west and turned on the sprint. At Sixth Avenue—Avenue of the Americas—he turned south toward West Third.

"Good God *almighty*," Curley whined, leaning back in his wheelchair and shaking his bandannaed head in disbelief as Savage trotted up to the corner newsstand. "Mad dogs and po-leece-men go out in the midday sun," he recited sarcastically. "What are you, nuts, it's gotta be a hundred freakin' degrees out there, for crissakes."

"Marvel Super Heroes are never affected by that which would bring mere mortals to their knees," Savage teased with a half grin. Truth was, he'd overdone it and knew it. He slipped the top *Post* from beneath the iron hold-down weight. "How're they treatin' you, Curley?" he asked, pulling a soggy fiver from the back pocket of his shorts and tossing it onto the counter.

"Tips and all . . . not bad," the paraplegic Vietnam vet replied through a wildly overgrown red mustache that bore traces of his lunch—possibly yesterday's lunch. Without even being asked, he handed Savage a roll of his favorite Life Savers. After making change, Curley spun in his chair, leaned over, and spit a gob of chew into his gook pail.

It wasn't a pretty image, but chewing Red Man was one of Curley's few indulgences in life. He'd picked up the habit in a Pleiku foxhole when doing outer-perimeter duty with some rednecks from Tennessee. His other indulgences were the multiple dark tattoos that covered most of his arms and neck like a busy paisley print, and a wack-a-doo "roommate," Karl—who eked out a living writing porn and playing bass for Fistula, a local heavy-metal band. Karl also claimed to have been one of the co-inventors of the vacuum-assisted penile pump. Striving always to be as nonjudgmental as possible in matters concerning Curley, Savage figured that there wasn't much else for a mid-fifties man who hadn't moved his legs since he stepped on a claymore days before his nineteenth birthday. The poor bastard certainly had paid his dues.

"You working the late shift tonight?" Curley asked. Savage nodded.

"How do you stand that goddamned job?" Curley inquired, shaking his head and making an ugly face.

"I stand it quite well, actually," Savage said in earnest, always ready to defend The Job. "Couldn't imagine myself doing anything else."

"When I was a kid growing up here on the West Side, I was a cop wannabe," Curley said. "I figured after my hitch with Uncle Sam, I'd take the test . . . but things didn't quite work out that way."

Savage nodded again.

"Gotta run, buddy," he said, stepping out of the way of a new customer who was waiting to peruse the kiosk's extensive magazine display. He tucked the *Post* under his left arm, gave Curley a casual salute, and ambled down Sixth Avenue toward Bleecker.

As he turned off Bleecker Street into Sullivan, he saw a marked radio car from the Sixth Precinct parked directly in front of his apartment house, number 184. Police officer Billy Cox, a savvy and squared-away honor cop whom Savage had known for many years, was behind the wheel. At Savage's approach, he rolled the driver's window down.

"Sergeant Savage, sir," Cox called out. "Got a minute for an old pal?"

"Always," Savage responded. He stepped to the edge of the curb and squatted beside the driver's door.

"Hop in," Cox said. "I'm losing all my AC."

"If I hop in now, I'll wind up with pneumonia," Savage replied, tugging at his sweat-soaked shirt. "What's doin', Billy?"

"I called your office an hour ago, looking for you.

They told me you weren't due in today until four o'clock, so I swung by hoping to catch you at home. I got no answer when I rang your apartment bell, so I figured if I sat here at least an hour, you might show up for lunch."

"Here I am," Savage said. "Wanna come up? I've got a pot of hot on."

"No time," Cox replied tersely. He turned the noisy AC blower down a notch and looked seriously at Savage. "You know I'm just a uniformed radio-car cop," he began. "My job is first response. I take reports of past burglaries, I handle chickenshit fender benders, and I break up domestics between warring husbands and wives—regardless of the gender of either."

"Plus a million other things," Savage pointed out, knowing that patrol was the toughest part of the job.

"Right," Cox agreed, conceding the point. "Thing is, I don't do investigations; that's not my job. At least that's what I've been reminded of by my commanding officer. I'm not a detective. So I need to ask you to follow up on something for me."

"What kind of something?"

"A supposedly natural DOA. It was the first job my partner and I handled as soon as we turned out on a Tuesday morning back in late May."

"*Supposedly* natural?"

"The guy *supposedly* dropped dead while being treated by a neurologist in his office over on West Thirteenth. Or so the neurologist said, but . . ."

"But what?"

"Something was really wrong with it, Thorn. I knew it then, and I know it now. Believe me, I know it as sure as God. That goddamned doctor caused this guy's death."

"There's a lot of that going around," Savage replied, half in jest. "People die each and every day because of some physician's ineptitude. But according to article fifteen of the New York Penal Law, in order for it to be a crime it requires an accompanying culpable mental state on the doctor's part."

"And those culpable mental states are?"

"Intentionally, knowingly, recklessly, or with criminal negligence. Any of those four fit the scenario?"

Cox thought deeply, then, after clearing his throat, replied, "It could have been all of them."

"Okay," Savage said soothingly, giving his friend the benefit of the doubt, "let's hear it."

Cox exhaled hard and shook his head. "I just don't believe the damn doctor. His name is Janus—R. Charles Janus—big-deal Ivy Leaguer type."

"*R.* Charles Janus?" Savage questioned, emphasis on the *R.* "I don't like him already. I've got this thing about people who have an initial for a first name. Something about unbridled ego, pomposity, or self-importance."

"If you're talkin' mega-ego, you're right on with this guy," Cox said with an ironic snicker. "Anyway, I don't believe the DOA was there in his office for medical treatment, and I don't believe he died in the way this Dr. Janus said he died."

"Why don't you believe him?"

"Who goes to see a neurologist at four in the morning for a heart problem?" Cox said, making another face. "And what neurologist do you know would come in to his office at that hour to see you?"

"Four in the morning? That's odd office hours."

"*Ya think?*" Cox said, grimacing ironically.

"What do *you* think they were doing there, Billy?"

"Don't know. A sex thing, maybe. Maybe drugs. Something definitely wasn't kosher."

"How did the doctor say the guy died?"

"Heart attack. Said the guy died right in his goddamned office an hour after he got there."

"How do you think the guy died?"

"I'm not sure," Cox admitted, again shaking his head. "But I'm telling you, Thorn, the whole thing stunk right from the beginning. It was well beyond flagrante delicto, so we called for our precinct detective squad to respond."

"And?"

"They thought it stunk pretty good too. So they declared it a suspicious death and requested a sexual-assault analysis be performed. The ME on the scene even collected and preserved some specimens."

"That meant the body *had* to go for autopsy," Savage said.

"Right. And that pissed off that Dr. Janus pretty good. He was all ready to certify to the cause of death as heart attack and sign off on the death certificate. Then the body could have been released directly to a funeral home." Cox swiped his hands together cymballike. "End of problem."

"What did the autopsy show?"

"I couldn't believe it, but when I got back from my vacation two weeks later, I found out that the damn autopsy had agreed with that schmucky doctor," Cox replied. He chewed angrily on the inside of his cheek. "They declared it a natural death. A heart attack."

"End of story," Savage declared with a casual shrug. "If the ME signs off on a suspicious death as a natural, you can't open a case. That's just the way it is. You know that."

"I'm telling you it wasn't a natural, Thorn," Cox said forcefully. "You know how sometimes you just *know* something ain't right?"

"What did your detective squad say when they got the word about the ME's finding?"

Cox made a face. "I'm guessing they were as surprised as I was," he said with a smirk. "At least that's the feeling I got from the squad boss, Lieutenant Barone, when I talked to him about it. They were somewhat surprised, but they accepted it—said they had no choice."

If it had been someone other than Billy Cox telling him this, Savage would probably have sloughed it off, but he had a great deal of respect for Billy's instincts. And besides, he recalled, he'd solved many a case down through the years that had been set off by a mere hunch.

"Okay, Billy. Start at the beginning. Tell me more about the DOA."

The veteran street cop walked Savage through a chronological and concise commentary of all the events of that Tuesday morning in May, and his attendant suspicions. He focused on the DOA's cold body, the busy signals Janus supposedly encountered at the station house and 911 phone lines, and the absurdity of his having done forty-five minutes of CPR. "There were just too many damn inconsistencies. Know what I mean?" Cox said. "And now there's even more."

"Like what?"

"The DOA had some red marks on him. On his chest, sides, belly—random. They looked like freakin' hickeys. The doctor had said he'd given the guy an EKG during his examination, so at the time I wrote them off as being caused by the suction-cup-type leads."

"So what are you thinking now?"

"Looking back, I don't think that all those marks were from an EKG. I think some were caused by something else," Cox said flatly. He made strong eye contact, begging the question.

"Okay," Savage said. "I'll bite. What made 'em?"

"A stun gun."

"A stun gun?" Savage was taken aback. "This doctor we're talking about, you said his name was Janus, not de Sade."

"Yeah, well, maybe that's what it oughtta be."

"Man, this one's really eating at you, Billy," Savage said. "You clearly believe there's more here?"

"Yeaaaah," Cox replied with a nasal drawl. "I *know* there's more. I found out a little tidbit when I came to work last Friday. Information that dumps a whole lot more fuel on this fire for me."

"Talk to me."

"One of our steady-midnight sector teams, Cavonis and Hildebrand, were just getting off as I was coming in. I overheard them in the locker room telling a great story. Said they were doing a midnight about three months ago when they got flagged down by some half-drunk guy at around one o'clock in the morning. Guy said he'd been assaulted by a doctor right in the doctor's own damn office on Thirteenth Street.''

"Dr. *R*. Charles Janus?"

"Guy claimed Janus had attacked him with a stun gun. He showed Cavonis and Hildebrand a bunch of red marks all over his chest and arms."

"Christ. Did they collar Janus?" Savage asked.

"Nope." Cox shook his head and grimaced. "When they took this guy back over to Janus' office, they found out that the two had met hours earlier at an S&M club down off Houston. Seems both Janus and this complainant are very much into pain. You know," Cox said, raising his eyebrows and clearing his throat derisively, "this is the Sixth Precinct . . . do I need to say any more? As a matter of command policy we have, shall we say, a bit greater tolerance when it comes to certain sexual *behaviors* and *proclivities*. Therefore, Hildebrand and Cavonis wound up writing the whole thing off as a lovers' quarrel. No hits, no runs, no errors . . . no men left on."

"And no collar."

"Right. No collar."

"It could be said that these two events were simply coincidental," Savage offered. "But I'm not a big fan of coincidence."

"That's how I see it, but apparently it didn't impress Lieutenant Barone up in the squad or, more importantly, the precinct commander who pulls his strings. That morning, I ran right upstairs with this new information, but after Barone spoke briefly to Captain Dipson, he wasn't about to reopen any damn thing. He even ordered me not to do a Complaint Follow-up Informational. That's why I tried contacting you. I'm really pissed."

"But we still need the ME to tell us we've got a crime," Savage murmured. "No crime . . . no case. Did

Cavonis and Hildebrand get that earlier complainant's name and address, a phone number? I'd really like to talk to that guy."

"They said he gave the name of Timothy DiBona. They described him as a bit spacey. He told Cavonis he had no phone. I've checked the address he gave, but he's since moved—left no forwarding. I've asked around, but I'm getting nowhere."

"What would you like me to do, Billy?"

"You've been in Homicide a long time, and I know you're very well connected over at the ME's office . . . you know a lot of people there. Maybe you can inquire about this one. I just wanna know that they're absolutely certain about supporting the doctor's diagnosis. I'll sleep a lot better."

"You think they're going to change their story now?" Savage asked with a jaded snicker. "Months later? I don't think so."

"What's the matter?" Cox said with an edge. "They can't ever do any reviews?"

"I'm sure they can, Billy," Savage assured him. "But you've gotta figure the body is long gone. It's probably been buried . . . maybe even cremated."

"Unh," Cox grunted. "Could you ask the head guy over there to review the reports—you know, just do a follow-up?"

"So happens the head guy over there is a head gal. But if she does review it—and tells me that there is no doubt—will that satisfy you?"

"Ehh. In my heart, I'd still think something stinks, but I'd have to go with it." Cox held out a large manila envelope. "Here. I've made Xerox copies of all my reports and memoranda from that morning. You'll find it contains all the pertinent info: times and names of all who responded from EMT, the ME's office, patrol supervisors, and our detective squad. It also contains the names and phone numbers of those I made personal notifications to, blah-blah-blah. Beyond that, I've also written down all the questions that I asked that schmucky doctor that morning and some of his ridiculous answers. Take a look at them when you get a chance. You'll be amused."

"What was the DOA's name?" Savage asked, tucking the envelope into the pages of the *Post*.

"Granger. George Granger. Male, white, forty-five years. It's all written down in those notes."

Savage stood. "I'll see what I can do."

Cox slipped the cruiser into gear. "Gotta run, Thorn. Thanks a million."

Belfast, Ireland

The late afternoon was not hot, nor was it humid, but a somber, dull dark gray and raining like hell as the black Austin crossed the Queen Elizabeth Bridge in the heavy traffic and made a tight left onto Oxford Street. John Boyer Holloway sat anxiously in the backseat, rechecking his notes and directions; so far, it seemed, the horse-faced, sullen, and untalkative cabdriver was on the right course. The taxi continued southbound on Oxford and made a right turn onto Chichester Street as directed. It flew past the courthouse complex, crossed Victoria Street and Cornmarket, and made another right onto Arthur Street. At the middle of the quaint shop-filled block, the driver flipped off the meter and pulled abruptly to the curb. Through the rain-sprinkled window, Holloway could make out the shingle sign hanging above the business location's door. Sure enough, it read: EAMMON BRADLEY—PHOTOGRAPHY.

Holloway handed over a fresh twenty-pound note for the fifteen-pound ride, popped his umbrella, and stepped from the cab. A thank-you was not forthcoming from the driver.

As he let himself through the shop's red-enameled and multipaned front door, a small bell bracketed to the inside jingled loudly. Seeing no one about, he collapsed the umbrella and called out a mild "hello," but got no response. The showroom was small but not claustrophobic, with a squeaky floor of well-worn planks, a sales counter far too large for the limited amount of space, and, at the far wall, a curtained entry into a rear area. Holloway noted the elaborately framed enlarged portraits that graced every available space along the high walls: smiling brides, handsome grooms, brides and grooms together, freckle-faced, redheaded, and blue-eyed little girls in communion white. The usual photographer fare.

"Can I be helpin' you, sir?"

The brogue was heavy, Holloway thought. And the short, white-haired, wiry-eyebrowed gent who stepped from the back room appeared as if just sent up from central casting for the role of the classic older Irish man. Even his Kelly green vest and plaid pants looked the part.

"I certainly do hope so," Holloway replied, looking tightly into the man's intense blue eyes. "Are you Eammon Bradley?" he asked.

"That I am. And who might you be?"

"Is there anybody else about?" Holloway asked in a soft tone, ignoring the man's query while nodding toward the back room. "We need some privacy," he continued. "I guess you could say that I have something of a delicate business proposition to discuss with you."

"And what might that be, sir?" Eammon Bradley said. "You may speak freely; there is no one else in the shop. Fact is, I was about to close shop for the day."

"I am advised that when one needs a British passport—an *authentic* British passport—one can come to Belfast City to see Eammon Bradley and, shall we say, have the whole process somewhat . . . accelerated."

"Is that a fact now?" the diminutive photographer intoned. His eyes were squinted suspiciously. "And just where might you have heard such . . . things?"

"From Benjamin Franklin," Holloway said, holding up a fanned fistful of hundred-dollar bills and slowly waving them.

"You're a Yank," Bradley said, his eyes still asquint.

"Yes, but I want to be a Brit."

"Become naturalized," Bradley offered with a shrug.

"I don't want to become naturalized."

"What do you want, then?"

"I want to be a by-birth citizen of the UK, complete with a brand-new name and identity."

"Is that all?" Bradley said through an amused laugh. "Sounds to me as if you were probably born in New Jersey. Or maybe you were born in California . . . or Pittsburgh, or Denver. You just can't change that and decide that you were born in Liverpool, or Glasgow, or Newcastle."

"I'm told I can," Holloway said. "And I'm told that you're the guy who can do it. For a nice round fee, that is." He tossed the pile of century notes onto the sales counter.

"Sir, do you have any idea of the state the damn world is in just now?" Bradley asked, tightening his focus on Holloway's eyes. "Do you have any idea of the shit that's been goin' on in the world for the past damn decade? Does the word *terrorism* mean anything to you?"

"Look at me, Eammon," Holloway said forcefully, meeting the cunning man eyeball to eyeball. "I'm a damn Yank. I'm certainly not some al-Qaida asshole prepping for a suicide mission, nor am I an agent of the British government here to run some sort of integrity test on you."

Long pause. "Those are American dollars," Bradley finally said with a sneer, brushing the stack aside. "They're only worth about half that of the pound sterling."

"You name your price, in American dollars, British pounds, or fucking Euros . . . I'll pay it."

There was a long pause as Eammon Bradley continued to stare deeply into Holloway's eyes, studying him, deciding. John Boyer Holloway could see the powerful gears of greed beginning to engage inside the diminutive Irishman's head.

"It usually takes seven days," Bradley said flatly.

"I don't have seven days to wait."

"Despite my connections, that is one aspect of the process over which I have no control. The United Kingdom Passport Service requires that seven-day period—and a seventy-pound fee—for the issuance of a first adult passport."

"Get around it. I'm due back in Amsterdam tomorrow evening."

"I've got someone on the inside who might be able to speed up the process . . . but he's a greedy fella."

"No problem."

"Why don't you step into my studio?" Bradley said, sweeping back the curtain. "The first thing we need to do is get two nice, identical, full-face photographs of you . . . for your application, of course."

"Of course."

"And while we're at it," Bradley added, scrunching his wiry eyebrows and narrowing his gaze, "we can be discussing *my* fee."

Thorn Savage let himself into his three-story brownstone apartment building and climbed the squeaky wooden stairs to the second floor. Upon entering apartment 2, he quickly shed the Nikes, stripped off the sticky wet T-shirt and shorts, and dropped them into the clothes hamper behind the bathroom door. The hamper was about to overflow; washday was nigh. Clad only in white socks, he ambled through the living room into the small kitchen and found Ray curled up in his usual spot atop the Kelvinator.

"You gonna sleep all day?" Savage asked, reaching into the wall cabinet above the sink for a water glass. The cabinet also contained his supply of vitamins, medicines, and herbal supplements.

The sharp question elicited a single quick swipe of Ray's battle-scarred tail and a long, gaping yawn, followed by an intense glare of sour annoyance from tightly squinted yellow eyes. For sure the fifteen-year-old tom never had liked being disturbed when he was busy doing that which he did best. But there seemed to be something else—a quality Savage couldn't quite put his finger on. Maybe Ray was coming down with something. He would keep a close eye on him in the coming days.

Savage filled the glass at the tap and downed a 425 mg vitamin C, two ginkgo bilobas, and an 80 mg Diovan HCT. Having recently heard that ginseng might be contraindicated for those with high blood pressure, he again avoided taking one. He missed ginseng, and the vitality-generating, memory-enhancing, feeling of well-being it used to bring.

He wondered where his BP stood today; it had been moving around quite a bit lately. At his last office visit, Dr. Sahay had read him the riot act and directed that he take at least one reading each day and keep a diary that she could review at his next scheduled visit, which would be two weeks hence. He glanced at the Omron BP monitor sitting on his dinette table and thought briefly about slipping his arm into the cuff and taking a reading. Nah, he decided. If it was high—as it probably was—he'd be bummed. Screw it.

The coffeepot beckoned. He poured a cup and added just a splash of expired half-and-half from the fridge. According to the digital clock on the microwave, he still had ample time to do one load of laundry, shave, shower, and possibly finish off the last six chapters of *Tale of Two Cities*—only fifty-six more pages—before heading into work. Since high school, it was the third time he'd gotten wrapped up in Dickens' twin-themed story of two cities, two heroes, good and evil, love and hate, life and death, where the worst of times surely outnumbered the best. But, he decided, first things first. He took a tentative sip of the French roast Maxwell House, plucked the wall phone from its cradle, and dialed a number he knew only too well.

"This is the Office of the Chief Medical Examiner, New York County. How may I direct your call?"

"Dr. Karyn Hartman, please."

FIVE

Dr. Karyn Hartman, senior pathologist at the New York County medical examiner's office, had taken Savage's call and, as a special favor, agreed to review the George Granger file. She also suggested that he call her back in several hours to discuss it over the phone. But because he'd made the special request, he felt it more appropriate to get the information in person. It was just good protocol. Before heading to his office at Manhattan South, he went directly to the ME's office on First Avenue at Twenty-ninth Street. He arrived shortly before three p.m.

Savage popped a Wint-O-Green as he pushed through the dinged, dented, and dirty aluminum swinging doors of the basement delivery entrance. Plainly and simply, the initial sense awakened upon entering the gory workshop of the New York County medical examiner's office was olfactory. One immediately smelled meat. Some days, the meat odor wasn't too bad—no worse than that of a neatly kept butcher shop. Other days, the stench of rotted human innards could curl the hair of a bald man. He thoroughly hated the place.

Every medical examiner's office he had ever been in shared the same cold, nonporous decor. There was the abundance of glass and stainless steel, and each wall surface, ceiling to floor, was constructed of glazed ceramic block, usually bisque or beige in color. Floor surfaces were also ceramic, though not highly glazed. A multitude of drains allowed for necessary and periodic hose-downs. He controlled a mild shiver as he let himself into the large, brightly lit autopsy room—twelve slabs, no waiting.

"Good afternoon, Sergeant Savage," Dr. Karyn Hartman said. The attractive, though somewhat plump, pathologist was poking around inside the open chest of a partially decomposed black female customer stretched out before her.

"That's a rather ripe one," Savage observed drolly, squinting his eyebrows and doing his best not to breathe.

"Her skull's been crushed in two places. She was found beneath a viaduct of the Henry Hudson Parkway. Probably been there three or four days." The pathologist looked over at him and shrugged. "In *this* weather . . ."

"Unh," Savage grunted, siphoning in just enough air to keep from turning blue.

"Close her up," Hartman said to a female assistant who was clad in what appeared to be a full-length hazmat suit. Pulling off a pair of elbow-length surgical gloves, Hartman moved away from the station and let the bloodied objects drop into a medical waste container.

Savage sucked a little harder on the Life Saver. It was clear that today wasn't a particularly good meat day at the butcher shop.

"As you requested, I did a review of that postmortem you called me about . . . George Granger."

"The verdict?" Savage asked, praying that Hartman would suggest they leave the nightmarish space and adjourn to her office. As she reached into a wall cabinet and plucked an Oreo from an open package, he realized that wasn't going to happen.

"Mr. George Granger had a host of medical problems," she said, raising her clear-plastic face shield with the side of her wrist. "But first and foremost, I must tell you that I have to concur with the pathologist who performed the autopsy and the physician who attended the death—a Dr. R. Charles Janus—as to the cause of death." She bit into the cookie, taking half.

"You concur absolutely?" Savage asked.

"After completion of my evaluation and analysis of all the materials, it is my professional opinion, based upon a reasonable degree of medical certainty, that George Granger died as a result of heart attack precipitated by severe intoxication."

"Is there no room for any doubt?" Savage said, pressing.

"No one can ever be one hundred percent sure of anything in this world, Sergeant," Hartman replied, almost condescendingly. "You of all people should know that. And without benefit of having the body before me, all I can do is go by the report. In which event, I would have to say *no doubt*."

"All right," Savage said, giving her that one. "But as long as I'm here you may as well give me the whole picture."

Hartman moved briskly to a stainless-steel writing counter that ran the length of the large room and picked up a bright orange folder labeled GEORGE GRANGER. Printed in bold block lettering, the name was followed by a six-digit code beginning with the letter *N* for New York County. She opened the folder, removed a packet of color photographs, and handed them to Savage.

"Taking you literally," she joked. "Here's the whole picture."

Savage quickly scanned through the ME's photos of the supine nude body of George Granger. They were taken just prior to, during—with chest cavity fully open and organs removed—and immediately after the postmortem. Consistent with Billy Cox's observations, he noted some red blotches on the chest area in the first photo. One of those abrasions—quite small and saw-toothed in appearance—was unlike the others and was located on the left breast just above the nipple. He also studied the man's face. Although his hair was thinning and he was no movie star, the guy looked pretty damn good for forty-five years.

"You said he had a host of medical problems . . ." Savage ventured.

Hartman flipped slowly through several pages, running a delicate index finger across lines of notes. "Beyond having nonspecific focal myocarditis," she began, "Mr. Granger was also HIV positive. Also, at the time of death he had a point two-nine ethanol-alcohol level. Must have been doing some *real* heavy boozing in the hours before."

"Whew," Savage said, impressed. "Guy was a walking can of Sterno. Twenty-nine's a pretty hefty number, almost four times the legal."

"Very high," the pathologist agreed. "Maybe the alcohol was Mr. Granger's way of dealing with his HIV condition—if, in fact, he even knew he was infected—but it certainly didn't help his cardiac problem in any way."

"Okay, Doc. Now what was that first thing you said again . . . nonspecific *focal myocarditis*?" Savage inched out the words, unsure of their proper pronunciation. "Could you explain that condition a little bit for me?" He reached into his pocket for a Wint-O-Green. He was already down to his last one.

"Briefly, myocarditis is an inflammation of the muscular walls of the heart. The condition may result from bacterial or viral infections, or it may be a toxic inflammation caused by drugs or toxins from infectious agents. The most common symptoms of *acute* myocarditis are pain in the epigastric region or under the sternum . . . dyspnea."

"Dyspnea?" He peeled away the foil from the final Life Saver, popped it into his mouth, and sucked hard.

"Difficult or painful breathing. It's a symptom of a variety of disorders and is primarily an indication of inadequate ventilation, or of insufficient amounts of oxygen in the circulating blood."

"Gotcha."

Hartman reached into the folder and extracted a short length of EKG strip. "We also have the decedent's EKG, which was taken just before he died. Basically, all I see here is evidence of sinus tachycardia—

fast heartbeat. Which is quite consistent with someone under the influence of alcohol."

"I see. Does the EKG strip indicate, in any way, that the person was about to drop dead of a heart attack?"

Hartman made a tentative face and inhaled the remainder of Oreo. "No," she replied, chewing slowly. "Not in and of itself, but . . ."

"If someone is about to die from a heart attack, shouldn't certain abnormalities be present and detectable on the EKG?"

"I would say, yes . . . in *most* cases."

"But not in this one?"

"Apparently not." She swallowed, wiped her mouth with a napkin, and dropped it into a medical-waste bin.

"Was there any bruising or hemorrhage in the area of the rib cage?" Savage asked. "You know, the kind one would expect if CPR had been administered for a prolonged period?"

"Some faint discolorations that followed the contours of the costal margins of the central chest," Hartman replied. "Which would be consistent with resuscitative efforts and/or lividity. Otherwise the rib cage was intact."

"Hmm. What about any bleeding below the scalp, or bruising elsewhere on the body? This guy was supposed to have fallen from an examining table and made a loud thud."

"Abrasions on right wrist and knee in which there was no inflammatory response; therefore they occurred within one or two hours of death." Hartman quickly added, "But both would be consistent with such a fall."

"Could they have also been consistent with trauma, say, from an assault . . . or some form of restraint?"

"The small size of the abrasions on the wrist, and the lack of pressure marks, would argue against any type of restraint which would have encircled the wrist and made more broad and circumferential lesions."

"What mention was made of the red marks present on the body? In the area of the chest, sides . . . arms?" He held up photograph 1 and pointed to the small saw-toothed mark he'd seen above the DOA's left nipple. "Specifically, this one."

"Hmm," Hartman uttered. "Odd little mark." She flipped ahead several pages in the folder.

"I ask because the officer on the scene remembered seeing some red blotches on the torso," Savage continued. "At the time, he wrote them off as something related to the EKG testing. But, to me, this little mark looks like the impression of a key—a house key, perhaps. It may have absolutely no significance whatsoever, but it certainly is nothing at all like the other red blotches."

"Why don't I just read you the pathologist's summary," she said, flipping back a page. " 'The body is that of an unembalmed Caucasian male, middle-aged, who appears younger than the stated age of forty-five years. Lividity is fixed posteriorly, and on the right side of the head and neck. There is beard stubble on the face. There is patchy reddish-yellow discoloration of the skin around the mouth and left lower lip. Not patterned, they appear very superficial, and possibly represent an irritated area, such as from shaving. This could account for the stubble on decedent's face; he may not have wanted to have worsened it by shaving again. The chest shows pectus excavatum.' "

She looked up briefly at Savage before continuing. She emphasized the next sentence. " '*A number of small red abrasions on chest consistent with heroic resuscitative measures*. There is a small yellow-red abrasion at the inferolateral aspect of the right patella measuring 0.6 x 0.5 centimeters and another small red abrasion on the dorsum of right wrist. The decedent went into cardiac arrest at his doctor's office. He had been complaining of severe chest pains and headaches and arranged to meet at his office. He never went to see a cardiac specialist. Previous medical records indicate complaints of chest pain going back at least one year and more. Cause of death consistent with natural causes.' "

"You mentioned that bacterial or viral infections, or a toxic inflammation caused by drugs or toxins from infectious agents, could be the underlying causes of this myocarditis. Were any tissues checked for signs of viral or bacterial infections, or the presence of any poisons or drugs?" Savage asked.

"Of course. Other than the high-octane moonshine or Wild Turkey—or whatever it was—preliminary tests indicated no toxins in his blood. Beyond that, just last week we received the gas chromatography results on a number of his tissues—all were negative."

"I'm told that a sexual-assault analysis was to be performed," Savage said. "Anything there?"

"Rectal swab was negative. However, a foreign antigen, type B, was discovered on an oral swab taken from the deceased. The DOA happened to be type O."

"What can we conclude there?" Savage asked, knowing full well the answer.

"Someone was deep French-kissing Mr. Granger shortly before, during, or after his death. But as far as I know, there's no law in this town about making out. No matter how you look at it, it just comes out as a natural, Sergeant. We have no evidence of a crime having been committed." Hartman glanced up from her notes. "I do have a few questions, though, just out of my own curiosity."

"Shoot. I'll answer them if I can."

"Why was a man with a heart condition seeing a neurologist for treatment—in the neurologist's private office—at some ungodly early hour of the morning? Why didn't he just go to an emergency room? St. Vincent's Hospital was right around the corner."

"Dr. Janus was asked that very question by the police officers at the scene. Supposedly, this guy Granger was a longtime patient of his with an intense—almost psychotic—fear of emergency rooms and hospitals. The doctor indulged the man by meeting him at his office in the middle of the night. He claimed to have just performed an EKG on Granger and had stepped momentarily from the room. After hearing a thud, he came back in and found the guy unconscious on the floor."

"Weird-o-rama. But this did happen over in the West Village, right?" she said, flashing intelligent brown eyes.

"Right," Savage agreed, replying with a half laugh. "Many peculiar things do seem to occur down there." He knew his remark was at least an understatement. It was no secret that if one was seeking the truly bizarre—or the really weird—in New York City, one might look first in the Village. "What else can you tell me that I can pass along to the officer?"

The doctor stuck her nose back into the folder and began to read off information in a mildly bored manner. "The heart weighed 348 grams; the ventricles were dilated. The lungs had a combined weight of 1,406 grams and were clear and healthy."

"Clear and healthy?" Savage interrupted.

"Surely a nonsmoker," she replied offhandedly and read on. "There was a 0.3-inch yellow-white lesion on the surface of the liver. The stomach contained 45 cubic centimeters of a gray-brown fluid without admixed food particles. The organs were otherwise unremarkable."

"Okay, okay," Savage said, shutting her down.

"Just for your own edification, though, you may want to know that Granger's body was additionally identified by, and subsequently released to, his business partner, a Mr. John B. Holloway. The body was then removed from here by Fairlawn Mortuary—the Bronx—on May thirtieth."

Savage jotted those two pieces of information down.

"Is there anything in your reports that would tell us if the body was to be buried or cremated?"

"No. We don't normally require such information."

"You said, 'business partner,'" he mumbled. "Were there no family inquiries, from blood kin?"

"The technician who performed the postmortem personally checked with Dr. Janus on that. According to his patient records, Granger listed only Holloway to be notified in case of emergency. Notes here say that the guy flew in from Columbus, Ohio."

"The pathologist who performed the autopsy spoke *directly* with Dr. Janus?"

"According to these notes," Hartman said after flipping another page, "yes. And"—apparently to head off the next question—she added, "under the circumstances, such an inquiry would not be considered out of the ordinary."

"Does it say whether that contact occurred before, during, or after the postmortem?"

"Probably very near completion."

"Probably?"

"Apparently she just wanted to hear some of the doctor's insights to see if they gibed with what she found."

"She?"

"Althea Blanchard, an associate pathologist who was working here at the time."

"An associate?" Savage said. "A rookie doing a postmortem on a suspicious death?"

Dr. Hartman cleared her throat and composed herself. "That happens all the time," she said. "But I assure you, had she found *anything* suspicious, she would have consulted with a senior pathologist."

"So this Althea Blanchard . . . she is no longer working here?"

"She's now over at the Kings County ME's."

Jesus, Savage thought while fighting off a shiver, *that fuckin' place is even worse than this*.

"Let me ask you this," he said. "Are there still any of Granger's tissue samples in your custody?"

"Of course," Hartman replied. "Heart, liver, lung, esophagus . . ."

"His clothing?"

"Clothing went with the body."

"Hmm. Okay," Savage replied, scribbling notes.

"So then it's a wrap, right, Doctor? Your office is going with natural causes."

"It's a wrap."

Dr. Karyn Hartman smiled and snapped on a fresh pair of surgical gloves. She pulled them up to her elbows, snatched another Oreo from the wall cabinet, and plunked the entire thing in her mouth. Chewing eagerly, she turned her attention to the unopened body of a young white male on table 5.

Savage left the ME's office and walked out into the roasting afternoon sunshine and clear, nonputrefied air. He climbed into his unmarked, started it, and drove slowly up First Avenue, deep in thought.

He both liked and respected Dr. Karyn Hartman; she was considered at the top of her profession. Down through the years she had proven her abilities on countless occasions, and she had always been approachable and reasonable. But he liked and respected Officer Billy Cox every bit as much . . . perhaps even an ounce or two more.

He didn't know quite what it was, but he felt unsatisfied by the interview he'd just conducted. It all sounded quite legit, all right, but . . . as Billy Cox had said, "Sometimes you just *know* something ain't right."

SIX

Every afternoon, rain or shine, at around 1530 hours, the area of East Twenty-first Street in front of the Thirteenth Precinct station house becomes clogged with police tour-change activity. Overworked radio cars—most with that beaten, worn-out, tongue-dangling-from-the-grill look of high-mileage fleet taxicabs—rest only briefly while being hot-seated by fresh crews taking them over from fatigued day-tour teams who spill slowly out. This is the routine that plays three times a day, seven days a week, 365 days a year at all the seventy-six NYPD patrol precincts that cover every neighborhood of the city's five boroughs.

Knowing he'd never get a spot nearby at that hour, Savage parked his unmarked department auto around the corner on Third Avenue. It was a nice day; he enjoyed the short walk and the clean air. As he entered the hectic station house, he snapped a customary salute to the Stars and Stripes displayed behind the desk and gave a friendly smile to Lieutenant Jimmy Dugan. The gaunt and balding uniformed desk officer, a neighborhood Bronx Irish kid who had been a few years behind him in high school, was talking on two phones at once, and had a couple of fresh-faced rookies standing by hoping for his attention. Dugan motioned Savage to wait until he completed his calls.

Being a desk officer in one of the busy NYPD commands ranked very near the top of things that the AMA strongly recommended against if one had a peptic ulcer—or did not want one. Savage had been a desk officer in Midtown South, the busiest precinct in the world, when first promoted to sergeant years ago; he knew the drill. Among a million other things, the DO was charged with knowing everything that was going on within the confines of the entire precinct at any given moment. He knew—or at least was charged with knowing—the whereabouts of every radio car and every footman as well. Like a hockey coach, he made constant changes in assignments to meet the needs of conditions as they changed from moment to moment on the street. He reviewed and approved the charges for every arrest, was responsible for safeguarding every piece of evidence and every piece of property vouchered for safekeeping for arrestees and DOAs. He dealt with the division and borough offices, argued with Downtown, pampered the press, handled the complaints of harried crime victims, dealt with any allegations of misconduct by any of the troops—and so much more.

Every so often, however, most desk officers have a chance to slip from behind the demanding desk, sneak into a rear office, and gulp down an overbrewed black coffee. The high-octane java was a necessity if one wanted to stay sharp enough to make the day without leaving one's own ass hanging out in harm's way . . . but it sure did raise holy hell with that damn peptic ulcer.

When Dugan hung up the phone, he penned in some quick changes on the roll call, spoke briefly to a patrol sergeant, then quickly joined Savage at the side of the desk.

"Heard about the Street Crime Unit reunion?" he said.

"No," Savage replied, wanting to hear more. Both he and Dugan had worked many years ago in the now defunct but well-remembered unit. "Where and when?"

"Marina Del Rey. You know the joint, up in the Bronx next to the Throgs Neck Bridge. Eighty bucks a head. It's on a Saturday night, August seventeenth. Six thirty till . . . whenever."

"You going?" Savage asked, nagged by a sense that the mid-August date had some meaning but not yet able to bring it up on his screen.

"You kiddin'?" Dugan responded with a smirk. "Wouldn't miss a Street Crime racket for the world. It's gonna be a good one."

"I think I might already have something on for that night," Savage said, hedging. "In fact, I think I'm booked for that whole weekend." There was absolutely no doubt in his mind that he would hate to miss the Street Crime racket—probably even more so than Jimmy Dugan would hate to miss it—but he recalled the Hamptons beach house promise and Maureen's sour prediction that something related to his job *"will"* definitely come up to ruin the plan.

"Hey, you've gotta make it, man," Dugan pressed. "Everybody's gonna be there, and everybody will be expecting to see you."

Savage nodded his understanding and noticed that the two rookie cops had inched gingerly closer to speak with Dugan. He recalled his own trepidation about approaching a lieutenant when he was a rookie.

"Be right with you," the feisty lieutenant told them, pointing to a far corner. "Wait over there." The two fresh faces turned about and marched off immediately.

"They from the class the academy graduated last Friday?" Savage inquired.

"Yep," Dugan said. "First day on the street for those two." Then, mumbling out of the side of his mouth, he added, "Don't know where they're finding these kids anymore. Look at that one guy, the tall one, Henderson. He just looks too soft, you know . . . too prime-time to make it in this game. Don't he?"

Savage looked the shiny rookie over. Dugan was right. The Henderson kid was as handsome a poster boy as the job could ever ask for. He was a lean six-footer with a chiseled chin, and he made the uniform look great. "Guy should'a been a movie actor, for crissakes," he commented.

"That's what the troops thought too. Wouldn't you know it, they've already dubbed the poor bastard 'Hollywood.' "

"That name'll stick for his whole twenty," Savage observed.

"But," Dugan said, shrugging and flashing a look of resignation, "even he'll eventually adapt. It might take six months or a year to get that cop look and attitude, but it'll happen."

"Always does."

As Dugan moved off to parlay with the two eager rookies, Savage made his way to the back staircase and took the diamond-plate steps two at a time up to C-Deck and the offices of the Manhattan South Homicide Unit. He went right to the command log kept beside the wheel desk and signed himself in. The wheelman, Eddie Brodigan, greeted him with his usual friendly smile and corny thoughts for the day.

"Hey, Sarge," Brodigan whispered, after looking warily over both shoulders, "why is lemonade made with artificial flavoring, while dishwasher soap is made with real lemons?"

"Don't know," Savage whispered back, looking over both shoulders. "But that's a pretty *tart* question."

"And another thing," Brodigan went on, an amused gleam reflecting from his Celtic browns. "If beef comes from a cow and ham from a pig, why do they put beef in hamburgers?"

"You're in *rare* form today, aren't you?" Savage replied, playing the word game with the office punster. "But I must tell you, Ed, I'm losing my *appetite* for the *flavor* of these questions."

"Do you think them in bad *taste*?"

"Can't say that I *relish* them."

Brodigan broke into a laugh. "Sarge," he said, shaking his head, "you're pretty good at this shit."

Savage nodded hello to partners Diane DeGennaro

and Richie Marcus, two of his three veteran detectives, and moved easily through the large and well-lit eight-desk office to the small sergeants' room he shared with Billy Lakis and Jules Unger. This afternoon Savage had the space to himself. Lakis was off on vacation in the Bahamas, and Unger was somewhere out in the field. After hanging his suit jacket beside the neatly pressed uniforms in his locker, he sat down at his desk and quickly jotted down all the ME's findings on George Granger. When he finished, he slipped the folded sheet into a multi-use envelope addressed to Officer Billy Cox, Sixth Precinct, and flipped it into the outgoing department mail.

Savage looked up at the clock; it was almost four—showtime. Unlike today, Savage usually arrived at least a half hour early for work. It mattered little whether he was doing a day duty or, like today, a four p.m. to midnight; the early start allowed him some quiet time to catch up on any in-basket reading, and if that was squared away, a chance to nip away at the Sunday *Times* crossword, which he kept stashed in his top desk drawer and always did in ink.

"Got a minute, Sarge?" Jack Lindstrom, the erudite and quiet-spoken third member of his team, leaned his slender frame into the office.

Lindstrom was again wearing that same old out-of-date J.C.Penney gray suit. Baggy, it had cuffs that didn't quite make it to the vamps of his tired brown Thom McAns. Homicide was easily the most prestigious assignment in the Detective Bureau, and most assigned there prided themselves on being clothes-horses. Not Jack Lindstrom.

"C'mon in, Jack," Savage said.

"Just want to let you know, I'll be out of the office for an hour or so. I'm heading downtown. I've got to swing by Photo to pick up something on that Mendoza case, and then make a quick stop at Latent Prints. Do you need anything while I'm out?"

"No, Jack. Thanks."

Lindstrom turned to leave, then changed his mind

as Richie Marcus and Diane DeGennaro entered the sergeants' room. Richie and Diane were longtime partners both on and off The Job. Their romantic involvement—and the fact that they lived together—was an open secret within the command.

"How was your weekend?" Diane asked, her cool Wedgwood blues taking Savage's eyes.

"Good," Savage replied, flashing a grin. "Maureen and I took a nice ride down to the Jersey shore on Saturday morning, spent the night."

"Go to the beach?" Marcus asked.

"Actually, no," Savage responded, rocking back in his chair. "I drove down to buy a replacement wire wheel for my T-bird. Some guy in Toms River had one advertised in the *Hemmings Motor News*."

"Jeez." Marcus looked surprised. "Seems to me you bent that wheel months ago—Memorial Day weekend—when you and Maureen was out in the Hamptons. You just now getting around to replacing it? That don't sound like you."

"Took that much time just to find one," Savage replied. "You can't just go and buy an authentic wire-spoke wheel for a nearly fifty-year-old classic car in Sears or Target. I was lucky to locate this one. Paid three bills for it, and before it goes on the car it has to be replated."

"How much is that going to be?" Lindstrom asked.

"Another three," Savage said stoically.

"Any good saloons down on the Jersey shore?" Marcus inquired. His voice, the product of an inclination toward coffin nails and the now and then pull of a cork, was pure rasp.

"Figures that would be *your* first concern," Jack Lindstrom said, verbally goosing the slightly older detective. "That, or were there any good pool halls, OTB parlors, or pinball arcades nearby. Boy, you sure are consistent."

Marcus shot Lindstrom a quick middle-finger glare, then turned back toward Savage. "Let me amend my question, boss. Were there any fine-dining establishments down there?"

"Matter of fact, there are several really nice places," Savage commented. "A bit on the heavy side pricewise. But nice."

"If I won the freakin' lottery," the paunchy, but not soft, Marcus mused contemplatively, "I'd sit down there on the Jersey shore, soak in the sun, and drink cocktails all damn day. Might even buy myself a boat; something with a small cabin. Would that be the good life or what?"

"He's not kidding," Diane chimed in, her eyes wide and earnest. "He'd love to have nothing to do but relax or fish all day."

"You wouldn't be any happier," Lindstrom said simply.

"Whaddaya mean, I wouldn't be *happier*?" Marcus growled. "If I hit one of them hundred-million-dollar lotteries I'd be freakin' ecstatic."

"Not for long."

Savage knew the brainy Lindstrom was about to go off on some kind of deep discourse.

"Research has proved that if you're dreaming of a wonderful life of leisure, if you hit the lottery—or if your wealthy uncle Wally remembers you in his will—you're just not going to be happy," Lindstrom said, looking Marcus straight in the eye.

"What are you, out of your mind?" Marcus drawled. He made a disgusted face that would have stopped a crosstown bus.

"It's true," Lindstrom went on. "It all has to do with the striatum—the part of the brain associated with reward processing and pleasure."

"The *who*?" Marcus muttered blandly.

"The striatum," Lindstrom repeated.

"You telling me there's some part of *my* brain that won't let *me* be freakin' happy if I win a hundred million bucks?" Marcus said. He laughed scornfully, his pale blue eyes beaming incredulity.

"Well, that's presuming one *has* a brain," Lindstrom said with a sardonic smile that somehow made his lined and rubbery brow even more prominent. "It's been proven by research that *some* reward centers of the brain get activated whenever we receive money. However, the striatum is activated only when people worked for their rewards."

"If I won the lottery," Marcus said emphatically, crossing beefy forearms to reveal a faded, but still distinguishable, eagle, anchor, globe, and *Semper Fi* tattoo on his left and a more colorful Dennis the Menace on his right, "I'd be happy . . . screw the damn *street-atom.*"

"There's substantial evidence that people who win the lottery are not happier a year *after* they win the lottery," Lindstrom continued. "It's also fairly clear from the psychological literature that people get a great deal of satisfaction out of the work they do."

"Lindstrom," Marcus said scornfully, "you're a nut."

Miami Beach Office of Dr. Herbert Koremvokis, M.D.

Dr. Herbert Koremvokis plucked the patient file for Mr. Eric Von Deutsch from the door pocket, turned the knob, and let himself into examining room 3. When he entered, he found the slender Von Deutsch dressed in his typical casual manner: a bright-colored Hawaiian shirt, baggy pants, and a pair of loose-fitting two-strap Birkenstocks. His patient was leaning close to the examining room mirror and pulling at his facial features with stubby, albeit recently manicured, hands. A husky diamond, easily two carats' worth, twinkled from the third finger of his right hand and matched the diamond stud he wore in his left ear. The man's greenish eyes were narrowed into slits, and he was making a series of exaggerated facial expressions. The doctor's sudden arrival did not interrupt him.

"*Ahem. Good morning,* Mr. Von Deutsch," the plastic surgeon said pointedly, not accustomed to being ignored. "How are we doing today?"

"Not so hot," the abrasive man grunted without turning away from the mirror. He pulled down on his lower lip and began to study his yellowed and crooked teeth.

"And why is that?" Koremvokis inquired, achieving only brief eye contact via the mirror. He opened the file folder and slowly scanned the patient's pre- and post-surgery reports and entries from prior visits. He thought it time to clear up the name discrepancies that appeared on several medical questionnaires that the patient himself had filled out. Once the doctor sensed that he'd finally gotten the man's attention, he off-handedly motioned for him to step away from the mirror and be seated on the examining table.

"What is the proper spelling of your last name, sir?" he asked, clicking his ballpoint.

"Von Deutsch," the patient replied. "V-O-N D-E-U-T-S-C-H." He smiled unnaturally and eyed the doctor suspiciously. "Why are you asking?"

"Well, it seems that on the registration card you filled out for us on your first visit, back in April, you spelled your surname somewhat differently than you did on the surgical questionnaire you filled out for us in June. On the first visit you were a Van, not a Von as you later spelled it, and you were Deutch—no *S*—not Deutsch. One version, I believe, makes you a Dutchman . . . the other a German." The doctor made strong eye contact. "For our records, sir, which spelling is the correct one?"

"It's Von . . . Von Deutsch. I'm German, full-blooded," the patient murmured in a low, deliberate tone, effectively closing the issue. "Gotta tell you, Doctor," he moved on angrily, "I'm not at all happy with the way these damn scars are healing."

"Well, let's have a look." The physician set a pair of magnifiers onto the tip of his nose, raised Von Deutsch's face into the light, and began a close examination.

Typical dried-out, lined, and leathery smoker's face, Koremvokis thought. He also noted heavy wrinkling, shrewd small eyes situated close together, and a pronounced projection of the thyroid cartilage . . . the Adam's apple. The man was virtually bald on top. This was no Brad Pitt—and a million dollars more in cosmetic surgery wasn't going to make him that—but when compared to the pre-op photos, he was certainly much nicer looking now than he had been.

"I see you've grown your hair much longer on the sides and back of your head."

"And the stringy gray is gone too," Von Deutsch mumbled. "I think the brownish-blond Clairol suits me. What do you think, Doc?"

"Yes, it looks good," Koremvokis replied, tactfully salving the always edgy, strangely intimidating man who was there to complain. "I also like your thin mustache," he added. "That's new too, isn't it?"

"Yeah. It's new . . . not completely grown in yet."

The doctor released the man's head and stepped back. "Well, Mr. Von Deutsch," he said, removing the magnifiers, "the upper and lower blepharoplasties seem to be healing quite nicely. Granted, the suture lines are still somewhat red and apparent, but that will fade with time. The tightening we did next to the eyes to get those crow's-feet, though still somewhat red, also looks very good."

"Well, what the hell is taking so long for the redness to fade, Doc? Even in the areas where you removed those facial moles it's still very red," Von Deutsch said, his thick fingers slowly stroking his tanned cheeks.

A gentle knock came to the examining-room door, and Ellen Plotski, Koremvokis' office assistant, stuck her head in.

"Sorry to interrupt," she said in a soft voice. "Doctor, Stephan just called. He said he was able to get those two tickets for tonight's baseball game. He also said to tell you they were third-base box seats right behind the dugout."

"Thank you, Ellen," Koremvokis replied. The assistant nodded and gently closed the door.

"My son," the doctor briefly explained. "I'm taking him to a Marlins game tonight."

"Unh."

"May I ask how many packs of cigarettes you smoke each day, Mr. Von Deutsch?"

The surgeon felt a shiver of alarm race through his spine as the man stared back at him with the cold-eyed intensity of a coiled diamondback about to strike. Finally Von Deutsch responded.

"Three . . . four packs, maybe. What of it?"

Doing his best to conceal the odd trepidation he felt, Koremvokis gently cleared his throat while deciding on a carefully worded and tactful response.

"Well, Mr. Von Deutsch, the healing process for scars is always greatly slowed by excessive smoking." The same was true for the illicit drug use that he suspected Von Deutsch to regularly engage in, but he opted not to imply such by mentioning it.

"When I came here to see you for the first consultation in April," Von Deutsch snarled, "you assured me that any scarring left by these procedures—should I decide to undergo them—would quickly heal. They haven't."

"These procedures were only done in early June, Mr. Von Deutsch," Koremvokis reminded him nervously, scanning the file to ensure accuracy. "That's just barely two months ago. Because of your heavy smoking it is simply going to take more time. But those scars will eventually fade, I assure you."

"All right," the patient said, his mood seeming to have suddenly become more conciliatory. "Maybe you're right. Maybe it is my smoking that's behind it. But now I want to move ahead. I want additional surgeries to make me look younger and even more different. What do you recommend from here?"

"Nothing."

"*Nothing?* What do you mean, nothing?" Von Deutsch countered loudly. "Hey, Doc, I clearly remember discussing things like a rhinoplasty, a brow lift, hair transplants . . . microdermabrasion. And, don't forget, just like the last time, your fee will be paid in full . . . *in cash,* just the way you wanted it."

"Please, Mr. Von Deutsch," the surgeon said. "Please lower your voice."

"I'll lower my goddamned voice when you begin to hear me, Koremvokis." Rapping his knuckles mockingly against the side of his own head, he added, *"Hello . . . is there anybody home?"*

"You must understand that there is a limit to the amount of facial surgery that can be performed within a short amount of time."

"I understand that, and I'm willing to take the risk," Von Deutsch said, his small eyes squinted and focused tightly on Koremvokis.

"I'm not," the physician said pointedly. He sensed his jaw begin to tighten as he dug his heels in. This situation was about to get ugly.

"I'll pay you a premium."

"I'm sorry, Mr. Von Deutsch," he said, his voice coldly professional, "or is the name *Van Deutch*? I'm simply not interested." The two men glared at each other for a long moment, then Koremvokis played his high card, adding, "But maybe the authorities would be?"

Eric Von Deutsch's hazel eyes squinted into an even more foreboding and icy glare. Lips pinched and quivering in barely controlled anger, he slid slowly to his feet and shouldered his way past the surgeon. The fuming man swung the examining-room door wide and faced Koremvokis one last time. His features were drawn into a venomous mask.

"You have made a very serious mistake, Doctor," he uttered in an ominous whisper.

Koremvokis shivered as his physical and spiritual guidance systems switched to full alert. He had just seen the true face of evil. Struck dumb, the doctor watched in fear-driven silence as Von Deutsch stormed from the office, elbowing staff out of his way as he moved.

Inadvertently interrupting the latest round of the on-going Jack Lindstrom/Richie Marcus battle of wits, Eddie Brodigan leaned into the crowded sergeants' room. "Sarge, pick up on line two-three," he announced. "It's an Officer Billy Cox from the Sixth. Says it's important."

"Billy," Savage said into the mouthpiece. "I just sent you out a quick recap of the discussion I had with the ME less than an hour ago. Long and short of it is, they're staying with natural causes on that Granger matter."

"Not a surprise." The veteran policeman let out an exasperated sigh. Then he put the question: "Did you really press them on it?"

"As much as I felt I could, based on what little I know. Pathologists—all doctors, for that matter—don't like being pressed too hard."

"Yeah," Cox snickered. "Tell me about it. Good old Dr. Janus sure didn't like *his* word being questioned that morning. I believe he was banking *totally* on the idea that nobody would have the balls to really question him. After all, *he* was a fucking doctor. Prick acted like he was some kind of damn deity."

"It doesn't take some of them very long after med school to develop that physician's passive-aggressive I-am-God attitude," Savage commented. "Any more than it takes for some rookies out of the academy to develop that cynical, active-aggressive, I'm-in-charge-here cop attitude."

"Unh, I never thought of it that way," Cox said. "But what do you think, Thorn? Were *you* completely satisfied with the ME's finding?"

"*Ehh.*" Savage hesitated. He thought a moment, then confessed, "Can't say that I'm one hundred per-cent satisfied . . . but where to go from here?"

"Jeez, Thorn, if you don't know where to go, I sure as hell don't."

"Billy, I was told that you had something important you called me about. What was it?"

"I spent a little time over in St. Vincent's Hospital since I last spoke with you. I've got a couple of good friends who've worked there for years. Nurse-type friends, know what I'm saying? And I made some pointed inquiries about Dr. R. Charles Janus."

"And?"

"And, it seems that Janus no longer has privileges at St. Vinnie's. He lost them about a month before this Granger thing went down. Has yet to get them back—probably never will. The guy's got an absolutely shit reputation among the staff there. And not only did he lose his privileges at St. Vinnie's, but they told me he'd lost them over at Joint Diseases also."

"Did your nurse friends happen to know why he lost those privileges?"

"Something about performing surgical procedures that he was not certified to perform. It was that issue, plus the citing of both of those hospitals as codefendants in some heavy malpractice suits against him."

"This guy is beginning to sound more and more like Dr. Death."

"Where *do* we go from here then, Thorn?" Cox said, his voice a plea. "Don't tell me we just have to drop it."

"The way I see it, Billy, the next logical step would be to find Timothy DiBona. The guy who was supposedly attacked by Janus with a stun gun a few weeks prior to the Granger death."

"I'll keep beating the bushes over here on the West Side," Cox offered. "Maybe I can turn him up."

"Gotta tell you, Billy," Savage stressed, "before I would even *think* about trying to carry this Granger matter any further, I would have to hear precisely what went on with DiBona in Janus' office."

"I fully understand," Cox replied. Then with happily renewed enthusiasm, he quickly related, "Now, according to Cavonis and Hildebrand, this guy DiBona's more than a bit of a flake. But he's probably fairly well known within the Village's gay underground. More specifically, I'm told, the S&M and B&D wings."

"Well, then, you keep working it from your side," Savage said. "I think I might have a knowledgeable source over there who may be able to feel around as well. No pun intended."

"Terrific," Cox replied. "If I'm able to come up with anything, I'll call you right away."

"Something starting to smell down in the Sixth?" Diane DeGennaro asked as Savage hung up the phone.

"Don't really know yet," Savage responded contemplatively. "But we're getting some very strange aromas." He stood, jerked his suit jacket from the hanger, and turning to Jack Lindstrom, asked, "Did you say you were heading downtown to Latent and Photo?"

"Yep," Lindstrom replied.

"I'm going to take a ride with you," Savage said. "While we're out, I want to make a quick stop at the newspaper kiosk over on West Third."

"Your friend Curley's place," Lindstrom said knowingly.

"Yeah," Savage replied, patting his empty jacket pocket. "I've got to get some Life Savers, and I'm also going to ask Curley to do me a little favor."

"By the way, Jack," Richie Marcus piped up, snapping his stubby fingers as if suddenly remembering, "while you're out, stop at your stationers. They called. Those pocket protectors you ordered came in."

SEVEN

After Jack Lindstrom had taken care of several investigative errands down at Latent Prints and the Photo Unit, he and Savage stopped at the property clerk's office to drop off a piece of evidence Lindstrom had presented before a grand jury earlier that afternoon: a bloodied and splintered thirty-two-ounce Louisville Slugger. The collector's item, used in the 1971 All-Star Game by Thurman Munson and autographed by Luis Aparicio, Reggie Jackson, and Carl Yastrzemski, had been used by Freddie "Three-to-Five" Ferrara to bash in the noggin of the late Peter "Rabbit Ears" Donatelli in the parking lot near the Lunas Restaurant on Mulberry Street.

Though Ferrara was employing the silence of *omertà* and had thus far made no statements about his extreme batting practice, it was known that old Rabbit Ears, a fringe Mob guy from Little Italy, had gone from being a good listener to being a *real* good talker—especially to a couple of agents from the DEA. Word on the street had it that Ferrara's intention was not to totally silence old Rabbit Ears that night but to simply tone him down a bit and teach him a lesson, *but . . .*

The final stop while they were out was Curley's Sixth Avenue newspaper stand. The Runyonesque paraplegic had not recognized the name Timothy DiBona, the spacey local believed to travel in rather bizarre circles. But as Savage had suspected, Curley knew more than a thing or two about those bizarre circles and promised to make a few calls on his cell phone. He knew people who "might know people."

It was nearly eight thirty p.m. when Savage and Lindstrom got back to the Manhattan South office from their downtown jaunt. Savage had just gotten comfortable at his desk when his telephone rang out; it was Curley.

"Guess who's slinging mahimahi over on Christopher Street as we speak?" Curley said. The man spoke loudly enough to be heard over the roar of a city bus moving past the kiosk.

"Don't tell me you found him already?" Savage responded, not expecting such quick service. "Timothy DiBona?"

"You got it."

"Jesus," Savage clucked. "You're in the wrong line of work. Want a job? You should have been a detective. How'd you find him so quickly?"

"I got with my roommate, Karl. If nothing else, Karl usually knows all the freaks. He wasn't sure he recognized the name, so he made a few calls around. He found out that there's a Timmy DiBona working tables over at The Deep."

"Great."

"Now, I just made a little phone call over to The Deep and asked if I could speak with Timothy DiBona," Curley said. "When they told me to hold on, I hung up . . . so he must be there now."

"You're a piece of work, Curley."

"Karl also found out that in his off hours this DiBona's a leatherboy. Seems he likes the nip of the whip. He's probably your guy."

"Thanks, buddy," Savage said.

"Don't mention it . . . *literally.*"

"I won't," Savage assured.

"You know I can't have the locals thinking I'm some kind of squeal to the cops."

"My lips are sealed."

"Oh . . . and one other thing," Curley tagged on.

"Word has it that the chow at The Deep sucks. Joint should be called The Dump."

"Traffic has lightened up some in the last half hour," Savage observed as Jack Lindstrom steered the department Ford left from Third Avenue onto Twenty-third Street and headed westbound toward The Deep.

"It's after nine on a slow Monday night," Lindstrom replied. "I guess there's not much doing around town."

"Getting ready for the wedding?" Savage asked, making small talk with a topic that he knew Lindstrom would like. "What is it, a week away?"

"Twelve days," Lindstrom replied, a contented smile breaking out across his face. "Next Saturday afternoon, the seventeenth." Jack Lindstrom had always been a notoriously doting father to his only daughter. Even a terribly messy divorce hadn't changed that one damn bit.

"How old is Cheryl now?" Savage inquired.

"Twenty-one. Would you believe it? Seems like she was born only last week. It's hard to believe that she's already completed college." The man looked across at Savage and added, "She's getting a good guy. I really like him."

"Yeah, I know," Savage acknowledged with a gentle nod. "He's the young man she met while up at Villanova. The one who's going on to medical school, right?"

"Gonna be a plastic surgeon," Lindstrom said proudly. "The kid's some kind of brain."

"I'm happy for you, Jack."

Conversation between the two men fell away as the Crown Victoria sped across Park Avenue, then slowed down and stopped for the light at Madison.

Savage's mind drifted off to thoughts of his own daughter, Jenny. He wondered if she would have completed college. Of course she would have. He wondered if she would have married. Perhaps. If she had, he would have thrown the biggest damn wedding he could possibly have afforded. After all, he too had been a world-class doting father to an only child . . . a priceless daughter.

Savage then realized that the date was August 5, and that it had been on a rain-soaked August 6 evening, so many years ago, when he had gotten the phone call at work informing him of the terrible car wreck that would forever cost him his beautiful little Jenny and his wife, Joanne. Casually turning his head to gaze fully out the passenger-side window, he lightly cleared his throat and blinked away a forming mist. The traffic light at Madison went green.

Savage and Lindstrom arrived at the West Village seafood restaurant and announced to a calm and poised Timothy DiBona that they wanted to speak with him. After arranging with the snooty-looking maître d' to have his wait stations covered, DiBona led the detectives down a long, narrow hallway, through a busy kitchen that smelled like a cross between Manhattan's Fulton Fish Market and Brooklyn's Fountain Avenue landfill, and out through a delivery door into the partially lit rear alleyway filled with scattered litter and lidless garbage cans. Once outside, the very slender, almost emaciated man shook a generic-brand cigarette from a soft pack, placed it squarely in the center of his chapped lips, and fired it up. He took a deep drag and slowly blew out the smoke. Savage noted the nicotine-yellowed middle and index fingers of DiBona's almost skeletal right hand.

"Glad you guys came by," DiBona said calmly, in a smooth soft, controlled voice. "I needed a smoke break anyway. I just hate that I can't smoke inside anymore. You do know that we're losing all of our rights, right?" With the cigarette dangling from his mouth, he added, "So you wanna talk to me about that prick doctor, eh?"

"What can you tell us about him?" Savage asked, sizing up the odd man, whom he placed in his late thirties. DiBona was green-eyed, clean-shaven, and had a pale oval face beneath a head of thinning light brown hair. He also had a mildly pockmarked complexion and possessed that aloof, almost anesthetized, aura of a Beat Generation sax player just returned for the second set after a smoke break. Savage also noted a fair resemblance to Billy Cox's description of George Granger. Perhaps Dr. Janus had a "thing" for a certain type.

"Got an hour?" DiBona replied tartly.

"Sounds as if you can tell us quite a bit," Lindstrom said. "Why don't you start at the beginning?"

"First of all, you've gotta remember one thing," Timothy DiBona began, looking earnestly into Savage's eyes. "S&M people are looked upon as outlaws. We are way beyond the distant fringes of what regular folks will tolerate sexually. So that's why we need to congregate together. That's why we have our own private clubs. Nobody bothers us; nobody fucks with us in those places. That's how I came to meet Janus."

"Exactly *where* was it that you met him?" Savage asked.

"The Meat Hook. It's a private club down on Houston."

"The Meat Hook," Lindstrom repeated, unfazed, scribbling notes onto a memo pad.

"Yeah," DiBona replied matter-of-factly, enjoying another deep drag. "Now you gotta understand, Detectives, there is no neon sign hanging on the front of the building that says MEAT HOOK. It's just a loft space where we all congregate. The name is just something we call it."

"What's the address?" Savage asked.

The way-cool sax player stiffened, suddenly taking on the look of a mousy, cornered cellist.

Sensing the man's reluctance to give up the location, Savage said, "We've got no desire, or intention, to affect their operation in any way. And we won't. But we do need to know where it is."

"Three-o-four Houston," DiBona murmured, peeling a fleck of dead skin from his chapped lower lip. "Fifth floor."

"Who runs the joint?" Lindstrom asked.

"A big burly tough-man type by the name of Omar. He's got a shaved head, a thick broomlike black mustache, and a shitload of tattoos."

"Omar what?" Lindstrom pressed.

"Don't think I ever knew his last name. But you can usually count on Omar for two things: a real bad attitude and a *real* good time."

"What hours would we be likely to find Omar there?" Savage inquired.

"I'd say anytime between nine at night and dawn," DiBona replied, lifting bony shoulders in a mild shrug.

"Would he be there now?" Savage followed up, glancing at his watch. "It's just after nine."

"Prob'ly," DiBona said, nodding. He took another deep drag and added, "Why all the sudden police interest in Janus? He zap somebody else?"

"Do you go to the Meat Hook frequently?" Savage asked, opting not to respond to the query.

"As often as I need to," DiBona replied.

"How often is that?" Lindstrom asked.

"At least every Wednesday night—that's my night off. Sometimes I go on Saturday nights too, late. It all depends."

"Depends on what?" Lindstrom asked.

"My work schedule, man . . . and how horny I might be." DiBona grinned and flashed his eyes suggestively. "Man does not live by bread alone!"

"Is Dr. Janus a regular at the Meat Hook?" Savage asked. Out of the corner of his eye he saw a pair of well-fed super-rats appear from the cluster of lidless trash cans and scurry clumsily into a nearby drain.

"I've only seen him there twice. First time was in late April, early May maybe. We struck up sort of a friendship that night."

"What night did you hook up with him?" Lindstrom inquired.

" 'Bout a week or so later. I don't remember what day it was . . . a Saturday, I think. But I do remember the exact date, May eleventh."

"How can you be so sure?" Lindstrom followed up.

"Because it was my birthday, and the very next day was Mother's Day. I remember thinking that it might be my last birthday, and that my mother might never see me again. I've come across a bunch of weird people in the lifestyle, but never anything like this fucking guy." DiBona made a stern face. "He is really twisted . . . know what I mean?"

"I can get behind what you're saying, Tim," Lindstrom acknowledged, playing along, still scribbling.

"And you've not seen him at the Meat Hook since that night?" Savage asked.

"No, I haven't. But after this all went down, I asked around. He's considered somewhat of a regular there. People also remember him from years ago at some of the old clubs too. Places that are now closed."

"Like which older clubs?" Savage asked.

"Like the Mine Shaft, down on Washington," DiBona replied, an air of fond memory lilting in his voice. "Now, that place used to be really good. 'Bout a year ago, somebody actually went to the trouble of painting the whole damn building pink, but it still stands empty."

"Tell us what happened on the night of May thirteenth," Savage said.

"We met, shared a few drinks, and became friendly. He told me he was a doctor and asked if I would like to go elsewhere for a few more cocktails."

"And?"

"And I said yes. Hell, he was buying. We went down to his car—an absolutely *stunning* Jaguar—and headed out. He told me he needed to stop briefly at his office to make a phone call and asked did I mind. 'My God,' I said, 'I don't mind at all.' "

"About what time was that?" Savage asked.

"Late. I'd say about eleven, maybe eleven thirty.

When we got to his office over on Thirteenth he asked if I'd like to come in for a free EKG."

Savage and Lindstrom exchanged a millisecond glance. *"And?"* Savage asked.

"And," DiBona said with a mild laugh, "I figured, why not. It turned out to be one of the worst moves I ever made. But by then I was already pretty whacked on booze."

"Once you were up in his office, did he, in fact, make a phone call as he had said he was going to?" Savage inquired. Again, peripherally, he picked up the furtive movement of a huge rat near the overflowing trash pails.

"I'm pretty sure he did. Left me sitting in an examining room, went into his private office, and closed the door. I heard him talking, but couldn't understand what he was saying—not that I much cared. He came back out in about five minutes."

"Do you know who he called?"

DiBona shook his head.

"Did he actually do an EKG on you?" Lindstrom asked.

DiBona nodded. "Wired me up for sound and fired away. Only took about ten minutes. He said my heart was strong and healthy."

"Did he have you undress for this test?" Savage asked.

"Yep."

"What exactly did you remove?"

DiBona flashed his eyes in mock modesty. "Everything . . . even my socks."

"After the test what happened?" Lindstrom asked.

DiBona shrugged.

"Did you and Janus get it on?" Lindstrom pressed.

DiBona took a final drag on the cigarette, dropped it to the pavement, and squashed it beneath his rubber-soled shoe. "Yeah," he replied. "We got it on, and we both got off."

"Let me ask you something, Tim," Savage said,

moderating his tone to one of sincere earnestness. "While you and the good doctor were 'getting it on,' did you and he swap spit?"

"But of course," DiBona replied, rolling his eyes. "Doesn't everybody swap spit when they're getting it on?"

"Continue," Savage said.

"Then we both started to get dressed." DiBona shook his head. "That's when the whole fucking thing went wacko."

"How so?"

"As I was cinching my belt, suddenly the crazy bastard attacked me with a damn stun gun. He zapped the bejesus out of me. I didn't know what the hell was going on. I can still see his face, the look in his eyes; it wasn't part of the game—know what I mean? The bastard *was* trying to kill me."

"How did you get out of there?" Lindstrom asked.

"I grabbed up the rest of my freakin' clothes and ran for my life. Janus followed me down the hall and out onto Thirteenth Street. Once we were out on the sidewalk, he started to cop some plea that he was very emotionally disturbed and that I should please forgive him. Said he couldn't help himself." DiBona rolled his hooded green eyes emphatically. "Weird-o-fucking-rama, huh?"

"Yeah," Savage intoned flatly. "Weird-o-fucking-rama."

Dry and huddled beneath the overhang of the upper deck on the third-base side, Dr. Herbert Koremvokis and his seventeen-year-old son, Stephan—and what yet remained of the more than seven thousand faithful who had shown up—watched while the whimsical Miami skies continued to dump a mini-monsoon onto the manicured Bermuda grass of the city's most famous sports venue.

Joe Robbie Stadium, located on Northwest 199th Street in Miami, Florida, had been rechristened in 1996 when Pro Player—a division of Fruit of the

Loom—bought the naming rights. Nine years later, the park underwent yet another name change and became Dolphins Stadium. Home in winter to the NFL's Miami Dolphins—who always packed the house—and in summertime to baseball's Marlins—who never did—it stands just a good line drive from the border of Dade and Broward Counties.

Citing Miami's unpredictable weather as the main reason for the poor attendance for baseball, the Marlins ownership had long sought public financing to help pay for a new retractable-roof stadium for their team. They insisted that a new park was essential if the Marlins were to stay in Florida.

Unfortunately, the stadium, with a capacity of something over 47,000, rarely came close to one-tenth that number for baseball attendance—except when the Mets came to play. Then, like tonight, South Floridian ex–New Yorkers, with their shared allegiance to both ball clubs, actually showed up in some numbers and made the place seem less like an outdoor echo chamber.

It was the top of the fourth inning, with the Marlins thumping the Mets by seven runs, when the rain began. That was an hour ago. Koremvokis knew that if it didn't let up within the next few minutes the game would be called and he and Stephan would have to head home early. Also, if the rain didn't let up, they would probably get soaked dashing across the parking lot to his gold Lexus. But that would not be the first time they'd come home wet from a Florida Marlins game.

"Figures," Stephan said glumly, crunching on the icy remnants of his second giant Coke. "Lousy rain couldn't wait one more inning to make this game official. You could probably bet anything if the Mets were winning, it would have surely gone the necessary five."

Koremvokis shrugged. Inwardly, he was happy, but he declined to say so. Born and raised in Flushing, New York, he was still a true Mets fan. Unlike his son, who was raised in Miami, he was glad the game would not count. It would keep the Mets from sliding one down in the loss column, and allow them to maintain their tie for second place in the eastern division with Atlanta. Struck suddenly with the urge to pee, he looked around for a sign pointing out the location of the nearest restroom. There was one farther up the left-field side.

"I'll be right back," he said to his son, then teased, "don't go getting lost on me."

Stephan nodded with a smile.

Koremvokis made his way through the light and rapidly dwindling crowd. He passed an idle vendor station that apparently couldn't even give away its inventory of teal-and-black Marlins hats and pennants, then had to worm sideways through a line at the Budweiser stand. The men's room was empty. He stepped up to a urinal, unzipped, and as he relieved himself, thought how little time was left for him to take his only son to baseball games. Stephan was a great kid. They had always been close, but in the past couple of years they had become dependent on each other. Ever since they'd lost Shirley to the virulent leukemia that had come out of the blue and devastated the family, he'd been both father and mother to his son.

In just a few years, Stephan—with an IQ hovering beyond 150—would be headed off to college. Surprisingly, the boy wanted to attend Florida State up in Tallahassee, not the University of Miami as he would have expected . . . and preferred. After that, of course, Stephan would be off to medical school—Duke, no doubt. Koremvokis sighed loudly, zipped up, and crossed to the bank of sinks.

He pushed the soap dispenser twice and lathered his hands. As he rinsed them with several strong blasts of the hot water, he thought about Shirley and how much he missed her gentle laugh. Preoccupied, he only half heard the men's room door swing open. He did not bother to look around, but he soon sensed that his space was being invaded. With a room so large, with so many stalls and sinks, that should not be happening.

Koremvokis raised his glance to the mirror. The man was standing immediately behind him. Glass green eyes fixed on him with a vacant stare. He knew the face.

"Mr. Von Deutsch, what . . . what are *you* doing here?" Koremvokis stammered. He tried to turn, but Von Deutsch pushed him against the sink, locking a thin arm around his throat. The man was far stronger than Koremvokis would ever have suspected. In the mirror, Von Deutsch smiled coldly, his dead eyes watching, relishing. He pressed the gleaming tip of a large serrated-back hunting knife to Koremvokis' exposed neck. It was . . . surreal.

The man was obviously insane. Koremvokis fought the rising fear that threatened to immobilize his mind as well as his body. He had to stay calm. "What do you want from me?" he cried in a strangled gurgle.

"You fucked up, Doc," Von Deutsch murmured eerily into his ear, the words enunciated in a haunting singsong whisper. Von Deutsch then plunged the blade into the doctor's neck. He pushed it hard, all the way to the hilt. After twisting it forcefully, he slowly withdrew it. He then plunged the blade over and over into Herbert Koremvokis' back and side, striking ribs but most times penetrating deeply. Then he released him and stepped back to watch.

Uselessly clasping a hand over the geyser of blood that pumped in spurts from his severed carotid, Koremvokis knew he had only seconds left of life. He quickly made peace with his God, dropped to his knees, and with vague thoughts of his beloved son tracing through his mind, fell forward onto his face.

EIGHT

Savage and Lindstrom parked their department Ford sedan directly in front of the postal station on Houston Street, a mere two doors down from the seven-story converted warehouse at number 304. Based on the drabness of its utilitarian architecture, which lacked cornices or any decorative lintels, Savage figured the redbrick structure had been there since the late twenties or early thirties. It just had that Depression-era look.

Once inside the dimly lit and dank building, they waited several long minutes as a slow-moving and whiny freight elevator made its way to the ground floor. When the huge over-and-under doors finally parted, a pair of masculine females strolled out. The taller of the two, Savage decided, must have undergone more body-piercing procedures than the average Port-au-Prince voodoo doll. The shorter one, by far the more attractive of the two, appeared to be her slave. Both were decked out completely in men's casual clothing and men's-style work shoes, and both wore their slicked-down short hair in a fifties DA.

The androgynous pair took a long, studied look at the two buttoned-down men, exchanged annoyed glances with each other, and strutted toward the building's exit like a couple of Jets extras from *West Side Story*.

"Lookin' for the Meat Hook," Lindstrom called out to the pair as he and Savage boarded the graffiti-decorated freight box.

Neither woman turned around to face them, but as

they let themselves out of the building, the one with the studded doggie collar around her neck replied, "Fifth floor to the right. Can't miss it. Have fun."

Savage closed the elevator doors and rang for floor 5. "You get a load of those two?"

Lindstrom nodded. "And they gave *us* the fisheye as if *we* were the ones from Mars."

"How did you know to ask them about the Meat Hook?" Savage asked rhetorically, already knowing the answer.

"They looked like two very satisfied customers to me. Did they not?"

"The one chick had rings in her ears, her eyebrows, her lip, and a damn pearl tie tack pushed right into her nose," Savage said, shaking his head and grimacing in question as the elevator inched past floor 2.

"Those were merely the rings we could see," Lindstrom said flatly. "I'll guarantee you she's got lots more. Tongue, nipples, navel, clitoris, labia . . ."

"What in God's holy name is the deal with that whole body-piercing bit?" Savage said, never having heard anything as to its rationale—if there was one. But if anybody could help explain it, the erudite Jack Lindstrom was the man. With a bachelor's in behavioral sciences, a master's in Oriental philosophy from Columbia, and currently doing a thesis on abnormal psychology, Lindstrom knew a good deal about what made odd people tick.

"It's three things," Lindstrom began. "It's reclamation, it's enhancement, and it's self-expression—an affirmation of their personal individuality." He thought for a moment and added, "Make that four things. It's also a means of enhancing sexual gratification and stimulation."

Savage immediately regretted asking the question. The encyclopedic Lindstrom would probably now go on to tell him much more than he wanted to know. They were only at the third floor.

"Men are doing it too," Lindstrom offered. "Penis, scrotum . . ."

Savage shivered. "If it's self-expression, then just what the hell is it that they're trying to say?"

"Body piercing lets a person express their individuality in a new way. Not that body piercing is a new phenomenon. No, no. According to the Association of Professional Piercers—"

"The association of *what*?" Savage didn't know whether to laugh or cry.

"Oh, yes, it's an organization which helps keep the practice of body piercing safe," Lindstrom advised matter-of-factly. "Anyway, it's claimed that piercing can be traced to the Native American ritual known as O-Kee-Pa, or Sundance."

"O-Kee-what?"

"O-Kee-Pa. It consisted of making deep piercings behind each nipple, into which hooks were inserted. Ropes were then attached to the hooks and the person was spun around in circles until he fell unconscious. It was sort of a tribal initiation that involved a year of preparation. It's still practiced every summer by the Cheyenne as a means of spiritual, mental, and emotional cleansing. It allows a renewal and revitalization of their culture."

Savage got a reprieve when the elevator bumped to a halt and its doors opened onto the fifth floor. They exited, turned to the right, and found themselves moving to the eerie and demanding pulse of a single-note booming drum that seemed to echo throughout the level.

"Sounds like a slow row tempo on a slave galley," Lindstrom said.

"Probably is."

At the very end of the hall they came to a black-enameled metal door, from behind which the drum sound was definitely emanating.

"Shall we?" Savage said. He grasped the handle and slid the heavy door back on its well-greased rollers.

The detectives stepped into a large, well-illuminated showroom filled with sexually explicit adult material, both straight and gay but apparently geared primarily to those with leather-love on their minds.

Displayed on hooks that lined one long wall were harnesses for chest, torso, and full body, available in either studded black leather or plain black rubber. They ranged in price from eighty to a hundred and fifty bucks each.

At least a dozen browsers—men mostly, some women—aged from their early twenties to late sixties were sprinkled throughout the space, drifting quietly and wide-eyed from aisle to aisle. A gray-haired couple busied themselves examining and fingering the leather goods in the apparel aisle while discussing the virtues of patent and Lycra shorts, shirts, and tank tops. Another pair, mid-thirties, eyeballed the vast collection of head and face harnesses, blindfolds, and muzzles displayed around a huge poster of a head-harnessed Hannibal Lecter. At the female's sudden urging, though, they turned their attention to the variety of riding crops, paddles, and restraints of every description. The man seemed to be paying special attention to the wrist and ankle restraints, while the woman fluttered her fingers through the lashes of a cat-o'-nine-tails.

Hundreds of adult-video tapes, broken down into straight and gay categories of S&M and B&D, lined one entire wall. Sex toys and kinky gizmos—both battery powered and manual—were displayed on several counters, and a number of freestanding racks scattered throughout were filled with glossy magazines with outrageously graphic cover photos. A big bald guy who perfectly fit Timothy DiBona's description of Omar was talking to two men who had stepped up to his sales counter. Tattoos covered most of his visible flesh from the neck down. Savage figured the guy could have been half of a WrestleMania tag team.

After handing the bald man a sum of money, the two men, each totally decked out in black leather from head to toe, moved to a large metal door that was several steps removed from the counter and waited. The door bore an eerily painted sign that read, ALL HOPE ABANDON YE WHO ENTER HERE. After pocketing the men's money, the bald guy reached beneath the counter, a buzzer sounded, and the two men pushed through the black door and disappeared into a murky darkness beyond. In the instant that the door was open, the drumbeat had gotten momentarily louder.

Two other middle-aged men, apparently a couple, then approached the sales counter. They had made selections from the shop and were ready to purchase. It was interesting to Savage that everyone was so pre-occupied that no one seemed to have noticed his and Jack Lindstrom's entry or presence.

"One-stop shopping," Savage mused aloud, looking around the huge space. "Need anything while we're here, Jackie boy?"

"I could use a new set of handcuffs," Lindstrom replied. "I've worn all the pink faux fur off my old set."

"Well, now that you mention it . . ." Savage played along. "I wonder if they take Visa?"

All of the ceiling, wall, and floor surfaces within the large space were painted a flat black. Sketched across three of the walls in wild fluorescent paints of orange and green—and made luminous by black lighting— were superficial illustrations of stark human forms twisted into unnatural shapes and doing unnatural things to one another. Most of the forms were de-picted nude, and all were anatomically correct—some very much so.

"Place stinks from burnt candle wax and stale sex," Lindstrom observed in a loud whisper, scrunching up his nose.

Savage agreed. He popped a Wint-O-Green into his mouth. He offered one to Lindstrom, who quickly accepted.

Moving to the sales counter, Savage was shocked to find himself suddenly face-to-face with attorney Louis Armbruster, one half of the apparently gay couple who'd been standing there making a buy. The former legal aid counsel, and now high-priced defender of the indefensible, was an old-time courtroom nemesis. Savage and the high-profile, headline-grabbing bleeding heart had gone toe to toe in a number of trials down through the years. In each instance, Savage's well-prepared testimony had stood up, and Armbruster's dirtbag clients wound up going bye-bye to Attica or Greenhaven—or taking that long dark ride on the night-night needle. During one murder trial, Armbruster had made a vicious and baseless complaint to Internal Affairs that Savage had perjured himself on the stand and had altered evidence to fit tainted testimony. IAB, never one to reject making a case against a cop, no matter how thin the allegation—especially on the complaint of an attorney—took the transparent ball of lies, ran with it, and investigated the matter to death. That unsubstantiated cloud of bullshit had hovered over Savage's rep for years. To say that Savage disliked Armbruster—and vice versa—was a colossal understatement. It was all-out nuclear war.

"Well, I declare," Savage said, approaching the pear-shaped and cocky lawyer, who had just laid two crisp one-hundred-dollar bills on the sales counter to cover the purchases of a heavily studded bandolier-style rubber torso harness, a few tubes of K-Y, and a fair stack of gay S&M mags. "Look who's here, Jack. The great arbiter of truth, justice, and the American way. It's our good pal, the policemen's friend, attorney-at-law Louis Armbruster." He leaned down and got right in Armbruster's face. "You and your *friend* picking up some toys, Lou?"

At the sight and sound of Savage, the lawyer's eyes flashed like he'd taken a jolt of high-amperage Con Ed. He reared back in stunned disbelief, and his weak jaw dropped enough to reveal his mouthful of expensive porcelain implants. The big-nosed prick didn't know whether to stand and nonchalance his way through the situation or bolt for the door, but he certainly wasn't happy.

"Savage," he finally mumbled. "What—what brings you here?"

"Apparently not the same thing that brings you here," Savage responded positively, thoroughly enjoying the moment. He made a show of picking up one of the tubes of lubricant from the counter and examining it. "I'm here on business," he said, tossing the tube back. Then, looking Armbruster's quiffy boyfriend up and down, added, "You and your bleach-blond buddy are obviously here picking up a few of the necessities of life. How nice. So tell me . . . how are the wife and kiddies?"

"Fuck you, Savage!" Armbruster snarled, quickly regaining some of his notorious, yet momentarily misplaced, arrogance. "What I'm doing here is none of your goddamned business."

Savage had considerable difficulty controlling the need to get some measure of revenge on the lying little bastard. Truth was, he would have liked nothing more than to punch the creep's lights out right on the spot. He slowly gazed all about the decadence-filled room, turned back to Armbruster, and asked, "Find everything you need, Lou? Have you checked out the dominant enema bags?"

At that instant, the door adjacent to the sales counter swung open on squealing hinges, and three people, two real hard-looking women and a heavily sweating black man, emerged from the darkened back room. They gave a cursory wave to the bald man behind the counter and immediately left the premises. This was a busy place.

The bald man counted out twenty-six dollars in change to Armbruster and placed the goodies the lawyer had purchased in a plain brown bag. He then turned his attention to Savage and Lindstrom.

"Come on, Garth," the snotty lawyer snapped to his companion. He grabbed his bundle, pushed past the policemen, and headed for the exit, with gorgeous Garth following an obedient three steps behind.

"Can I help you?" the bald man drawled, his voice

a surly and imposing deep baritone, but with a slight lisp.

"You Omar?" Lindstrom inquired, pulling his shield case from his pocket.

"Could be." The man briefly reached beneath the counter. "Who the hell are you?"

"We're the music police," Savage ad-libbed, knowing the man had just sounded a silent alarm. Everybody in the private back area probably had to drop their whips and chains and run for their street clothes. "We're here on a complaint about your lousy sound track."

"That a fact?" Omar replied casually as he stepped from behind the counter, trying to appear unfazed. "I always thought it had kind of a nice beat."

"Yeah," Lindstrom piped up. "It's, sort of, music to torture by."

"Gotta remember," Omar replied, shrugging his massive shoulders, "some people actually do come here for that sweet agony."

"Well, if that's the case," Lindstrom said, "I suggest you pick up some Manilow, or Gary Lewis and the Playboys." He opened the case and showed his gold shield. "Got a place where we can talk?"

"Hold on a second," Omar said. He clicked on the intercom. "Holly, we have a couple of uh . . . people, here, *official* people that want to talk to me for a few minutes. I need you to come out and keep an eye on the front."

A gruff but panicky-sounding female voice from somewhere unseen replied, "Uhh, yes. But give us . . . uh, me, two minutes. I'm tied up right now in dungeon . . . uh . . . room number three."

Moments later, when the heavily made-up, clearly dominatrix Holly appeared from the back room, Omar motioned for the detectives to follow him. He led them out into the main-floor hallway, past the freight elevator entrance, to a much smaller, dimly lit room that contained a metal desk with a broken leg and one dusty antique of a swivel chair.

"What's your last name?" Savage asked, leading off.

"Kawaloczyk," Omar replied, then with a sneer added, "It's Polish."

"Gee, never would have guessed," Savage murmured.

"This it for you?" Lindstrom inquired offhandedly. "You a professional, full-time dungeon master?"

"I do other things."

"Like what?" Lindstrom pressed.

"For a couple of years I was the day manager of the Zum-Zum up on Broadway," the big man said thoughtfully. "Right now, though, I drive a taxi during the day."

"Hmm," Lindstrom observed with a sarcastic snicker. "No wonder you do this at night."

"What do you want to know?" Omar said, apparently weary of the banter. He slouched his huge form down into the dusty chair, and rested his size 13 booted feet atop the desk.

"Tell us about Dr. R. Charles Janus," Savage said.

"Who?" Omar replied, putting on a dumb face.

"Janus," Savage repeated. "He's a doctor. He's also one of your, shall we say, clients."

"Don't know him," Omar said flatly.

"Oh, I can see that we're getting off on the wrong foot here, Omar," Savage said evenly, then clucked his tongue. "Janus is a regular here. We know it, and you know it. If you're gonna play dumb, we're gonna raise the ante. We can finish this discussion down at *our* office. And you might have to leave old Holly in charge of the dungeons for the rest of the night."

Omar shifted the glance of his dark, almost black eyes back and forth between the two detectives. The man was not a good liar but apparently was a fair judge of character. He also knew when the other guy was pretty much holding all the cards.

"I don't know that much about him, except that he's a switch," Omar said.

"A *switch*?" Savage repeated.

"Goes both ways."

"You mean he's a switch-hitter? AC/DC? He likes boys and girls?" Lindstrom asked.

"Well, he might be that too," Omar said, "but when I say 'switch' I mean that he enjoys both dominant *and* submissive roles in his sex play."

"How often does he come here?" Savage asked.

"Used to be one, two nights a week. Now I hardly ever see him anymore."

"What else can you tell us?" Savage asked.

"That's it," Omar said with a dismissive shrug. "That's all I know."

Savage sensed otherwise. "I think you know more," he said. "I think you can move us up a notch on this thing, but you're gonna hold out."

Omar again shrugged, but he did not deny Savage's pointed observation.

"Can't force you to tell us more," Savage went on matter-of-factly. "But neither can you force us not to drop a dime to the city's Department of Finance and Taxation about your sweet little operation here. Once they swoop down, they'll be followed by the IRS, the city marshal's office, and God knows who else."

"I'm on the up-and-up," Omar declared angrily, propelling himself up and out of the chair, chased by a rising cloud of dust. "Don't go trying to intimidate me."

The big man was clearly a believer in the old adage that the best defense is a good offense. But Savage noted particles of antique dust settling on nascent beads of sweat gathering at his brow.

"I noticed that you didn't attach any sales tax to that last sale you made," he said. "I also didn't see any business license prominently displayed over there, as it is required to be."

"Yeah," Lindstrom observed. "The fire department would have a ball with this place. Ridiculously slow access and egress, no fire escapes." He turned to Savage and added, "Why, I don't even recall seeing one damn fire extinguisher in there. Did you?"

Omar's square jaw protruded, and he breathed

heavily; he was definitely stung. This was a complete off-the-books phantom operation and Savage knew it. And Omar now knew that Savage knew.

"I don't own the joint," Omar blurted. "All I do is merely run it."

"Well, be that as it may, Omar," Savage replied, "my partner and I can easily develop some amnesia about you and this whole damn place, as if we'd never been here. But in return, you're gonna have to give us the whole enchilada on Janus and his playmates." Savage tightened his focus into Omar's eyes and dropped his voice a full octave. "And you're going to have to convince me that it *is* the whole damn enchilada."

The gears in Omar's pumpkin head were smoking. He pressed his thick lips together, then, after many seconds, finally spoke.

" 'Bout a year ago, Janus used to come in regularly with one of two different guys. Seemed like he alternated them. He never came in with both of them at the same time."

"You remember their names?"

"One guy's name was John; real handsome dude. Janus always referred to him as 'John Boy.' Don't remember much about the other guy; kinda balding, plain-looking, had a dangerous aura . . ."

"How do you mean 'dangerous'?" Lindstrom asked.

"It's in the eyes, man," Omar said with a knowing laugh. "I shouldn't have to tell *you* that. Anyway, most people come to places like this because of fetish. Not that guy. That son of a bitch was flat-out evil."

"Getting back to this guy John Boy," Lindstrom pressed, memo pad at the ready. "Do you know his last name?"

"No. I'm sure I never heard it. Most people who come here generally only go by their first names."

"We're going to need a coupla last names, Omar," Savage announced flatly. "Otherwise all bets are off."

The big man's barrel chest heaved with an exaggerated inhale as he pondered. His rubbery lips then fluttered in exasperation, blowing the wind out. "The guy you need to talk to, the guy who knows Janus—and probably his handsome buddy, John Boy, and that other guy—as well as anybody, just left. You were talking to him. Seemed like you knew one another."

"Louis Armbruster?" Savage said.

"He and Janus have been playmates. I also know that they've both partied with that evil guy I was telling you about. Not really sure about that John Boy guy, though."

"You know that Armbruster is a lawyer, right?" Lindstrom inserted.

Omar nodded. "We get *lots* of lawyers up here, Detective. They happen to be very much overrepresented in the B&D scene."

Omar hesitated a moment, looked back and forth at Savage and Lindstrom, then added with a tentative shrug, "So are cops. A lot of them like being doms."

NINE

Brilliant rays from the early-morning sun reflected like industrial lasers off the modern glass-sided towers and ancient gilded steeples of storied Belfast City, almost blinding John Boyer Holloway as he trailed the bellman to the idling taxicab in front of the Hastings Europa. Squinting and shading his eyes, he regretted having packed away both pairs of sunglasses. The four-day stay in the four-star hotel's executive suite had cost him slightly over sixteen hundred British pounds, or nearly three thousand U.S. dollars. Eammon Bradley had cost him another five thousand British. He was just becoming accustomed to the UK exchange rate and here it was, time to leave the fair city and the pound sterling. Beginning this afternoon it would be back to Amsterdam and Euros.

The young bellman unloaded Holloway's two pieces of leather luggage from the wheeled cart and unceremoniously chucked them like sacks of potatoes onto the taxicab's backseat floor.

"Hey, be careful with those," Holloway snapped in disbelief. "That's brand-new Louis Vuitton."

The bellman turned, pinched the brim of his red cap, and nodded in apology. Though fuming, Holloway tipped him two quid and climbed into the cab.

"Belfast International, please," he said to the driver. The red-faced man smiled, nodded, and started the meter.

"That's about twenty-nine kilometers from here," the driver said as the boxy Austin began to lumber down Great Victoria Street. "You just be sittin' back there and enjoyin' the ride, sir. It will be a pretty one, especially on such a sunshiny day as this."

Holloway acknowledged with a friendly thumbs-up and a broad smile. Despite the thoughtless actions of the stupid bellman, he was in a particularly excellent mood today, feeling as if a knapsack full of bricks had finally been removed from his shoulders.

As the black Austin wound its way through the busy streets of the heart of Belfast, Holloway plucked a small, unsealed envelope from his jacket's inner pocket, removed two typewritten pages, and—for the third time this morning—read them. He would commit the in-depth information to instant-reflex memory.

John Anson Conover had entered the world at five thirty a.m., on the nineteenth day of February, 1968, at Queen Alexandria Hospital, in Portsmouth, in the southeast of England. According to Eammon Bradley's in-depth account of Conover family ancestry and descent, it had been a Monday, as if that was important—but if the quirky photographer and genealogy nut was anything, he was certainly a detail freak. The boy was the only child born of the late Miles Peter Conover, a chief welder at the Portsmouth Naval Dockyard, and his wife, Mildred Anson Conover—née Hathaway, both now planted beneath the rolling green of Highland Road Cemetery, Cosham, Portsmouth. The blue-eyed child had only just entered his tenth month of life when he was found dead in his crib; sudden infant death syndrome, no doubt, Holloway concluded.

He carefully folded the neatly typed biography and placed it back in the envelope. He would read more of it later at the airport, and then again on the plane, until he knew it by rote; then he would destroy it. As the taxicab sailed past Hampton House on Belfast's High Street, he tapped his jacket pocket and felt the firmness of the freshly issued British passport. Contented with his latest coup, he could not control the smile that kept stealing across his face.

He was now John Anson Conover, a British subject,

born and bred in Portsmouth, Hampshire, England. At least, that was who his just-issued official British passport said he was. And if an authentic British passport—containing *his* photograph—identified him as John Anson Conover, a British subject, then, goddammit, he *was*. The smile grew wider.

The new John Anson Conover looked out the window and took in the view. He decided that he had come to like Northern Ireland in the brief time he'd been there; perhaps someday he would return and tour it in its entirety. Perhaps.

His KLM flight would arrive in Amsterdam late morning. He couldn't wait. He would go immediately to the ING bank, where John Anson Conover would open an account. Shortly thereafter, John Boyer Holloway would wire to that account seven hundred thousand dollars. After taking care of the money business, he would proceed to his suite at the fashionable Blakes Hotel, unpack his bags, and arrange a late lunch with Darrin in the courtyard garden. After lunch they would spend what remained of the day at the Van Gogh Museum. There was a Van Gogh and Gauguin exhibit that concentrated on the autumn of 1888, when the two volatile artists worked on sunflower paintings in Arles. Then, if they had the time, they would also visit the Rijksmuseum, eyeballing its trove of Rembrandts and Vermeers. Then . . . he and Darrin would have a steamy matinee before dinner.

Early tomorrow, though, perhaps after a hot wakeup scene with Darrin, they would climb into his new red Porsche and together begin the long road trip that would take them through Bonn, Stuttgart, Zurich, Milan, and Pisa to Italy's Tyrrhenian coast. Pressing, the drive would easily take fourteen hours; he intended to do it in thirteen, or perhaps less. *Carpe Diem* waited for him in the seaside town of Marina di Grosseto. There, he would pay for and take ownership of the freshly restored old ketch in cold, hard cash. John Anson Conover and his new friend Darrin

Greavey would immediately set sail to the island of Sardinia for a few weeks of wanton pleasure.

Ahh, Darrin. With that thick head of long blond hair, piercing blue eyes, and tanned, rippling abs, Darrin Greavey was movie-idol handsome, only two years his junior, pretty much alone in the world, and extremely needful. He was also hung like a stud bull and horny as hell. They'd met in Amsterdam only a few days before he'd left for Belfast and were immediately attracted to each other; God, what a find, Holloway thought. And, thank God, he knows me only as John.

There was something else too. While out and about together bouncing the gay clubs of Amsterdam, he and Darrin had already twice been asked if they were brothers. Apparently they looked a good deal alike. They had played along and found themselves invited to several very-very private soirees where he and Darrin performed what everybody believed was a brother-brother act. It was just too hot.

Life was just so damn good . . . and he was just so goddamned smart.

When Savage signed in on Tuesday morning, he found a note on his desk directing him to see the unit's commanding officer, Lieutenant Pctc Pczzano, ASAP. After pouring himself a mug of coffee at the squad java pot, and ignoring the tempting contents of the Dunkin' Donuts carton sitting alongside it, he walked directly to the lieutenant's office and rapped on the steel doorjamb.

"C'mon in, Thorn," Pezzano said, slipping off heavy dark-rimmed glasscs. The hulking man set aside a stack of DD-5s he had been wading through and leaned back in his desk chair.

Pezzano's office was as plain as they come. Only slightly larger than the cramped sergeants' room, it had the same enamel-over-block walls, decorated only with the blue and white NYPD calendar and two framed photos: one each of the police commissioner and the current chief of detectives. Opposite his desk, on the far wall, was the unit's stat board. Pezzano, a total family man, kept a photo of his wife and kids on his desktop.

"What's doing, boss?" Savage asked in a deferential tone. Although he and Pete Pezzano went way back, Savage never failed to give superior rank its proper due.

"Not a whole lot, Thorn," Pezzano said, sweeping a thick arm toward one of the chairs opposite his desk. "Sit down."

Savage took a quick sip of the steaming joe, winced at its acrid taste, then sat.

"How are your cases going?" Pezzano asked flatly.

"Good," Savage replied, sensing something much more lurking in the lieutenant's unusual query. Pezzano always knew exactly how the squad's cases were going; he didn't need to ask.

"Anything in particular on your mind, boss?"

"I got a call from Lieutenant Barone over at the Sixth Squad," Pezzano replied directly, his expression pained. "He's somewhat concerned that we're doing a follow-up on something that they've already closed, and something which they never referred to us. He figures that puts him in a bad light. I figure maybe he's right."

"It's not an official follow-up," Savage explained. "We haven't opened a case on it."

Pezzano exhaled hard. "Sal Barone's a decent guy. We were promoted to lieutenant on the same day. I like him, and I would hate to see any hard feelings develop between his squad and our unit. We've always enjoyed a good working relationship with them."

"Procedurally, at the outset, there's no question that Barone did the right thing," Savage said. "The ME determined that there was no case, so there was no case."

"The ME is *still* saying that there's no case," Pezzano said firmly. "And damn it all, it's not as if we're so low on cases around here that we've gotta be poaching work that rightfully belongs to others. We're loaded up. Your team is already carrying more than their quota of cases, aside from being one member short."

Savage acknowledged with a slight nod. "Boss, I'm not looking to upstage Barone, or in any way make the Sixth Squad look bad. But, now, eleven weeks later, the matter is crying out for just a little bit more attention."

"Why?"

"Because there may be something there. Some new information has surfaced. Information, incidentally, that was first brought directly to Barone's attention, but he opted to pass on it. He simply decided that he's not going to reopen."

"And *you* see something to this new information?"

"I do see enough to warrant looking a little further, boss." Savage sipped at his overbrewed coffee but maintained steady eye contact with Pezzano.

"How much is a little further?"

"I'm not sure yet," Savage said, shrugging. "But I promise I'll wrap it up as soon as possible. Unless what you're telling me is to outright drop it. If that's what you want, boss, then that's what I'll do."

"You know, of course," Pezzano said, exaggerating a clearing of his throat before continuing, "Sal Barone is finding himself in a bit of squeeze over this one."

"The precinct commander up his butt?"

Pezzano said nothing, but said everything in his blank-faced, definite way.

"I figured as much," Savage said, irritated but acknowledging Pezzano's silent assent. " 'Compstat' figures, right?"

This time Pezzano nodded.

The acronym stood for the chief of the department's weekly, monthly, and yearly computerized statistics process that precisely measured the crime-reduction effectiveness of every precinct commander in the job.

"Good report cards mean promotion," Pezzano said, with a palms-out shrug. "The less crime in a command, the better for the commanding officer."

"Bad report cards mean . . . no promotion," Savage echoed. "And reassignment to such inglorious places as the Memo Book Stapling Unit, or the Sam Browne Belt Repair Squad."

"Where some of them no doubt belong," Pezzano said reflectively, rolling his eyes. "Compstat's a terrific measuring stick," he went on. "It separates the wheat from the chaff. Some of these guys who've gotten themselves promoted to captain only because they were bookworms—and never spent a damn day on the streets—finally find out that there's a lot more to police work than knowing what the goddamned book says."

"You know there's been some rumors coming out of the Sixth, that the commander over there, Captain Dipson, has been ordering the downgrading of felony complaints to help improve his Compstat figures."

"He wouldn't be the first one to do it," Pezzano explained. "Compstat started out being a good thing. But, as you know, it can be adulterated. And Dipson is probably figuring that if the ME has determined that there's no case, then there's no case. He's flat out told Barone to let the matter die. He's also told Barone that if your pal Billy Cox doesn't lighten up, he'll find himself out of his sector seat and doing eight-hour fixers as station-house security and catching all the damn fly assignments."

Savage angrily bit at the inside of his cheek. Damn department politics was once again rearing its ugly head. "If there's a true homicide here," he said forcefully, "there's no way I'm going to close my eyes to it to get Captain *Dipshit* a nice report card this semester."

"Awright, Thorn. Awright." Pezzano groaned, both reluctance and acceptance in his tone. "Do what you've got to do, but do it quickly and keep me informed. If it's a damn dry hole, we drop it immediately."

"I understand."

"There's a matter of professional courtesy involved here." Pezzano pulled his stack of paperwork back to center desk and refitted his glasses. "We both know that Captain Shit-for-Brains will eventually be either promoted or transferred out. But Barone is a fixture there, and the day may come when we need him."

"Well, let's take Barone off the hook," Savage said. "If we keep pulling this string, and find we keep wanting to continue to pull the string, let's call in our big gun."

"The chief of detectives?" Pezzano asked.

"Right. If we can sell Chief Wilson on reopening this case, Captain Dipson becomes insignificant."

Pezzano nodded. "We just may have to do that. But before we call the damn chief in, we better damn well know what it is we got."

The meeting was over.

Savage strode back through the maze of desks in the squad room and collected his three detectives. After quickly refilling their coffee mugs, they all adjourned to the unit's war room. Marcus brought along a French cruller and a chocolate-coated cream-filled.

"We've got no official case on this, boys and girls," Savage began. "And despite some objections from the commander over at the Sixth, I think we still need to look just a little deeper into the world of Dr. R. Charles Janus."

"I got a feeling you're right on this one, boss," Lindstrom said. "Anyway, I know Captain Dipson. I worked for him when he was a lieutenant out in the One-oh-nine. They name streets after him . . . One-Way. I also know he's currently gunning for the exec's job over at the Employee Management Division. The only way he can get it is a promotion to deputy inspector. . . ."

Savage nodded. He was always amazed at Jack Lindstrom's vast collection of knowledge.

"Where would you like *me* to begin?" Lindstrom asked.

"I want you to contact the DOA's next of kin."

"The only name we have to go on is that guy John B. Holloway. The ME's report showed him as the guy who flew in to claim Granger's body."

"He was supposedly Granger's business partner," Savage said. "Contact him. See what he can tell us about the relationship between Granger and Janus— if he even knows anything. Was it merely doctor, patient, friend, as Janus said it was, or was it something more sinister?"

"What else?" Lindstrom asked.

"Find out from Holloway if Granger had any blood kin, and who they are. If he doesn't know offhand, he might be able to tell us if Granger had any life insurance." Savage recalled Billy Cox's sage remark, " 'Where there's a will, there's a relative.' "

"Ten-four," Lindstrom replied. He then looked over and glared at Marcus, who was licking icing from his fingers after stuffing most of the French cruller into his mouth.

"Don't you eat at home, Richie?" Lindstrom said. Marcus mumbled something back. Though his words were unintelligible, it was probably X-rated.

"Also," Savage said, restarting the meeting, "I think we'll contact the mortuary up in the Bronx that handled the disposal of Granger's body. Maybe *they* have some information on next of kin."

"Should I give them a call?" Lindstrom asked.

Savage shook his head. "You've got enough on your plate, Jack." He turned to Richie Marcus and Diane DeGennaro. "I want you both to take a ride up there today."

"Looks to me like Marcus has got more than enough on *his* plate too," Lindstrom inserted sarcastically.

Marcus eyed Lindstrom, gave him a quick bird, and burped. He then looked at Savage, smiled, and nodded.

Savage adjourned the meeting, returned to his office, and decided to put in a call to Attorney Louis

Armbruster. Maybe Omar at the Meat Hook was right; maybe Armbruster could shed a little more light on Dr. R. Charles Janus. If Armbruster could, though, Savage was betting the obnoxious cop-hating lawyer wouldn't part with any of it willingly; it would probably require shaking his tree a bit. Savage wouldn't mind doing that at all.

Armbruster had already left his office for court, or so his secretary, Ms. Kranick, informed him. Savage would have bet otherwise. He would try again later.

TEN

Detective Richie Marcus counted his winnings—two fifties, four twenties, and one ten—then stuffed the crisp bills into his trouser pocket and stepped with a broad smile from the offtrack-betting office on Forty-second Street. He walked briskly to the silver Taurus parked at the curb, opened the passenger-side door, and slid in.

"Okay," he growled, in his gruff Brooklynese, "*now,* we can go to the Bronx."

Diane DeGennaro slapped the shift handle into gear and worked the Taurus into the busy noontime traffic. "You're smiling," she said, keeping her gaze focused on the line of taxicabs and buses directly ahead.

"Hit a good one," Marcus replied. "Picked up a hundred bucks. I shouldn't brag about it because it was a sure thing. The damn horse *couldn't* lose."

"How could you tell it couldn't lose?" she asked, glancing over briefly.

"I just know these things, Diane. I follow these horses very closely. You know me, I don't ever bet hunches. I pay attention to the odds; I do my arithmetic. Let me tell you something, you don't come out ahead in this game by mistake, you know."

"Well, how come you don't *know* these things and come out ahead far more frequently?" she asked.

"You being a smart-ass?"

"Me? Never. It's just that I've been sitting here doing a bit of arithmetic myself."

"Yeah?"

"This is purely anecdotal, you understand. But

based on my calculations, it seems that we stop at OTB to drop *off* money many times more than we stop at OTB to pick some up."

Marcus let loose with a nervous snort. "Just drive."

Diane headed uptown on FDR Drive and crossed the Triborough Bridge into the Bronx. From there, she picked up the Bruckner and exited at East Tremont Avenue in the Schuylerville section. At the corner of Lafayette and Tremont, she pulled the Taurus into the driveway of Fairlawn Mortuary Associates and parked in the rear lot. Marcus noted that the building looked a little run-down; its peeling fascia boards could have used some fresh Benjamin Moore.

The detectives let themselves into the location through the double-door front entrance, and a quick glance around revealed that the building's interior needed as much cosmetic help as the exterior. Dated flocked wallpaper peeled at some of the corners, and paisley carpet runners were worn threadbare in spots. An aura of mildew hung heavily in the air. Marcus sneezed loudly, twice—allergies.

"I'm Roberta Klemp. May I be of service to you? We're not actually open for viewing for another twenty-five minutes." The words came from an osteoporosis-bent slender woman in a dark pin-striped business suit who greeted them in the main lobby. The name tag pinned on her lapel read: R. KLEMP—DIRECTOR.

Roberta was easily in her later sixties and had a long and narrow equine face. Her pale complexion was exaggerated by liberal use of dark lipstick and eyeliner, and parts of her milk-white scalp were visible through sparse head hair dyed an impossible jet-black. Arthritically deformed fingers were bedecked in garish rings and fragile, bony wrists in turquoise-encrusted bangles. She wore a large purple flower—an orchid, Marcus guessed—above her right ear. He couldn't figure out if she was Vampira or Holly Loki, but he immediately made Roberta Klemp as a nut.

"I'm Detective Marcus, from Manhattan South Homicide," he said. He held up his gold shield, pointed a stubby thumb at Diane, and added, "This is my partner, Detective DeGennaro. We'd like to speak to somebody in management."

"I am the management, Officers," she said in a gentle funeral director whisper. "May I suggest that we get comfortable, though?" She motioned with a bony arm down a hall toward rear offices.

Bangles a-jangle and turquoise-studded earrings a-dangle, the odd lady led them down the long carpeted hall past three large viewing rooms, only one of which, Marcus noted, was in use. Room 2 contained a cheesy pressboard coffin draped with a biker's black leather jacket bearing the colors of "The Outlaws." On one side of the plain bier was an easel-supported blown-up photograph of an obese biker. Clutching a long-neck Bud in a huge fist, he was replete with hoop earring, untended beard, distended belly, and surly scowl. An attached placard identified him by the sobriquet "The Falcon." Opposite was a large standing flower arrangement made up in blacks, whites, and oranges to form the Harley-Davidson logo. Nothing like a theme funeral, Marcus thought, rolling his eyes.

"That's Mr. Falcone," Roberta Klemp said without being asked. "Got his wings clipped the other night on the Cross-Bronx Expressway by a Toys 'R' Us tractor-trailer. Oh, Lordy, was he a mess. Had no choice but to go with a closed casket." At the end of the corridor, she turned right and opened a door marked PRIVATE.

"This is our pre-need and arrangement room," she said, motioning the detectives to tired chairs that faced each other across a large round mahogany table. "This is where the bereaved decide on their choices for disposition. This is where we draw our contracts."

"I see," Marcus uttered. As he sat, he exchanged a millisecond glance with Diane. The one-word coded message flashing back from her blue Irish eyes was, as he expected it would be, "Nut."

"Now," the woman said, squirming and shifting in her thickly padded leather chair. "How can we at Fairlane Mortuary Associates be of service to New York's Finest?"

"Back in early June, this year, you handled the disposition of a deceased, a one George Granger," Marcus said. "You picked up the body at the medical examiner's office in Manhattan and handled its cremation at the direction of a Mr. John B. Holloway."

"Uh-huh." The woman nodded. She suddenly plucked a mirror from her desk drawer, held it up to her face, and adjusted the orchid. "I think I recall that matter very clearly," she said with an apparent edge.

"Are you saying you recall this one more than usual?" Diane asked.

"You could say that," the woman replied, offering a blasé shrug. "You know," she confided flatly, "dealing with the dead can be a really fucked-up business." She placed the magnifying mirror back in the drawer and looked across at Diane. "The Granger disposition was a real pain in the ass, if you don't mind my saying."

"How so?" Diane inquired.

"Several reasons. First of all, the man who made the arrangements for Mr. Granger, this Mr. Holloway, was a real putz."

"Why was that?" Marcus asked.

"Mr. Holloway was merely Mr. Granger's business partner, not a true next of kin. I much prefer dealing directly with the family, not with some disinterested third party."

"Did you have any contact at all with any true next of kin?" Diane asked.

"Not a one. The only person we had any dealings with was Holloway. There were no calls or visitation by anyone else."

"Why was Holloway so bad?" Diane asked.

"Holloway was cheap," Roberta said, narrowing her gaze to pinpoints. "It was like dealing with Scrooge looking for a discount burial for Marley, for crissakes."

"Tell us about it," Marcus pressed.

"Holloway demanded a direct cremation, no embalming, no formal visitation, no clothing, cosmetics, or ceremony—no nothing. He didn't even want to see the body, for God's sake. Isn't that sad?" As she spoke, one of her fake eyelashes broke loose from its moorings. Without missing a beat she again dug out her mirror, a tube of cement, and quickly made the fix.

"Sad maybe," Marcus replied with a mild shrug. "But what was the problem? After all, you do advertise the cheapest cremations in town."

Roberta smirked. "Yeah, we do offer the *least expensive* cremations in town . . . but for crissakes, let us sell you *something*. But not only did Holloway want this whole thing done on the super cheap, he was also in a terrible hurry and wanted the cremation performed immediately. Said he couldn't—wouldn't—leave town until it was done."

"Did he say why he was in such a hurry?" Marcus followed up.

"Oh, he was bellyaching that being away from his business in Ohio was costing him daily." The strange woman frowned deeply, rolled her eyes, and added, "He didn't give two you-know-whats about his damn partner."

"Was there a problem for you to do the cremation right away?" Diane asked.

"You bet. He wanted us to fire up the retort and do it that day—that minute—for God's sake. I told him that we only did the cremations one day a week. Besides that, he also wanted us to immediately scatter the ashes out over the water. Long Island Sound."

"How immediately?" Marcus pressed.

"I mean *immediately*! We don't normally do that until we have a number of urns on hand. We make one trip out of City Island and do twenty, twenty-five at a time. We ain't chartering no boat to do one damn scatter job. Get me?"

"I getcha," Marcus replied, marveling at the crusty old broad. After exchanging another quick glance with his partner, he asked, "So what did you do?"

"We went ahead and did everything exactly the way Holloway wanted. But . . ." Roberta looked coyly at Marcus. "We had no choice but to charge him a little extra for complying with those special wishes."

"How much extra?" Diane asked.

"Four-fifty."

"Did he balk?" Diane followed up.

"Didn't like it, but he paid it. Hell, it was worth every damn penny of it. You got any idea what it costs to get that cremator up to two thousand degrees for three hours? Just to do one body?"

"Was there any life insurance involved in the payment of your fee?" Marcus asked.

"Not in the payment of our fee, but there *was* life insurance."

"How do you know?" Diane asked.

"We always ask about insurance. As a normal part of our service to the family, we will acquire the necessary number of death certificates that they may need. Where life insurance exists, we will even file the death certificate with the particular carrier. It saves the family, and/or the beneficiaries, any of that annoying bullshit."

"Do you have the name of the insurance company?" Marcus asked.

"I'd have to look it up in my files," Roberta Klemp said, "but I'm sure I have it."

"If not by insurance, how did Mr. Holloway actually pay the bill for Mr. Granger's funeral?"

"He paid the entire bill in cash."

"Any other reasons that this *funeral* was such a problem for you?" Diane inquired.

"Oh, yeah. We got really jerked around by the medical examiner's office. We sent our van down there to collect the body and they wouldn't release it. We had to make another trip the next day to get it."

"Why wouldn't they release it?" Marcus asked.

"No death certificate. They hadn't signed off on it yet. There had been some sort of *delay*." Again the woman rolled her eyes.

"Why was that?" Marcus asked.

"Really don't know. But the next day, after Mr. Holloway went ballistic and made some calls, everything was cool. The death certificate was signed off on, and we got the body released to us with no problem."

"One more thing," Marcus asked. "Did you happen to notice any unusual red marks or blotches on the decedent's torso, chest, arms?"

"No. I never actually looked closely at the body and I'll tell you why. If this had not been a *direct* cremation, we would have washed and disinfected the body, sutured or packed any openings, then embalmed and dressed the body. But because of Holloway's demands we did none of that. Mr. Granger's body was simply placed into a cardboard receptacle and . . . incinerated."

Roberta Klemp stood, stepped to a four-drawer file cabinet, and opened the drawer marked A–G. Pulling out a manila folder, she flipped quickly through its contents and jotted something down on a Post-it. She slipped the small yellow square and some other papers into a letter-size envelope.

"Here you are, Officers," she said, returning to her desk. "I've written down the name of the insurance company I forwarded a copy of George Granger's death certificate to. I've included their policy number as well as Mr. Granger's Social Security number."

"Thank you very much," Diane said.

"I'm also providing you with one of our brochures, in the event that you, or someone you know, may one day need our services." She smiled a forced smile. At that very instant, the glue-on eyelash on her other eye broke free.

Marcus and DeGennaro left Fairlawn Mortuary Services by the same side door they had used to enter. As they crossed the parking lot, they were stopped in their tracks by the thunderous roar of several dozen unmuffled and chrome-heavy Harleys wheeling onto the funeral home's property. Every one of the scruffy-looking riders, and their biker-chick passengers, were decked out in leathers with the Outlaws colors.

"Coming to bid their fond farewells to the late, great Mr. Falcone, I presume," Marcus rasped sarcastically over the continuous chopper clamor.

"As only the Outlaws know how," Diane acknowledged, clicking the remote to unlock the car doors.

"The Falcon has left the building," Marcus announced in feigned Elvis solemnity as he climbed in on the passenger side. Then, quickly shifting gears, he added, "On the way back, let's stop at OTB. There's a three-year-old going tomorrow by the name of Falcon's Fancy."

Diane snickered slightly as she pushed the key into the Ford's ignition switch.

"What's the matter?" Marcus asked, letting go with one of his involuntary nervous snorts.

"That sure sounds like a fine example of real solid arithmetic to me."

ELEVEN

It was one thirty in the afternoon when Richie Marcus and Diane DeGennaro returned to Manhattan South. After signing back in at the office, they gave Savage a complete rundown of their late-morning visit with the strange Roberta Klemp up at Fairlawn Mortuary Associates. They then contacted Winona Escalante, chief claims investigator at the Aurora Occidental Insurance Company of Fort Wayne, Indiana. Escalante took the information on George Granger and promised to get back to them before the end of the day. By two o'clock, the pair had again left the office to go have a late lunch around the corner.

Though nothing that Marcus and DeGennaro related could in any way be construed as evidence of any crime in the Granger matter, neither was anything revealed that could in any way rule that possibility out. But based on the detectives' report, and their personal impressions, Savage did conclude one thing for certain. Before dropping the very odd matter entirely, he now would insist that Mr. John B. Holloway, Granger's business partner, at least be interviewed.

"Sarge," Eddie Brodigan said, leaning into the sergeants' room. "Pick up on two-three. It's a lady."

"Sergeant Savage."

"Hi, honey. It's me," Maureen Gallo said.

Hmm, Savage thought. Apparently, the New Jersey ice had thawed. He was back to being "honey."

"Just got off the phone with Doreen Heimgartner. She just wanted to confirm that we'd be using their beach cottage for the weekend of the sixteenth to the eighteenth. I told her yes. I just wanted to make sure it was still a go with you."

"It's still a go," he responded, deciding not to mention the Street Crime Unit reunion he'd have to forgo in order to live up to his promise.

"Because if there's any problem with you being able to make it, we can back out now. I won't mind. I just don't want to leave them hanging."

Yeah, like hell you won't mind, Savage thought. "There's no problem," he assured her evenly.

"Doreen and Randy are leaving on a cruise on the fourteenth, so they just wanted to make sure that we would be taking the place. If not, they could arrange to rent it that weekend for a bunch of dough. But they've gotta know now."

"I'm still up for it if you are."

"Okay," Maureen said. "Talk to you later." As Savage hung up the phone, Jack Lindstrom ambled in.

"I think we're going to have a bit of difficulty getting in touch with George Granger's next of kin," Lindstrom began, sitting on the edge of Jules Unger's desk. He glanced down at notes scribbled across a memo pad and added, "The only reference we had to go on was the Ohio phone number that Officer Cox said he called from Dr. Janus' office that morning."

"Right," Savage replied. "Said he spoke to Granger's business partner, notified him of Granger's death, a guy named Holloway. That guy absolutely must be interviewed. Can't you reach him?"

"Nope. Got an Ohio Bell recording that tells me at the customer's request the service has been disconnected. I then contacted Patti Capwell over at Telephone Security. According to her, Ohio Bell said they did have a listing for a John B. Holloway, in Columbus, but the service was disconnected three weeks ago . . . with no forwarding."

"Hmm." Savage removed a fresh roll of Wint-O-Greens from his desk's kneehole drawer. He peeled away the end foil, popped one into his mouth, and held out the roll to Jack Lindstrom, who waved him off.

"Get back with Telephone Security. Have Patti get us a printout of *any* Granger, or *any* Holloway, who does still have phone service in Columbus."

"Already done," Lindstrom said. "She'll get back to us with a printout by midday tomorrow."

"Just to make certain that we're talking about the same guy, at the same phone number," Savage said, "let's go about it in reverse. Ask Patti to also get us a printout of all the toll numbers that were called *from* Janus' phone that morning. Billy Cox claimed he made that notification to Holloway somewhere around eight a.m."

"She's going to require a case number in order to do that," Lindstrom reminded him. "And since we have no case, we therefore have no case number."

"Use your charm," Savage whispered, narrowing his gaze conspiratorially.

The detective smiled and nodded, turned on his heel, and strode back into the squad room. Lindstrom and Patti Capwell were old friends—for him she would bend the rules.

Struggling to keep his mind off of his own problems, most of which circulated around money—or rather the lack of it—Dr. R. Charles Janus hurriedly finished the general neurologic examination of Mrs. Debra Monk, his next-to-last scheduled patient for the day.

The zaftig mid-fifties widow had been a referral from Harold Cousins, the questionably competent internist up on the second floor. She had presented with complaints of extreme fatigue and exhaustion of the muscles aggravated by activity and relieved by rest. She had also presented in threadbare clothing, well-worn cheap shoes, and an untended wiry salt-and-pepper mane that hadn't seen a beauty parlor in decades, if ever. This was not a relative of the Rockefellers or the Vanderbilts; this lady was broke, and Janus could empathize.

"When did you first notice this fatigue?" Janus asked, having already concluded a diagnosis. He'd seen this condition a thousand times before.

"I first started to notice it when I would climb my stairs," the woman replied. "Especially when carrying bundles. I live on the top floor of a four-story walk-up. I can barely make those stairs anymore."

"I see," he said. "And how long ago was that?"

Debra Monk thought for several seconds, then replied, "A year . . . maybe a little more."

"And now?" he probed.

"Now it happens whenever I get up from a sitting position, raise my arms over my head, or lift anything heavy. Up to now, Dr. Cousins has been telling me that all I needed to do was lose some of this excess weight and I'll be okay. I'm worried that there's something more involved here. My heart maybe."

The woman was right. Something more was going on, but it was likely not to be the result of any cardiac problems. Although Janus' examination had revealed no muscular atrophy or loss of sensation, her additional symptoms—drooping of the upper eyelids, double vision, and difficulty chewing and swallowing—all pointed to a singular diagnosis.

"You can get dressed now," he told the woman while jotting a prescription. Moving toward the door, he added, "I'm going to start you on something, and you must take it exactly as directed. My office assistant will have the prescription waiting for you. You can pick it up on the way out." Janus discerned the momentary worried grimace that flashed on the woman's bone-weary and life-lined face. Poor soul probably didn't have the price of a bottle of aspirin, he concluded, let alone an expensive fourteen-day prescription.

"What do you think it is, Doctor?" the woman asked, while stepping behind the privacy screen.

"I'll see you in two weeks," Janus replied. "Let's see how you respond to the medication. I'll be better able to evaluate then." He knew that if the woman responded well to the cholinergic drug during that period, his diagnosis of myasthenia gravis would be all but confirmed.

Janus moved quickly from the examining room and

dropped Mrs. Monk's patient file and prescription for neostigmine onto Guillermo's desk. "Don't charge her anything," he said to his assistant. "And fill that prescription from our physician sample locker."

Guillermo nodded.

"Weren't we supposed to have one more patient?" he asked, looking out at the empty waiting room.

"Mr. Vitale," the assistant replied. "But he canceled about two hours ago. A 'death in the family.' "

"Bill him."

"But . . . Doctor?" Guillermo said, shrugging. "He's been your patient for years. Besides, he called and canceled, it's not as if he just didn't show. . . ."

"Bill him, I said. Twenty-four hours' notice on all cancellations . . . office policy. No exceptions, do you understand? Besides, the son of a bitch is loaded. He can well afford it."

Guillermo nodded. "I'll be leaving as soon as Mrs. Monk leaves," Guillermo informed him. "I've got to stop at Gristedes—we're out of bread, coffee, and toilet paper. Can you think of anything else we need?"

Janus rolled his eyes and sighed. "I can think of a whole lot of things that we need." Without another word, he disappeared into his private office, pulled the door tightly closed, and checked his watch. It was three thirty p.m., as good a time as any to make the call to Columbus. He sat at his desk and dialed. The call was answered just after the third ring by a deep and assertive female voice.

"Hello."

"Hazel? Hazel Holloway?"

"Speaking."

"This is Charlie Janus. How are you today?"

"I'm fine," the woman responded curtly.

"Been waiting to hear from you, Hazel," he said. "I've been patiently watching for FedEx or UPS to deliver that box of green stuff."

"Green stuff?" the woman asked, sounding confused.

"Don't play dumb with me, Hazel," he said with a

sharpening edge, feeling his anger grow. "You know damn well what I'm talking about. Cash . . . moolah. I was to have received at least part of my share by now. John Boy was to funnel it to me through you."

"I don't have it yet to send to you," Hazel Holloway said flatly.

"Look," Janus snarled, "I know for a fact that John has already received a million and a half from the insurance company. And that was three whole weeks ago. I should have had my share no later than one week after that. But I haven't seen so much as a fucking nickel. Where's my share, goddammit?"

"Last I spoke to my son, he told me that he's a little leery of making any *major* disbursements quite yet. It just wouldn't look good. Think about it."

"Ohhh," Janus moaned angrily. "I'm thinking about it, all right. I'm also thinking about having to ride goddamned overcrowded buses when they repossess my fucking car—which is going to happen at any moment now."

"Relax, Charles," the woman said soothingly. "How much will it take to get your car payments up to date and get you straight for the few more weeks that John feels he needs?"

"Screw what John Boy feels he needs," Janus yelled. "The agreement was the damn agreement. I was to get my share as soon as the settlement was made. The settlement was made three fucking weeks ago, and it still hasn't happened. I'm warning you, I do not appreciate getting jerked around like this. Just who the hell do you think you're dealing with?"

"I don't like the way I'm being talked to," the woman snapped. "And I certainly do not appreciate your filthy gutter language. Unless you want me hanging up, you better tone it down, buster."

"Unh," Janus grunted, wishing to God that he had some sort of solid recourse—but, damn it all, he had none. He was being strung along, smoothly jerked around by Holloway's always-doting mommy. The woman was running interference for her little faggot

son, and was every bit as treacherous. "You know," he said, bluffing, "all it would take from me is one goddamned phone call. . . ."

"Don't you threaten *me*, Doctor," a poised Hazel Holloway countered. "That kind of nonsense isn't going to get any of us anywhere. You know," she added with a laugh, "it amazes me how supposedly brilliant people can sometimes be so goddamned stupid. Do I have to remind you that if anybody is culpable in this matter, it's *you*? So don't go blustering about making any damn phone calls, do you understand?"

"I need my fucking money."

"You're just going to have to be a little more patient, Doc. You'll see your share in due time. Now, tell me, what do you absolutely *need* in order to tide you over?"

"I must have twenty thousand right now."

"Too much. I don't have that kind of money kicking around. You gotta cut that number in half, at least."

"All right," Janus replied, fuming. "Ten."

"Make it ninety-five hundred. I'll wire it today."

"Why not the whole ten?"

"Because any wire transfer of ten thousand or more gets the IRS notified. *Duh!*"

"Okay."

"I'll wire it, but I will not wire it directly. Do you have someone who you can trust? Someone who will allow me to wire it into his or her bank account? That way there's no paper trail from us to you."

Janus pondered for a long moment. He wanted to accept the lousy pittance like he wanted a hole in the head. What he really wanted was his full share: five hundred thousand bucks. But reality was reality. He would have to wait for the big chunk, but right now he needed to stop the sharks from circling. He pressed the intercom.

"Guillermo," he said sharply.

His office assistant, studio apartment roommate, and casual lover replied, "Yes, Doctor?"

"Has the last patient left?"

"Yes. I gave Mrs. Monk the prescriptions you ordered, and she's gone. The office is empty."

"Good. Guillermo . . . you have a bank account at Chase, right?"

"Yes."

"Would you be good enough to come in here for a moment? I need to ask you for a favor."

It was fifteen minutes past quitting time when Diane DeGennaro—née Fallon—left the female locker room on C-Deck after freshening her makeup and running a brush through her shoulder-length red hair; Richie was already downstairs waiting for her. Today was her daughter Sandy's twenty-seventh birthday, and she and Richie planned to stop by Sandy's claustrophobic Sunset Park apartment with their gift of a new toaster oven—which Sandy sorely needed—and then take her and the children out for a veal Parmesan dinner over at Mario's on 9th Avenue. There, they would all put the finishing touches on the Fallon family reunion they'd been planning for the last six months. They'd already booked the back dining room of the Boardwalk restaurant; it would easily hold the sixty-some guests due to attend, and because Richie was old buddies with the owner, the price for the room and food catering was very right. The reunion was scheduled for Saturday, August sixteenth, and time was running short. Dozens of people were going to be flying in from all over; they wanted everything to be just right.

Sandy had divorced a year ago and was barely squeaking by financially. Her creep ex-husband had skipped town, and with two small kids to rear by herself it was a rough spot in her life, no question, but she would survive it—Diane would see to that. She often helped the younger of her two daughters with rent money and utility expenses. Richie knew cash was sometimes being funneled to Sandy, but Diane felt it better if he didn't know to what extent—hell, he'd probably have a conniption fit if he did. But, hey, he was never straight with her about his pony losses . . . or winnings, for that matter.

Diane returned to her desk, quickly organized the DD-5s into the folder of her most recent case—a hooker homicide over in Midtown South—and slipped it into the file drawer. She was close to making collars on this one; in fact, one of the two slimeball perps was already in custody, rooming at Rikers while awaiting trial on an unrelated robbery. She would pay the mope a visit tomorrow and drop the homicide rap on him; she was certain that by telling him he'd be taking all the weight, she could get him to give up his murderous accomplice—the slimeball type always did. Diane locked the file and snapped off her desk lamp. The phone rang as she stood to leave; she picked it up.

"Detective DeGennaro, Manhattan South Homicide."

"Yes, Detective. This is Winona Escalante from Aurora Occidental Life calling. We spoke earlier this afternoon about one of our insureds, a Mr. George Granger."

"Oh, yes, Ms. Escalante."

"I have our complete file before me. I have reviewed it in depth. What is it that you would like to know?"

Diane quickly unlocked her desk, retrieved a fresh memo pad, and set it down before her. "What can you tell us about Mr. Granger's next of kin?" she asked. "Beneficiaries, that sort of thing. We would like those names and ways to contact."

"Before we get to that, Detective," Escalante said, her voice even and refined, "I must tell you that, on its face, at least, this matter appeared perfectly normal; legitimate in every way . . . do you know what I mean?"

"I'm not sure that I do, Ms. Escalante," Diane replied. "What exactly do you mean?"

"What I mean is this: Once upon a time, Aurora Occidental Life had a policyholder by the name of George Alan Granger. Mr. Granger was in the final year of a term policy that the company had determined they would not again renew. Mr. Granger then died—in the presence of a licensed physician, I might add—a mere five days before the expiration of said policy. Aurora Occidental then paid off a very handsome sum to the sole beneficiary, who was many states away at the time of the insured's death."

"Let me have the name of the sole beneficiary," Diane said.

"John Boyer Holloway of Columbus, Ohio."

"Did you say John *Boy*-er Holloway?" Diane asked, her voice an octave higher.

"I did. Why?"

"It just triggered something," Diane replied, opting not to explain just yet. After all, the similarities between the names of Granger's beneficiary and that of Dr. Janus' supposed handsome Meat Hook playmate, John Boy, might just be coincidental. Might be, but she doubted it.

"And just how handsome a sum did Mr. John *Boy*-er Holloway receive?"

"One million, five hundred thousand."

"Jeez."

"Yes . . . Jeez. Furthermore, both the attending physician *and* the medical examiner, who subsequently performed an autopsy, have declared Mr. Granger's death one of natural causes—a simple heart attack."

"So far that's what we've got," Diane agreed. "But—"

"Like I said," Winona Escalante interrupted, "on its face it comes across as legit. However, in reviewing this case—which I have come to study only because of your inquiry contact—and looking somewhat deeper into it, I see some stuff here that is really sounding alarms. I'm surprised this one wasn't flagged by us for at least a cursory investigation before we made the payoff."

"Do tell," Diane said, snapping the lamp back on while getting comfortable.

"Are you ready to copy?"

"I'm all ears," Diane said, clicking her ballpoint. Richie would just have to wait.

TWELVE

Natty yet still business conservative in a custom-tailored gunmetal-blue pinstripe that set off graying temples and a lean outfielder's build, Chief of Detectives Ray Wilson arrived at Manhattan South Homicide. Punctual to the minute, the tall black man strode directly to Squad Commander Pete Pezzano's private office. When he entered, both Pezzano and Savage stood. Pezzano moved from behind the desk, relinquishing the seat to Wilson.

"At ease, gentlemen," the chief said tersely. He unbuttoned his suit jacket and sat himself at Pezzano's desk. "I'm here on very short notice, at your request, but I've got a ten o'clock with the PC, so we've gotta make this quick."

"Coffee, boss?" Savage asked.

"No, thanks," the chief replied with a shake of his head. "Sonya's got me off the caffeine. Let's get right down to business."

Savage and Pezzano sat.

"We want to move ahead with an official investigation on a somewhat dated matter which involves a physician over in the Sixth Precinct," Pete Pezzano opened. "At the very minimum, we want to be able to subpoena one of his patient files."

"And at maximum?" Wilson asked Pezzano.

"We would very much like to secure a search warrant for his entire office, and thereby get a look at some of his other records—telephone, billing, the like."

"We may also need official access to some of the medical examiner's records and reports," Savage inserted. "They may go ahead and freely give them to us just for the asking, but without a case number they don't have to."

Wilson nodded almost imperceptibly, his expression neutral, void of decision. The room was quiet for many seconds.

"Are we talking about the one from a few months ago?" he said. A frown line wrinkled his brown forehead. "Janus. Dr. Charles Janus. The one where a guy dropped dead right in his office at some ridiculous hour of the morning."

"Right," Savage responded, amazed always at the chief's incredible powers of recall, especially when it came to names.

Gesturing toward Savage, Pezzano added, "Thorn's crew has . . . unofficially . . . taken a little closer look at this thing because of some new information that has recently surfaced. Information that brought with it more than a slight aroma."

The chief trained his dark mahogany eyes on Savage. "What have you got now?"

"We got us a pretty good stench, boss," Savage replied flatly.

"I'm not totally unaware of the genesis of this thing," the chief said. "I had a conversation about it with Lieutenant Barone several months ago. Subsequent to that I've also heard from the precinct commander, Captain Dipson. According to Dipson, there's nothing there."

"Thorn feels strongly that there *may* be something there, Chief," Pezzano pushed.

"But in order to find it," Savage tacked on, "I think we need to look a lot deeper."

Wilson leaned back in Pezzano's chair, folded huge hands in his lap, and gazed thoughtfully at Savage.

The large nails and cuticles on Wilson's long fingers were trimmed and neat, almost manicured; the man's knuckles, however, were calloused and the right thumb badly misshapen. Savage recalled that the chief's screwed-up digit was the result of a violent tussle with a psycho perp years ago; the crazed crackhead moron had damn near bitten the finger off as Wilson tried to collar him for armed robbery. Wilson had the scarred hands, the intense eyes, and most notably, the even demeanor of a cop who'd worked his way up in The Job—a cop who had more than paid his dues on the street.

"It's my understanding that it was a collection of circumstantial factors that put Janus in the spotlight in the first instance," the chief went on, turning his gaze back to Pezzano. "But, beyond that, the Sixth Squad was unable to open an investigation because of the ME's finding. Case closed. Why the hell do we want to go back in?"

"We think now it's justified," Savage said firmly, knowing the chief could sometimes be a hard sell. "We've been doing some digging, peeling away some peripheral layers of this doctor's very strange life." He gave the chief a rundown on the information that had come to light in the last few days, focusing heavily on the Timothy DiBona scenario.

"Granted," Wilson said, his tone still doubtful, "in your eyes, you may well feel that you've established 'reasonable cause to believe.' But, open case or not, after this much time has elapsed—coupled with a natural-causes finding from the ME and no body to exhume—it's my bet that a judge is not going to sit still for some fishing expedition and simply grant you a warrant to search this doctor's office." The chief took a breath, then added, "The same thing goes for getting a subpoena issued for medical files, billing, and telephone records. I think you're gonna have to show them a lot more."

"We have more," Savage said, aware that the chief was probably correct on his last point.

Wilson continued, "Even then, at best, most any judge would limit such a warrant to only those specific items possessed and used in the commission of the alleged crime, and *also* limit the scope of the actual search to within arm's reach." The chief shrugged and threw open his palms. "What specifically can you tell a judge you're going to be looking for in that one examining room?"

"The stun gun he's alleged to have used on Di-Bona," Pezzano said.

"We'd really like to pursue this matter, Chief," Savage said firmly, matching his words with a determined look. "But we're dead in the water without your imprimatur."

"Keep talking."

"In speaking with an investigator from the Aurora Occidental Insurance Company, Detective DeGennaro discovered that the DOA—George Granger—was insured for a million and a half," Pezzano said.

The chief's benign expression did not change. "Is that it?" he asked flatly.

"The annual term policy under which he was covered was due to lapse on June second, this year. He died just five days before that expiration date," Pezzano continued.

"The insurance company had notified Granger last December of its decision *not* to renew that policy upon its scheduled expiration," Savage added.

"Why not?" Wilson asked.

"They uncovered the fact that Granger had tested positive for HIV. A fact that was also proven at autopsy."

"Okay," the chief said. "If a guy dies five days before the clock runs out on his life insurance, that's a matter of terrific timing, but completely circumstantial. And we've still got a 'natural causes' finding from the medical examiner. How do you plan to overcome that?"

Savage exhaled hard. "If we can reopen, dig a little harder, and possibly show them a much higher probability that a crime has been committed, maybe we can get the ME to reconsider. If we can't get them to move from natural causes all the way to homicide, we might at least get the middle ground—unknown causes. Hell, it wouldn't be the first time that's happened."

Chief Wilson rolled his eyes. "Don't hold your breath. Before they go against the word of another doctor, especially one who was present at the time of death, they are gonna want a real smoking gun. If there's a benefit of the doubt to be given here, believe me, it'll go in Janus' behalf."

"That's precisely what Janus might be banking on," Savage said. "From what I understand, he's a self-important and pushy son of a bitch. Arrogant enough to consider himself above any question."

Pezzano went on. "We've also established that in the three weeks since the insurance company paid off the mil and a half to Granger's sole beneficiary—his business partner, John B. Holloway—Holloway has abandoned that business—simply walked away from it and seemingly vaporized. We now also know that the business, and both Holloway and Granger, were very deep in debt."

"How deep?" Wilson asked.

"Millions," Pezzano growled sharply.

"You implying that the business partner had something to do with Granger's demise?" Wilson asked, raising graying eyebrows. "Lieutenant Barone told me that on the morning of Granger's death, this guy Holloway was physically in Columbus, Ohio. That's six, maybe seven hundred miles away. Barone said he personally spoke to Holloway, called him right from Janus' office that morning."

"That's true," Savage said, piping up. "We've accounted for that particular call; it was made by Barone at nine-oh-five a.m. from Janus' office line. We can also account for an earlier notification call to Holloway placed by Officer Cox at oh-eight-hundred."

"So where's the problem?" Wilson asked.

"According to Telephone Security," Savage replied reluctantly, having hoped he would not need to reveal to the chief the out-of-procedure peek made into Janus' phone records, "there were two other calls to Holloway's residence from Janus' office number earlier that Saturday morning. One was placed at oh-two-thirty hours, another at oh-three-eleven."

"Is that a fact?" Wilson replied curtly, glaring at Savage through perturbed slits. "Maybe it was Granger himself who made those calls to his partner's home?"

Savage shook his head. "According to Janus' statements that would be impossible. He claimed to have been awakened at home by Granger at around oh-three-thirty. Claimed he arrived at his office at around oh-four-hundred, and stated that Granger didn't arrive until several minutes later."

"Continue," Wilson said, still inscrutable, but now leaning forward in his chair.

Pete Pezzano broke in. "We've also uncovered information that Dr. Janus himself is not only broke but also in debt up to his friggin' ears."

"Yes," Savage said. He decided to reveal the additional out-of-procedure steps he'd exercised. "But the clincher for us concerns Janus' telephone records of last May the eleventh, the date he is alleged to have assaulted Timothy DiBona."

Wilson, stone-faced, listened intently.

"Two calls had been placed from Janus' office number just prior to the time of the alleged assault, within only moments of one another," Savage said. "One call went to a hotel listing in Miami, Florida; it lasted two minutes. The other went to the now disconnected Columbus, Ohio, residence listing registered to one . . . John B. Holloway."

"Holloway?" the chief of detectives said. He pursed his lips and rested his chin between thumb and forefinger.

"Holloway," Savage repeated. "That's not all, Chief. Thirty-eight minutes later, shortly *after* the time of the alleged assault on DiBona, those same two numbers were again called from Janus' office."

"Do we know who he was calling at the Miami hotel?" Wilson asked.

"No way of knowing, boss," Savage replied. "We contacted the hotel, the Delano, and they informed us that on that night they had sixty-seven rooms occupied. Calls for guests come in on their main switchboard, where they are redirected to guests' rooms. No records are maintained as to what room got what incoming call. They only keep a record of outgoing calls."

"What's your feedback from the insurance company, now that some of this stuff has come to light?" Wilson asked, frown lines again beginning to form at the center of his brow.

"They want a closer look too," Pezzano said. "Matter of fact, they're sending their lead investigator in from Indiana to huddle with us."

The chief of detectives went quiet. He looked off into nowhere, pondering. Long seconds passed until he stood up, rebuttoned his jacket, and moved toward the door. "I'll call Lieutenant Barone over in the Sixth," he said decisively. "I'll have him package up everything they've got on this matter and deliver it to you here, forthwith."

"Thank you, boss," Savage said. "I've got Jack Lindstrom standing by to chase after warrants and subpoenas. Marcus and DeGennaro are going to pay a visit to the ME."

Wilson stared intently at Savage and Pezzano. "It's now your case, fellas. Get to the bottom of this goddamned thing once and for all. But if there's nothing there, you will have pissed off a lot of people."

Though the chief had stopped just short of saying so, Savage knew that he was including himself on that roster of pissed-off people.

The current time and temperature flashed alternately in large digital numerals that were part and parcel of the strip mall's sign at the edge of U.S. 1 in

Marathon, Florida. It was two forty-five p.m. as the Avis rental Mercury pulled into the parking lot, drove past the Bank of America, and parked in a spot between Hanlon's Men's Store and Katy's Hallmark Card Shoppe. It was a paint-peeling ninety-eight degrees; such were the Florida Keys in the dog days of August.

Allowing the engine to remain running with the air conditioner on high, the driver opened one side panel of a vinyl valise that lay on the seat beside him. He dumped the contents—papers, driver's licenses, and other assorted documents—out across the front seat and began to organize them by name. Who would he become today?

The unfortunate episode at Dolphins Stadium two nights before, for which he had no alternative, had forced him to vacate the Miami Beach rental condo he'd called home for the last five weeks and blow town. Hell, he'd wanted to settle in Key West anyhow, so maybe it was fortuitous. There was no time like the present to make that move.

Of course, there were serious residual problems that had resulted from the Dolphins Stadium affair. First and foremost, it was time for a different identity. The name he'd used for the last many months, Eric Von Deutsch, now had to be shit-canned. It just made good sense not to use it anymore; Eric Von Deutsch would simply evaporate into thin air. But in ditching Eric, Granger now would need a new bank account—in a new name—from which he could draw cash, write checks, and conduct the business of buying a place down in Key West. People down there—Realtors— would probably become suspicious if he tried to purchase expensive real estate with cold cash. But who could he now be?

He still had his California driver's license in the name of George Granger—but, hell, he could never use that name again. And with the Eric Von Deutsch stuff now having to be retired, he'd have to start all over again in building an identity. While shuffling through the pile of documents, he came across the identification he'd taken from the body of Elvin Welch after he and Janus had snuffed the dumb schmuck up in Janus' office. There were two credit cards—a Visa and a Discover—an Oklahoma driver's license, and a dog-eared Social Security card. *Hey,* he thought with an ironic chuckle, *that jerk took over my identity. . . .*

Granger returned all the documents to one side panel of the valise. He then unzipped the other side panel and looked in on his fully loaded Browning Mark III; beside it was an additional clip with thirteen extra rounds. Then he opened the much larger center panel of the valise and gazed at dozens of wrapped stacks of hundred-dollar bills. He shut off the car's engine and stepped out onto broiling, almost bubbling, asphalt. Toting the heavy valise, he strode confidently past Katy's Hallmark, window-shopped the shirt display in Hanlon's, then walked into the Marathon branch office of Bank of America and went immediately to the tellers' counter.

"Good morning, sir," a female teller said. "How can I help you?"

"New accounts?" he replied.

She directed him to an open adjoining room. It was separated from the teller area by a door marked SAFE-DEPOSITS and beyond that a mildly ornate brass railing. He was greeted there by a very friendly Gloria Garibaldi, who motioned him to sit down in the chair at the edge of her desk.

Granger smiled, sat down, and crossed his bare legs. "I wish to open a checking account," he said, "and I'm also going to need one of your large-size safe-deposit boxes."

"Have you banked with Bank of America in the past?" Gloria Garibaldi asked, gathering a packet of forms from her desk file drawer.

"Uh . . . no."

"Well," she said with a big plastic smile, "then we would like to welcome you, *Mr. . . .*"

"Welch. Mr. Elvin Welch."

* * *

Unusually hungry for lunch, Savage trotted across Twenty-first Street and took the three metal stairs down to Carl's, the subterranean deli in the basement of the building across the street from the Thirteenth Precinct station house. It was exactly noon and, as usual, there was a long line waiting at the sandwich counter. He kicked himself for not coming over ten minutes earlier. Before joining the line, he picked out the coldest can of root beer he could find in the beverage cooler, Hires. The line moved quickly, and in five minutes he stood before the aproned and mustachioed deli owner.

"Ham and Swiss?" Carl asked knowingly.

Savage grinned and nodded, having long ago learned to live with his predictability when it came to his simple choices in food.

"Ham and Swiss," Carl barked to his eager-looking assistant at the slicing machine. "Poppy-seed bread, go heavy on the hot mustard, no lettuce or tomato." Turning back to Savage, he asked, "Anything else, Sarge?"

"Slice me up a quarter pound of the imported pepperoni," Savage replied, setting the can of soda down on the counter.

"That for your roommate?" Carl asked, chuckling.

Again Savage grinned and nodded.

Carl's sandwiches were a treat, especially for a finicky meat-and-potatoes kind of guy like Savage. He had often thought that if he ever wound up on death row, his choice for a last meal just might be a large hero sandwich from Carl's. Carl sliced the lean ham so thin you could read an eye chart through it, but at the same time he really piled the stuff on. The imported Swiss was creamy, not hard at the edges like you got at some places, and he used just the right amount to add that cheese component but not overpower the delicious ham.

But what made Carl's sandwiches really exceptional was the Italian bread. Slate-hard crust on the outside and soft as a cream pie on the inside, it was the best Italian bread Savage had ever had. He usually alternated between a poppy- or a sesame-seed loaf—he never got the plain. Only in New York can bread like that be baked, Carl had always told him; it was "all in the water."

The total for lunch and the side package of pepperoni came to $8.74. Savage trotted back across the street, took the rear stairs two at a time up to C-Deck and the offices of Manhattan South Homicide. Before getting comfortable at his desk, he slipped the package of pepperoni into the office refrigerator.

True to his word, Chief Ray Wilson had contacted the Sixth Squad and directed Lieutenant Barone to turn over everything they had on the George Granger/ Dr. Janus matter to Manhattan South Homicide. By twelve twenty, just as Savage was about to bite into his lunch, their case folder on the Janus affair was hand-delivered to him at his desk.

As he went to work on the sandwich and washed it down with the ice-cold root beer, he pored over each and every piece of paper in the Janus file. Not surprisingly, it was a typical dead-end case, with banal reports that contained nothing beyond that which he already knew. It did, however, contain several photographs of a fully clothed George Granger lying dead in Janus' examination room.

Photo Unit had responded that morning and taken shots from several different angles. Granger was wearing a fancy western shirt with those mother-of-pearl snap buttons running down the front placket and also on the breast-pocket flaps and at the snazzy cuffs. He also wore faded blue jeans and fancy snakeskin boots; all he'd needed was a neckerchief and a ten-gallon Stetson to be the Midnight Cowboy.

Held in place by a paper clip on the case folder's edge were two separate and short EKG strips that had been confiscated by Lieutenant Barone on the morning of the occurrence. Both were dated on the reverse side in black ink, presumably in Janus' hand. One represented an EKG performed on Granger by Janus on February 18; the other was dated January 11. Savage recalled that the medical examiner's records also included one EKG strip, supposedly taken only moments before Granger died in late May. He wanted to get another look at that one. The three strips might provide a good way to track Granger's alleged heart failure in his final months. Maybe he would even have his friend Axel T. Moonvie give them a look and offer an opinion. Moonvie was a fellow of the American College of Cardiology and always made himself available to Homicide.

As Savage swept fugitive poppy seeds, bread crumbs, and the empty Hires can from the desktop into his wastebasket, Jack Lindstrom entered the sergeants' room.

"I'm back from Manhattan Criminal Court," he announced glumly. "Struck out big time on the warrant and the subpoenas."

"Unh," Savage grunted, recalling the chief's admonition. "What judge did you see?"

"Cromarty."

"Figures," Savage said, annoyed. "Should have gone to Judge Rothmann."

"Vacation," Lindstrom advised with a shrug. "But both Cromarty *and* John McVeigh of the DA's office balked."

"McVeigh's a real schmuck. What did he say?"

"Told me we were close, but no cigar. Said he's not about to join us even in a preliminary criminal investigation against a medical doctor without something far more damning."

"Hmm. How are we coming on the next-of-kin question?" Savage asked. "Telephone Security gotten back to us?"

"They've given me a list of six other Holloway listings in Columbus. Of the four that I've been able to reach, none are related to, or have any knowledge of, a John B. Holloway. But I've still got two more to go."

"Any Granger listings?"

"Five of them. All were dead ends."

"He's gotta have family somewhere," Savage murmured.

"Apparently not in Columbus."

Right on Lindstrom's heels, Diane DeGennaro and Richie Marcus arrived back at Manhattan South from the administrative offices of the New York County medical examiner. Though not anxious to release any of it, the ME had finally provided the persuasive detectives with copies of everything that office had regarding George Granger.

"Surprisingly," Diane said, "though everything else they gave us was a photocopy of their forms and work sheets, they retained a photocopy of the EKG strip and gave us the original." She handed the small strip to Savage. "Said it was actually PD property."

Savage noted that the EKG strip looked very much like the two in the Sixth Squad case folder. All three were signed and dated by Dr. Janus, and all three looked pretty damn kosher. He felt a sudden pang of doubt. Was he spinning his wheels on this one? Was he trying to create something out of nothing—which he hoped would never be his style? To be sure, the office had more than enough homicide work to go around already; his detectives did not need to be burdened any further by investigating wild-goose chases based on hunch or whim. Should he just drop the whole damn thing, fold up the tent, and move on? Where the hell to go from here?

It was nearing three thirty in the afternoon, almost quitting time. He decided to take just one more step.

Savage picked up the phone, dialed the Park Avenue office of cardiologist Axel T. Moonvie, held a brief conversation, then hung up.

Popping up from his chair and snatching his suit jacket from his locker, he said, "I'm going to run everything over to a heart specialist on Park Avenue."

"Moonvie?" Jack Lindstrom asked.

Savage nodded and quickly gathered all the case

documents in one folder. Raising his chin toward the office wall clock, he announced, "There's no point in my coming back to the office today. I'll see you all tomorrow."

Case folder tucked under his arm, he strode from the sergeants' room, signed himself out, and left the Manhattan South office. Two minutes later, he returned. He went directly to the office refrigerator and collected the neatly wrapped quarter pound of thinly sliced pepperoni.

THIRTEEN

Axel T. Moonvie was born in India, the only son of a New Delhi physician and a British businessman who did not live to see his only son's first birthday. Shortly after the death of his father, his mother relocated them for a time to London, where she continued to practice internal medicine; five years later she accepted a prestigious research position at Columbia-Presbyterian Medical Center in New York City. Axel attended the very-very Dalton School, did his premed studies at Cornell, then graduated NYU Medical School—Class of '72.

The mild-mannered Eurasian spoke seven different languages, including Farsi, Cantonese, and, believe it or not, two different dialects of Swahili. He hated the New York Yankees, loved the Mets and Jets, and like many others in his profession, had a true passion for the game of golf. He was also a big-time NYPD buff.

"You're lucky," Moonvie said, reaching out across his wide desk to shake Savage's hand. "Normally on a Wednesday, I'd be out at Bethpage Black Course working on my handicap as well as my waistline. You've gotta walk that course, you know; no carts allowed."

"Really?" Savage replied, trying to sound interested in the game of golf. "So, how come you're not out there today?" he inquired.

"A patient of mine needed emergency surgery this morning. The procedure went longer than I expected. By the time I got done, it was too late; I'd never make my tee time. It's a thirty-five-mile drive." The diminutive Moonvie sat and was nearly swallowed up by his overstuffed, almost thronelike, swivel chair. He motioned Savage to one of the two leather wing chairs opposite his desk.

Savage nodded. He didn't understand the game of golf; never had. Whatever it was about the game that seemed to captivate so many had somehow eluded him. Whenever asked, he had always joked that he preferred games that required much bigger balls. Fact was, he did.

"So," Moonvie said. "You've brought along some stuff you want me to look at."

"That I did, Doc," Savage said, leaning forward and laying the Granger case folder on the physician's desktop.

"Anything you want to tell me about it before I begin?" the cardiologist asked, leveling his wire-rimmed glasses at the tip of his finely shaped nose.

"Don't want to influence your conclusions," Savage replied. "I'd just like your flat-out medical opinion based strictly on what you see."

"Fair enough."

"I'd like you to first look at these EKGs," Savage said. He stood and laid the three approximately eight-inch strips in dated order across Moonvie's desk. "And tell me whatever it is you see."

Moonvie quickly eyeballed the narrow paper strips, looked up, and commented: "Tell you one thing. These were done on an old machine."

"How can you tell?"

"The fan folds on the paper," he said. "And these." He pointed a slender brown finger at a pale pinkish dye line that ran partially through the length of the strip dated May 28, and a similar, yet more pronounced dye line that ran completely through the strip dated January 17. The March 19 strip bore no dye line.

"But those dye lines have nothing to do with the actual EKG," Savage said, "right?"

"Correct," Moonvie replied. "They run along the outer edge of a strip, perpendicular to the actual peaks and valleys. They let the technician know that the machine's roll of continuous paper is about to run out."

Savage nodded his understanding. "Getting back to the test itself, what do you make of the heartbeat?" Savage asked.

"Sinus tachycardia," Moonvie replied with no equivocation.

"Fast heartbeat."

"Exactly."

"I'm told that alcohol consumption could be responsible for creating that condition?"

"Oh, yes, that could certainly be," Moonvie said, drumming the fingers of his right hand on the desktop. "But I would have some slight problem with that in this case."

"Why?"

"One would have to wonder if the person was highly intoxicated while undergoing three separate EKG tests—on three separate occasions—all taken months apart." Moonvie chuckled and leaned forward in his chair. "Not that it's impossible, mind you. But if alcohol were the underlying cause, the person would have to be almost in a permanent stupor, for God's sake."

"We happen to know that on at least one of these occasions the person was, in fact, severely intoxicated."

Moonvie shrugged.

"What else could cause a consistent reading of sinus tachycardia?"

"Oh, a variety of things. It could be atrial, junctional, orthostatic, supraventricular—which is a combination of junctional tachycardia and atrial tachycardia. . . ."

"Anything in those EKGs which would indicate that the person was about to drop dead?" Savage asked.

"No," Moonvie replied. "They all appear virtually identical; none of them would indicate a potentially fatal abnormality. But EKGs are not necessarily the be-all and end-all in diagnosing every form of heart problem."

Savage handed Moonvie the pathologist's description of Granger's heart. The man readjusted his glasses, leaned back comfortably in his chair, and read. When he was done, he looked up. "How old was this person?"

"Forty-five. A male." Savage slid color copies of the on-scene and medical examiner photographs across Moonvie's desktop. "According to his life insurance company *and* the ME, he was HIV positive. But do you see any signs of heart disease, atherosclerosis?" Savage asked.

"No," Moonvie replied, shaking his head while looking at the photos. "There is no indication of cardiac atherosclerosis, which would be fatty deposits beneath the intima, the innermost lining of the heart. Nor are there signs of an infarction, new or old, or ischemia—obstacles to arterial flow. Also, I find that the heart was listed at normal size, another feature which I find unusual due to the medical examiner's listed cause of death as myocarditis." Still holding the photographs, Moonvie looked across at Savage and again shrugged. "Maybe this guy *was* drunk all the time. What else have you got there?"

"The pathologist's reports on some of the other internal organs—lungs, et cetera."

"Let me see." Again, while drumming his fingers on the desktop, the man read quietly. After perusing the balance of the ME's reports, he commented, "Man's lungs were pristine, extremely healthy."

"What does that tell you?" Savage asked, certain of the answer but wanting to hear it from an authority. He recalled that he had heard a similar remark about Granger's lungs from Dr. Karyn Hartman at the ME's office.

"Pulmonary functions appear to have been fine," Moonvie answered. "At the very least, it doesn't appear that this guy ever invested in Liggett and Myers or the American Tobacco Company."

"A nonsmoker?" Savage asked.

"Assuredly." He closed the folder but held on to

the DOA photos. "These pictures interest me, though," he said.

"Talk to me."

"This guy is blue, almost purple."

"What does that show?"

"Lack of oxygen," Moonvie replied, his face pinched into a pondering frown. "It might suggest strangulation here."

"The ME considered that," Savage responded, "but said there were no signs of it. No marks at all on the neck or throat."

"Then go back and take another look."

"Can't. The body has been cremated."

"Unh. Then I'd have to consider asphyxiation," Moonvie suggested.

"How does one asphyxiate a grown man without meeting and overcoming a whole lot of resistance?"

"One way in which it could be done," Moonvie said, "would be to already have the victim unconscious . . . say, as in this case, by superintoxication."

"Or by stun gun?" Savage suggested.

"Possibly." Moonvie shrugged. "But I would think that method would probably require additional help . . . in order to physically restrain the victim. In any event, once the victim is passed out, then all one needs to do is tie a plastic bag around the victim's head. The rest will happen all by itself. Eight, ten minutes, tops."

"Gotcha," Savage said, at the same time reaching for his roll of Wint-O-Greens and peeling one loose. "In this case there was only one other person present."

"Of course, then too there's always 'burking,'" Moonvie went on, almost talking to himself. "But that also generally takes two people."

"Burking?" Savage said, popping a candy. He held out the roll to Moonvie, who declined.

"Burking occurs when pressure is placed on the chest at the same time the mouth and nose are obstructed."

"Where did it get the name . . . *burking*?"

"What kind of Scotsman are you?" Moonvie asked with a light laugh.

"Tell me all about it," Savage said. He uncrossed his legs and leaned forward in his chair. The topic sounded very intriguing.

"Goes back to the early eighteen hundreds," Moonvie began. "It involved a William Burke and a William Hare, who were a couple of grave robbers. The two dug up fresh graves and sold the bodies to medical students, and to Dr. Knox, an anatomist at Edinburgh Medical School. But soon growing tired of the strenuous shovel work, and being the two very resourceful chaps that they were, they found a much more convenient way of coming up with fresh corpses."

"Murder."

"El correcto," Moonvie replied, somewhat out of character. "They usually picked on vagrants and prostitutes, people they figured wouldn't be missed. Burke would sit down heavily on the victim's chest, and Hare would pinch the nostrils and cover the mouth. Very efficient."

"Suffocation."

"Yes. Best of all, the method produced few or no marks of violence, thereby allowing them to sell the body for dissection. But, as opposed to your case, it does take two to tango. I don't believe one man could do burking alone."

"Interesting," Savage mused, recalling the unusual jagged impression on the DOA's left breast.

"How long would the process take?" he asked.

"Again, eight to ten minutes."

"Let's suppose the burking victim had a house key in a shirt pocket," Savage said. "Just a thin cotton shirt, mind you . . . no undershirt. Is it conceivable that an impression of that key could be pressed into the soft tissue above the victim's nipple?"

"Why not?" Moonvie replied with a chuckle. "Especially if the sitter had a bony ass." He handed back the photos. "So, Sergeant. Have I helped you?"

"Don't know, Doc," Savage replied. He chewed the Wint-O-Green. "I really don't know. I think maybe you've given me more questions than answers. But maybe that's good."

Moonvie jotted down a name and phone number on a prescription blank. "Dr. Sheldon Lowenstein," he said, tearing the form from the pad and passing it to Savage. "His friends call him Shelley."

"I know who he is," Savage replied. "He's probably the most prominent cardiac pathologist around."

"I suggest that you bring him in on this one. Without a body, he's the guy whose opinion you'll want to have."

Savage got up from the comfortable chair, moved toward the door, then stopped and turned. "Tell me, what happened to Burke and Hare?" he asked.

"They hung Burke," Moonvie replied.

"And Hare?"

"Because of the lack of evidence, the prosecutors offered Hare the chance to turn Crown's evidence. He did—he got a walk."

"Hmm," Savage grunted ironically. "Nothing much has changed in criminal justice down through the years, has it, Doc?"

FOURTEEN

"Truly amazing," Darrin Greavey said, gazing adoringly as he leaned across the console divider toward Holloway. "You've never made this drive before, yet you calculated it to the damn minute. How did you know that it would take us precisely thirteen hours and fifteen minutes of actual driving time to get from Amsterdam, Holland, all the way down to Marina di Grosseto in Tuscany?"

"There are a lot of things I've never done before," Holloway replied, slowing the Porsche Boxster and craning his neck to see around a slow-moving oxen-filled truck that was blocking his path. "When I tackle something for the first time, I always lay it out completely. I don't do *anything* without careful preparation."

"Totally anal?" Greavey said with a sly snicker.

"I guess. . . . But then, you would know . . . wouldn't you?"

"Yes, I suppose I would," Greavey said, smiling salaciously. "But this is truly uncanny, John. I want to know just how you did it."

"According to the map, its eight hundred and forty-five miles from Amsterdam to Pisa," Holloway began.

Greavey nodded, hanging on every word.

"I calculated that, obeying speed laws, it would take most people about thirteen hours plus to make that drive. An additional ninety-two miles from Pisa to Marina di Grosseto would take the average driver about two additional hours. The rest was easy."

"By my figures, that adds up to fifteen-plus hours,"

Greavey said. "Not thirteen hours and fifteen minutes."

"You didn't factor in my driving skills, my penchant for speed, and the fact that I'm driving a brand-new Boxster S."

Greavey made another flattering comment to him, but Holloway wasn't listening. He finally saw the opportunity he had been waiting for, and moved the car left of the center line into the oncoming lane of the twisting road that connected the Tuscan inland agricultural center of Grosseto and the nearby beach resort town of Marina di Grosseto. Nimbly downshifting, he floorboarded the gas, calling on all 280 horsepower, and roared past the dawdling cattle truck.

"Ugh!" Darrin Greavey said, scrunching his nose and closing the passenger window as they shot around the open-back lorry. "What a terrible stink."

"Smells like a mix of bovine dung and burnt brake linings," Holloway advised, steering back into the proper lane, leaving the offal truck far behind. "Not very appetizing, was it, Darrin?"

"Disgusting," Greavey replied, reopening the window to allow the blasting fresh wind to clear the cockpit air. "But speaking of appetizing, don't you think we'd better start thinking about dinner?" Greavey glanced at his watch. "It's nine thirty already. We haven't had a thing since we stopped in Stuttgart."

"We're not very far from our destination," Holloway assured him, realizing that it was now the middle of the afternoon back in Columbus, a good time to check in with his mother. "If we can't eat in the hotel dining room when we get there, we'll find a nice place nearby."

"Good," Greavey sighed, rolling his eyes. "My God, I'm simply famished."

"Relax and enjoy the ride. Look at these little hill towns we've been passing through," Holloway said, smoothly upshifting to sixth gear. "They're so damn neat and clean, it's hard to believe that this area of

Italy is actually referred to as the Wild West of Tuscany."

"It's known as Maremma," the knowledgeable Greavey interjected, raking the long fingers of both hands through his rock-star-like blond mane. "It's a strip of coastal plain which begins just below Livorno and runs from the Tyrrhenian, east to the Apennines, and south to the very end of Tuscany."

"How do you know so much about Italy?" Holloway asked. "Have you ever lived here?"

"No. Never lived here. Just studied it a good deal in school."

"Sounds like you got a thorough education at St. Lawrence Boys Academy for well-heeled young men," Holloway chuckled. "Not to mention learning the finer points of how to get along with other young gentlemen. I'm envious."

"That's true." Greavey shrugged. "That was where I discovered I liked boys, but at the time I really didn't want to go to a private school. My father insisted on it, wouldn't have it any other way."

"Speaking of dear Pater," Holloway segued casually. "Tell me about him. Matter of fact, why don't you tell me about your whole family? I want to know all about you."

"I grew up in Batley," Darrin Greavey said, pleased with the attention. "It's a little city in central England. No brothers, two sisters. Haven't shared a word with my sisters in years, though."

"Stay in touch with the folks?"

"My mother is gone," Greavey said solemnly. "I really miss her."

"What about your father?"

"Pater's still around. My parents sort of disowned me when they found out I was gay. Not my mother so much, she could have handled it, but definitely my old man. And if my old man decided to disown me, my mum didn't have very much to say about it. She had to go along with him on everything." He gazed out across the rolling hills. "He really is a prick. I hate him."

"When did you last speak to him?" Holloway asked, making sure to appear sympathetic.

"Day before yesterday," Greavey said. He made wistful eye contact with Holloway. "I told him I was leaving Amsterdam and that I was going to sail the Mediterranean on a small ketch. I thought it would sound very macho to him." His expression soured. "It didn't go terribly well."

"What did he say?"

Darrin did not immediately answer. Holloway realized that Greavey was choking up. Struggling for control, Darrin finally replied, "He said he hoped I'd drown."

"I'm sorry," Holloway murmured softly. He placed his hand on Greavey's thigh and gently patted it. Darrin then totally broke down.

"You know how to do everything," Greavey said, wiping his nose with a tissue. "Your confidence, your poise; you're exactly what my father would have wanted me to be like in so many ways."

"Except that I like boys too," Holloway reminded.

"Unh," the effeminate Greavey murmured. "But unlike me, no one can tell that by your exterior. And besides, you also like girls sometimes."

"Don't worry, Darrin," Holloway said. "As long as you're with me, you're safe."

"I know that, John," Greavey replied, sniffling. "I can just sense that." He gently stroked Holloway's arm. "I've never felt this way about anyone before."

Two miles from the seaside village of Marina di Grosseto, John Boyer Holloway pulled the Porsche into a scenic overlook at the side of the roadway. "Enjoy the view," he said to Greavey as he climbed from the car. "I've got to make an important phone call. I'll only be a few minutes."

Holloway walked fifty paces from the sports car and dialed his cell phone. Hazel Holloway answered in the middle of the third ring.

"Mother?" he said.

"Oh, Johnny," Hazel Holloway replied. "How are you, my darling?"

"Just fine, Mother. I've left Amsterdam, and I'm now talking to you from Italy."

"Florence? Rome . . .?"

"No, just a little seaside town. I've bought a boat. I'm going to sail her to Sardinia in the morning."

"Alone?"

"With a friend."

"Oh, how exciting. But you be sure to be careful, darling. I can't have anything happening to the most important person in my life." Hazel Holloway let out a long sigh. "I'll bet it's just beautiful there. . . ."

"Yes, it is, very. But you'll be able to see it for yourself soon. Why don't you come join me for a while?"

"Well," she replied, "that would be nice. But right now I'm packing. The mover will be here first thing in the morning."

"Vegas?"

"Yes. I've found the most wonderful condo there."

"Will you be happy in Las Vegas?"

"Oh, I'm sure I will, darling. You know how I love that city. And now, with the money and everything, I can afford to live there decently. But as of tomorrow you will no longer be able to reach me here at this number—it'll be disconnected with no forwarding. I'll contact you with my new number as soon as I get situated."

"Get yourself a cell phone also."

"I'm going to."

"I'm happy for you, Mother."

"I know you are, darling. And I couldn't have done it without you. Listen," Hazel Holloway continued, "I heard from your self-important friend yesterday."

"Janus?"

"Yes. And he didn't treat me very nicely."

"What did he want? As if I didn't know."

"He wanted money."

"What did you tell him?"

"I jerked him around. Sent him ninety-five hundred to get him off my back. By the time he realizes he's not going to get any more, I'll be gone. I'll be living in Vegas, and he'll be totally screwed."

"*Ehh,*" Holloway groaned. "Something's come up. I think we may need to rethink some of our original plan."

"Like how?" Hazel Holloway replied defensively. "Like give that bum more money?"

"Maybe."

"Darling," Hazel Holloway reminded, "you told me that I could keep that creep doctor's share. You said he'd never be able to find you *and* he'd never go to the police. . . ."

"I know what I said then, Mother. It's just that I've come up with a new plan."

"What new plan?"

"You know, of course, that I am still covered by a million-and-a-half life insurance policy. And after Georgie's terrible and untimely demise, I canceled him as my sole beneficiary and replaced him with you."

"Uh-huh. I know that."

"If something were to happen to me . . . like, say, an accident, or something on the order of what happened to Georgie . . . there would be another windfall of cash for us."

"But you would need Janus again."

"That's possible."

"So what do you want me to do?"

"Continue to string him along. You may have to give him a little cash here, a little cash there. But don't alienate him. It would also be a good move to give him your new Vegas phone number. We have to keep him in the fold, at least for now."

"I think I understand what you're saying," Hazel Holloway muttered. "But would you mind being a bit more specific about *something happening to you*?"

"I met this most interesting fellow," Holloway said, looking back at the car, where Darrin was examining his tear-streaked face in the mirror on the sun visor. "He's a Brit. People have been mistaking us for brothers. He's never been to New York City. I thought that perhaps I might treat him to a short vacation there someday soon."

"And?"

"And while we're there, he and I might look in on good old Dr. Janus."

"I'm beginning to get the picture. What do you want me to do?"

"Simply be around to answer the telephone when a call is made to give you the bad news. That call might even be made by the police, so don't get alarmed. Then go to wherever and identify your son, John Boyer Holloway. Then make absolutely sure that his wish to be immediately cremated is taken care of."

"I love you, darling. I miss you."

"I love you too, Mother."

Looking up intently at Savage, Ray sat at feline attention, his back ramrod straight, his front paws side-by-side with a ragged tail curled neatly around them, his eyes wide and yellow. The expression on the cat's face was one of barely controlled anticipation as he watched his roommate peel slices of pepperoni from the deli wrapper and place them on a saucer. Happy days were here again.

"If I allowed you to," Savage said, "you'd sail right through this entire quarter pound in one sitting, or, in your case, one damn standing. Wouldn't you?"

"Murrr." Ray was a cat of few words.

"But that ain't gonna happen tonight, pal," Savage said firmly. He was certain of Ray's ability to make short work of vast quantities of pepperoni. He'd seen him do just that on more than one occasion.

"Tonight, I'm going to limit you to half of what I've bought." He looked down at Ray, who had totally abandoned his earlier poise and was now sucking up with the ankle-rub treatment while crying piteously.

"It's for your own damn good, man," Savage assured. "You're getting a little flabby, a little bit out of shape. We'll save the rest for another night, okay?" He set the pepperoni-draped saucer down on Ray's food mat and then refilled his water bowl.

After putting the remainder of the pepperoni in a Ziploc sandwich bag, Savage stashed it in the refrigerator and withdrew a Tupperware bowl of meatballs, sausage, and rotelle pasta that Maureen had given him to take home. He slipped the week-old leftovers into the microwave and punched REHEAT, setting the timer for three minutes. When he again looked down at Ray, unbelievably the old tom was not eating. Instead, he was glaring back with a very pissed-off expression. Savage knew immediately what was wrong. Whenever Ray dined on pepperoni or—his favorite—pepperoni pizza, he needed to wash it down with something a bit more dynamic than water.

Savage reopened the refrigerator, grabbed a Miller Lite, and exchanged the water in Ray's bowl for half the can of frosty suds. Ray took a sample lap and glared back at Savage.

"Look," Savage groaned, "I know you're a Bud Light man, but tonight I'm afraid you're just going to have to go with the Miller Lite, okay?"

"Murrr?" Ray groaned back.

"Because, my friend, that is all we currently have in stock, that's why." Ray went back to lapping. *"Jesus Christ,"* Savage muttered under his breath, "I'm arguing with a cat."

When the saucer was licked spotlessly clean and the bowl of cold beer was lapped dry, Ray licked his chops, leaped somewhat unsteadily onto the kitchen counter, then sprang up to the top of the old refrigerator. Within seconds, the husky tom was curled into a ball off somewhere in pussycat dreamland. Savage always envied the feline ability to lie down and knock right off.

Savage downed the other half of the can of beer while waiting for the reheated pasta leftovers to cool. All through dinner, and afterward while pecking away at the Sunday *Times* crossword—which was a bitch this week because it contained several long phrases that were spelled backward—he found himself unable to think of anything else but the Granger case and how much it was bothering him. There was something about the whole matter that was so crazy, so weird . . . so damn unfathomable.

He would absolutely need warrants and subpoenas if the thing was ever going to move forward. But the judges down at the courthouse and the assistants in the DA's office wanted more incriminating evidence—even if only circumstantial—against the doctor before issuing any such thing. Savage didn't know if he had it to give them, or would ever have it.

He did know, however, that a hard case could often be very much like a difficult Sunday *Times* crossword, where it is virtually impossible to get all the answers on the first pass, or the second . . . maybe not even the fiftieth. The trick is to stay with it and keep looking at it, because you know it *is* solvable. If you put it down and keep coming back, eventually things start to fall into place. The underlying thread—the necessary key words with intentionally missing letters, or phrases purposely spelled backward—to solving a difficult one will finally become clear. You can then approach the rest of the puzzle, seeing it through different eyes, until you triumphantly fill in the last box. But the absolute key was to keep coming back to look at it.

Savage opened a fresh beer, sat down at the dinette table, and reopened the case folder. He placed the three EKG strips chronologically beside one another at the top of the table, then began to pore over every word of the Sixth Squad's reports and the medical examiner's file. For the next two hours, he read and reread every scrap of paper, including all the information that Billy Cox had initially provided him.

He had it, he knew he did. He just couldn't put his finger on it yet. But it was there, all right; it was there somewhere in Granger's medical file. Of that he felt certain.

Axel Moonvie was right, and the doctor's reservations about the odd similarities of the EKGs kept ringing in his ears. Unable to figure why the strips had so captivated his attention, he continued to gaze down at them, studying them, until, at nine thirty, Maureen Gallo telephoned and again reminded him of the upcoming weekend at the Hamptons. The call totally broke his concentration.

At ten o'clock, he moved to the comfortable old denim-blue chesterfield in the living room. He clicked the TV on with the remote, tuned in to a Discovery Channel documentary on tropical storms and hurricanes, and stretched out. Two hours later, he awoke, got up, and went to bed. Sleep was fitful.

At three thirty in the morning, he awoke once again and lay there for ten minutes in deep thought. The key was dawning on him—he was sure of it. He left the bed and ambled back to the dinette table and the three EKG strips. He stared down at them again. Chronologically, starting with the earliest taken, based on dates penned on them by Dr. Janus, he butted the three strips together side by side. The fracture marks of the tears did not match up or align, nor did the dye lines. Then, ignoring the handwritten dates, he repositioned the strips, moving them around one another as if dealing a game of three-card monte. On his third shuffle alignment, he saw it . . . clear as three sevens on a Reno blackjack table.

"That ballsy son of a bitch," he murmured in disbelief. He smiled broadly and went back to bed. He slept well. He slept like a cat.

FIFTEEN

Forensic technician Howard Winkler set his horn-rims on the top of his balding head, then pressed his chubby, cherry-cheeked face to the high-powered electron microscope's viewer shield and slowly turned the focus adjustment.

"There's no question that you're correct on this, Savage," Winkler said, stepping aside. "Come have a look."

Savage placed his face to the viewer and took a long gaze. "They line up perfectly," he said, turning then to face Winkler. "I told you they would."

"The one long strip came from a single examination," the lab-coated Winkler said. "It was torn into thirds and a separate date was scrawled on each of them to make it appear as though there were three different EKGs taken on three different occasions."

Savage looked back into the viewer. "The *you're-running-out-of-paper* pink-dye trace lines up as well. The first section has no line, then it begins faintly on the second and continues perfectly into a broader expanding dye line on the final strip." Looking up again, he added, "This now also explains the time-stamp question as well. Both test two and test three bear a stamp of one minute after midnight, while test one bears a later time stamp of two minutes after."

Winkler nodded sagely.

"We can now show that test number three actually occurred before test number one," Savage said, having already concluded everything that the forensic technician was scientifically proving for him.

"But the clincher in this whole thing is the graph lines and the paper tears," Winkler said. "The edge fractures—which, of course, I'm going to photo in great enlargement for you."

Savage popped a Wint-O-Green and mused. Maybe this accounted for Janus' inexplicable delay in contacting 911 that May morning when, regardless of how George Granger actually died, Janus decided to cover his ass by peppering Granger's patient file with notations indicating long-term heart symptoms. He then added the sections of tape to prove that there was no previous evidence of heart attack on the EKGs. That surely would have taken a bit of time. Also, Janus claimed to have performed an EKG on Granger shortly before he died—perhaps these three pieces were it. In hasty panic, Janus simply tore it into thirds and, failing to notice the telltale dye line, scribbled each piece with a different date. When he was finally ready, he dialed 911.

Armed with Winkler's written report and several enlarged photographs of the microscopically matching fracture marks between the torn strips, Savage left the department's Jamaica, Queens, forensics office and headed back to Manhattan in the damnable traffic of the Long Island Expressway.

The clock on Janus' EKG machine wasn't broken, he thought, as he entered the Queens Midtown Tunnel. Nor was it set at the wrong time, as Janus had suggested to Cox that it might have been. And to carry the thought a little further, it occurred to Savage that the time stamps did not jibe very well with the Granger timeline—which supposedly didn't begin till around three or four in the morning. But they did jibe very nicely with the times when an EKG was supposedly performed on a heavily liquored-up Timothy Di-Bona two weeks before.

If Janus was capable of such blatant fraud as planting postdated test results in George Granger's patient record, then he would surely have no problem substituting and representing Timothy DiBona's EKG as

Granger's. Savage knew, however, that the latter could never be proven; EKGs were not positive identifiers like DNA or fingerprints.

Savage didn't have as much as he wanted—or needed—to start kicking over tables and demanding answers from anybody, but he had enough to begin pushing a little harder on the expanding circle of those who might be in the know. One of those on the list was Louis Armbruster. He would continue to call the attorney's office and press for a meeting.

He turned off Second Avenue onto East Twenty-first Street and parked the dark green Crown Victoria in a tight spot several doors beyond the Thirteenth Precinct. Climbing from the car, he wondered whether the damning pieces of conjured EKG would be enough to finally satisfy Judge Cromarty and John McVeigh of the Manhattan District Attorney's Office, and get them to issue subpoenas and warrants. He knew that before the morning was over, he would have Jack Lindstrom or Diane DeGennaro downtown finding out.

As he approached the entrance to the station house, Savage stepped aside and waited as two uniformed cops led a dozen daisy-chain-connected prisoners from the building. He recognized one of the escorting officers—the taller of the two in the crisp new uniform with the shiny handcuffs on his belt and the tentative what-the-fuck-am-I-doing-here look on his handsome face. It was the rookie, Hollywood Henderson.

The rookie years in the NYPD could be tough. Upon graduating the academy and arriving at their first command, rookies were almost always selected for the less-than-desirable assignments. Jobs like prisoner escort, rainy-day parade detail, fixed posts on subzero nights, and babysitting stinky old DOAs in roach-infested flop hotel rooms, always went to the new kid on the block; that's just the way it was and always had been in The Job. Random thoughts, visions, and some less-than-happy recollections of his own rookie years flashed in a fleeting montage through his mind. He had come to love The Job down through the years, but he would never want to do the early years again.

He watched as Hollywood held back the regular pedestrian flow while the other officer guided the red-eyed and scraggly group of prisoners across the wide sidewalk and led them one by one into the rear of an idling paddy wagon for the bumpy ten-minute ride down to the Manhattan Criminal Court building at 100 Centre Street. There, they would be arraigned on their charges. Some, with less serious charges, roots in the community, and little or no criminal background, would in all probability be released into their own custody and directed when to report back to court. Others would have to make bail. Those with more serious charges, or a rap sheet as long as the Declaration of Independence—or no means of making bail—would invariably be shipped over to the nightmarish Rikers Island to await further court action.

As Savage watched the now loaded paddy wagon lumber away from the curb, he thought how arrests, though important, represented only a small aspect of the overall police function. But just as bread bakeries delivered warm, fresh rye and pumpernickel each and every day to the markets, and the *Post* and *Times* delivered warm and fresh morning papers each and every day to the newsstands, the NYPD was expected to deliver warm and fresh bodies each and every day into the funnel end of the criminal justice system.

Once inside the station house, he trotted up the three flights of stairs to C-Deck, signed himself in to Manhattan South Homicide, and motioned Richie Marcus immediately into the sergeants' room. In only moments, he described the forensic findings of the bogus EKGs to the detective.

"Jesus Christ," Marcus sneered in disbelief. "Where does that son of a bitch get the friggin' balls?"

"Have no idea," Savage replied.

"Guy's either incredibly stupid or diabolically brilliant," Marcus offered.

"I'm going with the incredibly stupid," Savage replied. He took off his Hickey Freeman suit jacket and carefully hung it in his locker, then added as he sat at his desk, "Janus claimed that he was unable to get through to 911 that morning."

"We know that's bullshit," Marcus replied, lighting up a Winston and exhaling the first drag of smoke down the front of his shirt.

" 'Course we do," Savage said with a knowing grimace. "But we've got to touch that base and have a rebuttal established for that claim. I want you to get hold of Linda Jensen, the supervisor down at OTSD. Ask her to have an audit done of all the 911 activity between the hours of midnight and eight a.m. of May the twenty-eighth. Tell her we also need to determine whether 911's lines were ever busy during that period."

"Ten-four," Marcus said and slipped from the office just as the phone on Savage's desk rang.

"Is this Detective Savitch?" the mildly distressed voice on the other end asked.

It was an old female voice, old but not fragile, and it was peppered with Yiddish undertones. It was his octogenarian upstairs neighbor, Mrs. Potamkin. What the hell could she want? He reminded himself to get over to that Ukrainian bakery in the Ninth Precinct and pick her up some of that baklava she loved.

"Yes, Mrs. Potamkin," he said in his friendliest tone. "This is Thorn Savage. What can I do for you? Is something wrong?"

"Ray is sick," she said. "I found him lying still on my fire escape just a little while ago. You know how he sometimes comes up here to visit mit me."

"What's wrong with him?" Savage asked, alarmed. "Can you tell?"

"When I reached out to pet him, the meshuggener didn't move—not even a whisker. He just looked up at me with very tired and sad eyes. I knew right away something vas bad wrong. I think you should come see, Mr. Savitch. I think you should come right away."

SIXTEEN

Dr. Jane Figueroa had been Ray's veterinarian for the last five and a half years, ever since taking over the Hudson Street practice from Dr. Furrer, who'd retired to Arizona because of seriously debilitating rheumatoid arthritis. Savage thought she was a nice woman and very competent. More important, though, Ray, the curmudgeon, got on well with her.

"I'm afraid I have to tell you something that I'm sure you don't want to hear," she said to Savage, while stroking the cat's head and thick neck as he lay motionless on the stainless-steel examining table.

Savage grimaced unhappily.

"I'm afraid Ray has suffered a stroke," she said flatly.

"How do you know that for sure?"

"First of all, he is very weak and not very responsive on his right side." The vet then pointed to Ray's face. "Also, you can see that his mouth is asymmetrical, distorted, his upper lip is slightly curled, again on the right side."

"Yeah," Savage agreed glumly. "Makes him look kinda like Elvis."

"Also, he's able only to take a few wobbly steps before collapsing," she continued.

"Okay, so what are we going to do?" Savage asked, glancing momentarily down into the cat's golden eyes that seemed to plead. He gently stroked Ray's furry chin.

"Not very much, I'm afraid," Figueroa replied. "A number of critical hours have already passed. Now it's solely up to him. He can stay exactly the way he is, almost inanimate. He could get worse, or—"

"Or he could get better," Savage broke in, anxious for any sign of hope.

"He could," the lady vet acknowledged half-heartedly. "But I have to tell you that's not very likely."

"Why?" Savage asked. "Are cats different? People sometimes recover quite well from a stroke."

"Age, Mr. Savage. We must remember, that to the best of your knowledge, Ray is fifteen, possibly sixteen years old."

"What is it you're suggesting, Doc?"

Figueroa grimaced and gently shrugged. "Ray has had a very good life with you," she counseled softly. "You've given him a good home all these years. But frankly, I think you'd be doing Ray a favor by . . . letting him go."

"Putting him down?" Savage said, looking askance. She nodded. "Yes."

Savage reared at the word. "That is just not going to happen," he replied unequivocally. "Let's talk about other alternatives."

"The only other alternative is keeping Ray here. We can keep him on an IV, watch him, and hope for a miracle of some kind. But you must understand that can run into some money, and there is simply no guarantee that I can give you that he will recover, or even survive."

"That's what we're going to do," Savage said, looking strongly into Dr. Figueroa's keen brown eyes. "There's just no way I'd consider anything else."

Again, he looked down and winked at his old friend and longtime roommate. They were kindred spirits; they understood each other. Like him, Ray was a fighter, a warrior. "We're gonna beat this, right, buddy?"

Looking back through tired eyes, Ray struggled and forced what looked like a grateful smile.

*   *   *

The Lazy Parrot Cottages were six separate one-bedroom rental units clustered together in a zero-lot-line grouping on magnolia-lined Fleming Street just off William. The white-clapboard, green-roofed, pink-shuttered cottages were neat and clean, reasonably priced, and conveniently located a mere three blocks east of busy Duval Street, the boogie-down-and-dirty heart of funky Key West, Florida. Another perk was that the Parrot also offered a very private, clothing-optional swimming pool for all the guests. Where the hell had Key West been all his life? George Granger mused, still half asleep. Or for that matter, he thought, Ramon Mendez. Jesus, what a piece of ass.

George Granger rolled over on the extra-soft queen-size mattress and sensed that Ramon was no longer in bed beside him. He glanced at the red numerals of the digital alarm clock. It was a few minutes before ten a.m., and the appealing fragrances of fresh brewing coffee and frying bacon hung heavily in the air. Manna from heaven, he thought.

Eyes closed and lying perfectly still, he rehashed the intensity of the steamy night before. There was no question about it, he decided, Ramon was an animal, a walking, talking wet dream, a goddamned sexual acrobat. How glad he was that he'd decided to call Ramon and invite him down for the last two days. Exhausted still, and groggy, but realizing it was time to get up, Granger slowly untangled himself from the twisted sheets and swung his calloused and flat size elevens down onto the coolness of the travertine floor. He pushed off from the rack and plodded naked from the tiny bedroom.

In the narrow kitchenette, he found a bare-chested and sexy Ramon setting two places at the L-shaped breakfast counter. Half a dozen strips of well-done bacon were draining on a paper towel, a serving platter was piled high with scrambled eggs, and two English muffins stood poised in the four-slot toaster. The radio beside the toaster was turned down low, tuned to a local Key West station; it was playing something by the Eagles.

"My," Granger said, grinding the heels of his hands into watery, scratchy eyes, "do your talents know no end, Mr. Mendez?"

"Flattery will get you everywhere," Ramon replied with a sly smile.

"Will it get me back in bed with you?"

"Umh," Ramon sighed dreamily, acting the coquet. "I would love it," he purred, "but I'm afraid I must be getting back to Miami. I've got to be back on the hotel desk by two."

"Stay."

"I've got to earn a living," Ramon snapped in a get-real tone. *"Some* of us in this world *have* to work, you know. Not all of us are rich like you."

"Ouch," Granger replied. "Am I detecting a hint of jealousy?"

"You like your eggs soft or hard?" Ramon asked.

"Hard. I like everything *hard.*"

"Good," Ramon chuckled. "Because that's how they came out. Slightly, shall we say . . . *overdone.*"

"Screw the eggs. Why don't we just adjourn to the bedroom and have us a quickie?" Granger pressed, tightening his gaze into Ramon's dark eyes.

"These pots, these pans, and all these utensils," Ramon said, turning away. "Are they yours, or do they come with the place?"

"No," Granger snapped, annoyed at the rebuff. "They come with the cottage."

"That's wonderful. They're really nice, extremely good quality. I like this place. It must be very expensive, though. Is it?"

"Not too bad," Granger replied.

"Just what do you consider not *too* bad?"

Seeing an opportunity to impress the clearly wealth-conscious hot-blooded Cuban, he said casually, "Four grand a month."

"Madre mia. That's more than I gross in *two* months."

"You've also gotta remember that it's August. Come January they'll be getting twice that."

"How long are you intending to stay here?"

"Not sure. Probably until I buy something."

"Are you intending to buy here in Key West?"

"Oh, yes."

"Property is *very* expensive in the Keys, and most especially in Key West," Ramon announced. Then, clearly probing, he said, "You must be a millionaire, or something. Are you?"

"What time did you get up?" Granger asked, opting not to respond to the prying question about his finances. All this fucking guy thinks about is money, he thought, sitting himself at one of the two counter barstools.

"About a half hour ago," Ramon replied, pressing down the toaster. "I thought I'd surprise you with a nice breakfast. It'll only be a few more minutes."

"Jeez," Granger murmured. "You're not a bad guy to have around. What would it take to have you quit that lousy hotel job and come stay here in sunny Key West?"

"Is that a proposal?" Ramon asked coyly.

"Maybe."

"I'm not rich like you," Ramon replied. "I could not afford to live down here. Maybe someday I'll have money, though," he added dreamily. "Then . . . who knows?"

"What makes you think I'm rich?"

"Oh, I can tell," Ramon quickly replied with a knowing laugh. "I can smell money."

"You seem to have a preoccupation with it," Granger observed.

"I really have to be on the road in about twenty-five minutes," Ramon advised with a rueful shrug. "I wish we had time for more sex, but the drive to Miami is going to take at least three hours. I'm afraid there's just no way."

"When are your next days off?" Granger inquired, nibbling at a crispy bacon slice.

"Next week, Wednesday and Thursday. The fourteenth and fifteenth. You want me to come back?"

"Definitely."

"Then I will," Ramon Mendez replied, setting out two cups. "To firm it up, I'll call you here next Tuesday afternoon. Make sure you give me the number before I leave. Milk and sugar in your coffee?"

"I take my coffee black," Granger replied.

He knew he could easily talk Ramon into a quick fuck before leaving, but he would let it go. He had important things to do today, and he'd best be getting about them. Once Ramon headed back to Miami, he would bathe, dress, and do the dishes. When everything in the apartment was neat, clean, and squared away, he would take a nice slow mope into town for some daytime reconnoitering.

He needed to further familiarize himself with his new and probably long-term surroundings. But so far, so good, he thought, extremely pleased with his new living quarters, even if they were just temporary.

Today he would begin to explore the quieter side streets just off raucous Duval, with their seemingly endless T-shirt emporiums, noisy saloons with their attendant drunken tourists, and busy, overrated, and overpriced restaurants. On the side streets, however, he'd been told, were many smaller bars and clubs frequented almost exclusively by the locals, or "Conchs," as they referred to themselves. George Granger—now to be known as Elvin Welch—was now a permanent resident of the Conch Republic. He would work on becoming a Conch, and he would eventually fit right in.

As Ramon poured the coffee, a loud knock came to the cottage door. Not bothering to cover himself in any way, Granger rose from the stool and answered it.

"Good morning, Mr. Welch," an older man in short khaki pants and paint-splattered tee said. "I'm Jacob, the caretaker here. I'm just going to be doing a little touching up of the trim around your cottage. I didn't

want you to become alarmed if you heard somebody
rustling around outside your windows."

"Go right ahead, Jacob," Granger replied. He
closed the door and returned to his coffee.

"Mr. *Welch*?" Ramon questioned, a queer look on
his face. "I thought your name was Von Deutsch. Eric
Von Deutsch. At least that's what you've been telling
me right along."

"I'm a man of mystery, Ramon. Get used to it. Oh,
and one other thing. I don't want you to be calling
me here next Tuesday. If I can get together with you
next week, I'll contact you at the hotel. Okay?"

"Why?"

"Never mind why. That's just the way I want it."

Ramon flashed his best cabana-boy smile. "Whatever you say, *Mr.* Welch."

SEVENTEEN

"I was only able to secure a warrant to search the doctor's examination room number two," Jack Lindstrom said, letting himself into the sergeants' room upon his return to Manhattan South from 100 Centre Street.

"I attempted to get one which would allow a search of his whole damn office, but, as Chief Wilson predicted, Cromarty balked. He specifically limited the scope of the search only to the room in which Granger's body had been found."

"Which fortunately happens to be the same room where Timothy DiBona alleges to have been assaulted," Savage said, then grunted. "But the odds of that stun gun—if there ever was one—still being somewhere in that specific room would seem slim at best. . . ."

"But we gotta go with what we've got," Lindstrom said with a shrug.

"What about the subpoenas?" Savage asked.

"No problem. The DA loved the gimmicked EKGs, thought that Janus must be a real fuckin' nut. Seems to think that if nothing else, we could possibly nail Janus for falsifying business records. If it was done to conceal the commission of a crime, it's an E felony. At any rate, for now we can take George Granger's complete medical file and Janus' telephone logs—if he has any."

Armed with the warrants and subpoenas and several photos of the death scene from the Sixth Squad's case file, Savage and Jack Lindstrom left Manhattan South and headed directly over to Janus' medical offices on Thirteenth Street. Having worked straight through lunch, both Savage and Lindstrom were hungry; they'd have to grab a sandwich later.

A weary-looking and watery-eyed older male with an unshaven angular face that flinched constantly from tics, and fragile-looking, veiny hands that vibrated in tremor, was seated in Dr. Janus' nondescript waiting room opposite a morbidly obese middle-aged woman wearing a cervical collar when Savage and Lindstrom entered the physician's Thirteenth Street medical offices.

It was never their style to come on like gangbusters in a nonthreatening situation such as this—that would unnecessarily alarm the two patients and surely piss off the respondent—so they approached the Hispanic male seated behind a receptionist window at the far wall in a quiet, businesslike fashion. Savage had learned after decades of police work that you always start out nice—you can always get *not* nice. Hell, as far as the two patients would know, the two suited gentlemen might just be pharmaceutical salesmen.

"May I help you?" the slight receptionist said, a frown of concern crossing his dark olive-face. He apparently knew the difference between detectives and pharmaceutical sales reps.

Savage leaned partially into the window and spoke in a low tone. "I'm Sergeant Savage from Manhattan South," he said. Then he asked, "And you are?"

"My name is Guillermo . . . Guillermo Cabrera," the receptionist whispered back. "What's wrong, Officer?"

Savage displayed two neatly folded documents. "We need to speak with Dr. Janus. I have a subpoena for the office telephone log and the medical records of Mr. George Granger, a former patient of his. I also have a warrant to search one of the examination rooms."

The frown deepened, and the receptionist stuttered

apologetically. "The doctor is busy with a patient just now," he whispered back, glancing up at a wall clock. "He'll probably be at least another ten, maybe even fifteen minutes. Would you gentlemen mind . . . waiting?"

"I'm afraid that's not possible," Savage replied evenly. "I suggest that you interrupt the good doctor and ask him to join us for just a moment."

The receptionist rose from his seat and quickly disappeared into a hidden hallway. Moments later, the door leading from the waiting room to the inner offices opened.

"Please come this way, gentlemen," the receptionist said. He motioned the detectives into the inner hallway, closed the waiting-room door behind them, and immediately led them into a nonmedical, well-decorated private office.

A wall plastered with framed diplomas and certificates—the focal point of which was a Dartmouth Medical School sheepskin—formed the backdrop for a carved mahogany desk. A slender man, wearing a shirt and tie and herringbone slacks that hung from his bony ass like a sack, rose abruptly as they entered. Savage guessed him to be in his mid-fifties, medium build, with an unhealthy pastelike complexion. He wore a very deep scowl.

"Just what is the meaning of this?" the man demanded, his words equal parts anger and surprise. He motioned to his assistant to remain, but to shut the office door.

"Are you Dr. R. Charles Janus?" Savage inquired. When the man nodded assent, Savage handed him both the warrant and the subpoena and informed him of their purpose.

The physician looked up from the court-ordered documents and began his not unexpected objections.

"You can't just go ahead and do this," he argued, his brown eyes bugged and flashing. "You can't just come storming into my medical offices and begin rummaging around as if you own the place."

"Oh, but I'm afraid we can, Doctor," Savage replied evenly, continuing to half peruse the framed certificates hanging on the wall. His eye caught an honorable discharge certificate from the U.S. Army. "You were in the service, eh, Doc?"

"Yes."

"Tell me," Savage asked in his most sincere tone, "how does one manage to do military service time and also earn a medical degree from Harvard?"

"Some of us can walk and chew gum at the same time," Janus said sarcastically. "But to answer your question, I wasn't active. I was in the reserves. It was an obligation I fulfilled after my schooling was finished."

"I see." Beyond the snotty attitude, Savage was getting creepy vibes from the mouthy medic. Maybe it was the cut of the man's sideburns—they swept strangely forward.

"We've been through all this," the doctor said. "Months ago, for God's sake. It was tragic—no question—but nonetheless, George Granger died of natural causes . . . a goddamned heart attack. Why are you continuing to persecute me this way? Haven't you guys got anything better to do? Go catch a real criminal and leave good, decent people—like me— alone." He laid the warrant and subpoena on his desktop.

"Does the name Timothy DiBona mean anything to you, Doc?" Savage asked.

"Who?"

"DiBona. Timothy DiBona," Savage repeated, raising his voice a few decibels.

"Never heard of him," Janus snarled, momentarily breaking off eye contact with Savage.

"Funny," Savage said. "We're told that you picked him up at the Meat Hook, your kinky little playground down on Houston Street, and invited him back up here for a midnight EKG."

"That's absurd," Janus sneered.

For all Savage knew, Janus might very well be a

lousy doctor, but he could tell by the man's bold face
and cocky body language that he was a good liar—a
damn good liar.

"DiBona tells us that once you got done testing his
heart, you decided to road-test his joint," Lindstrom
inserted.

"And when you were done with the fun and games,
you then assaulted him with a stun gun," Savage said
flatly. "Mr. DiBona is absolutely certain that you were
trying to kill him. All this happened about two weeks
before Mr. Granger happened to pass away here—in
the very same examination room."

In barely controlled rage, Janus sputtered, "I'll sue
you. . . . I'll sue the city. . . . I'll sue the goddamned
mayor. This isn't going to stop here—I can assure you
of that."

Having been threatened with lawsuits more times
than they could remember, Savage and Lindstrom
stood silent and impassive. Both held Janus in an un-
flinching no-nonsense stare.

Reclaiming a modicum of his composure, Janus
reached for his phone. "Before you do a thing, you're
just going to have to allow me some time to contact
my attorney." Without consulting a Rolodex or phone
book, he began to dial.

"Know the number by heart, eh, Doc?" Lindstrom
said. "Does he handle all of your malpractice suits
also?"

Still wearing his angry snarl, Janus glared at the
detectives but continued dialing.

"Do feel free to contact your lawyer," Savage advised sternly, realizing that the time had come to get
not nice. "But first have your assistant get us any and
all medical files for the late Mr. George Granger and
your telephone log, then have him show us to examination room number two. Failure to immediately comply
leaves you open to arrest for obstructing governmental
administration, and I would have no qualms about
snapping cuffs on your wrists."

"I'm not afraid of some minor arrest on some puny

trumped-up charge. Just who in the hell do you think you're dealing with here? Some mindless street jerkoff?"

"I don't think you'd like those two patients out there to see you escorted out of here in handcuffs. From what we understand, your reputation in the community is already somewhat suspect," Savage tagged on.

Exasperated, Janus looked over at his assistant. "All right, Guillermo," he said, angrily jerking his head for the man to comply. "Do as they direct and give them Mr. Granger's file, or, more accurately, what's left of it. Hell," he mumbled, "they've already taken part of the damn file anyway and never returned it." The physician then sat and drummed his fingers angrily on the desktop, telephone receiver still at his ear.

"This way, Officers," the assistant said, motioning them toward the door.

He led them from Janus' private office, down a wide enameled hallway that was devoid of any décor—no plants, no pictures, no wall hangings of any kind. The entire office complex, not unlike the doctor himself, was nondescript and . . . cold.

Guillermo stopped at a wide bank of metal file cabinets, knelt, and pulled open a lower drawer marked G-H-I. He quickly thumbed through the hanging files and extracted one bearing the name George Granger. Without a word, he stood and handed it over to Savage.

Savage opened the folder and noted about two dozen various forms held in place by a Sparco prong fastener. Flipping through them, he saw that they all pertained to George Granger. "Is this *all* of the files the doctor would have on George Granger?" Savage asked directly.

"Oh, yes," the assistant replied courteously and, Savage thought, believably.

Guillermo closed the file drawer with the toe of his loafer and continued farther down the hall. He stopped at a door plainly marked with the numeral 2, turned the old-fashioned white porcelain knob, and gestured the detectives into a high-ceilinged space illuminated by two pipe-suspended schoolhouse light fixtures with white opal glass shades.

The room contained a paper-covered examining table, an EKG machine that looked like a fugitive from the Smithsonian, and white enameled cabinets set against the far wall. There was also a sink beneath a paper towel dispenser, a wall telephone exactly where Billy Cox had said it would be, and a Ritter Speed-Clave sterilizer. Two large, brilliantly colored posters decorated the left-side wall: one was of the central nervous system, the other depicted the peripheral nervous system. Savage compared the entire space to the photographs in his pocket; this was the room.

"Let's do it," he said.

Jack Lindstrom nodded and started the search at the examination table that stood in the middle of the room. Every built-in drawer, save the one that contained two rolls of Graham standard white table paper, was empty. Lindstrom then turned his attention to the wall cabinets. Moving from left to right, he opened and examined the contents of all three uppers. They contained standard medical supplies: rolls and pads of gauze, bandages, swabs, wrapped packets of paper towels for the dispenser, urinalysis reagent strips and specimen containers, a gallon of Banicide instrument disinfectant, and several sixteen-ounce bottles of isopropyl alcohol. Again moving from left to right, he squatted down and checked the lower base cabinets, and again he found nothing suspect.

The sink countertop held the autoclave, a box of Kleenex, and a supply of DermAssist powder-free latex exam gloves. Between the countertop and the lower storage cabinets were four drawers, the first two of which contained a variety of surgical instruments including forceps, scissors, hemostats, dermal curettes, and disposable biopsy punches. Drawer 3 contained a supply of tie-on surgical masks and a selection of 3-0 and 4-0 sutures in silk, nylon, and Vicryl. When Lindstrom opened drawer 4 he was taken aback. After gazing into the open drawer for several long seconds, he helped himself to a pair of the latex surgical gloves and snapped them on.

"What've you got?" Savage asked.

Lindstrom made wide eyes, reached into the drawer, and held up a large, flesh-colored dildo. After placing the item on the counter, he again reached into the drawer and began removing a vast collection of condoms, lubricants, vibrators, and other sex toys.

When both detectives looked over at Guillermo for a reaction to the find, the slight man shrugged helplessly.

"Did you know the doctor had this kind of stuff in here?" Savage asked. "Right in his examination room?"

Guillermo stuttered something unintelligible that did not answer the question. It was his body language that gave the response. Guillermo was clearly embarrassed by the finding, but Savage saw something else there as well.

"Let me ask you a question, Guillermo," Savage said smoothly, seeing an opening. "Are you aware that the doctor uses this room for sex?"

The man nodded a reluctant yes.

"Have *you* ever had sex with the doctor in here?" Savage pressed the even-tempered and gentle man.

Again Guillermo nodded. "The doctor and I live together," he volunteered, "but we sometimes have used this room for sex."

"I see," Savage said calmly. "Do you know if the doctor uses this room to have sex with others?"

Guillermo exhaled hard. "Yes."

"How often?"

"On very rare occasions."

"Did he ever have sex in here with George Granger?"

"I don't know."

Behind the assortment of sex goodies, and beneath a pile of gay magazines—more toward the rear of the drawer—Jack Lindstrom dug out a small nylon case. The item had a belt loop, and an opening flap bearing the trademark "Raptor."

"What do you know about this?" Lindstrom asked Guillermo.

"Never saw it before," he said assuredly. "What the hell is that thing, anyway?" he uttered, bemused.

"It's a holster," Savage said. "And judging by its somewhat larger size, it once contained a very powerful Raptor stun gun."

"I've never seen that *holster,* you call it," Guillermo said, firmly. "And I can tell you I've never seen any *stun gun* anywhere around this office either."

An intense re-search of the entire examining room by Savage and Lindstrom failed to turn up the actual stun gun itself. Although it wasn't in that room, Savage would have bet the ranch that it was somewhere else in the offices.

"What time have you got, Jack?" Savage asked.

"One twenty-five," the detective responded.

Savage checked the clock reading on the old EKG machine. It was only three minutes off.

"We done?" Lindstrom asked.

"As soon as Guillermo here gets us the office telephone log we are," Savage responded.

The office assistant led them back to his receptionist desk, opened a lower drawer, and handed over the log. Having exhausted the limits of the search warrant, Savage and Lindstrom returned to Janus' private office.

"Found your little toy cabinet, Doc," Savage said. "You must do some pretty interesting examinations in that room."

"As far as I know, there exists no law prohibiting possession of anything you may have found in there," he replied smoothly.

"You're probably right, Doc," Savage conceded. Then, holding up the stun gun holster, he asked, "Just for the record, can you tell me what you have a stun gun for?"

"I have no stun gun," he snarled. "That is merely a holster. Haven't you heard, there's a law against stun guns in this town; a class A misdemeanor, I'm told. And, besides, if I did have one, I'd have it for protection."

"From whom, your apoplectic patients?" Lindstrom said, screwing his rubbery face up into a grimace of disbelief. He held out a receipt for the confiscated medical records, telephone log, and stun gun holster. Janus snatched it angrily from his hand.

"Just so we're correct on this," Savage said, holding up the medical file labeled GRANGER, GEORGE. "Is this the *entire* medical file for Mr. Granger?"

Janus glanced over and nodded with a smirk.

"Are you also stating that it is a true and authentic representation of Granger's past medical history with you?"

"Yes, for God's sake."

"Just for the record, Doc," Savage inquired, handing the file back to Jack Lindstrom and deciding to rattle Janus' cage, "who is John Boy?"

"John Boy? John Boy who?" the man said straight-faced.

"The John Boy who is another one of your regular playmates down at the Meat Hook," Savage responded.

"I don't know any John Boy," Janus snarled, his eyes squinted into horizontal arrow slits.

"We think you do," Savage said. "We actually think his whole name is John Boyer Holloway, who, besides being your kinky playmate, also happened to be the sole beneficiary of George Granger's very big life insurance policy. Nice tie-in, don't you think?"

"I wouldn't know anything about that."

"One more thing, Doctor," Savage said. "Would you mind telling me your blood type?"

Janus reared back. "Why? What the hell do you need that for?"

"Just curious."

"All right, that's it. I will not answer any further

questions," Janus snapped arrogantly and pointed toward the door. "Show the officers out, Guillermo."

"No big deal, Doc," Savage announced as he and Lindstrom left the room. "We'll get it from your army records."

Having sensed an innocent openness in Guillermo's overall attitude, Savage waited until the medical assistant had escorted them through the waiting room and into the outer hallway, then casually asked what would appear to be a benign question.

"Did you happen to know this particular patient, George Granger?" he asked Guillermo.

"Oh, yes," the man responded. "Not very well, mind you, but I did know him. After all, he was a patient here."

"Do you not think the circumstances around his death somewhat questionable?" Lindstrom inquired.

"Since you ask," Guillermo replied, the innocent openness quickly morphing into bitter defense, "I'm of the opinion that this whole investigation is a shameful persecution of Dr. Janus. Why, he would no more hurt one of his patients—especially his friend—than the man in the moon."

"But it was a shame that Mr. Granger died such a young man," Savage said, fishing.

"Well," Guillermo responded under his breath, looking over his shoulder as if taking Savage into his confidence, "it really didn't come as any surprise to me."

"Why is that?" Savage asked, staying casual.

"Terrible chain-smoker."

Stunned, but careful to keep his poker face, Savage held Guillermo in his gaze and asked, "Just how heavy a smoker was Mr. Granger?"

Guillermo harrumphed and did an exaggerated eye roll. "The man smoked with both hands."

"Where did you see him smoke?" Savage asked.

"In the waiting room. Anytime he came in to see the doctor, he always had one of those damn things burning. My God, the man's fingers were yellow."

"Is smoking not prohibited here in the office?" Savage asked. "As far as I know it's been banned in almost every building in the state."

"Only one time did I make the mistake of telling Mr. Granger to put out his cigarette while in the office." The small man gave a dramatic shiver of fear. "I never made that mistake again. Mr. Granger could reduce you to nothing with just his glare. Know what I mean? Besides, he was a good friend of the doctor's. I couldn't tell him what to do."

"If he was a heavy smoker, then I guess he must have been a big drinker too," Lindstrom said, also fishing. "Most smokers I know are."

"Oh, no," Guillermo said, shrugging innocently. "As far as I know, Mr. Granger never touched the stuff. He was a regular teetotaler."

"Thank you, Guillermo. You've been most helpful," Savage said. Then, as he and Lindstrom turned to leave, he did a stutter step and, as an afterthought, asked, "Tell me, what is *your* blood type?"

"I'm O," Guillermo replied. "O positive. And since you're going to find out from the army anyway, I may as well tell you right now that Dr. Janus is also a type O."

"You're certain of that?"

"Absolutely positive. Hey, check it out with the army."

Savage and Lindstrom nodded and let themselves out of the building.

"A guy with 'healthy pink lungs' who happened to be a heavy chain smoker?" Savage said incredulously as he waited for Lindstrom to unlock the doors to the department auto.

"The same guy—who we're now told never touched the sauce—who just happened to have a little bit of actual blood in his booze at autopsy," Lindstrom said, continuing the muse.

"There's also the matter of the property that Billy Cox and his partner removed from the DOA at the scene," Savage said, shaking his head in puzzlement.

"Which is?"

"What man just happens to be walking around carrying only a copy of their damn birth certificate and three expired credit cards? Nothing else. No driver's license . . . no photographs . . . not even a damn library card."

"I didn't like that either," Lindstrom agreed. "It was too damn convenient, but . . ."

"We've got a complete pedigree on Granger," Savage said, sliding into the passenger seat. "Name, address, DOB, height, weight, hair and eye color, Social Security, blah-blah-blah."

Lindstrom nodded, fastening his seat belt.

"I think it's time we tried to get into this thing through the back door," Savage said. "Besides Dr. Janus, and the AWOL beneficiary, John Boyer Holloway, let's also do a complete background check on the supposed victim, *Mr. Granger*. Let's run them all through BCI, go after any of their military records, motor vehicle records, driver's licenses . . ."

"Wants and warrants?"

"The whole round-robin," Savage replied.

"You know it's very likely I won't get anything back from the military until tomorrow, possibly even Monday," Lindstrom advised, starting the Crown Victoria's engine.

"We've got plenty of time," Savage assured. "Mr. Granger sure ain't going anywhere, and the good doctor is too damn arrogant to think he might have to."

"And it looks as if Mr. Holloway already has," Lindstrom added, then asked, "A little late lunch?"

"Sounds good," Savage replied. "Let's do Katz's. I've got a thing for corned beef and rye today." While there, he thought, he'd also pick up a little lean pastrami and some chilled gefilte fish for Ray.

Man oh man, he thought, his mind quickly returning to the Granger case as they pulled away from the curb. The stench of this thing was getting worse and worse . . . and more and more damn confounding.

One thing was for certain, though—Dr. R. Charles Janus was not the only person present in that examining room the night that George Granger died. Someone else had to be there, someone with type B blood.

EIGHTEEN

When Winona Escalante appeared in the bustling Manhattan South Homicide squad room at nine o'clock on that Friday morning and asked Eddie Brodigan if she could speak with Sergeant Savage, every head in the office turned—both male and female. The unlikely-looking insurance investigator from the Midwest wore a dark business suit with fine white vertical pinstripes set wide apart, like those of an old Eliot Ness double-breasted. But the lady was not old, nor was she anybody's Eliot Ness—she was an absolute knockout.

Winona Escalante had straight, gleaming black hair that had it not been held up in a tight French twist would have cascaded to somewhere around the middle of her slender back. She viewed the world through doe-size ebony irises and, though svelte, was moviestar curvy in all the proper places. She owed the richness of her classic mane and perfect high cheekbones to a Native American mother and her exotic coloring and sensuous aura to a high Castilian father whom she'd never met. All eyes stayed locked on her as Brodigan led her through the office to the sergeants' room.

They waited just outside as Savage finished a phone call with Dr. Figueroa, Ray's vet. The report he got was not encouraging. Nothing had changed. The old tom had made little or no headway in the last twenty-two hours. He decided he would break away early today and make a visit.

"Please come in," Savage said, rising from his chair

after hanging up the phone. He smiled warmly when the woman entered the cramped space and extended his hand in mannerly introduction. "I'm Thorn Savage."

He could have looked into her incredible big eyes for days. She was neither a redhead nor small-breasted . . . but this was a pretty lady. He also caught the unmistakable scent of Tabu; he hadn't smelled that stuff in years. He had always liked Tabu—which was the counterpart to the male scent Canoe—but thought both had become passé. His high school steady, Marguerite Cassidy, used to wear it by the gallon; but, then again, Marguerite also wore a lot of Clearasil. For just an instant, he wondered how Margie was doing.

"Winona Escalante," she said, grasping his hand firmly, but not too firmly. "Aurora Occidental Life and Casualty, Fort Wayne, Indiana."

"Have a seat." He quickly borrowed the lopsided and squeaky swivel chair from Billy Lakis' desk, slid it across the gray vinyl tile floor, and set it alongside his desk. She sat, demurely crossing long, shapely legs; he put Winona Escalante at five eight.

"I was informed during my phone conversations with a Detective Diane DeGennaro that you are the supervisor in charge of an investigation that is looking into the death of a Mr. George Granger," she began.

Her millisecond assessment of him—if that's what it was—had been discreet, very discreet, but Savage knew that she had looked him up, down, and sideways before setting her expensive leather Tumi portfolio on the floor beside his desk.

"At this point, let's just say we feel there exists some cause to believe it *possible* that George Granger did not die from natural causes," he said, prudently hedging. "And we're looking into it. If it turns out to be so, the question then becomes, Can the real cause ever be determined—or proven."

"Can it?" she asked straight out, folding finely man-icured hands into her lap. The yellow-gold-and-sapphire band on her right ring finger matched well her simple but elegant gold earrings. She wore no jewelry at all on her left hand. Her watch was a slender gold Piaget with a white face. The woman exuded both Corn Belt naïveté and big-city sophistication.

"Don't know," Savage offered forthrightly. "But I *do* know this: We'll keep pulling the string until we find out one way or the other."

"My company has sent me here to gather all the facts and to offer any possible assistance to your investigation. Perhaps we can help one another."

"That would be fine, Ms. Escalante. We'd welcome anything you can bring us."

"I trust you won't feel that I would be in the way."

"If you start to get in the way I'll let you know."

"Fair enough," she replied with an agreeable smile and prolonged eye contact, just as a jacketless Detective Jack Lindstrom entered the room. Cuffs rolled, necktie knot askew, he carried with him Janus' confiscated medical file on George Granger, which he'd been poring over since yesterday afternoon.

"Detective Lindstrom, meet Ms. Winona Escalante," Savage said.

"Ah, the insurance company . . ." Lindstrom acknowledged. "Welcome aboard." After shaking hands with the woman, he sat down on the edge of Jules Unger's desk.

"What have you got, Jack?"

"I've just about exhausted all the Granger phone numbers in Columbus."

Savage turned to Escalante. "We've been trying to get through to Granger's next of kin—his real family—blood. Jack's been contacting all the Grangers listed in Columbus, Ohio, with no results."

"That's because his family is all from Schenectady, New York," she replied, digging into her briefcase and coming out with a list. She handed the document to Lindstrom, who perused it.

"You'll find names, addresses, and phone numbers for his mother, brothers, and sister."

"They were not listed anywhere as beneficiaries," Lindstrom said.

"Once upon a time they were," she countered with a crooked smile.

"I'll get right on this," Lindstrom said, slipping the form into the medical file folder.

"Anything back on the round-robins?" Savage asked.

"Here's the deal," Lindstrom replied. "I'm getting nothing back on John Boyer Holloway. Apparently, he was never arrested, never in any of the military branches—nothing. Can't even find a driver's license on him. What I'm getting back on Janus we already know."

"And Granger?" Savage asked.

"Waiting for a fax back from the U.S. Army as we speak. Did two years, never saw any action, some minor disciplinary—honorable discharge. Also waiting to hear back from California, where he held a driver's license. They're gonna send me everything they've got." Lindstrom stood and turned to leave.

"Has that medical file shown us anything at all?" Savage asked, stopping Lindstrom in his tracks.

Lindstrom shook his head. "I can't say that it has. One of Janus' earlier entries, coupla years ago, indicated a San Francisco address which is the same one that supposedly appears on Granger's California driver's license. The license information I got over the phone also jibes with Janus' file as to Granger's DOB, brown hair, hazel eyes, five ten, one fifty-five, blah-blah-blah."

Savage turned toward the insurance investigator and quickly brought her up to speed on the previous day's search of Janus' downtown medical office and the items he and Lindstrom had confiscated under subpoena and warrant. "Jack's our detail man," he went on to explain. "He's our maven of minutiae, as it were. If there's anything in that medical file that would add any weight in this case, he's the guy who will find it."

"Other than the clearly bogus EKGs that you came

up with," Lindstrom said, "the balance of the file appears pretty comprehensive and very well put together. There is nothing jumping out of it that we might want the doctor to answer for. Yet."

"Well, I can't help you very much with Dr. Janus," Winona Escalante said, looking back and forth between Savage and Lindstrom. "But maybe I can shed some more light on Mr. George Granger."

She picked up her briefcase, opened it, and removed several photocopied documents. "Yesterday, on my way here to New York, I flew first into Columbus, Ohio. While I was there, I spent several hours at the Franklin County courthouse."

Savage motioned Lindstrom to again sit down.

"I made extras, so consider these your copies," she said, handing one page to Savage. "That document is a photocopy of the Change of Life Insurance Beneficiary form which George Granger filed with our company back on the seventeenth of January, this year."

"It made John Boyer Holloway the sole beneficiary of his life insurance policy," Savage murmured, scanning the form. Then, raising his brow, he added temptingly, "A one-million, five-hundred-thousand-*dollar* life insurance policy."

"Yes, it did," she said, immediately handing Savage another photocopied form. "Coincidental with filing that change of beneficiary for his life insurance, you can see that on that same date, Mr. Granger also appeared at the probate court in Franklin County, Ohio, to file for an amendment to his last will and testament."

"Uh-huh."

Handing over a third document, she continued. "The official proceeding was then held on February seventh. On that date, Granger appeared there in probate court and testified before a magistrate. The will changes he sought went uncontested, so the changes were immediately made official." She then handed each a three-page copy of Granger's will.

Savage placed his glasses at the tip on his nose,

slouched slightly, and quickly read through the entire document. "Says here, he revoked all wills and codicils heretofore made, bequeathed all property, both real and personal, of every kind and description, wheresoever situate, to his friend John Boyer Holloway, absolutely and in fee simple."

"Right," Winona Escalante said. "You will also note that he appointed Mr. Holloway as executor with full power and authority to sell and convey all or any part of his estate."

"And," Savage picked up, "that's when he completely disinherited his mother, his two brothers, and a sister, Gwendolyn. Nice guy."

"Look at this notarized affidavit," she said, handing over the final document. "It was filled out and signed by George Granger back on March nineteenth. In it he spells out to his executor, John Boyer Holloway, detailed instructions for his funeral."

Savage scanned the form and noted that Granger directed that his body be immediately cremated and that no relatives, either by blood or adoption, be notified of his death unless a subsequent probate proceeding required it.

"This is all well and good," Savage said, playing devil's advocate while testing the woman's instincts. "But we've got to remember that Granger *was* HIV positive. It could be argued that believing that his time was short, he was simply putting all of his affairs in order."

"What you say is true," she acknowledged thoughtfully. The attractive lady sat back in Lakis' squeaky chair and pensively looked off into nowhere.

Savage could almost see the gears turning behind the intelligent eyes. Winona Escalante clearly had a nose for this sort of work. He knew that—just like him—she also smelled the pungent odor that usually accompanied dead things that just won't stay buried.

"It could also be argued that maybe Granger *or* Holloway had some sort of plan to beat the policy lapse date," she finally said. "Or"—her eyes grew wider—"perhaps Granger *and* Holloway had a plan to beat the lapse date."

"Or," Savage said, upping the ante, "perhaps Granger, Holloway, *and* Dr. R. Charles Janus had a plan to beat the lapse date."

"I like the way you think, Sergeant."

"Ahem." Jack Lindstrom cleared his throat. "Let's go over the date you mentioned a moment ago," he said, opening the Granger medical file. Then to clarify his statement, he added, "The date that Granger appeared in the probate court in Franklin County, Ohio."

"The date he was there to file for the amendment to his last will and testament was January seventeenth," Winona Escalante replied. She handed Lindstrom a copy of that court record.

"No, not that date," Lindstrom said, further scrunching up his already rippled and rubbery brow in analytical left-brain concentration. "I mean the date he appeared in probate court and, in an official proceeding, testified before a magistrate for amendments to his last will and testament."

"February seventh," the insurance investigator replied. She quickly dug another copy of that record from her briefcase and handed it to Lindstrom.

"What've you got, Jack?" Savage asked, all too familiar with the dawning look spreading over the detective's face.

"Looks as if we've got us a miracle," he muttered. "We've got a guy capable of being in two places at one time."

Winona Escalante stood and positioned herself to read over Lindstrom's shoulder.

Lindstrom continued. "This probate court amendment order—complete with a time and date stamp—shows Granger present at the courthouse in Columbus, Ohio, at fourteen-thirty hours on February the seventh."

"Okay," Savage replied patiently, knowing more was coming. He tore the cellophane from a Wint-O-

Green he'd pulled from his top drawer and popped one into his mouth.

"According to Dr. Janus, however," Lindstrom went on, running his finger along a document from Granger's medical file, "Mr. Granger was present at his office the afternoon of February seventh. Janus claims here to have then performed a general examination on Granger, administered a flu shot, and again recommended to Granger that he see a cardiologist." Lindstrom looked up at Savage.

"Somebody is lying," Winona Escalante intoned in rhythmical singsong, eyes wide and tongue in cheek.

Savage bit down hard on his upper lip, feeling the shift of his mind-set. For whatever reason, this little tidbit was the final straw, the trigger that pushed him over the invisible line. His thinking on the case had just passed from the good possibility of a crime having occurred to the strong probability of a crime having occurred. He knew too what lay ahead—from here on in it would be a full-court press to prove the certainty that a crime had occurred. But without a body . . . where next?

"Where are you staying, Ms. Escalante?" Savage asked, hoping his query would not be misconstrued as a lame come-on.

"The Grand Hyatt. Forty-second, right next to Grand Central Station. Perhaps we could have dinner there one evening and talk this whole case through," she suggested boldly. "I do have an expense account."

"Perhaps," he replied, with a noncommittal shrug. "The Grand Hyatt. Your company treats you very well."

"Yes, they do," she agreed firmly. Then she added temptingly, "But with me they get a great bang for their buck. And please, Sergeant . . . everybody calls me Winnie."

"Okay, Winnie," he said, standing. "Come with us. We'll introduce you to Diane DeGennaro, Richie Marcus, and a few of the others."

As the woman gathered up her briefcase, Eddie Brodigan rapped on the office doorjamb.

"This just came in for you, Jack," Brodigan said, handing Lindstrom a one-page fax. "It's from the California Department of Motor Vehicles."

Lindstrom quickly glanced at the form. "Blown-up copy of Granger's driver's license," he said, and handed the fax off to Savage.

Savage stared at the fax, focusing in on the driver's license photograph. He felt the hairs at the back of his neck spring to full attention.

"This is not our DOA," he said.

"Whaddaya mean it's not him?" Lindstrom asked, the rubbery brow again heavily lined. "All the information jibes with Janus' medical files—date of birth, height, weight, eye color. Even the Social Security number . . ."

"Even the autopsy report confirmed that he was HIV positive," Winona Escalante inserted.

"Oh, I do believe that what you have here *is* a photograph of Mr. George Granger," Savage said evenly. He kept studying the still-warm fax and, in his mind's eye, watched as all the jagged pieces of the confounding mosaic suddenly integrated into one clear design. "It's just not a photograph of our DOA."

"Well, if that *is* a photo of George Granger, but is *not* a photo of the DOA," Winona Escalante said, her attractive face now lightly lined by a severe frown, "then who the hell *was* the DOA?"

"Oh, I can't tell you who he *was*," Savage answered, deep in thought. "All I can tell you is who he *wasn't*." He handed the fax photo back to Lindstrom. "And he wasn't the guy in this picture."

NINETEEN

It was the beginning of a gleaming golden sunrise on the calm emerald waters of the Tyrrhenian when, after two days at sea, a shirtless and tanned Darrin Greavey called out the first sight of land from the helm. John Boyer Holloway killed the propane flame beneath the omelets he was cooking in the small galley and, wiping his hands on a paper towel, climbed the three short steps that led out to the main deck. He blinked and focused on the vast, uneven, and undefined terrain rising out of the western horizon. To the distant port side he could see also another speck of land, the tiny island of Tavolara, gateway to Olbia.

"We're here," he said, letting go with a satisfied smile. Without even thinking, he pushed Greavey aside and took over the helm.

Twenty minutes later his view was much improved. Set into the Smeralda Coast at the northeast corner of Sardinia—at latitude 40.9 degrees north, longitude 9.5 degrees east—he could see the hill-surrounded port town of Olbia dead ahead.

"I've heard it said that the Smeralda Coast of northeast Sardinia is the summer home of Italy's paparazzi," Greavey called out from the foredeck.

"We don't know that for certain," Holloway replied, tongue in cheek. "But we can sure hope."

Fifteen minutes later, the *Carpe Diem* slipped into Porto Cervo and sailed past Yacht Club Costa Smeralda, the sponsor of some of the greatest Mediterranean regattas ever.

"You're beaming," Darrin Greavey pointed out as the boat rocked in an outgoing cruiser's wake. To steady himself, he reached overhead and grabbed a jib line, revealing a small heart-shaped port wine stain in his left armpit.

"Because I'm ecstatic," Holloway replied.

"Let me ask you a question," Greavey said. "Why Sardinia . . . and why the Costa Smeralda?"

"The serenity, the exceptional but very demanding hiking trails . . . the tradition," Holloway replied, thinking it the kind of answer that Greavey would like to hear.

"Tradition, you say?"

"I do say. While most of the population of mainland Italy is killing themselves trying to stay up with the latest styles, the locals here cling to traditions that have gone unchanged for generations. I like that."

"Like old Italian men sitting in doorways smoking stinky little cigars, sipping wine, and watching silently as the world goes by?"

"That, and widows walking through town dressed completely in black, as tradition has taught them. This place is in a total time warp. You could say it's just what I need in this stage of my life."

What he had said was true, but Holloway also knew that this area of Sardinia was a perfect place to be very much anonymous. It was also a haven for the rich and famous, as witnessed by the many Hatteras and Azimut yachts—owned by some of the biggest names—that dotted the harbor. Rich and famous with whom he could rub shoulders, and perhaps other parts of his lithe and athletic anatomy.

"What time is it?" Darrin Greavey asked.

"0645 hours, CEST," Holloway replied.

"Exactly the time you said we'd arrive," Greavey murmured, shaking his head. "That's simply amazing. The other day, you asked me where I went to school, so now I want to know where you learned navigation."

"My father taught it to me," Holloway lied, seeing an opportunity to further cement his new identity with his current lover. "Although he was merely a welder at the Portsmouth Naval Dockyard, he loved to sail. My mother loved it too."

"They dead?"

"Yes, a long time. I was an only child."

"How did you get on with *your* parents?" Greavey queried.

"Very well, actually. I miss them both terribly—especially my mum. She was a great cook."

"Hmm," Greavey uttered, then casually asked, "Is that where you got your middle name? From your mother?"

"Yes," Holloway replied, feigning thoughtfulness. "She was a Conover. A real good lady."

"What can I do now?" Greavey asked.

"Why don't you go down into the galley and finish cooking our breakfast while I find us a place to moor."

"Then what?"

"Who knows?" Holloway murmured with a sly wink. "Maybe we'll both get lucky."

Greavey smiled seductively, turned, and carefully let himself down the three steps into the cabin. Holloway noted how terrific Darrin's buns looked in those extra-short cutoffs. Breakfast would be a quickie, Holloway thought. Dessert, however, was bound to take a bit longer.

Most everybody has a strong point, an unusual talent for which there exists no real explanation. Some, like the chief of detectives, Ray Wilson, have the uncanny ability to remember names: first, middle, last—nicknames even—over the span of many decades. Others excel at recalling dates, like the birthdays and wedding anniversaries of everybody they know—and a lot of people they don't know—and perhaps the day and date they themselves got their first piece of ass and whether or not it was a Tuesday or a Wednesday.

But Detective Sergeant Thornton Savage's undeniable strong point was that he never *ever* forgot a face.

The countenance of the male DOA photographed lying on the floor of Dr. Janus' examination room and the face of the male DOA photographed during autopsy at the New York County medical examiner's office several hours later were one and the same. However, though bearing a close resemblance in general shape, eye and hair color—even down to the partial balding—the face appearing on George Granger's California driver's license was very similar but, Savage discerned, different.

By late Monday afternoon, ID photographs of a younger George Granger, provided by the U.S. Army, began arriving at Manhattan South. On Tuesday morning, when compared by Savage and his crew to the California driver's license photo of George Granger, they were found to be right on. However, when compared to those of the DOA, they were close but definitely no cigar. The most apparent differences, to Savage's keen eye, lay in the variant prominence of the Adam's apples—the Granger in the license photo had an inordinately large one—and the size and shape of the ears—again in contrast, the DOA had almost no lobes. It wasn't until later that morning, after the fingerprints of George Granger provided by the U.S. Army were compared with those of the DOA autopsied as George Granger, that the question was positively settled.

And then there was also the discrepancy of blood type. The DOA had been type O; the army records indicated, however, that Mr. George Granger was type B. The reeking stench of a doctor-involved deadly flimflam was now overwhelming. The type B third man in that examining room that night might well have been Granger himself. Granger and Janus, Savage thought, a two-man burking team.

"Where to from here?" Lieutenant Pezzano asked no one in particular.

The squad boss was seated at the head of the conference table in the Manhattan South war room. Thorn Savage and his three detectives, Richie Marcus, Diane DeGennaro, and Jack Lindstrom, sat evenly spaced around the rest of the table. Also present was insurance investigator Winona Escalante, who had somehow managed to scare up a cup of tea. Marcus, Lindstrom, and Pezzano had mugs of steaming coffee before them. Sitting cross-legged in his chair, elbows on the armrests and fingers of strong hands clasped in his lap, Savage sucked on a Wint-O-Green, pondering the lieutenant's question while at the same time wondering how Ray was making out at the vet's. As of last night, the progress had been minimal, but as Dr. Figueroa pointed out, every day that he hung on was, in itself, progress of a kind.

"In order to make a solid case against Dr. Janus et al., we need three things," Savage finally said. "For starters, we need to determine the true identity of our DOA. We need then to determine if the real George Granger is still alive. And we absolutely need a finding other than 'natural causes' from the medical examiner."

"Where do we start?" Pezzano asked.

"We could start by breaking down Dr. R. Charles Janus," Richie Marcus suggested. "Collar his ass."

"My senses tell me that Janus won't be an easy nut to crack," Savage said.

"We know he's got the answers," Lindstrom pointed out. "If not for question number one, then at least to question number two."

"Once we confront Janus with proof that the DOA is not who he says it was, we should have him on the ropes," Pezzano said. "If nothing else, the creep'd probably look to cut himself a deal—no?"

Unsure of Pezzano's conclusion, Savage shrugged. "Janus will lawyer up right away—if he hasn't already. My bet is he'll stonewall. I don't know where he'd get the balls to do it, but I'll bet you he'll swear till the day he dies that the DOA was George Granger."

"Could we collar him now?" Jack Lindstrom asked.

"We'd have to run it past the prosecutors first," Savage advised. "And I don't think we're quite strong enough yet."

"You telling me that the DA wouldn't go with *suspicion* of murder?" Pezzano said. "And maintaining fraudulent medical records?"

"Conspiracy to commit insurance fraud," Lindstrom added.

"How about his litany of lies and obfuscations?" Winona Escalante suggested angrily.

"If we went and collared every asshole who ever lied to us," Marcus piped up in his raspy growl, "*nobody* would ever have any problem parking on the streets of Midtown."

Savage spoke. "Our ends, which also include finding those other two, George Granger—if he's actually still alive—and the mystery bastard who got all the money, John Boyer Holloway, would be better served if we don't jump the gun."

"Why is that?" Winona Escalante queried.

"Because once those two hear that Janus has been collared, they'll definitely go to ground," Savage answered. "But even beyond that, I deem it essential that we get a new ruling from the medical examiner before we even think about fitting Dr. *R.* Charles Janus for handcuffs. I don't want us to waltz him in one door down at the courthouse and have his barrister immediately waltz him right out another."

"In the meanwhile, shouldn't we be concerned that he'll split?" Pezzano asked.

"The son of a bitch is too damn arrogant," Savage replied surely. "Even when we do eventually take him down, he won't think of folding, or talking, until we have every damn thing we need to really put the squeeze on him—and probably not even then."

Lindstrom nodded to Savage. "At your direction, boss," he said, "I contacted the Delano Hotel in Miami Beach this morning, hoping to find that a George Granger had been registered there on the night of May thirteenth, the night that Janus twice

called there around the time that Timothy DiBona
was assaulted in his office.''

"And?" Savage asked.

"It was a negative," Lindstrom replied. "They
checked from January one to present for me. No
George Granger was registered there at any time during that period. Just to make sure, I also had them
check all variations on the name John B. Holloway.
Same deal—*nada*.''

"That would have been too easy," Savage quipped,
then, struck with an idea, asked, "Did you get a contact name at the Delano Hotel?"

Lindstrom checked his notes. "Dempsey," he replied. "Daphne Dempsey. Said she was the reservations manager. Nice gal.''

"Why don't we try this?" Savage said, taking an
outside shot. "Fax her our photographs of George
Granger. Ask if she'd be good enough to show them
around to her staff. Who knows? Maybe someone will
remember seeing the face."

After a slow sip of his coffee, a half smile of understanding came to Lindstrom's face. "I see where
you're going," he said. "Granger might have been
checked in there under a false name."

Savage shrugged.

"Speaking of Miami," Pezzano said, "we've got
some geography to concern ourselves with on this
case. Costly geography. The beneficiary, Holloway, is
MIA from his home and business in Columbus, Ohio.
He could be anywhere. This guy Granger, if he is still
alive, was born in Schenectady, New York, has an
address in Ohio, lived also in San Francisco and God
knows where else. As far as I can see, all we can do
is put out arrest warrants on these gypsies and hope
they get stopped for passing a red light somewhere in
Keokuk or Oshkosh.''

Winona Escalante raised her hand, cleared her
throat, and directed her remarks to the lieutenant.
"While your Team Three was off enjoying a long
three-day weekend," she said, glancing teasingly at

Savage and his crew, "I've been spending hours on the phone with my company. Aside from providing me with some additional interesting information on this case, they've given me carte blanche to spend whatever may be necessary to pursue and prosecute. If any travel is required, by me or any of your detectives, my firm will underwrite all costs."

"Any restrictions on that?" Pezzano asked.

"The only requirement is that I be along," Escalante advised.

"Good to know," Pezzano said, grinning. "Because it usually takes an act of God—or a case of *extreme* importance—for the city to underwrite travel beyond the limits of driving distance."

"Yeah," Marcus chimed in again with his sarcastic rasp, "which they consider to be a five-mile quickie through the Holland Tunnel to Newark, maybe, and back."

"If they don't consider a murder to be a case of 'extreme importance,' " Winona Escalante asked, sincerely puzzled, "just what would they consider underwriting out-of-state travel expenses for?"

"The last time that I heard they sprung for airline tickets," Jack Lindstrom announced, "was over forty years ago. They actually sent two detectives down to Miami to cut a deal with Jack Murphy—Murph the Surf—to recover the Star of India sapphire he'd glommed from the Museum of Natural History. That, Ms. Escalante, is their idea of extreme importance."

"Jack's exaggerating, of course, Winnie," Diane De-Gennaro said, with a friendly laugh. "But," she added, "not by a whole lot."

"You mentioned something about additional interesting information?" Savage asked, staring intently at Escalante. It was as if she had been awaiting his eye contact.

"Since I left home, my staff back in Fort Wayne has been doing great work," she began. She pulled a legal pad from her portfolio, flipped back a page, and began to summarize her notes.

"On June second last year, while operating their athletic clothing store business in the state of Ohio, George Granger and John Boyer Holloway each purchased term life insurance policies totaling one million dollars. As we all know, Granger purchased his policy from my company, Aurora Occidental. Holloway, however, purchased his policy from a firm in Omaha, Calpernia Fidelity. Several months later, in October, those policies were both increased to one million five in value."

"Who were the beneficiaries?" Savage inquired.

"Initially, Granger's beneficiaries were his family— mother, sister, brothers."

"And Holloway?" Savage asked.

"Holloway's original beneficiary was his mother, Hazel Holloway, of Columbus, Ohio."

"I know that name," Jack Lindstrom interrupted. "That's the Holloway phone listing in Columbus that was disconnected with no forwarding just last Thursday."

"Gee," Marcus mumbled sarcastically. "No freakin' coincidence there."

"Two things of particular interest," Escalante continued. "Both men eventually changed their beneficiaries. As we all know, Granger made Holloway his sole beneficiary back in March. We now know that Holloway made Granger his sole beneficiary at about the same time."

"Disinheriting his mother?" DeGennaro asked.

"Yes. However," Escalante was quick to add, "since Granger's death, Holloway has again reinstated his mother as his sole beneficiary."

"How thoughtful," DeGennaro mumbled.

"Just what was the second thing of interest?" Pezzano queried.

"When each completed medical questionnaires for their respective policies," Escalante replied, "they each listed Dr. Janus of New York City as their previous and current physician."

"Nice neat package," Marcus said, grimacing as he

flipped the filter of a fresh cigarette between his lips. "These three boys had a plan right from the get-go." He began digging in his pockets, looking for his lighter.

"How do you want to break this up?" Pezzano asked Savage. The lieutenant turned and glared daggers at Marcus, who quickly slipped the unlit Winston back into his shirt pocket and nervously cleared his throat.

"With a view towards getting her to reconsider her original findings, and maybe finally calling this damn thing a homicide, we need to get with Althea Blanchard, the pathologist who performed the postmortem on our DOA," Savage replied flatly.

"But before we do that," Pezzano said, "before we can really expect that she'd reassess, we need to know the real identity of our victim and provide Blanchard a true medical history on him."

"Richie and Diane have already gotten to work on that," Savage advised.

"What have you done?" Pezzano asked, glancing back and forth at the two detectives.

"We've already touched base with a Detective Ragusa up at Missing Persons," Diane responded. "We've provided him with a complete pedigree on the DOA, the clothing he was wearing, and the date of death—around which he might have been reported missing."

"All of that is contingent on him even being a resident of the city, and reported missing from one of the five boroughs," Pezzano pointed out.

"True enough, boss," Marcus spoke up. "But for now we've asked Ragusa to run an administrative informational search of our NYPD records. He's gonna get back to us. If that comes up dry, then we start contacting Nassau, Suffolk, Westchester County Missing Persons Units, in an ever-broadening circle."

"You know, of course," Pezzano said, "the DOA falls well within that gray area of someone between eighteen and sixty-five years of age who may have left home voluntarily because of domestic, financial, or similar reasons. In which event he would not have qualified as a 'missing person,' and a report of such would never have been taken."

Both detectives nodded their understanding; Diane spoke. "That's true, boss, but we're hoping that maybe he'll fall into the 'absent under circumstances indicating unaccountable or involuntary disappearance' category. In which event a missing persons report *would* have been processed."

Pezzano offered a conceding smile. "You know your Patrol Guide, Diane. You studying for sergeant?"

"Meanwhile," Savage broke in, speaking to Pezzano, "I've been attempting to get through to an old lawyer friend of mine. It's very possible he may know something."

"And Ms. Escalante?" Pezzano queried, nodding toward the insurance investigator.

"Ms. Escalante can float between our two teams," Savage replied. "Fill in and assist wherever needed." He looked over at the lady. "Does that suit you?" he asked her. She nodded squarely back, holding her eye contact just a beat too long.

"Anything else?" Pezzano asked.

"Heard back from Linda Jensen down at OTSD-911," Richie Marcus said. "She confirmed what we already suspected. Their Investigations Unit did a full audit of everything called in to the Public Safety Answering Center from midnight to oh-eight-hundred hours on May twenty-eighth. The audit showed that 911 was not ever down or ever in a stacked-up busy mode during those hours. Their records account for only the one call from Dr. Janus. It was received at oh-seven-thirty."

"We'll need her to put that on paper," Savage advised. Marcus nodded.

"Can 911 *ever* be busy?" Lindstrom asked, shrugging.

"Linda said it's possible—it does happen," Marcus replied. "After all, they took twelve million calls for service last year that accounted for almost five million radio runs."

"I understand that, Richie," Lindstrom said. "Communications Section does a fine job. But, I'm going to repeat," he added impatiently. "*Can* 911 *ever* be busy? That's what I want to know. And, if so, what conditions have to exist in order for that to happen?"

"According to Jensen, it would take an extreme shortage of communications personnel on a given shift, Jackie my boy," Marcus snapped back, a raw edge to his voice, "coupled with an incredible flurry of calls in order to bring it about."

"An incredible *flurry*?" Lindstrom questioned, creasing his brow.

"Surely a man with your education," Marcus replied, really pouring on the surly, "a man with your mercurial psyche and intelligence, should know what a goddamned 'flurry' is." He shook his head and made a face.

"This," Lindstrom announced, "from a man who thinks that holistic medicine is the practice of proctology."

Winona Escalante stifled a giggle. Savage too thought the remark a good line.

"I was just looking for an example, Richie," Lindstrom then said. "That's all. Don't go getting all weird on me."

"A *flurry* might be something on the order of a plane crash in the middle of Brooklyn," Marcus responded, tight-jawed. "Or a fifty-seven-car fender bender on the Gowanus, where a great number of people are calling in all at once. That, Mr. Lindstrom, is an example of a freakin' flurry at 911."

"*Ahh,*" Lindstrom murmured, nodding his head in overdramatic understanding, and obvious put-on. "Now I see."

"Every 911 call is digitally recorded and logged," Savage said, breaking into the never-ending game of one-upmanship the two detectives had engaged in with each other for years. Looking directly at Marcus, he continued, "And they're saved for at least ninety days—which means we're pretty close to running out of time. So get right on it and ask Linda Jensen to send us a transcription of Janus' actual call."

"Already in the works, boss," Marcus replied. He slowly turned toward Jack Lindstrom and shot the man a screw-you glare.

"What's your problem, Richie?" Lindstrom asked.

"Nuthin. No problem, Jack. We'll talk about it later, after you've taken your Prozac."

Pete Pezzano stood. "All right, boys and girls, let's get to it."

TWENTY

Richie Marcus had been an NYPD detective for more than two decades and was now entering his twelfth year as a homicide investigator. He had spent the first five of those years working the violent and depressing ghettos of Brooklyn North, where crime is usually very high and where life is usually very cheap, where people can die in unbelievably violent ways for little reason—a drug transaction gone bad, a few lousy bucks, because they inadvertently "dissed" some hothead who was packing a Saturday night special—or simply for no reason at all. He had spent the last seven years, however, working within the confines of prestigious Manhattan South, where crime is usually lower and where life has some greater value, but where people still die in unbelievably violent ways because of drugs, money, and pistol-packing hotheads—or for no reason at all.

Marcus, justifiably cynical and jaded after years of wallowing around in man's inhumanity toward man, had a chest full of ribbons and, aside from a long-ago reputation as a swordsman and carouser, a few insubordinations, and some other minor alcohol-drenched transgressions, a reputation within The Job of being a pretty nice guy—if you could get past the saltiness. He also had a case clearance and conviction rate that was the envy of any investigator.

The somewhat paunchy, yet ruggedly handsome ex-marine should have long ago seen a promotion to detective second grade, and then, like his partner both on and off The Job, Diane DeGennaro, been moved on up the ladder to detective first grade; but it hadn't happened. There were those with very long memories still sitting on the bureau's promotion board who possessed little regard for onetime carousers and swordsmen. Others disliked reformed boozers and were pure death on anybody with an insub in their personnel jacket. Still others on the board didn't care much for the taste of salt. So Marcus was still a third grader. In Savage's mind, however, Richie was easily the most street-savvy cop in the office.

After all these years as a detective, Marcus knew only too well that there are many times in an investigation when nothing much seems to go right. An investigator could seek and seek for weeks, fruitlessly tracking down dead ends and groping through endless blind alleys, and come up with zilch. Many times Marcus had busted his cojones to finally take one step forward in a case and, the very next day, found himself five whole steps to the rear. But then, every once in a while, for whatever reason, something does go effortlessly right. Maybe the correct phone call is placed at the perfect moment? Maybe the right button is pressed, or perhaps the right door knocked on and the right questions asked? Whatever. Some days it just works out the way it's supposed to—just like on TV. Today, it seemed, might be such a day.

"Manhattan South, Marcus."

"Yeah, Marcus. This is Carmine Ragusa up at Missing Persons. You called me late Friday afternoon to see if we had anything that could match up with an unidentified male DOA from last May twenty-eighth."

"Right," Marcus responded. He motioned to Diane, who was seated at her desk directly opposite, to pick up on the same line.

"Other than the age being off a bit, I feel strongly that I've got something for you."

"Go," Marcus said, flipping the notepad before him to a fresh page.

"We got a guy reported missing from a residence in the Bronx on June third. However, he had last been seen on the morning of May twenty-seventh. Says here that he had taken up temporary residence with some relatives just after relocating from out of state."

"Where, out of state?" Diane asked.

"Oklahoma."

"Ok-la-ho-ma . . . Okay!" Marcus sang off-key, while scratching out his notes.

"The guy you're lookin' for was supposed to be forty-five, right?" Ragusa asked. "Problem here is, this guy is only thirty-seven."

"Unh," Marcus grunted. "Don't let age bother you, Ragusa. Keep goin'."

"Well, anyway," Ragusa continued, "the clothing matches to a freakin' T. When last seen, this guy was wearin' a white-and-blue-striped western shirt, faded blue jeans, cowboy boots. . . . Way I see it, this has gotta be your man."

"Sounds good," Marcus replied. "How about faxin' me a photograph and whatever else ya got, ASAP?"

"No photo. The aunt and uncle, a Mr. and Mrs. Clem Buckner, didn't provide one. I'll send you all the rest, though."

"You got an address and phone on the Buckners?" Marcus asked.

After Ragusa read off the information, he added, "Let me know how you make out. I'd like to close this one."

"Ten-four," Marcus replied. He hung up his phone, tore the page of notes from the pad, and motioning for Diane to join him, made straight for the sergeants' room.

It was gonna be a good day, he thought; he felt it in his bones. It might even be a lucky day, he reasoned. It's definitely *gonna* be a lucky day, he then concluded. He'd wait till lunchtime and call his bookie. He'd like to go ten dimes on that up-and-coming filly running in tomorrow's third. But that was tomorrow, which might not be so lucky. However, the Mets were going against Cincinnati this afternoon at Shea; he'd go ten dimes on the Mets—Gonzaga was pitching, and his ERA against the Reds was horrendously bad. He oughtta be able to get some long odds; hell, freakin' Gonzaga was due.

The normally quiet fax machine suddenly gave a short beep and a gentle whir. Daphne Dempsey then heard the sound of paper scraping against paper as it pulled a sheet into the printing tray. Because the toner is blown onto the paper much the way a copier works, the printing that followed was very quiet. When the fax was completely received and printed, there was another short beep, and the machine went back to its quiet hum. She pulled the printed sheet—a blown-up photograph of a man—from the machine and laid it faccup on her desk. At first glance, the man's face did seem familiar, but only vaguely.

While the Delano Hotel reservation manager was trying to study the picture more closely, her attention was suddenly drawn to a raised voice spouting angry words at one of her clerks at the counter just outside her office. She quickly discerned that it was a guest having some difficulty understanding his final bill, which, in this business, was something that happened from time to time.

She listened intently as the clerk professionally responded to "Mr. Hartnett," carefully explaining to him each and every one of the charges for which he had been billed. As the discussion continued, it became clear that the guest was calming down, having been nicely mollified and well handled by the newest member of her front-desk staff.

After Mr. Hartnett had settled his account with his Visa, and left the building with at least somewhat of a smile on his face, Daphne Dempsey motioned for Ramon Mendez to step into her office.

"I must tell you that you handled that situation very well, Ramon," she said, still seated at her desk when the slender man entered. "You're doing a fine job—very professional."

"Thank you, Ms. Dempsey," the handsome Cuban

replied, nodding with a charming smile. "If it were not for you giving me the chance, I'd still be lugging bags as a bellman."

"Oh, you're way too bright, and have far too much on the ball to have been lugging bags for a living," she replied earnestly. "So when we had an opening, we moved you up." She also thought that the young man had much in the way of ambition—some thought possibly too much.

"Thank you," Ramon replied. "You're very kind." His dark eyes suddenly widened, and his mouth fell partially agape when his glance fell on the freshly faxed color photograph lying on her desktop. "Oh, my God!" he muttered reflexively, then, as if gathering control, seemed to quickly stifle himself.

"What's the matter?" she asked, surprised by Ramon's momentary shock.

"This picture," he said, holding up the photo and studying it. "Where . . . where did you get it?"

"A detective from New York City just faxed it through to me. I just got off the phone with him five minutes ago. Why?" she pressed. "Do you recognize that man?"

"I'm—I'm not sure," Ramon stuttered. He cleared his throat nervously and seemed to be struggling for composure.

"According to the detective, his name is George Granger, and it's possible he stayed with us on several occasions. But we have no record of it."

"*Granger?*" Ramon echoed, looking puzzled. "When was he supposed to have stayed here?"

"Last May."

"Is he *wanted* by the police in New York?" Ramon asked guardedly.

"Well, I guess so."

"Did the detective tell you what he was wanted for?"

"Not really, actually. Just said they needed to talk with him."

"About what?"

"Didn't say exactly," Daphne responded softly, studying Ramon's responses, watching him process the information—or lack of it. "I seemed to get the sense, however, that it must be something pretty serious. The detective said he worked in a homicide unit."

"Hmm," Ramon muttered and handed the photo back just as the phone rang on Daphne's desk.

"Delano Hotel," she answered in her friendliest tone. "You're speaking with Reservations. How may I help you?"

"Yes. I'd like to speak with Ramon Mendez, please."

"May I tell him who's calling?"

"Elvin Welch."

"Just a moment, Mr. Welch." She handed the receiver up to Ramon. "It's for you."

Daphne Dempsey busied herself with some filing as Ramon held a brief and stilted phone conversation. Though not eavesdropping, she thought the call seemed somewhat odd, as if Ramon was unable to speak freely. He voiced only some agreeing grunts, a few "uh-huhs," and a "yes" and "no" or two. It clearly was not a business call; it surely was personal—which was frowned on by company policy. She would not make an issue of it, not this time, but if it became a steady thing . . .

"Since I'm off tomorrow and the next day, I was wondering if I could have the rest of today off," he said immediately upon hanging up. "I'm afraid I'm not feeling very well."

A new hesitancy seemed to have dawned in Ramon. Though nothing of his initial shock remained evident in his demeanor, Daphne sensed that the man had somehow shifted his emotional gears. He appeared to be retreating, as if wishing he were somewhere else.

"All right," Daphne replied, not for a moment believing that he was really sick. But she decided to cut him some slack, especially since there was plenty of desk coverage on hand. "When you punch out, bring me your time card and I'll initial it."

As she gazed then at the photo, it finally came to her. "Now I remember him," she blurted out. "Don't you recall the guy who you said had those terrible yellowed fingers?"

"Not really," Ramon replied flatly.

"Nicotine stains," she pressed. "The guy smoked like a chimney. Don't you remember?"

"Do you actually think that's the same guy?" Ramon responded with a dismissive shrug.

"Oh, yes. I'm sure it is," Daphne replied definitively. "He looks a bit different in this picture, but of course he would; he's the same guy who had all those bandages all over his face for about a week while he was here. Everybody was figuring that he'd had plastic surgery. I'm sure that was back in late May . . . early June, just like the detective said. Don't you remember?"

"That was when I was still carrying bags," Ramon said. "I really can't say that I recall him."

"He had a strange name," Daphne muttered to herself, straining mightily to bring it to mind. "And it certainly wasn't George Granger. I'm pretty damn good on names."

She sat down at her computer and brought up the guest lists for May and June. She scrolled quickly through them, hoping for a trigger.

"Can't help you," Ramon replied, his air still defensive.

"Von Deutsch," Daphne finally exclaimed. "See here," she said, pointing to the name on the monitor screen. "Eric Von Deutsch. He was here twice in May. Both times we put him in fourteen twenty-two; he always requested a smoker suite."

She reached for the phone and punched in the New York City number shown at the bottom of the fax.

"Detective Lindstrom, please."

Cleaved in two by the monoxide-gray, busy east-west leg of the Major Deegan Expressway, which soon turns northbound at the Harlem River and runs right past Yankee Stadium, the Mott Haven section of the Bronx perhaps was not the worst part of New York's most northern borough, but it certainly wasn't New York's answer to Beverly Hills either.

Avenues with names like Lincoln, Alexander, Brook, and St. Ann's intersected with numbered streets running from the low 130s to the high 140s. The area's lower half was primarily industrial, warehouses and such, with a large section devoted to the Harlem River Rail Yard. Mott Haven's upper section was lined with old tenement apartments, some older row houses, but was mostly marked now by overpopulated, graffiti-scarred municipal housing projects. The section, once totally Irish, was now a mixture of working-class blacks, whites, and Hispanics.

"You have to wonder what the hell makes people move to New York, of all places, from Oklahoma," Diane DeGennaro said in mild disbelief as Marcus aimed the silver Taurus across the Willis Avenue Bridge, crossing into the Bronx from Manhattan. He turned right at 138th Street.

"Seems the husband, Mr. Buckner, got himself a halfway-decent-paying job with some big water tunnel project that's going on up here. Told me he's only a laborer, though, not an engineer or nuthin'. Said he was skilled in well drilling, which, after all, makes sense, coming from Tulsa."

"Did you tell him that the guy we're coming to see them about, who might well turn out to be their nephew, is DOA?" she asked.

"No," Marcus replied, letting loose with a nervous snort. "I didn't. I just told them we was coming to see them to follow up on their outstanding missing person complaint. Routine."

"Huh," Diane acknowledged, thinking how much difficulty crusty Richie always had when it came to delivering death notifications. He always dreaded it. Not that it was a positive in this case—and would not be until Mr. or Mrs. Buckner actually made the photo ID—but it was certainly a very good probability. She decided to change the subject and discuss the upcoming family reunion.

"We're all set for the weekend, by the way," she said. "Every *I* is dotted, and every *T* is crossed."

"What about your pain-in-the-ass uncle Harry?" Marcus inquired, stopping for the traffic light at Brook Avenue.

"I was finally able to get him situated at the Ocean View Motel down in Bay Terrace."

"The one on Hylan," Marcus replied, making a face. "Place is a dump."

"Uncle Harry won't mind. Not for three days. Hell, he's flying back to St. Pete first thing Monday morning. And you know him, he don't go for spit. I'm amazed he's even coming."

"What's the final head count going to be?" Marcus asked.

"Aunts, uncles, cousins, sisters, brothers, children, grandchildren, great-grandchildren, in-laws, and miscellaneous," Diane replied, "brings us to a total of fifty-three people. Good God, I hope the weather is going to hold up."

At Cypress Avenue Marcus made another right turn and crossed 137th Street. One block later, he pulled the unmarked car to the curb beside the Mill Brook Houses.

"Ready?" he asked, flipping off the air conditioner and shutting down the motor.

"Let's do it," Diane replied, popping her door.

"You wanna handle this one?" he said, acting nonchalant but letting loose with one of his involuntary nervous snorts as they let themselves into the building at 620 East 135th Street and scanned the resident directory.

"Not really," Diane replied flatly. "But I can tell that you don't want to . . . so, therefore, I guess I will."

Mrs. Clem Buckner was a rail-thin, rawboned, and sinewy woman of about sixty-five. Despite being short—five one, five two at most—with heavily wrinkled skin and a deeply lined face, she hardly came

across as fragile. She had big, alert eyes, set close together like an owl's, and though slightly bent and
stooped from osteoporosis, she had the hard, tough
aura of iron rebar. Shoeless and wrapped in a terry
robe when she answered the door, she motioned both
detectives into her sparsely furnished and strange-
smelling project apartment and asked if either would
care for a cup of coffee. Both declined.

"Is Mr. Buckner at home?" Diane asked.

" 'Fraid not," the woman replied. "Clem had to go
leave for work 'bout ten minutes ago. But I can answer your questions probably better than he could
anyhow. Elvin was my sister's son, and I know'd him
since he was just a little child. My sister's gone, ya
know, went to be with the Lord nigh ten year ago."

Mrs. Buckner nimbly sat in a grime-stained Barca-
lounger near the living room window and raised un-
washed and badly calloused bare feet to an olive green
vinyl hassock that was losing its straw. Every one of
her toenails was something beyond belief. Most of
them were at least two inches long. Some, like those
on both great toes, were even longer, curled into gro-
tesque talonlike hooks. No wonder she was barefoot,
Diane concluded, having never seen anything quite
like it before and wondering what the hell it was all
about. At any rate, there was no way those feet went
into shoes. Diane tried to divert her eyes. Though
strangely captivating, the Okie's feet were just straight
out disgusting.

"My condolences on your sister," Diane finally
said softly.

"What can I help you detectives with?" she asked,
motioning them to sit on the brown sofa that probably
used to be a pale yellow. Again they declined. "Do
you need some more information on Elvin?"

"Uhh, yes, we do, as a matter of fact, ma'am," Marcus said. "For starters, how was your nephew's
health?"

"His health was good. Why, I can't remember Elvin

even having a damn cold. To my knowledge, that boy never ever missed a day's work. Very reliable."

"What kind of work did he do?" Diane asked.

"He's always worked as a patient care assistant. Usually in old-age and convalescent homes . . . that sort of thing. Elvin likes people, old people. He's a very gentle man."

"Did he have a job here in New York?" Diane followed up.

"Not yet. He was lookin' for one. He'd only been here but a few days before he disappeared on us. But he worked fifteen years for St. Angela's Manor House back in Tulsa. You could call them, they'll tell ya all about Elvin."

"Getting back to his health, ma'am," Diane interrupted. "Had Elvin ever been treated for any heart problems that you were aware of?"

"Not that I ever heard. Like I said, Elvin was never sick."

"To your knowledge, was Elvin ever a smoker?" Marcus asked.

"Never," Ms. Buckner said emphatically. "Elvin never smoked. Despised those damn cigarettes. His dear mother passed from a lung cancer. I'd give anything to get Clem to quit."

"Okay," Marcus said. "Now, how about alcohol? Would you say that your nephew was a man who liked his drink?"

"Now that's a fact," the woman replied, crossing her unshaven legs and clucking her tongue. "If my dear nephew has him a devil-inspired weakness, then it surely has to be the drink. I'm ashamed to say it, but the boy does like his alcohol. He can get hisself just plumb stupid sometimes. Actually he's a lot like his father was."

"What about his social life?" Diane inquired. "Would you say that he was a . . . ladies' man?"

Mrs. Clem Buckner scrunched her lined and wrinkled face into something resembling that of an apple-head doll. "Now there you got me," she said. "Elvin got hisself hitched there one time. But it didn't last too long. Except for that I don't really recall too many women in Elvin's life." She unscrunched her face and looked up coyly at both detectives. "You might say that he had *other* fish to fry."

"Was your nephew homosexual?" Diane said flatly.

"Yes, I believe he was. It wasn't something that the family ever really talked about too much. But I guess you could say it was something we all somehow know'd."

"We understand that back in June when you reported your nephew missing, you were unable to provide Missing Persons a photograph of him," Diane went on.

"That's true!" Mrs. Buckner replied, springing impulsively to her bizarre feet as if catapulted from the chair. "But since then I've come across a few I had in a old cardboard box filled with pictures. Would you like to see them?"

Diane DeGennaro nodded, and the barefooted woman shuffled off briskly into another room. Several moments later, she returned and handed across three grainy photographs of her nephew, Elvin Welch.

After a quick comparison to the photos taken of the clothed DOA in Janus' examining room and those of the nude DOA in the medical examiner's autopsy photographs, it was clear to the detectives that the mystery as to the identity of the DOA in Doctor Janus' office had now been solved.

"I regret to inform you, Mrs. Buckner," Diane stated, coating her words with as much empathy as she could, "but I'm afraid your nephew is deceased."

"Oh, please don't say that," Loreen Buckner groaned, allowing herself to sink back onto her recliner while clutching the lapels of the terry robe and pressing them tightly to her breast.

The detectives stood by silently, allowing the idea to settle in.

"I have to admit, at first, I myself did have some bad feelings about this all," the woman continued, talking to no one in particular. "But I fought those terrible thoughts off. I know'd that it was strange for Elvin to leave without so much as a word, but I'm positive that he'll be comin' back."

"Do you think you'd be up to viewing some photographs for us?" Marcus asked, softening his gruff voice.

The misty-eyed woman nodded and accepted the packet of pictures that Marcus handed her. After only a tentative glance at one photo, she handed them right back.

"I don't know if that's him," she blurted, shaking her head disgustedly. "That fellow in them pictures is all purple and bloated and everything, I just can't look."

"Mrs. Buckner, we truly believe that the man in those photographs is your nephew, Elvin Welch," Diane said, suspecting that the woman was not only in deep shock but also in deep denial.

"Would you mind spending some time with us?" Marcus asked. "We've got an awful lot of questions. Good answers to which may help us in finding out just how Elvin did die."

The woman blew her nose in a tissue and dabbed at her eyes. "I'll tell you anything you want to know. But I'm not at all convinced that's my nephew in them pictures."

"Can you tell us if your nephew was a licensed driver?" Marcus asked.

"Yes, he was. He had him a Oklahoma driver's license. I remember Clem tellin' him the very day he arrived here that he'd have to go get hisself a New York State one, though."

"I see," Marcus said. "Did he usually carry that driver's license with him?"

"Well," the woman mused, "I would guess he did carry it around with him. Since the day he went missin', me and Clem been through his things any number of times . . . didn't find no driver's license, though. Just clothes, things like that."

"How about a Social Security card?" Diane asked. "Did you find one of those?"

"Not one of them neither."

"By any chance do you happen to know what his Social Security number was?" Diane followed up.

The woman shook her head. "Hell, I don't really believe I can remember what my own Social Security number is. But I bet if you call that there St. Angela's Manor House down in Tulsa, they sure would have a record of it."

"That's a good idea, ma'am," Diane said.

"That there dead fellow in the picture . . ." Mrs. Buckner started.

"Yes, ma'am," Diane replied.

"Was he carrying around Elvin's driver's license or Social Security card?"

"No, ma'am," Diane replied. "We've not recovered any of Elvin's identification as yet."

"See, I told ya . . . that man in them pictures ain't him."

"Ma'am," Diane said, "have you ever seen this before?" She held out the brass Kwikset house key that had been removed from Elvin Welch's shirt pocket when his body was first searched in Janus' office.

"That there looks kinda like the key to my apartment," she replied, shrinking farther into her chair.

"Did your nephew have such a key?"

"He did. I gave him one the day he arrived here."

"Would you mind, ma'am?" Marcus asked, nodding toward the apartment door.

"Mind what?" she asked, her weathered face scrunched into a flustered, preoccupied question mark.

"Would you mind if we tried this key in your door?"

"All right," she replied tentatively. "Go ahead."

Marcus took the key from Diane and tried it in the Buckners' front-door lock. It worked.

Loreen Buckner buried her lined face in bony, age-spotted hands and broke down into long, screeching, anguished sobs. Denial was over.

Richie Marcus cleared his throat and turned away.

TWENTY-ONE

A meeting requested by Winona Escalante had been set for eleven fifteen in Pete Pezzano's office. The insurance investigator had asked for the morning huddle in order to go over some new information that had just come into her possession.

After completing one of his monthly reports for downtown by 11:05, Savage placed two quick phone calls. One went to Dr. Figueroa—Ray had started to take some food and water, but other than that, he was not much more improved than last night when Savage had visited. He also placed a second call to the law offices of Louis Armbruster. Armbruster, according to Omar at the Meat Hook, was a rich source of information on his kinky playmate Dr. R. Charles Janus. But equally important now, it was likely that Armbruster had some answers about Janus' pal, the handsome guy known as John Boy, who might well be John Boyer Holloway.

After identifying himself to Armbruster's secretary, Ms. Kranick, with whom he'd become friendly, his call was put on hold. Five minutes later, Ms. Kranick came back on the line and again informed Savage that Armbruster had already left the office for court and would not be back to the office any more that day.

"Did you tell Louis that I had called several times and wanted to speak with him?" Savage asked.

"Uh, yes, I did," Ms. Kranick replied in a stutter. "I'm sorry if he has been unable to get back with you. . . . It's just that he's been so terribly busy. . . . I'm sure you understand."

"Oh, I understand, Ms. Kranick," Savage replied soothingly. "Just tell Louis that I called again."

Ms. Kranick was a terrible liar. The bullshit brush-off was precisely what Savage had expected. Louis Armbruster was evading him. Good.

At fifteen after, Savage left his desk in the sergeants' room, grabbed a mug of coffee, and joined the squad boss in awaiting Escalante's arrival. As he entered the lieutenant's office, Pezzano was just hanging up his phone.

"According to the chart, your team is scheduled for RDOs this coming weekend," Pezzano said, frowning slightly. "That right?"

"Right," Savage replied, taking a seat opposite the lieutenant. "We're doing a day duty on Friday and don't come back until a four to twelve on Monday. It's a nice swing."

"Anything planned?" Pezzano asked ominously.

"Matter of fact, yes," Savage replied guardedly. Somewhere in the back of his head Maureen Gallo's harangue of "if we make plans, something *will* definitely happen" began to echo—if not boom. "I'm committed to taking a beach house out in the Hamptons."

"Don't count on it," Pezzano said. "The borough office needs some warm bodies this weekend for special security details up at Gracie Mansion and the Waldorf. Some heavy-duty politico from Tel Aviv is gonna get the key to our city from the mayor Saturday afternoon."

"So what?" Savage said, annoyed, as his booming thoughts morphed to include a vision of an ice-encrusted yet steam-fuming stone statue of Maureen.

"Intelligence has gotten information that some Palestinian group intends to be at the ceremony too. They say they're gonna blow the friggin' place up. And if they don't get him during the ceremony at Gracie Mansion, they're gonna attempt a hit on him sometime during his three-day stay at the Waldorf."

"*Shit!*" Savage murmured.

Pezzano smirked, shrugged, and threw open his big palms. "Just another average weekend in the Big Apple. What can I tell you?"

"How many warm bodies are they looking for?" Savage asked.

"They've directed our office to provide one supervisor and three detectives."

"Lakis and his team are working the weekend," Savage said. "Give it to them."

"Can't do it," Pezzano replied. "Strict orders from the borough. All regular days off are to be canceled, and those bodies are to be put on ordered overtime and used for this security detail. No exceptions."

"Jesus!"

"Better let your team know what's coming down the pike," Pezzano suggested. "Give them some time to readjust any plans they might have made."

"Boss," Savage said, cocking his head and holding up his hands in a slow-down motion, "Jack Lindstrom's daughter is getting married on Saturday. If I tell him he's got to work, the man'll go sick—and I can't say that I would blame him. You would too."

Pezzano again shrugged and grimaced helplessly.

"Coincidentally," Savage went on, continuing to plead the case, "DeGennaro and Marcus are having a family reunion this weekend. They've worked on setting it up for months. People are flying in from all over the country. They're booked on flights and into hotels. There is just no way in hell that can be readjusted. Simply put, me and my entire team need our regular days off this weekend."

"Don't know how that can be done," Pezzano replied, again throwing open his huge palms. "These orders are from the freakin' borough. I can't just ignore or disregard them; you know that. We're stuck."

"Boss," Savage urged, "let Lakis and his team cover. As long as there's one supervisor and three detectives standing there, nobody is going to actually check to see if they are on ordered overtime, for crissakes."

Pezzano frowned. "Let me think about it," he said, just as a knock came at the office door.

Savage and the squad boss quickly stood as a prim, but very attractive, Winona Escalante entered. Dressed in a deep-blue form-fitting, knee-length business suit and businesslike black pumps, the insurance investigator shook hands with both men, then, pointing to the open chair next to Savage's, asked, "May I sit down?"

"Please do," Pezzano replied.

Gazing for only a millisecond too long at Savage, the woman slid gracefully into her chair. Savage inhaled a whiff of Tabu.

"One of my staff back in Indiana contacted me at my hotel this morning," she began, immediately crossing her leggy legs. "At my direction, they had tapped into several industry resources and uncovered some more very interesting facts about Mr. George Granger's background."

"If you don't mind, just what resources might those be?" Pezzano asked, curious.

"It's sort of a central repository of data and information provided by and shared among all insurance companies throughout the country."

Pezzano nodded. "Go on."

"It seems that when they entered Mr. Granger's name, his date of birth, and his Social Security number into the data bank late yesterday, bells went off like a jackpot-spewing slot at a Reno resort."

"Sounds good. What did they find?" Savage asked.

The woman made direct eye contact with him, eye contact that contained a subtle sultry gleam. It was a momentary look that he hoped Pezzano had missed.

"In particular," she replied, "they found an inordinately high number of personal-injury insurance claims put forth by him down through the years. Actuarially speaking, well beyond the pale."

Both Savage and Pezzano nodded.

"He's had any number of supermarket slip-and-fall claims; several in California and another two in New

Jersey. He has also made injury claims resulting from minor automobile accidents, one in Ohio, another in New York, and one in Pennsylvania. Further, he claimed to have once been injured on an icy platform of the Long Island Rail Road."

"Just what kind of injuries has he been alleging?" Pezzano inquired.

"Head, knee, wrist, cervical spine, lumbar spine, you name it." In one smooth, ladylike motion, Winona Escalante uncrossed the leggy legs while at the same time clasping slender arms tightly beneath her fine breasts. The action accentuated the alluring size and shape of the latter.

"Sounds like this guy should be considered either the Bionic Man or a complete basket case," Pezzano observed.

Savage knew the bland remark was typical of a Pezzano lame attempt at humor. He smiled wryly.

"True enough," the heads-up Escalante agreed, also allowing a diplomatic sly smile to creep across her finely made-up face. "But . . . that is not all of what we've found out."

"Let's hear it," Savage said. He leaned forward anxiously in his chair.

"We also looked in on the claims track record of Mr. John Boyer Holloway."

"And?"

"And we found pretty much the same thing," she said. "Holloway has had in excess of eight personal-injury claims in his lifetime. Any actuary worth his salt would tell you it's just not possible. But wait," she added again, her smile broadening even further. "There's more."

Pezzano now leaned forward in anticipation.

"Guess who the attending physician was who made the injury diagnoses in every one of those claims for both Granger and Holloway?"

Smiling, Savage turned his glance to Pete Pezzano. "Don't you just love it?"

*   *   *

The rattling old Toyota Corolla had a million miles on it. Its metallic red paint was faded to a chalky pink by the insistent South Florida UVs, it burned a quart of 10-40 every thousand miles, and it leaked almost as much when just sitting still. It needed a new set of tires, and the finicky AC hadn't worked since April; now, in the middle of a scorching August, it was like driving down the highway in a damn toaster oven. But that would all soon change, Ramon Mendez thought, as he steered the decade-old fugitive-from-a-scrapyard across the Seven Mile Bridge that linked Marathon Key with the Lower Keys. The marvel of engineering was one of forty-two bridges he would cross today while traversing the hundred-plus miles of U.S. 1 that terminated in Key West.

By this time next week, he allowed himself to daydream, he'd surely be driving a better car—a new car, for that matter, dammit. Maybe an Infiniti, or perhaps a Lexus. Maybe he ought to think about one of those two-seater roadster jobs—they were sharp. BMW made a nice one, and so did Porsche. But he wanted a sedan; it would be a Lexus, a bright red one. Ramon looked down at the odometer, which was one of the few things that still worked in the old junker. Key West was now only forty miles away. He estimated he'd be checking into the Beachside Holiday Inn there in something under an hour.

Eric, of course, had expected and wanted him to come directly to his Lazy Parrot Cottages hideaway—and probably hop right into bed—but Ramon had coyly declined. That wasn't going to happen; not today . . . and probably never again. Instead, they were to meet for dinner tonight at a busy downtown place called Mangia Mangia, and it would be during dinner, possibly over a heaping platter of the wonderful mussels marinara, that he would make his demands. Ramon knew that from that moment on, he would be well advised to keep a very safe distance from the flaky Eric and should continue to meet thereafter with him only in the relative safety of a crowded public place.

Americans were known to say that opportunity strikes but once. Mendez was not certain that the adage was true, but he would be taking no chances. *This,* as he saw it, was an opportunity, a big one, and he was going to wring it out for all that it was worth. Eric Von Deutsch, or Elvin Welch, or George Granger—whoever the hell the man was—had money, moolah, and apparently lots of it. Therefore, he should have no problem parting with a goodly amount of it to keep his whereabouts unknown to some New York City homicide detective.

How fortuitous it had been for him that Eric had given Daphne the name Elvin Welch when telephoning him at the hotel for the invite down. Had he used the name Eric Von Deutsch, this whole plan could never have materialized.

Just a mile or so past the Seven Mile Bridge, the Toyota struck a Route 1 speed bump that jarred the little car to its rafters. It turned out to be a good sign, however. The temperamental air conditioner that hadn't worked in months was suddenly blowing icy cold.

Ramon Mendez rolled up the driver's window and smiled.

Smart-ass Eric was sure to be thinking that when Ramon Mendez arrived, he was going to get laid. Truth was, Ramon knew, that Eric was about to get fucked . . . royally fucked.

The call from Diane DeGennaro had lasted only thirty seconds; it had come in only minutes after Winona Escalante left Manhattan South at the conclusion of the morning meeting. Unable to conceal the self-satisfied grin and accompanying sense of elation that he knew was lighting his face, Savage hung up the phone at his desk and strode next door to Pete Pezzano's office.

"You've either heard from the borough office that they've canceled that weekend detail up at Gracie, or you've heard back from DeGennaro and Marcus," Pezzano said, dropping the current set of Personnel Orders he'd been studying onto his desktop and yanking off his glasses. "Which one is it?"

"Just got off the phone with Diane DeGennaro," Savage replied happily, feeling his grin broadening. "We've struck gold."

The out-of-character tightness and strain so evident in Pezzano's expression since the last meeting with the chief of detectives fell immediately away. The pressure was off. He exhaled a relieved sigh and, flashing a comfortable, easy smile, said, "Tell me all about it, Thornton."

"We've got us a positive," Savage began. "The DOA, formerly known as Mr. George Granger of Columbus, San Francisco, and Schenectady, is now to be known as Mr. Elvin Welch of Tribbey, Oklahoma, and, most recently, the South Bronx."

"Yes!" Pezzano exclaimed, his lantern jaw thrust strongly forward, his two massive fists simultaneously punching short jabs into the air.

"DeGennaro already made contact with Welch's most recent employer—a nursing home down in Tulsa. Their employee health plan is also faxing us Welch's medical records. According to them, Welch had no history of any heart problems and had never smoked a cigarette in his life."

At that moment, Jack Lindstrom rapped firmly on the metal doorjamb. Savage motioned the detective into Pezzano's office and quickly brought him up to speed on the ID that had just been made in the Bronx.

"This thing is starting to build up a good head of steam," Lindstrom said. "And to make things better, I just got some good news back from Miami."

"Somebody recognized our boy?" Savage said.

"According to that Ms. Dempsey, he stayed at the Delano Hotel on two separate occasions," Jack Lindstrom began, reading from his hastily scribbled notes.

"On each of those stays he registered as and signed his name as Eric—Von—Deutsch."

"Jesus," Savage said with a snicker. "That is some damn handle."

"Just as an aside," Lindstrom went on, "he signed his name *Von* with a capital *V*."

"Yeah?" Pezzano said, puzzled. "So what?"

"I think he's got a problem spelling his own alias," Lindstrom pointed out. "As a general rule, Germans use the lowercase for the *von*."

"Now please tell me that this Mr. *Von Deutsch* was booked in there on the night of May thirteenth," Savage said firmly, not wanting to hear anything else but.

Lindstrom nodded. "On his first stay, he checked in at the Delano shortly after noontime on the ninth of May; he did not check out until the late morning of the sixteenth."

"Yes!" Pete Pezzano shouted again, smiling like a fat kid in a chocolate factory. Anxious then for further clarification, the lieutenant quickly said, "So what you're telling us is, Eric Von-*whatever-the-fuck*-his-name-is, was definitely booked into the Delano Hotel in Miami Beach on the night that Timothy DiBona alleges to have been assaulted by Dr. Janus."

"Yes, sir," Lindstrom said. "So I'd say it's pretty fair to say that the calls placed from Janus' telephone to the Delano Hotel in Miami at around the time of DiBona's assault that night were meant for our boy George Granger, now aka Eric Von Deutsch."

"There's that goddamned triple-play combination again," Pezzano mused, glancing over at Savage.

"Yeah," Savage agreed. "But in this game, instead of from Tinkers, to Evers, to Chance, it's Janus, to Holloway, to Granger."

"What other time period was this guy supposedly at the Delano?" Savage asked Lindstrom.

"It gets a little interesting there," Lindstrom replied. "According to this Ms. Dempsey, he checked in again on the evening of May the twenty-eighth and stayed until June eleventh."

"Not possible!" Savage gibed. "Didn't he know he was already dead on the morning of the twenty-eighth?"

"The morning of the twenty-eighth was the day the DOA was found in Janus' office," Pezzano observed through a wide grin. "Isn't this great?"

"What time did he check into the hotel on the twenty-eighth?" Savage asked.

"Eighteen forty-five hours," Lindstrom replied. "This Ms. Dempsey is going to fax us copies of all the registration cards he filled out."

"So if he was in Miami at eighteen forty-five, it's very possible that he could have been in New York City earlier that morning," Savage said. "Like around four or five a.m."

"Very possible," Lindstrom strongly agreed. "But here's the killer," he added. "I asked Dempsey to check the hotel telephone records. They indicated that very shortly after checking in on the twenty-eighth our boy made several phone calls from his room. One went to the residence of John Boyer Holloway, it lasted under a minute, and the other went to—"

"The office of Dr. R. Charles Janus," Pezzano broke in, smiling from ear to ear.

"Not to the office," Lindstrom corrected. "It went to Janus' residence line, which is registered to his roommate, Guillermo Cabrera. That particular call went on for more than seven minutes."

"Any other calls during his stay?" Savage inquired.

"Quite a few," Lindstrom replied. "Mostly local calls—Miami and such; a number of others in different area codes within the state of Florida. Besides the registration cards, this Ms. Dempsey is also faxing me the numbers of all his outgoing calls. Soon as I get them, I'll get Patti Capwell at Telephone Security to run them for names."

"Do me this too, Jack," Savage said, resting his chin between thumb and forefinger. "Check with every airline that services Miami from LaGuardia, JFK . . . even Newark. See if we can come up with a New York

City–to–Miami passenger traveling that day under either George Granger—"

"Or Eric Von Deutsch," Lindstrom said, nodding, finishing Savage's thought. The lanky man then about-faced and left the room.

"Where to from here?" Pezzano asked.

"First, I'm going to call Winona Escalante and give her the news," Savage replied.

"And speaking of *Miss* Winona Escalante," Pezzano segued through a devilish grin. "I'm sure I'm not telling you anything that you were not already well aware of, but unless I miss my guess, it seems to me that the fair lady may have taken somewhat of a shine to you."

"Unh," Savage groaned, supporting Pezzano's astute observation while at the same time shrugging it off. "I've got enough trouble with one woman in my life," he added, feeling that he had to somehow respond *and* effectively close the topic down.

"So after you notify *Winona,*" Pezzano teased, "then what?"

"Then I'm going to contact Dr. Karyn Hartman at the medical examiner's. I'm going to bring her up to date on this whole thing and have her arrange a time and place where we can interview the original pathologist, Althea Blanchard. I'm going to shoot for tomorrow morning. What she now has to say could be very critical." Standing then and moving toward the door, he turned to Pezzano and asked, "You?"

Offering a contented grin, Pezzano replied, "Soon as you're outta here, I'm gonna personally call Chief Wilson and get our good names restored."

Savage nodded and smiled. "While you're at it, boss, why don't you see if you can also get our names scratched from that weekend detail roster? I think the chief now owes us one."

TWENTY-TWO

George Granger parked his rented tan Mercury in one of the two available spots in front of Mangia Mangia, the Chicago-style pasta place on Southard Street. The corner Italian trattoria offered homemade pasta, alfresco or inside dining, and, best of all, it was off the Key West tourist's beaten track—it catered mostly to locals. Granger checked the time; he was five minutes early. He slouched comfortably behind the steering wheel and waited.

At precisely eight p.m., Ramon Mendez pulled beside him in his broken-down Toyota and waved. Granger motioned for Mendez to park the noisy hulk in the spot directly ahead. What a hunk of crap, Granger thought, as he stepped out onto the curb and tried to avoid breathing the nasty exhaust fumes it belched.

Dressed in tight white denims, a teal-and-white-striped polo, and with his jet-black hair smoothly combed, Ramon was the picture of sizzling Latino hot when he climbed from the beat-up junker. He acknowledged Granger with a quick nod and flashed that sexy smile of his, then reached into the car's rear seat and pulled out an overnight bag. Without a word, he stepped around to the back of the car and opened the trunk by twisting a flat-bladed screwdriver into the hole where, presumably, the key lock used to be. He chucked the blue nylon bag into the trunk and slammed the lid closed. Then he spoke.

"I just didn't want to leave it sitting on the backseat," he explained.

"When are you going to get rid of this piece of shit?" Granger said, throwing a dismissive hand in the direction of the sad-looking little sedan.

"I have a feeling, pretty soon," Mendez replied, again flashing a hint of that sexy smile.

"You're really going to like this place, Ramon," Granger said. "The food is great, and the ambience is superb. And they've got a wine list that'll knock you dead—three hundred and fifty different selections."

"I thought you didn't drink," Ramon said. "Wine, or anything else with alcohol."

"I don't," Granger replied, lacing his words with a lascivious tone. "But I happen to know that you do. And I figure if I can get you to drink enough of it, I can really take advantage of you when we get back to my place later. Tell me you're horny?"

"Always horny," Ramon murmured.

Although Ramon had spoken the desired words in response, Granger noted that the sly smile that would usually accompany them was suddenly missing from the man's face. In its place was a look of edginess, if not trepidation. He sensed that something might be up.

"Good," Granger said, looking directly into Ramon's dark eyes, trying to get a read. "Then let's go have us a nice dinner and conversation, and after dessert we can go to my place and play."

Granger led the way into the restaurant, through the noisy and bustling dining room, to the outdoor brick garden that was lit in twinkling pepper lights and crowded with specimen palms. At Ramon's strong insistence they took the small table for two in a far, quiet corner. They shared few words while perusing the extensive menu.

"For an appetizer I'm going to have the bruschetta," Granger finally said. "For dinner, I'm going with the Pollo al Quattro Formagio." Then, by way of recommendation, he added, "It's very good."

Ramon shook his head. "I don't feel like chicken tonight," he replied, his voice strangely lifeless, flat.

"You seem preoccupied," Granger said. "Is there something wrong? Is there a problem?"

"No," Ramon replied tersely, offering no further explanation.

When the waiter arrived, Ramon passed on having an appetizer, then ordered the Bollito Misto di Mare and a bottle of 1998 Robert Mondavi Chardonnay Reserve. During dinner, Ramon's distance seemed to increase. Granger found himself brooding and eating in uncomfortable silence.

The meal was delicious, Granger thought, as the attentive waiter bused the table. The dessert of Key lime pie was extraordinary, the warm backyard-dining garden extremely pleasant . . . but something was terribly wrong. Granger could just feel it. In the last half hour, the usually engaging Cuban had settled into an even more distant mode. With each glass of wine the man downed, he seemed to be steeling himself for something. Pondering a move, as one might when faced with the necessity of delivering bad news.

"All right," Granger said firmly, tired of the bullshit attitude. "Let's have it. What the fuck is wrong?" While awaiting Ramon's reply, he casually motioned for the waiter to bring him another cup of coffee.

"You've told me that your name is Eric Von Deutsch."

"I did, and it is," Granger replied in a terse monotone.

"You've rented your cottage under the name of Elvin Welch," Ramon went on.

"So happens I have," Granger answered directly, making his tone insightful. "And you want to know why, don't you?"

"I already know why," Ramon shot back, seeming to have fully discarded his earlier aura of reticence, fear, or whatever the hell it was.

"You *do*?" Granger responded, laughing out loud for only a second. The nerve of this little faggot bastard, he thought. Why is he being such a nosy prick tonight?

He leaned across the two-top, licked his lips in fomenting anger, then through gritted teeth said, "Go ahead, Ramon . . . tell me why."

"Because your real name is George Granger. And you are wanted up in New York by homicide detectives."

Granger, stunned, sat back in his chair. He maintained tight eye contact with Ramon, not knowing how to respond. On the one hand he wanted to deny, he *had* to deny. But his insides were churning; he needed to know every bit of information that Ramon might possess. Had the cops gotten onto the scam? Had that fucking Janus given him up? Had John Boy been arrested? As the waiter approached with the ordered coffee, Granger waved him angrily off with a swipe of his hand.

"My name is not George Granger," he swore, striving mightily to be convincing.

Ramon said nothing. He just locked eyes.

"This is ridiculous," Granger went on, almost pleading. "You've got to believe me, Ramon. For crissakes, I've never even been to New York."

"Simple," Ramon replied flippantly. "If you're not the George Granger they're looking for, then you have nothing at all to worry about, now, do you? After they come and talk to you, the detectives will then go away and leave you alone."

Granger felt his gears beginning to strip; he lashed out. "Now you listen to me, you little fuck," he muttered to Ramon through clenched teeth.

"No," Ramon replied coldly. "You listen to me. I want fifty thousand dollars. And I want it tomorrow. If I don't get it tomorrow, by noon, Detective John Lindstrom of NYPD Homicide gets you. Now, is that simple enough for you, Mr. Von Deutsch? Mr. Welch? Mr. Granger?"

"That's what you want for tomorrow," Granger snarled, knowing this was only the beginning. "What are you going to want next fucking week?"

Ramon did not reply. He just held his steely gaze.

Granger sat back and considered his alternatives. Caught flat-footed, he wished he had adequate time to strategize more fully. But he didn't. The best he could hope for at that moment was to buy some time. The only way to accomplish that, and keep the rotten bastard from giving him up, was to concede and hold out the carrot.

"I don't suppose you'd take a check," he said, lightening the heavy mood. He pulled a checkbook from his back pocket and waved it, struggling to maintain a cool exterior.

"I meant every word I've said," Ramon said calmly. "Please don't take it as a joke."

"My bank is not in Key West," Granger announced. "It's up on Marathon Key."

"I don't believe you," Ramon replied. "I can't believe a fucking word you say."

Granger tossed the checkbook onto the table. "See for yourself. Bank of America, Marathon Key, Florida. Those checks are for my money market account. It's totally fluid. You want the fucking money in cash, Mr. Mendez . . . that's where we've got to go to get it."

Ramon Mendez opened the small vinyl holder and studied the personal checks. "This account is in the name of Elvin Welch," he said warily.

"No shit!"

Satisfied, Mendez nodded and tossed the checks back.

"We'll drive up there first thing tomorrow morning," Granger said offhandedly. "We'll use my car. I ain't getting in that piece of shit of yours."

"You and me ride together?" Ramon questioned, an astonished twist of disbelief splashing across his face. *"I don't think so!"*

The mocking response and flat-out refusal to his offer was precisely what George Granger had expected from Mendez. After all, the man wasn't totally stupid. With the straight-faced misdirection skill of a chess master, designed to lure an opponent into a false sense of security, he then casually invited the Cuban to set the agenda.

"Well, why don't you just go ahead and tell me how you want to do this, Ramon."

It was ten o'clock when the high-pitched notes of the William Tell Overture blared into Janus' ear, startling him; he had been sleeping in. He threw back the sheet, quickly grabbed the cell phone from the lamp table beside the bed, and answered the call.

"Yes?" he grumbled sleepily into the phone.

"Do we have a problem?" The voice coming through the line was that of George Granger—an apparently very angry George Granger.

"Hold on a minute," Janus replied. Still not hitting on all cylinders, he blinked his eyes forcefully and shook his head, trying to gain full consciousness. He noted that Guillermo was nowhere about, but he heard the shower and the vent fan running in the bathroom. He rolled quickly from the bed, pulled on a pair of wrinkled slacks that he'd left draped over the recliner, and let himself out of the apartment. He stepped out into the hallway for privacy.

"Just what do you mean, do *we* have a problem?" he finally said.

"Because last night I got shaken down for fifty thousand dollars, that's what," Granger announced, the anger quotient still high.

"*What?*" Janus breathed, every one of his cylinders suddenly kicking in.

"Some little Cubano fruit fly that I've been bangin' down here in Florida is blackmailing me. The little bastard knows that I'm George Granger, and he also knows that some New York City detectives are looking for me . . . *homicide* detectives. What the fuck is going on, Janus? Are we under investigation?"

"He must be jerking your string," Janus said. "How could he possibly know that? Did you ever tell him that you were George Granger?"

"What, are you nuts?"

"What else does this guy claim to know?"

"Won't tell me a thing other than what I've already told you. Not until he gets his fifty grand, which, by the way, I have to fork over by noon today."

"Well, at least you've got the fifty grand to fork over," Janus snapped. "All I've seen so far is a promise for something under ten thousand. Your buddy John Boy is totally screwing me."

"Nobody's screwing you, Janus," Granger replied. "You're gonna get your share."

"When, George? When am I going to get *my* share?" Janus exploded. "When fucking John Boy finally decides to give it to me? Apparently, you've already got yours, and I'm freakin' broke here."

"What does John say to that?"

"Don't play dumb with me, George. You know damn well that I've been left out in the cold on this. I have no way of contacting John. Hell, I don't even know where the man is. He could be in freakin' Egypt."

"As I recall the arrangement, you were supposed to go through John Boy's mother."

"I've been made to go through his rotten bitch mother, all right. But now I can't even contact her. Her phone in Ohio has been disconnected. She's done a complete fade on me."

"What do you want me to do?"

"I want you to get a message to John Boy, George. I want you to tell that son of a bitch that he damn well better contact me ASAP. I want to talk directly to him . . . do you hear? Nobody else; not his mother, not his brother, not his freaking tailor . . . *him*, dammit. If anything is brewing, we all better damn well get our stories together."

"What do you know about the police?" Granger pressed. "Are they on to us?"

"I'm not sure," Janus conceded. "A couple of detectives paid me a visit at my office last Thursday. They searched the place up and down, confiscated

your medical file, broke my balls, and left. But I'm
sure they've got nothing, I tell you; nothing at all—
nothing more than they had on day one. They're
fucked."

"Then why are they still snooping around on this
thing, Janus?" Granger snarled. "And why are they
out looking for George Granger when they should be
believing that George Granger is long dead and
cremated?"

"I don't know," Janus replied in a murmur. "I find
that very puzzling."

"You find that *puzzling*?" Granger snapped. "I find
that absolutely frightening."

"Look here, don't you forget that I'm at the van-
guard of this goddamned thing," Janus announced.
"So it's going to be up to me to handle it. John Boy—
and you—should not be forgetting that. As I go, so
shall you both."

"I'll do my best to get in touch with him and deliver
your message. By the way, how come you're not at
the office this morning? I tried reaching you there."

"It's Wednesday, schmuck. The office is closed. If I
had any goddamned money—like I used to have—I'd
be out playing golf. Tell me, what are you going to
do about your greedy little Cubano friend?"

"Don't you worry about him," Granger growled in
venom-coated syllables. "That little spic bastard has
fucked with the wrong gringo."

"You better be careful," Janus urged. "That man's
expecting something from you. If you don't
deliver . . ."

"Oh, he's gonna get something delivered, all right,"
Granger murmured caustically. "But what he's gonna
get, he most certainly won't be able to take to the
bank."

TWENTY-THREE

A meeting to interview associate medical examiner Althea Blanchard was convened at the New York City Medical Examiner's Office conference room at eleven o'clock on Wednesday morning. In addition to detectives Thorn Savage and Jack Lindstrom from Manhattan South Homicide, present also were Dr. Karyn Hartman, chief of the New York ME's Office, medical examiner attorney George Albright, medical examiner investigator Cal Thomas, Manhattan assistant district attorney John McVeigh, and insurance investigator Winona Escalante.

As it turned out, Althea Blanchard, M.D., was a bookish black woman in her early thirties. She had light cocoa skin, wore heavy horn-rimmed eyeglasses, little or no makeup, and stood at a fragile five two. Her diminutive size, however, did not in any way interfere with her having a substantial attitude. In her short tenure at the Kings County Medical Examiner's Office, she had developed a reputation for being aloof and, at times, a true bitch on wheels. Also, she did not like cops, and never made any pretense that she did.

Before the meeting started, Blanchard spent thirty minutes huddled intently in the outer hallway with ME attorney George Albright. Albright, of course, was there to represent the best interests of the medical examiner's office, while at the same time advising Blanchard. Savage also knew that if push ever came to shove, however, Albright's overriding concern would be for the ME's office—Blanchard would be on her own. To Thorn Savage, who had viewed the huddle from a distance, the woman's whole demeanor seemed to be one of angry defensiveness.

When the meeting finally did begin, Dr. Karyn Hartman quickly introduced Dr. Blanchard to all those who were present and seated around the large conference table. The pathologist offered only a tight-lipped nod to the group and immediately showed her mettle by complaining to Hartman about having been inconvenienced. Judging by George Albright's annoyed expression, the act was clearly done against his best advice.

"I must ask you, Dr. Hartman," Blanchard began, waving a dismissive hand in the direction of the two detectives, who were seated directly opposite Hartman at the table. "Since it is the police who wished to speak with *me,* why is it that they did not travel out to Kings County in order to do so? Why have I been made to travel into Manhattan?"

"Doctor," Dr. Hartman said gently but quite firmly, "as you are well aware by now, this whole matter revolves around some very unusual circumstances—"

"Yes, I'm well aware of that, Dr. Hartman," Blanchard acknowledged tartly, cutting off the older woman, who was also her professional superior.

Unaffected by the mild insubordination and without missing a beat, Hartman moved right along. "And it was I who prevailed upon these gentlemen to hold this meeting here in Manhattan, in my office, as a favor to me, in order that I may be present not only on your behalf but mine as well."

"Yours?" Blanchard exclaimed, making a face. "It's me they all seem to be after."

"No one's after anybody here," John McVeigh immediately broke in.

The district attorney had the bland good looks and ivory smile of a smarmy maître d'. But, Savage thought, even though McVeigh had spoken the truth in an apparent attempt to calm the woman down, he did not come across as totally believable—McVeigh just didn't know how.

"You must remember, Dr. Blanchard," Karyn Hartman picked up, "that at the time of this occurrence
you were assigned here as part of my staff. If any
embarrassment were to arise because of this matter, it
would naturally have direct fallout on me. Therefore,
whatever small inconvenience you may have suffered
by having to come here was as a result of my request,
not a request by the police."

Well done, Savage thought, as the stung Dr. Althea
Blanchard blinked away her embarrassment, cleared
her throat self-consciously, and sat at the end of the
table. She opened a legal-size blue vinyl folder and
set several reports and some additional papers out before her.

Hartman nodded to Savage to begin.

"Dr. Blanchard," he said, "back on May twenty-
eighth, this year, you were the pathologist who performed the autopsy in New York ME's case no.
N052934."

"Yes." Blanchard nodded stiffly.

Savage could see that the strong-willed woman was
hunkered down into total defense. Understandable, he
thought. After all, her reputation could well be at
stake. He didn't know how it was going to be done,
but it was clear that it would not be an easy task to
pull Althea Blanchard away from her guns.

"In that matter," he went on, "you did a postmortem on a body once thought to be that of a Mr.
George Granger, but now·known to have been that
of a Mr. Elvin Welch. Do you recall that case?"

"I recall it clearly," she responded, squirming un-
easily in her chair. "However, Sergeant," she then emphasized with a sharp edge, "it is never a pathologist's
job to *identify* the bodies. That responsibility belongs
to the police and the police alone—"

"You're quite right on that point, Doctor," Savage
interrupted. He made sure to keep an even and
friendly tone, while at the same time cutting off what
he saw was going to be a lengthy impulsive mono-

logue. "However, now that the proper identity of that person has *finally* been established by the police, and that person's true health records made available to us, we find we must move on to other questions. And, therefore, in that regard, we sincerely do *need* your help."

Blanchard did not reply, but held a steady searching gaze in Savage's eyes. He seemed to sense a relaxing in her narrow shoulders.

Carefully expressing himself in respectful language to gain the proud woman's trust, Savage went on. "The purpose of this meeting is to now provide you with additional information, both medical and investigative, which might assist you in reevaluating certain aspects originally believed to be attributable as a cause of death of Elvin Welch."

"I'm aware of why you have me here, Sergeant." Though Blanchard's unpainted lips were still tight, the set to her jaw had visibly eased.

Savage continued. "As part of the evidentiary package we've prepared, you have been provided with a report by Dr. Axel Moonvie, a New York cardiologist. You have also been provided with an additional report prepared by Dr. Sheldon Lowenstein, a noted, and highly respected, cardiac pathologist."

"I have them both here," Blanchard replied, tapping the reports with the tip of her small index finger.

"Have you had a chance to review them yet, Dr. Blanchard?" he asked.

"I have."

"You'll note that both of those reports come to identical conclusions," Savage said. "But for now I refer you to Dr. Lowenstein's report."

Blanchard shuffled through the papers before her and came out with the document.

"Dr. Lowenstein has been contracted to conduct a far more detailed examination of tissue samples taken from Elvin Welch," Savage went on. "He was specifically asked to determine the presence of lymphocytes, the degree of necrosis in the heart muscle, and render an opinion as to myocarditis being a possible cause of death."

"Uh-huh," Blanchard uttered, adjusting her heavy glasses as she opened to the second page of Lowenstein's report. All in the room flipped their copies to the second page as well.

"I'm going to quote Dr. Lowenstein here," Savage said. " 'In my opinion, based on the material I have reviewed, I cannot conclude that this man died of myocarditis.' " Savage looked across at the woman and added, "A list of Dr. Lowenstein's education, credentials, and qualifications has been obtained and is available for your review."

"What say you about all this, Doctor?" John McVeigh suddenly called out, officious as ever.

"In their reports, both Drs. Lowenstein and Moonvie did agree with a finding of sinus tachycardium," Blanchard replied, her nostrils flaring. Savage saw that her shoulders were tensing again. She was headed back to full defensiveness.

"Yes, they did," Savage acknowledged positively. "But each points out the very high blood-alcohol reading as being the likely cause. Beyond that, however, much of their judgment—and, I'm suspecting, yours at the time—was based upon EKG reports which we now know to have been bogus." He turned to Lindstrom and said, "Jack."

Jack Lindstrom stood, walked to the end of the table, and handed Blanchard several enlarged photographs of those EKGs seized from Dr. Janus. After she perused them, he then handed her a copy of the "fracture identifications" report provided by Forensics. She read it stone-faced.

Savage went on. "Dr. Blanchard, our investigation has revealed that Dr. Janus has apparently prepared a false medical file for Mr. George Granger. It is our belief that certain medical diagnosis was part of Janus' scheme to defraud the police, the medical examiner's office, and the insurance company, and mask the death of Elvin Welch to appear natural."

Althea Blanchard sat back and exhaled hard. Pensive, she licked at dry lips as her stone face softened some. She glanced momentarily at George Albright. Albright offered a simple, reassuring nod.

"I think it is possible that I may have made the wrong decision as to nonspecific focal myocarditis," she finally said.

Thank you, Jesus! Savage thought.

"Would you mind telling us then just what it was that brought you to a diagnosis of myocarditis at the time of autopsy?" John McVeigh snapped, clearly speaking down to the woman.

Again she looked across at Albright; again he nodded.

"It was a diagnosis of desperation," she replied softly, looking momentarily into her lap.

"Please explain *that*," McVeigh said, again obnoxiously officious.

While flashing McVeigh a discreet icy look, Savage steamed inside. Of all the DAs they could've sent here today, he thought, why did they have to send freakin' Mr. Personality? The guy who wrote the book *How to Lose Friends and Blow Important Interviews*.

Once again Blanchard looked at Albright; once again the attorney nodded reassurance.

"I was having great difficulty in determining a cause of death," she answered softly. Then, after letting loose with a long, rueful sigh, added, "I could not find anything wrong."

"And *so*," McVeigh snarled coldly, ignoring Savage's steady glare, "what then did you do?"

"I deferred the cause pending further laboratory tests. But . . ."

"But what?" Savage said in a nonthreatening, smooth tone, wresting the questioning from the DA.

"But I was hounded by Dr. Janus and another man named John Holloway."

"To come up with a cause of death?" Savage asked.
"Yes."

"Do you recall how many times Mr. Holloway contacted you about this matter?"

"I believe three. In one instance he railed at my inability to locate a specific cause of death at the time of autopsy. In another, he wanted to know what the delay was in posting the final death certificate so that the body could be released to a funeral home."

"I see, Doctor," Savage went on soothingly. "Can you tell us what you might recall of the conversations you had with Dr. R. Charles Janus?"

"I explained to Dr. Janus my difficulty in locating an exact cause of death. I also explained to him the necessity for further laboratory analysis."

"And what was his response?"

"He wasn't very happy."

"Then what happened?"

"Sometime later that day, Dr. Janus called me back and told me that Mr. Granger had been complaining of left-sided chest pain for the past year. He also stated that Granger had been diagnosed one week earlier as having a viral infection."

"Did that information affect your opinion in any way?" McVeigh called out.

"I had to factor it in."

"Let me ask you this, Doctor," McVeigh pressed, his unnaturally white teeth gleaming from behind the newly found smug smile of a cat playing with a cornered mouse. "Would it be fair to say that your opinion was swayed by a need to assist Dr. Janus?"

"I—I don't understand," the woman muttered, shaking her head.

"To be more specific, Doctor, what I'm talking about here is you perhaps extending Janus—who was, after all, another physician—a far too wide degree of professional courtesy in this matter."

Althea Blanchard sat mute, her jaw clearly retightening. It occurred to Savage that she, like most physicians, had an intense aversion to—and an equally intense mistrust of—lawyers; could be she disliked them even more than she disliked cops.

This whole thing had boiled down to "shit happens," Savage decided. Clearly, he saw, there was never any intent on the part of Althea Blanchard to in any way thwart justice. If she had made mistakes in this case—as she surely had—they were simply mistakes of inexperience, not of a laissez-faire attitude toward her profession.

Again seeing the need to intervene in the questioning and cut off the surly McVeigh before his chesty style caused the woman to clam up completely, Savage broke in.

"Let *me* ask you this, Doctor," he said. "At that time, the day of the autopsy, did you believe that the dead man was a bona fide patient of Dr. Janus?"

"Yes," she responded with a sorrowful grimace. "I did believe that."

"And at that time," Savage gently continued, "did you trust Janus' stated diagnosis, evaluation, and opinion of the dead man's condition prior to death . . . and believe it to be thoroughly legitimate?"

"Yes. Yes, I did."

"Considering all the information available," Savage then asked, "could you have *ruled out* the possibility that Elvin Welch died from natural causes?"

"No, I could not," she eagerly responded, her tenseness relaxing further.

"Then I must ask you," Savage quickly followed up, "could you now rule out the possibility that Elvin Welch died as a result of criminal agency?"

"No," she said, hanging her head. "No, I can't."

"Based then on your statements, Doctor," the unwanted McVeigh suddenly broke in, "I must ask you to reconsider all the facts present in this case and render a *current* medical opinion as to mode of death." His smug ivory smile was gone; his expression was now one of firm demand.

Dr. Althea Blanchard turned to look first at George Albright, then at Dr. Karyn Hartman.

Dr. Hartman pushed her chair back, rose, and spoke. "Gentlemen. Our office will take the entire matter under consideration. We will thoroughly review everything and respond within twenty-four hours. Thank you all very much."

Before leaving the room, she glanced at Savage. He saw a thumbs-up in her eyes. Apparently so did Jack Lindstrom.

"Can we collar that bastard now?" he asked Savage under his breath.

"Patience, Jack. Patience."

Jack Lindstrom picked up the phone on his desk and dialed the Miami, Florida, area code and phone number. He was greeted with a recording: "You have reached the office of Dr. Herbert Koremvokis. Our office is closed and there is no one here to take your call. Our office will reopen again on Monday, August nineteenth, at nine a.m. If you were a patient of the doctor's and wish to collect your medical records, please contact us at that time. If you were a patient of the doctor's and wish for us to make a referral to another physician, please do the same. Your patience during this difficult time is gratefully acknowledged and appreciated."

Lindstrom scratched a big question mark beside the "Dr. Koremvokis" listing. It was the fourteenth and last telephone number on the list; he was striking out. Of the numbers dialed by Eric Von Deutsch during his two stays at the Delano back in May–June, all save one had now been accounted for.

Two of the numbers were attributed to Janus—one belonging to his medical office and the other to the apartment where he lived, the latter listed in the name of Guillermo Cabrera, Janus' roommate. One number went to the Ohio residence line of John Boyer Holloway, now disconnected. Another—which had been dialed at least a dozen times—belonged to Absolute Athletic Wear, the Ohio company owned by Granger and Holloway. The company now abandoned, that number too was disconnected.

The remainder of the telephone numbers belonged to a variety of real estate companies—one or two in Miami, but most in the Key West area—and the balance to restaurants around Miami Beach. No one who Lindstrom had been able to speak with at those probably benign numbers recognized either the name Granger or the name Von Deutsch. The medical doctor deal, however, intrigued him. The number had been dialed a total of six times during those stays at the Delano. It had to be followed up on.

TWENTY-FOUR

Carefully slipping the clutch to keep the beat-up Corolla from stalling until he finally got the damn thing rolling, Ramon Mendez pulled out of the parking lot of the Key West Holiday Inn and, in a cloud of blue smoke, headed north on U.S. 1. Though the Toyota surely was hurting, all it had to do was last him for just one more day—one more lousy hundred-and-ten-mile drive back to Miami—with only the briefest stop on Marathon Key to meet with Eric and collect his due.

Seeing the fuel gauge hovering near a quarter tank and the oil light flickering intermittently, Ramon decided it was no time to risk any form of auto malfunction. Nothing was to stand in the way of his making the meeting. He pulled into the very first service station he came to, topped off the fuel tank and crankcase, and, just to be sure, checked the spare tire—surprisingly, it was good. He got immediately back on the long, straight, scorching two-lane highway. Though it was only fifteen minutes after eleven, the Lower Keys temperature had already climbed into the mid-nineties—thank God the flaky air conditioner was still working. One more day, he thought again, just one more goddamned day.

Forty-five minutes later, at precisely noon—the agreed-upon meeting time—Mendez pulled into the crowded parking lot of Salty Sam's, located on a sandy spur at the southern tip of Marathon Key. He looked for but did not see Eric's tan Mercury anywhere about. Mendez parked the Toyota in one of the few spots still available in the side lot and walked around to the restaurant's main entrance. This, he knew, was going to be a great day—his life was about to take a quantum leap forward.

Mendez had carefully selected the popular restaurant for the meeting because it was wide-open and always busy for lunch. There would be lots of people around, just in case Eric had some idiotic notion of reneging on their fifty-thousand-dollar deal—or doing something even more stupid. Then, after they had settled up, Ramon would drive straight back to Miami Beach; his business with Eric would have been concluded. He smiled, thinking, *Concluded* for now at least.

The interior of Salty Sam's was the typical—if not totally predictable and tacky—American seafood joint. Rough-hewn board-and-batten walls, bleached a nautical silvery gray, were decorated with all the usual phony accoutrements. A ship's wheel here, a couple of splintered oars and paddles there, and cork-float-bordered seine nets draped everywhere, all in haphazard disarray. Used-up lobster pots hung randomly from the ceilings. The flooring was of a nailed wide plank that had been thickly shellacked.

Ramon asked to be seated at one of the high-back booths in a distant corner; privacy for this meeting was essential. He glanced at his watch—it was five after the hour and George Granger, aka Eric Von Deutsch, was still nowhere in sight. Odd, he thought, having expected him to already be there. Ramon ordered a coffee. The wait, he was certain, would be only a matter of a few minutes at most. Eric would appear, and he would have the money. Hell, what choice did he have?

At twelve thirty Von Deutsch still had not arrived. Mendez decided he would give the man until twelve forty-five. Maybe there had been long lines at the bank.

Two cups of coffee later, Mendez again checked his watch—it was ten after one. Much of the lunch crowd had subsided. He decided to wait until one thirty before giving up. Then, if the bastard didn't show, it would be off to Miami and a collect telephone call to the New York City Police Department.

At two fifteen, Mendez, jittery from five cups of coffee, paid his check and left the restaurant. That fuck, he thought, that lousy son of a bitch. Mr. George Granger will be sorry he screwed with me.

In barely controlled anger, Mendez quick-walked in the blazing sun back to his car. He started the motor, pulled from the lot, and immediately noticed that the air conditioner wasn't blowing. He reached over and fiddled with the controls—nothing. Damn it all, he thought, swiping budding beads of sweat from his brow, the goddamned AC was out of commission again. He kicked the dashboard—that didn't help either.

The recurring AC failure only worked to anger Mendez more. He floored the gas pedal; he wanted back to Miami ASAP. He couldn't wait to call New York City.

Despite the muggy warmth that enveloped the city like a steaming barber's towel, Savage was in a good, if not playful, mood when he left Manhattan South. He could sense the spring in his step. It was two fifteen when he steered the Crown Victoria onto FDR Drive and headed downtown at sixty miles an hour.

Any number of good things had happened that morning. It was clear that the confounding case involving Dr. Janus was finally coming together. The medical examiner's office, faced with overwhelming evidence that they had probably fucked up the original autopsy, was going to do the right thing—by tomorrow, hopefully. And, as soon as they did, he would then have all the pieces he needed to go place handcuffs on the wrists of Dr. R. Charles Janus.

The chief of detectives, Ray Wilson, had also done the right thing. By Wilson's decree, Savage, Lindstrom, DeGennaro, and Marcus were now off the hook for the weekend security detail up at Gracie Mansion and the Waldorf. Billy Lakis and his crew were now on that hook. Jack Lindstrom would not have to report sick in order to attend his daughter's big wedding on Saturday. Diane and Richie now had a steady green for their long-planned family reunion. And, thankfully, he'd be able to make the Hamptons gig with Maureen. All was good.

Savage pulled off the drive at the Brooklyn Bridge–Civic Center exit and, after ten minutes of searching, finally found a semilegal spot for his car beside Borough Hall Park. He tossed the department ID plate up on the dashboard, locked the car's doors and, as only a true New Yorker can, wiggled, darted, and slipped his way like Baryshnikov when crossing the hellacious bumper-to-bumper traffic of Lower Broadway.

At 233 Broadway, between Park Place and Barclay Street, he passed through the Romanesque entranceway into the sumptuous barrel-vaulted lobby of the Gothic Revival Woolworth Building. With walls done out in yellow marble and a profusion of neo-Gothic details, and an unbelievable mosaic ceiling in the Byzantine style, the lobby evoked an almost religious sense. One almost expected to hear Gregorian chants.

The structure itself, sheathed in a cream-colored terra-cotta, was Savage's third-favorite New York City building. It came in just behind the Art Deco Chrysler, and the Beaux Arts Grand Central terminal. At almost eight hundred feet, it was once the tallest structure in the world, and its fifty-seven floors were actually equivalent to a seventy-nine-story building when one considered its generous story heights that ranged between eleven and twenty feet each.

Savage rode a speedy burl-lined elevator to the twenty-eighth floor, walked quickly to the end of the south corridor, and let himself into the law offices of Louis Armbruster.

No surprise, he was greeted there by Ms. Hilda Kranick, the familiar voice on the phone. Hilda turned out to be a white-haired lady with a saintly face. How in hell did she ever get involved in working for this shyster bastard? he thought.

"Hello, Hilda," he said brightly, holding out his hand. "Though we've often talked, allow me to now introduce myself. I'm Detective Sergeant Thornton Savage."

Though somewhat startled, Ms. Kranick gingerly reached out her hand as well. He could see the gears turning inside her head.

"I'm here to speak with Louis," he said jovially, knowing what was coming.

"Well . . . uh . . . I don't believe uh . . . Mr. Armbruster . . . uh . . . is here right now." The poor woman finally managed to force out the entire ill-delivered lie.

"That's quite all right, my dear," Savage responded, moving right past the woman. "I'll just wait for good old Louis right there in his office. He won't mind." Without giving her a chance to respond, he let himself directly into Armbruster's private inner sanctum. The hateful lawyer was there, seated beneath framed diplomas and behind a mammoth black-walnut desk, speaking—no doubt lies—into a Sony tape recorder.

"Louis," Savage said loudly, acting happily surprised. "You're here. How nice."

Trailed closely by a flustered Hilda Kranick, he walked to a crimson leather wing chair that faced Armbruster's desk and plunked down heavily.

"What the hell are *you* doing here?" the lawyer blurted. After quickly switching off the tape recorder, he glared and added, "How dare you come busting into my office like this. Just who the hell do you think you are?"

"We have some things to talk about, Louis," Savage said, locking the man tightly in his best no-nonsense gaze. Then, forcing an almost maniacal grin, he added unequivocally and ominously, "So why don't we just get right down to it."

"You bastard." Armbruster seethed, his normally pale face aglow in a bright red. He looked up at his

frazzled secretary, who stood by helplessly. "It's all right, Hilda. You can step out."

As soon as the door closed behind the white-haired woman, Savage, pumped up with a perverse glee, started in. "So, tell me, Louis, how's the family?"

"You don't give a fuck how my family is," the lawyer shot back.

"And how is your, shall we say . . . *friend*?" Savage went smoothly on, thinking how terrific it felt to trifle with the chesty and arrogant lawyer who'd become a multimillionaire by sadistically grinding people into bits.

"My *friend*?" the lawyer said, scowling in feigned ignorance.

"That extremely good-looking fellow you were shopping with at that *very* interesting store nine days ago. Oh, what *was* that guy's name?" Savage murmured. He placed an index finger to his temple and feigned failed recall.

"I don't know what you're talking about, Savage."

Savage looked up with a satisfied grin. *"Garth,"* he said, positively. "Oh, he is a very handsome fellow. I can see why you two would be such good friends. I'm sure you have a great deal in common."

Fuming, Armbruster pressed an attack. "Just like the one-dimensional, stooge-fucking cop that you are, you've been trying to reach me now for over a week for reasons which escape me."

"And just like the third-rate shyster hump that you are, you've been avoiding me, Louis—like the freakin' plague. I've gotta tell ya, it's been like trying to swat a darting cockroach with a chopstick. Why, I think your behavior has been just plain rude. Old pals like us, who share a common aim in the world of criminal justice, should try to be more collegial. Don't you agree?"

"Why do I have the utmost sense that you're just here to twist my nuts until I scream, and then ultimately go out and embarrass me?"

"Louis," Savage replied with no pretense, "you are

absolutely correct that I am here to twist your nuts. However, there's no reason in the world why I would ever *want* to embarrass you."

"Unless, of course, I leave you no alternative."

"I've always said you were very quick on the up-take, Louis."

"What is it that you want?" the lawyer asked, deflated.

"I intend to put a buddy of yours, Dr. R. Charles Janus—and two of his scumbag confederates—in irons for a long, long time."

"Should I deny knowing, or even having any knowledge of, R. Charles Janus?" the pinch-faced Armbruster asked, with his tongue set firmly in cheek.

"No," Savage responded, playing right along. "I would advise against that, Louis."

"I see. And, just out of curiosity, why would you be wanting to put Dr. R. Charles Janus in irons?"

"Murder One."

Armbruster's face cramped up in disbelief. "*Murder . . . One?* Jesus Christ, what the hell are you talking about?"

"Now here's the ground rules, Louis," Savage said, leaning forward in his chair and again locking the man into his tight gaze. "We're not in a courtroom, so today I'm the one who gets to ask the questions. Are we square on that?"

The lawyer, seething, nodded. "I know I can't help you," he said. "True, I do happen to know Janus, but only socially. If, in fact, he's truly involved in a murder, that's entirely beyond my knowledge." Armbruster was a skank of the lowest order, but Savage believed the man's last sentence to be the truth.

"Here's the deal, Louis. What I need from you is information about one of his other playmates, a play-mate that we believe could be involved in this homicide along with Janus."

"What's the name?" Armbruster murmured tartly.

"John Boy."

The lawyer sat mute, eyes fixed, exhibiting a pretty damn good poker face. "Don't know anybody by that name," he replied finally.

"So happens that I know differently, Louis," Savage scolded. He jabbed a pointed index finger in the courthouse creep's direction. "So let's get back on track, shall we? Tell me about John Boy."

Armbruster sat back in his creamy-soft high-back leather throne and exhaled hard. "He's been a friend of Janus' for years. I really don't know the guy that well. Name's John Holloway. Janus sometimes referred to him as 'John Boy.' Don't know why, but at other times he would jokingly refer to him as 'the Visible Man.'"

Savage immediately recalled the educational science toy of that name that was out when he was in high school. The Visible Man was a model of a human male complete with skin, skeleton, vital organs, major veins and arteries, eyes, brain. The skin was made of see-through plastic so that when it was put together you could see the placement of all body parts. The model could be taken apart and reassembled as often as desired. It was a great tool for the study of anatomy.

"I can understand 'John Boy,'" Savage said, "but what did he mean by calling him the Visible Man?"

"Asked him once. He laughed lewdly and said that when they got down to hot business, he could see right through the son of a bitch. It definitely had some sexual connotation for him."

"Very good, Louis," Savage declared, smiling. "Now that was easy, wasn't it?"

"That all you want?"

"Oh, no," Savage replied. "Strap yourself in, buddy. We've got a long way to go."

George Granger made sure to stay close—but not too close. Traveling from key to key along the Overseas Highway, he tried to maintain a distance of a least several thousand feet between his freshly acquired green Lincoln Town Car and the faded red Toyota up ahead.

He had waited for Ramon to pull in and park at Salty Sam's. Once Ramon had gone inside the restaurant, it had taken him only seconds to slightly loosen the air valve on the Toyota's left rear tire. It took only seconds more to pop the gimmicked trunk and totally deflate the spare. No one had seen him though the parking lot was choked to capacity. Granger knew it was now only a matter of time before the left rear tire of Ramon's shit car became totally flat and he would have no choice but to pull over. Then . . .

Driving at speeds that sometimes reached well over the limit, the two cars passed quickly through Islamorada, then Tavernier and busy Key Largo. It was clear that Ramon was in a great hurry.

Just above Key Largo, Ramon steered his car onto the twenty-two-mile stretch of U.S. 1 that led to the Florida mainland. Still maintaining his discreet distance, Granger followed. Virtually shoulderless for its entire length, the string-line-straight two-lane road was tightly edged on the one side by mangrove-lined backwaters and estuaries of Everglades National Park and on the other by Barnes Sound. Those heading south to party and vacation in the Keys move along here at whatever speed the traffic will bear. Those heading north to home, their vacations and parties behind them, move on the button as well. As a result, this stretch was often the scene of terrible, fatal head-on collisions. George Granger knew there would soon be life-taking in a somewhat different format.

Finally, at around mile marker 100, the brake lights of the red Toyota came on. The junk car pulled over as far right as was possible and came to a complete stop. As George Granger roared past in the big dark Lincoln, he saw a frustrated Ramon climbing out.

Granger drove until the Toyota was no longer visible in his rearview mirror. There, he stopped, U-turned, and headed back. As soon as the Toyota and Ramon were once again in his sight, he pulled the Lincoln to the roadside, waited and watched.

This just wasn't possible, Ramon thought, fighting back an all-consuming rage. He'd actually taken the time to check that spare tire only a few hours ago. It was totally inflated then. A tire can't go flat in the trunk of a car just like that. *Jesus,* he thought, it has to be at least three or four miles back to any kind of civilization where I can get this damn thing fixed.

He jerked the flat spare from the Toyota's trunk, slammed the deck lid down as hard as he could, and rolled the tire across the highway. Surely, some southbound asshole will stop and give me a lift to the nearest station, he thought. They'll see my car jacked up, see me rolling this damn flat tire, and feel sorry for me. And once I get the tire fixed, somebody else will give me a ride back up here. Stay in control, Ramon reminded himself, don't get nuts, for this too shall pass. A disturbing thought then suddenly crossed his mind—he would keep a keen eye out for the approach of a tan Mercury Marquis.

Several things soon became apparent, however. Of the dozen or so cars that had already passed him, not one had slowed to offer a ride. Also, he had come to realize the difficulty in rolling an uninflated tire, especially along a lumpy grass surface in ninety-plus degree heat. He stopped and rested for what seemed like the hundredth time in the last five minutes, and again wiped away the beads of sweat that cascaded down from his burning brow.

Ramon blinked away the glare of the baking afternoon sun. A great blue heron swooped past and landed in the saw grass not more than fifty feet away. So graceful, he thought.

Then came the sound of another approaching car. Ramon looked up the highway to see that it was a big green Lincoln and, like every car he'd seen on this road, was moving at high speed. As the car grew closer, he held out his thumb. Maybe he'd get lucky this time.

The Lincoln did not appear to be slowing. In fact, at a point about a hundred feet from where he stood, the big car suddenly accelerated. At a point less than fifty feet away, it suddenly swerved off the ribbon of highway and headed directly for him.

Ramon froze. There was no place to go, and no time left to get there. At the very last instant before impact, he saw the glaring wide eyes and demented grin of the Lincoln's driver. *Oh, my God!*

Every bone in Ramon's body was fractured. Catapulted and flying as if in slow motion, through the warm air, he wondered why he felt not one scintilla of pain. In his very last thought, he concluded that his head must have been disconnected from the rest of him. Then the lights went out. His mangled body landed at the edge of the saw grass, his limbs twisted into unnatural angles like those of a rag doll tossed from a speeding car's window.

The big green Lincoln steered back onto the ribbon of highway and, moving at just below the speed limit, continued southbound.

TWENTY-FIVE

Savage's impromptu confrontation with Louis Armbruster the day before may have paid off big time. Not only did Savage now know that Janus' handsome friend and sometime fellow traveler to the Meat Hook, "John Boy," and the beneficiary of George Granger's life insurance policy, John Boyer Holloway—as suspected—were one and the same person, he had also uncovered information that Holloway had left the country several weeks ago, supposedly "for good." Because of this new information another meeting with Ray Wilson, the chief of detectives, was requested and held in Pete Pezzano's office at Manhattan South.

"Did your source know where Holloway was headed?" Chief Wilson asked. "What country he was supposedly going to?"

"He'd heard that Holloway was going initially to Amsterdam, but didn't intend to stay there very long—a week, possibly two on the outside. I pressed him on that, Chief, and he denied knowing where Holloway intended to next go. But he turned me on to someone who very well *might* have that information." Savage paused, shot direct eye contact at each man, then added, "Hold on to your hats—the name he gave me was Harley Hopkins."

"*The* Harley Hopkins?" Wilson said, staring wide-eyed at Savage. "Are we talking about the reclusive star maker? The Broadway impresario?"

"That's who we're talkin' about," Savage affirmed.

"That fat ugly bastard's gay?" Wilson said, cramping up his face in mild disbelief. "Not that anybody would ever say that he was heavy in the loafers, but . . ."

"Apparently he's very gay," Savage replied. "Publicly, he's definitely not out of the closet, but he is known within a super-discreet inner circle to which my source belongs. According to him, Hopkins is a hermitic screamer who has a thing for extremely handsome younger men—preferably wannabe actors. He gets his way with them by promising to land them big parts."

"What is Hopkins' way?" Wilson asked, frowning as if he really didn't want to know.

"He likes to be the top. My source also told me that he likes Holloway because Holloway enjoys being the bottom."

"Jesus. A variation on the old Hollywood casting couch, eh?" Pezzano observed.

"That's pretty heavy information," Wilson said, stroking his chin. "What did you have to promise your source to get them to give that one up?"

"My source and I go way back," Savage related. "The man absolutely hates me, maybe as much as I hate him. He's a real nasty bastard with a very high profile within his profession. But not long ago, I tripped over some rather interesting information about him."

"And he wants your silence," Pezzano observed.

"I flat out told him that I needed a name," Savage said. "Somebody who could place Holloway for me beyond Amsterdam."

"Or else the silence he wanted *might* just be compromised?" Wilson guessed, straight-faced.

"Come now, Chief," Savage replied coyly. "That would be extortion."

"He hates you, yet he trusted you?" Pezzano stated, looking askance.

Savage shrugged. "He hates me, but . . ."

"But he knows you're a stand-up guy," Wilson said unequivocally. "That's why."

Savage shrugged again. "Anyway, he revealed that there have been whispers within that inner circle that on the night before he left the country, our 'exceedingly handsome' John Boy—now, aka the Visible Man—spent the entire evening with Mr. Hopkins up in Hopkins' fortresslike apartment off Central Park West."

"Next step is to talk to Hopkins, then," Pezzano said casually.

"That's not going to be as easy as it sounds," Savage replied. "It might not even be possible, for that matter. According to my source, nobody gets up to the guy's twenty-third-floor fortress unless he rings them in. My source claims that he's only ever been there one time himself. Hopkins is tougher to get with than Howard Hughes was, and supposedly he can smell a cop a mile away."

"Why's that?" Wilson posed.

"Because he's so goddamned paranoid," Savage responded. "I'm told that he's so afraid of being outed, he's got all sorts of security cameras in the building's lobby to ensure that he can see exactly who it is the doorman is ringing his apartment about."

"And if he doesn't like what he sees?" Wilson asked.

"He won't respond to the doorman's call," Savage replied with a shrug. "A couple of crusty-looking detectives is just not gonna cut it."

"So you damn well better be a young, good-looking wannabe movie star who wishes to see him," Pezzano said. "If not, he just won't answer the buzzer; is that it?"

Savage nodded.

Eddie Brodigan rapped on the office door, stuck his head in, and interrupted. "Excuse me. Sergeant Savage, pick up on two-three, please. It's a Dr. Karyn Hartman from the medical examiner's office."

Savage picked up the receiver. "This is Savage."

"Dr. Hartman here, Sergeant," the chief pathologist said directly, then, without any fanfare, got right to the point. "We are amending our findings in the matter of Elvin Welch. Cause of death will now be 'Unknown, pending police investigation.' All necessary documentation to that effect is being prepared as we speak. As soon as it is ready, I will have copies couriered over to your office. Good luck."

"What's the word?" Pezzano inquired as Savage hung up.

"It's a go," Savage replied, smiling. He unhooked his Nokia from his belt and quickly dialed. When Diane DeGennaro answered, he gave her the green light to present warrant requests to a judge.

"Where to from here?" Pezzano asked, as Savage closed his cell phone.

"In anticipation of this, this morning I took the liberty of sending Diane DeGennaro downtown to get all the paperwork prepared for eavesdropping warrants on Janus' phones," Savage replied. "Meanwhile I have Richie Marcus already over in Janus' building setting up the wire. As soon as the judge issues the warrant—which I'm now certain he will—all Marcus has to do is throw the switch. Then, I'm going to head over and pay the good doctor a visit."

"Collar time?" Wilson asked.

"I'm not sure," Savage replied. "If he caves in, and wants to give up the whole game, absolutely. But if he wants to play this thing out to the very end, as I suspect he will, I'll hold off."

"Why hold off on the arrest?" Wilson asked, smirking. "Hell, we've certainly got reasonable cause here."

"In order for the district attorney to indict and mount a strong prosecution, we must show prima facie evidence," Savage respectfully replied.

"It's your call, Thorn," Wilson advised, clearly not in total agreement.

"I just think we need to make absolutely certain that all future moves on our part are well thought out before we act," Savage replied. "There have already been enough missteps in this case. I want to avoid doing anything that would give Janus et al. any further advantage whatsoever come trial. A few more days or hours of freedom for that creep doctor are not going to make a damn bit of difference."

"What will your threshold be?" Wilson queried.

"When we can show beyond any doubt that George Granger is still alive—preferably when we have the son of a bitch in a holding cell someplace."

"He checked into a Miami hotel some twelve hours after he was pronounced dead," Wilson said sarcastically. "Is that not prima facie?"

"Yes, Chief, I think maybe it is. But without Granger and Holloway physically in our custody, will we be able to reach 'beyond a reasonable doubt'?"

"All right," Wilson said, half convinced. "Once Marcus has the wire in place, and you find that Janus wants to play hardball, then what?"

"If I really rattle his freakin' cage, and then leave without collaring him, maybe he'll pick up his phone and make a few calls. It sure wouldn't hurt to have conversations between the Three Amigos recorded."

"Do you really think Janus would be stupid enough to use his phones at this point?" Wilson asked.

"No, I don't believe he's stupid enough, Chief," Savage replied surely. "So all we can hope for with the wire is that he's arrogant enough."

The lieutenant and chief both nodded.

"Getting back to the Harley Hopkins question," Wilson said, drumming his fingers on Pezzano's desktop blotter. "If you feel we've actually gotta talk to this guy to get more on Holloway's location, have you got a plan as to how we can get inside to even talk to him?"

"Yes, sir," Savage replied, "I do."

Disappointed, Jack Lindstrom dropped the telephone's receiver into its cradle on his desk. He had just officially struck out with all the airlines that serviced Miami or Fort Lauderdale from any of the three

New York metropolitan-area airports. On the date that Elvin Welch had died in Janus' office, no person by the name of George Granger *or* Eric Von Deutsch had been booked on any flights to Miami from New York City. He felt stymied, upset also that he would have to wait until Monday morning to again contact the office of Dr. Koremvokis, the final lead on the list of Von Deutsch phone calls made from the Delano. Surely there was something there; of that he was certain.

Lindstrom walked to coffee central on the other side of the squad room, poured himself a half cup of black, and considered one of the two donuts still left in the Dunkin's box. He didn't cave to them. Then, suddenly struck with an idea, he returned quickly to his desk. He picked up his phone and dialed the Delano Hotel in Miami. The call was answered on the first ring.

"Registration."

"Daphne Dempsey?" Lindstrom said, making it a question. Although he had recognized the woman's Bronx-derived accent, he did not want to appear presumptuous.

"This is Ms. Dempsey. How may I help you?"

"This is Detective Jack Lindstrom from the NYPD again. How are you this afternoon?"

"Just fine, Detective," the woman replied, a lilt in her voice. "Do you prefer the name Jack?" she asked. "I ask because you've signed off on all your written communications to me as Detective *John* Lindstrom."

"Jack suits me fine."

"Then Jack it will be. How can I be of service?"

"First I want to thank you for getting all that documentation up to us as quickly as you did. We truly do appreciate that."

"Not a problem," Ms. Dempsey responded. "I have a brother-in-law that's a policeman attached to a precinct in the South Bronx—a really nice guy. Maybe you know him?" she went on. "His name is Corcoran, Bill Corcoran."

"Gee, I'm sorry," Lindstrom groaned sadly. "Afraid the name isn't familiar . . ."

"Well, I just thought . . ."

Funny, he mused, how although there were now almost forty thousand people in The Job—sometimes referred to as the third-largest standing army in the world—many civilians still seemed to think that everybody in the department knew everybody else.

"Is there anything more that we can do for you, Detective?" Ms. Dempsey asked.

"Matter of fact, yes. Have you a few minutes to spare?"

"I'll make a few," she said solidly. Like most other detectives, Lindstrom loved it when he got hold of an eager supporter of the investigative function.

"You faxed us copies of registration cards in the name of Eric Von Deutsch," he began. "Beyond that, you have also provided us with all the telephone numbers which this guy Von Deutsch dialed from his room during his two stays there."

"That's right," Daphne said, great willingness riding in her voice. "Is there something else you need?"

"Our Telephone Security ran those numbers and provided me with the identity of the owners of those listings which he dialed. Most of those numbers belonged to restaurants, some others to real estate businesses—some of which were in Miami, most in Key West—and a couple of car rental agencies."

"Uh-huh, I see."

"Now, I have already contacted and talked with people at most of those places," Lindstrom advised. "Unfortunately, not one person recognized the name Eric Von Deutsch or George Granger. But I have been unable to get through to the one listing which I'm most interested in."

"That is?"

"I've got one Miami Beach listing here that is registered to an M.D.," Lindstrom went on. "And I recall that in our first conversation, you said you thought

Von Deutsch appeared to have had some plastic surgery."

"That's right," Daphne responded. "For at least several days during his second stay with us, I clearly recall him wearing some small bandages in several different places on his face. Didn't think much of it at the time. We see a lot of that sort of thing down here, Detective. Lots of vanity in Miami Beach."

"Well, it occurs that this medical doctor's listing might belong to the plastic surgeon who actually performed that surgery on Von Deutsch. In which event we definitely need to talk to him. However, as of yet I've not been able to get an answer at that particular number, nor do I know whether or not this physician is, in fact, a plastic surgeon."

"What's the doctor's name?" Daphne said. "I'll look him up in the Yellow Pages."

"Koremvokis," Lindstrom said. "That's K-O-R-E-M-V-O-K-I-S."

The phone fell silent for a long moment before Daphne Dempsey's voice, shaken and cracking, replied, "Would that be a Dr. *Herbert* Koremvokis?"

"That's correct."

TWENTY-SIX

As Pete Pezzano and Chief Wilson continued to debate the pros and cons of immediately making the Janus arrest, Thorn Savage excused himself from the meeting and strode out through the squad room to speak to Eddie Brodigan. He caught the familiar scent of the wheelman's lunch long before he saw it.

"Good grief," he said playfully to Brodigan. The man was leaning over his desk, mouth agape, about to take a first bite into a Carl's Deli Italian Special hero he had just unwrapped. "Got enough sandwich there, for God's sake?"

"The Lord hath sayeth that 'man does not live by bread alone,'" Brodigan replied, grinning impishly. "Therefore, I had Carl install a number of different ingredients upon his wonderful loaf."

"They are?"

"Salami, cappacola, pepperoni, ham, provolone, lettuce, tomato, cherry peppers, oil and vinegar, and a sprinkle of oregano."

"You figure you needed the oregano?" Savage asked sarcastically.

"Oh, yeah!" Brodigan replied. "Hey, you gotta have *something* for flavor." The impish grin was still there, only wider.

"Well, I'm glad to see you take the Lord at his word," Savage said. His thoughts flashed to the small package of Carl's Deli pepperoni at home in his refrigerator. He wondered if Ray would ever get a chance to finish it.

"What is it that your humble servant can provide

for you at this time, sir?" Brodigan asked, carefully setting the humongous oil-dripping sandwich back down onto the wax paper he was using as a place mat.

"Need you to do me a favor."

"Anything for you, my liege," Brodigan said.

"Take a run downstairs to the Thirteenth Precinct Roll Call office for me," Savage began. "Get the work schedule for one of their cops, a police officer named Henderson—don't know his first name. If there's any question *which* Henderson, should they have more than one, tell them he's one of the recent batch of rookies who's already been dubbed 'Hollywood' Henderson. I'm going to want him assigned up here for a couple of days."

"Ten-four," Brodigan replied. The man pushed his chair back from the desk, stood, and moved toward the squad room door. "By the way, Sarge," he said, turning back with that Irish gleam in his eyes, "you know what Pavlov said. 'Eat, drink, and be merry, for tomorrow you may *diet*.' "

"Pavlov?" Savage muttered quizzically, skewing his face into a question mark. "I'm sorry, Ed, but that name just doesn't ring a bell."

As a tickled Brodigan laughed cheerily and let himself from the room, the telephone on the wheel desk rang. Savage picked it up. It was Diane DeGennaro on the line.

"I'm calling you from the front steps of 100 Centre Street," she said. "I have the eavesdropping warrant for Janus' office telephones in hand."

"Run into any problems?"

"Not really. Once Judge Cromarty compared the photographs of Welch and Granger, he signed off on it immediately."

"What about the residence line?" Savage asked.

"Cromarty wouldn't sit still for it."

"Because that phone is in the name of one Guillermo Cabrera?"

"Precisely," Diane replied, then asked, "Where do you want me to go from here?"

"Still got the photos?"

"Uh-huh."

"Get right over to Janus' office," he said. "Janus has an assistant-slash-roommate-slash-boyfriend by the name of Guillermo Cabrera. I want you to tail him in the event he leaves. Stay with him, see where he goes, encounter him even, but most importantly, don't let him return to the office, not until I'm finished interviewing Janus himself. I'm not absolutely sure yet that this guy Cabrera is without complicity in this whole damn thing. We'll know when he views the photos."

"All right," Diane replied. "But I don't know what this guy Cabrera looks like."

"Stick your head in the office on some pretext," Savage said. "Take another tenant's name off the building directory and ask directions. Cabrera's gonna be the small Hispanic guy seated at the receptionist's desk. He wears really weird red horn-rimmed glasses."

"Ten-four."

Savage hung up and immediately dialed Richie Marcus' cell phone.

"Marcus here," came the gruff response.

"It's a go, Rich," Savage said. "We all set?"

"Does a bear have coitus in the woods?"

"Unh," Savage replied plainly, probably not giving Marcus the response he sought. "Oh, and by the way, as we suspected, it was ixnay on the residence line."

"Ten-four, boss. But we're good to go here, all of his office lines are covered, and my pickups are voice activated. He gets on a phone, we'll have every word."

Savage left the wheel desk and returned to Pete Pezzano's office.

"We've got the warrants," he advised the chief and his lieutenant. "And the wire is completely in place at Janus' office. I'm going to head right over there now."

At that moment Jack Lindstrom rapped on the doorjamb and let himself in.

"This thing is really snowballing," Lindstrom began. "It seems that the Miami Beach plastic surgeon that

George Granger was in regular contact with is now dead. He got stabbed to death ten days ago in a stadium men's room during a Florida Marlins baseball game. No arrests yet, and no leads."

"Coincidence?" Pete Pezzano mumbled, shrugging his ample shoulders. His suggestion was greeted with three "What, are you kidding?" blank stares from the others. He quickly conceded.

"How'd you find that out?" Chief Wilson asked.

"Just got off the phone with Daphne Dempsey down at the Delano Hotel. She knew the name right away; told me it's a big thing. Been all over the local papers and the tube down there since it happened. She's going to get hold of some clippings and fax them up. I'm also already in contact with the Miami police to get more information."

"As soon as you're finished with your interview of Janus," Chief Wilson said, staring directly at Savage, "I want you to select one of your team to get home and pack a bag. They'll be on the early-morning flight to Miami with that insurance investigator, Escalante. We gotta stop this prick."

"Hey, boss," Savage responded in disbelief. "Tomorrow is Friday."

"That's the rumor," Wilson replied snidely. "So what?"

"But you already guaranteed those people the weekend off. Remember . . . the family reunion deal for Marcus and DeGennaro on Saturday."

"And my daughter's getting married on Saturday," Jack Lindstrom piped up. "No disrespect, Chief, but there's just no way I'm not gonna be there. I'll go on sick report if I have to."

"I've already once taken your entire team off the hook for this weekend," Wilson reminded, looking back at Savage with his impenetrable no-nonsense glare. "It ain't gonna happen twice."

"But, boss—" Savage began.

"Somebody's going," Wilson interrupted firmly. "And it's imperative that it be someone thoroughly familiar with all the aspects of this goddamned crazy case. Therefore, it will either be Lindstrom, Marcus, DeGennaro . . . or *you*. It's your call, Thornton."

Dr. R. Charles Janus hung up the phone, leaned back in his plush leather office chair, and smiled. He had just gotten off the line with Consolidated Auto Leasing and arranged an accelerated plan to catch up on his car payments. Thank God Mother Holloway's promised ninety-five hundred had finally arrived in Guillermo's account. Would wonders never cease?

Under the new arrangement with Consolidated, he had agreed to overnight them five thousand in a cashier's check to stop a repossession order. After that, his monthly payments would be upped from seven hundred fifty to one thousand until the lease termination next December. He would be paying some vig, no question, but he did not want to lose the damn Jag. Hell, he needed transportation. Surely by December, he would have gotten the balance of his share from Holloway and he could order himself a new Jag.

With this first installment of ninety-five hundred now safely in hand, he thought, there was no time like the present to begin pushing Hazel Holloway for more. He reached for the phone and dialed her new number out in Las Vegas. It rang six times before being picked up by an answering machine. He hung up; he would leave no message. He would call back later.

Janus had already seen his last patient of the day, and Guillermo had left the office, off to his bank on Sixth Avenue to get the cashier's check made out for Consolidated. The physician looked up at the old Seth Thomas on his wall; it was ten minutes to two. With no further business, he decided it was time to call it a day. He stood, pulled off his lab coat, and slipped quickly into his summer-weight suit jacket.

As he arranged his desk and prepared to leave, thoughts of visiting the Meat Hook that night suddenly swirled temptingly in his head. He sensed an aching in his loins and felt that strange, compelling urgency he hadn't felt in a while. That was understandable, he decided—it had certainly been a long time since he'd gone off and partied hearty. He'd go home, later this afternoon take a nice nap, then tonight, see.

The phone rang. His first thought was to not answer the damn thing, but he was then struck with the thought that it might be Guillermo. Maybe there had been some sort of a problem over at the bank. Or perhaps it was Hazel Holloway. He stepped back to his desk and picked up the receiver. He was greeted by a familiar voice.

"Dr. Janus?"

The connection was not very good. It was scratchy and unclear as if coming in from great distance, but the voice was undeniable. "Well, well, the Visible Man," Janus said. "Or perhaps I should rename you the *In*visible Man. Where are you?" He was conscious not to use John Boy's name.

"Never mind that. I just thought you'd be happy to hear from me."

"Well, it's about fucking time!" Janus blurted, allowing his bottled-up anger to partially erupt. "Where the hell have you been? I've got a bone to pick with—"

"Never mind that, Doctor," the voice interrupted. "I know you've been somewhat concerned as to whether or not I was going to *pay my bill,* as it were. This is just a courtesy call to assure you that I have every intention of doing just that. But I must have a little bit more time. I do hope that you can be a tad more patient."

"Just how the hell much more patient do you think I can be?" Janus pressed.

"Well, I've just gotten some disturbing news from a mutual acquaintance. So happens he's also the fellow who referred me to you some years ago. He informs me that you may be having some problems there."

"Problems? What kind of problems?"

"*Legal* problems."

"Oh, that's bullshit," Janus replied. "It's all a big nothing."

"Are you certain, Doctor?" the voice pressed, clearly needing reassurance.

"Of course I'm certain, goddammit," Janus snapped. "If I really had terrible *legal* problems, the goddamned sky would have already fallen in on me—and you—a long time ago."

"Well, maybe it's going to fall in on you soon?"

"It's not going to happen."

"Tell me, then, what's all this noise I'm hearing about search warrants at your office? And about homicide detectives out looking for Mr. George Granger—who we all happen to know is long dead?"

"It's nothing, goddammit! Now, about your *bill*—"

"I had been making plans to visit New York City sometime very soon," Holloway said. "At that time, I intended to meet with you to straighten out all of our affairs in person. But I must tell you, Doctor, these latest revelations are giving me great cause for pause. Therefore, I am going to have to rethink all of my earlier plans."

Janus lost it. "I want my fucking money, Hollo—" He bit the name off in midstatement.

"I don't want to talk on this line anymore," the voice interrupted, "and I don't believe that you should either. I'll notify our mutual friend not to ever contact you there again. I think any further discussions should take place at a different time . . . and definitely on a different line."

"When?"

"Later."

"When later, dammit?" Janus snarled. "Don't go jerking me around like your goddamned mother did."

"Look, it's already eight o'clock here. What is it there, like around the middle of the afternoon?"

"It's two."

"I'll contact you at your apartment in exactly one hour and thirty minutes." The caller hung up.

Downstairs in the basement of Janus' office building, amongst the myriad pipes, tubing, ducting, and the spaghetti bowl of wiring, the stocky man in the telephone repair uniform removed the tiny earpiece from his ear and flipped a fresh Winston between his smiling lips.

"The Visible Man," he muttered with a chuckle. He flicked his lighter and took a deep first drag.

"Mr. Hollo. *Mr. Hollo* my ass."

TWENTY-SEVEN

It took the supremely competent Winona Escalante merely twenty-five minutes to carve most of tomorrow's travel arrangements in stone. The plan was simple: At seven thirty in the morning, Savage would stop at the Grand Hyatt and pick her up. From there, the two would drive to LaGuardia, grab breakfast, and catch the ten o'clock flight to Miami International. Jack Lindstrom had even gone to the trouble of contacting Daphne Dempsey at the Delano Hotel and arranging short-notice accommodations for them there at, of course, a greatly reduced rate.

Initially, at least, all of their expenses, including air transportation, car rental, lodging, food, fuel, would be covered by Escalante's corporate American Express and Visa and charged back to Aurora Occidental. The city could decide down the road if it wanted to reimburse Occidental for Savage's costs. Apparently Occidental didn't much care whether it did or not. That was good, Savage figured, because "the city" was as tight as a clam's ass . . . and that was watertight. As sure as hell, they would conveniently forget the debt—like a ne'er-do-well deadbeat brother-in-law.

When Savage had gathered up his folder of evidence and was preparing to leave Manhattan South for his planned confrontation with Dr. Janus, Winona Escalante was still busy finalizing a car rental deal with Budget.

"Would you want a Mustang convertible waiting for us?" she asked, cupping her palm over the phone's mouthpiece. "Or would you rather I get us a Lincoln Navigator?"

"I could just see the city springing for a convertible or a Lincoln if they were paying the tab," Savage remarked. Chuckling sarcastically, he added, "If we had to go on a city-sponsored trip, we'd be lucky to manage a Geo . . . or a two-place skateboard."

"We're going to eat good too," she replied with a sly grin and wink.

This trip might not be so bad after all, he thought, signing himself out in the log. As he opened the office door to leave, he turned and said, "Get the convertible."

Savage was happy to see that the Fourteenth Street traffic wasn't too bad, as he piloted the Crown Victoria westbound behind the usual cluster of city buses, garment trucks, and yellow taxicabs; he almost made every other light. He was going to Florida tomorrow morning with Winona Escalante, not normally something he would consider to be a bad thing. Problem was, because of that he would not be going to the Hamptons tomorrow afternoon with Maureen Gallo. Timing, his father had once told him, was "everything in life."

Stopping for the light at Seventh Avenue, Savage knew he should be applying all of his faculties to the imminent confrontation with the shrewd Janus. That was his usual modus operandi whenever getting right down to the nitty-gritty with an all-but-collared suspect. He should be planning his line of questioning, organizing his thrusts, and preparing for the clever man's possible parries. Like an actor about to step onstage, he needed to know his lines. But his thoughts were constantly invaded by another discussion he would have to have sometime later today, the one he would have to have with Maureen. *Jesus Christ!* Talk about thrusts and parries—the lady was not going to be happy. He reached into his pocket for a Wint-O-Green.

Exhaling hard, he peeled the foil back and popped the little candy into his mouth. The damn thing was soothing; they always were. Even when he was a kid, he always preferred the Wint-O-Green-flavored Life Savers. The fruity ones were too cloying, and he never really enjoyed the taste of peppermint. Many years later, after he tossed a full pack of Marlboros into a roadside snowbank from his car window and vowed never to light another cigarette, Wint-O-Greens became his constant companion. The traffic light went green without him noticing—it took the taxicab behind him one-sixteenth of a second to deliver a reminder.

His cell phone rang out as he parked the department Ford directly in front of the Thirteenth Street building that housed Janus' medical office. He answered.

"Boss, Diane here."

"Where are you?" Savage asked.

"The Chase Bank over on Sixth. I followed Cabrera here from Janus' office a little while ago. He seemed to be in a big hurry."

"I just now got to Janus' office," Savage said. "Stay with Cabrera till I get finished here. Don't lose him. If he heads back this way, jump him and stall him. When I'm done with Janus I want Cabrera to view those photographs and do a comparison interview. And I don't want to give Janus a chance to first prompt this guy."

"Oh," Diane chuckled, "I've got him stalled all right. After I watched him conduct a transaction inside the bank, and he made me, I decided that it was time for him and me to have a talk."

"Okay," Savage said. "You show him the photos?"

"Oh, yeah."

"And?"

"And, a *lot*." Brief and to the point, Diane DeGennaro brought him up to speed.

She was right, it was a lot . . . it was more than a lot, in fact. The added information she had so

smoothly finessed from Guillermo Cabrera filled in his
missing lines. Curtain up.

He gathered the folder of photographs and additional items of evidence he'd brought along, locked
the car, and strode quickly through the building's first-
floor corridor to Janus' office. As he entered, the doctor was shutting off the waiting room lights, clearly on
his way out.

"Half a day today, Doc?" Savage inquired.

"I've already talked to you," Janus said flatly. The
doctor's words were loaded with unvarnished disdain,
and he was not looking at all troubled or intimidated
by yet another police appearance. "I've already told
you everything that I know, and everything I intend
to tell you. So now, if you don't mind . . . *get lost.*"

Janus was wearing his PUNCH ME HARD sign right on
his wide forehead today. Good, Savage thought, the
man's dismissive arrogance and hateful attitude—
along with this case's interference in his own personal
life—would make his job that much easier, if not actually pleasurable. Of course, only Savage knew that
should he decide to, Janus could instantly be wearing
bracelets and headed for the Tombs and a gourmet
supper of baloney on day-old white bread. But, let the
games resume—he would test the doctor's mettle and
see if the man actually had the balls the man thought
he did.

"We've got some things to discuss, Doctor," Savage
began. "I have some points to go over with you, and
I have some photographs which I need you to look
at. You're going to have to give me the time."

"I can't be bothered with you now," Janus snarled,
making an ugly face. "I have an emergency that I must
tend to. We'll simply have to do this some other
time." He continued shutting off the lights as if Savage
wasn't even there.

"Oh, I see," Savage said evenly. "Mind telling me
just what and where that emergency is, Doc?"

"If you must know, I have a post-op patient over

at St. Vincent's who has suffered a setback. I must get there immediately." The room was now totally unlit.

"You lie with facility, Doctor," Savage said.

"I beg your pardon!" Janus glared. His face was an iron mask of contempt cast somewhere in hell.

"You lie with facility," Savage repeated. "However, you make the mistake of giving me absolutely no credit. I warn you," he said coldly. "I might just take that as an insult and turn this matter into a personal grudge. You really don't want that. Be nice."

"Are you threatening me, Officer?" Janus said through a tight frown.

Time to turn up the heat, Savage thought. "I'm not partial to people who think I'm stupid," he said. "I don't like being dismissed by those people, and I certainly don't like being lied to by them."

"No one is lying to you."

"You lost your privileges at Vinny's months ago, and you no longer have privileges at Joint Diseases either. So stop jerking me off. I'm starting to get pissed."

Janus froze, made hard eye contact, but said not a word in rebuttal.

"I suggest we go inside to your private office," Savage said evenly. "It's far more comfortable in there. We are going to be a while."

Jaws clearly Vise-Grip tight, Janus wheeled on his heel and led the way.

The physician took a seat on the leather throne behind his big desk, pulled the knot of his crimson tie open, and with a quickly rediscovered attitude, uttered, "Let's get this goddamned business over with. I've got things to do."

Savage opened the folder and dropped a blown-up color copy of George Granger's California driver's license photo onto Janus' desktop. "Recognize him?" he asked.

"No," Janus said unequivocally, without an apparent shred of concern. He looked directly up at Savage and added, "Should I?"

The man was measuring up, Savage thought—what an incredible poker face. The damning photo should have blown him right out of his seat . . . but it didn't. At the very least, Savage should have been able to discern some degree of concern, however slight, on the doctor's part . . . but he couldn't. This guy was good, Savage decided. The son of a bitch was probably the best damn liar he'd ever encountered—and that was saying a great deal.

"I would think you should recognize him," Savage said. "That's a photograph of George Granger. The man you allege to have been your patient for seven years."

"I don't know who that man is," Janus replied. "But that is not George Granger. At least not the George Granger who was my patient. Or certainly not the George Granger that died in my office last May."

"You're right on that one, Doc. He certainly wasn't the man who died in your office last May." He withdrew the enlarged Oklahoma driver's license photograph of Elvin Welch from the folder. "Do you know who *this* man is?" he asked, tossing the photo onto the desk.

Without missing a beat, Janus immediately said, "That's George Granger."

"You're sure of that?"

"I should know. He's been my personal patient for over seven years. Now is there anything else?" He began to rise from his chair.

"Sit down, Doctor," Savage snarled. "I'm going to play along here for just a moment, as if I'd been born yesterday." He then stated firmly, "The man you did not identify *is* truly George Granger. The man you did identify as George Granger is not."

"Well, why would the man who I treated for years pose as being George Granger?"

"Hey, Janus," Savage went on, mightily striving to control a burgeoning desire to slap the snot out of the lying hump. "We know the game. We know the entire game. We know about Granger's life insurance. We know about 'John Boy' Holloway's connection to both you and to Granger. Beyond that, we now also know that the man who died in your office was some poor schlep by the name of Elvin Welch. And we know that he was 'burked.' "

"Who the hell is . . . Elvin Welch? And what in the hell is . . . *burked*?"

"You're cute, Janus. But let's talk straight. I can tell you this: You're looking at a death sentence or, at the very least, life in prison. But you can make things a good deal better for yourself if you were to give it up and turn us on to your stooge partners, Messrs. Larry and Curly."

"I don't know what the hell you're talking about," Janus replied, holding his ground, not giving a fraction of an inch.

Savage picked up the photos from the desk and dropped them back into the folder.

"Where is your office assistant today?"

"Guillermo?"

"Yes, Guillermo. I want him to look at these photographs."

That one did it. The harpoon had struck a nerve. Janus went white.

"The thought of Guillermo being asked to identify just who is who in these photographs scares the bejesus out of you, doesn't it?" Savage said, starting to turn the screws. "And well it should."

"Guillermo will tell you exactly what I've told you," Janus barked back, nostrils flaring. The sudden concern in the man's voice was palpable, the sudden strain on his countenance undeniable. But he remained steadfast to his lies. "Guillermo was acquainted with Mr. Granger. He'll tell you."

"No, he won't," Savage said, fully enjoying the man's discomfort. "He'll pick out the other guy—the *real* George Granger. Where is Guillermo, by the way? I want to talk to him."

"He's . . . he's out of town," Janus fumbled slightly. He quickly regained composure and added, "Will be for the next ten days. Went back to Honduras to visit his family."

"Boy, you're good," Savage said. "You picked that one right out of the sky."

"You don't believe me?" Janus snarled, arrogance totally back on line. "That's your fucking problem."

"At your direction, Guillermo left here about an hour ago and walked to the Chase Bank over on Sixth Avenue. You sent him there to have a five-thousand-dollar cashier's check drawn from Guillermo's personal account, payable to Consolidated Auto Leasing."

Janus' eyes bugged.

"As we speak, Guillermo is in the company of one of my detectives," Savage went on. "He's already selected the photo of the real George Granger as having been your longtime bud and patient. Had no idea who Elvin Welch was—did not recognize his picture. He's also busy explaining all about how you had almost ten thousand dollars wired into *his* account. Chase has informed my detective that the ten grand originated from an Ohio money market account held by Hazel Holloway."

Trying not to show it, Janus gulped. "Are we done here?" he asked in a quiet monotone.

"Not quite," Savage said, knowing the man was on the ropes. "I'm curious—was it you who sat on Welch's chest while George Granger pinched his nostrils and cupped a hand over his mouth? Or was it the other way around?"

Janus looked away, but did not speak.

Savage gathered up his folder and stepped to the office door. "You're running out of time to make a deal, Janus," he said. "Once the hammer falls, there'll be no more offers."

Hoping he'd managed sufficient cage rattling to prompt the doctor to unthinking action, Savage left the building and headed immediately back to Manhattan South Homicide. Upon arrival, he discovered that Diane DeGennaro had already returned to the office with Guillermo Cabrera. The first-grade detective was still questioning Janus' assistant and securing a detailed signed statement. Savage let himself into the interview room and sat in to listen.

"And how long have you actually lived in the same apartment with Dr. Janus?" DeGennaro asked.

"It has to be close to three years now," Cabrera replied. "And all during that time I have been his office assistant as well."

"And you did know George Granger, did you not?"

"Absolutely."

"Just how and when did you find out that Mr. Granger had supposedly died right there in the office?"

"Dr. Janus told me later on in the day when he came home."

"So you never actually saw the body; is that right?"

"Right. All along—until you showed me the photographs a little while ago—I've believed that it was George Granger who died there."

"All right," DeGennaro went on. "But if you were Janus' assistant, how come you were not present at the office that morning? Isn't that a little convenient for you?"

"Dr. Janus gave me the day after Memorial Day off, a four-day weekend. The office was closed."

"Has Dr. Janus ever confided to you the basis of some of his financial problems?" Savage asked.

"Oh, yes," Cabrera replied. "Besides his divorce and some very terrible investments, the doctor owes an incredible amount of money to the IRS. Couple of years ago, they seized his bank accounts and everything else he owned. The man is basically penniless."

"How much does he owe Uncle Sam?" Savage said.

" 'Bout half a million dollars," Cabrera replied; then in a frightened tone he asked, "Tell me, Officers, what's going to occur here? I just can't go home now and act as if nothing has happened. Not knowing what I now know. Charlie will know the minute he lays eyes on me that I've talked to you. I have no place to go."

Jack Lindstrom rapped at the interview room door and stuck his head in.

"Sarge," he said, holding up a cell phone, "I've got Richie on the line."

Savage left the interview room and took the call. "What have you got?"

"Some good news and some not-so-good news," Marcus replied.

"Start with the good."

"At fourteen hundred hours, only twenty minutes after I engaged the tap on Janus' office phone, I intercepted and recorded an international phone call to him."

"Must have come in just before I arrived there," Savage mused.

"Caller was a male," Marcus went on. "I'm certain it was Holloway. I'd bet the freakin' ranch on it."

"Okay. What was said?"

"They danced around in fuckin' circles, but there's some good stuff there. Also, during the call, the male mentioned to Janus that the time at his present location was 'already eight o'clock.'"

"Morning or night?"

"Presumably night. Lindstrom figures based on the time the call was received by Janus here in New York, it could have only come from somewhere within the Central European Summer Time Zone. An area that he says includes Amsterdam, Holland, where we suspected Holloway had gone."

"Yeah, and about a hundred other places too," Savage said, frowning. "Like Rome, Paris, and freakin' Madrid."

"There's something else too," Marcus said. "Just moments before that call came in from Holloway, Janus dialed a long-distance number and got an answering machine. He didn't leave any message. Lindstrom's gonna have Telephone Security find out who owns the listing and just where the hell it is."

"How about the not-so-good news?"

"This office wire is probably DOA. They suspect it may be hot. Caller was gonna recontact Janus at his residence line at four thirty our time."

"In that case, head over to the residence right now," Savage directed. "Jack and I will meet you there in about twenty minutes."

Savage poked his head into the interview room and motioned for Diane DeGennaro to join him in the squad room.

"What's up, Sarge?" she asked, closing the interview room door behind her.

"Keep Cabrera here for now," he said. "The time has come to go put bracelets on the good doctor. Once that's done, I'll call you. Then this poor bastard can go home without any fear."

"Ten-four, boss."

The wacko case was finally starting to come together, Savage concluded during the drive with Lindstrom over to Janus' flat. The snowball had started to roll downhill and was quickly picking up dimension and speed.

Upon arrival at his West Side residence, the three detectives took Dr. R. Charles Janus into custody without incident. He was charged with murder in the first degree. The assistant district attorney's office would argue for no bail at his arraignment. Though having merely $1.36 on his person when strip-searched at Central Booking, the destroyed man still possessed a fortune in arrogance. Rikers Island and state prison would deal with that.

At six fifteen, Savage headed home. He had to pack for the morning.

When he arrived at his Sullivan Street apartment, Savage immediately placed a call to Maureen Gallo at her SoHo art gallery. He'd missed her. A recording stated that the shop had already closed for the day—not surprising. He then dialed her apartment. He dreaded the call. It wasn't going to be pretty, but he owed it to her to let her know the situation as soon as possible. Again getting no answer, he left a message for her to call him back ASAP.

He then contacted Dr. Figueroa and informed her that he would be out of town for at least several days. The report on Ray was that he was little improved, was barely taking food and on intravenous, but amazingly was still hanging on. Savage gave the vet Maureen's telephone number to call in the event some special problems should arise in his absence. Maureen would know where and how to contact him during his stay in Florida.

Always a light traveler, Savage packed four pairs of socks and four changes of neatly folded briefs and tees into his soft-sided overnighter. He tossed in his shaving kit, which contained razor and cream, toothbrush and paste, hairbrush, cologne, and a Mennen Speed Stick. From his closet he selected four short-sleeved shirts, three pair of dress slacks, a brown leather belt, and his most decent-looking pair of sneakers. He decided he would wear his brandy-colored weave loafers on the plane. As an afterthought, just before zipping the bag closed, he went to the bottom drawer of his bureau and retrieved a bathing suit—just in case he got the chance to hit the surf.

His cell phone rang. He took a deep breath.

"Thorn, I just got home and got your message," Maureen said. "Where are you, at the office?"

"No. As a matter of fact, I'm at home also," Savage replied.

"Home so early? What are you doing, honey, packing for tomorrow?"

"Uh, yes. But—"

"I'm already packed," Maureen broke in, her voice excited. "You know me, never last-minute. I can't wait to get on that beach. This has been one killer week, let me tell you. What time are you going to pick me up tomorrow afternoon?"

"Well, that's what I'm calling about," he began. He paused, hoping he would somehow divine the best words to enunciate the bad news. "I can't go to the Hamptons," he finally said right out. "Something very important has come up, somebody has to handle it, and I'm afraid that I'm it. Why don't you take my car for the weekend and go yourself?"

"Don't fuck around with me, Thornton Savage," Maureen uttered in an ugly monotone. She never used the *F* word. "Not on this one. Not even in jest."

"Mo, I'm sorry, but I'm not jesting."

Long, long silence. "Do you know where this leaves me?" Maureen finally said.

"I'm sorry for that. But I have to go to Miami for a few days. I'll be leaving first thing in the morning."

"Sorry isn't good enough, Thorn. Doreen and Randy left for their cruise yesterday. There's no way I can get in touch with them now and let them know what's going on. They could have rented the place for thousands this weekend, but they were good enough to *give it* to us. And now you're turning your nose up at it."

"Look," Savage said softly, "there's nothing I can do about this. If there were any way I could have gotten off the hook, I would have done so. Believe me, Mo, I tried . . . but this is my work."

"Why you?" she whined. "You've got three detectives working for you. Why can't any of them handle this business in Miami?"

"It's a long story, but as it turns out it was impossible for any one of them to—"

"You mean to tell me that you have to go down to Miami *all alone*? By yourself?"

"Eh," he replied, "there's an insurance company fraud investigator who will be going as well." Savage decided that this was probably not the ideal moment to mention that his traveling companion on this jaunt was a *female* insurance investigator—a sexy single chick with a come-and-do-me persona. There was no reason why Maureen would ever have to know, he thought. Certainly no possible good would be served by it if she did.

"One of your own detectives isn't going with you?" she inquired incredulously. "They're gonna get to skate for the weekend, and the *sergeant* has to do all the work?"

The conversation with Maureen lasted only about another thirty seconds. But during that time, she vented her deep disappointment and frustration with a well-reasoned catharsis of her distaste for the NYPD and her pointing out how these things always seemed to happen. She also declined the offer of the use of his car. But in the end, Maureen agreed to take messages from Dr. Figueroa and forward them to him—if necessary—at the Delano, or wherever. When done, she hung up with a clipped "good-bye," but no "have a nice trip."

Savage knew that Maureen had a justifiable beef. She had been planning this weekend for months. He totally sympathized with her, and he wondered how he could make it up to her. An answer was not readily forthcoming.

He also knew that Chief Wilson had been one hundred percent correct—at least one member of Manhattan South's Team Three absolutely had to immediately go to Florida. This Granger maniac was killing folks, and Savage knew that, like it or not, he was the best hope of dropping the bastard before he got to do it again.

TWENTY-EIGHT

Friday, August 16, 1:25 P.M. Central Europe Summer Time

The slow climb up, across, and along the poorly marked twenty-mile trail was exhausting to the human body, especially in the blistering midafternoon heat of the unforgiving Sardinian summer. Designed and created by Mother Nature during what must have been a particularly nasty bout of PMS, the path bordered the stony and jagged cliffs that lay between the coastal towns of Porto Rotondo and Porto Cervo to the north. It is meant for only the most stouthearted and physically fit of hikers, nimble mountain goats, or complete masochists.

Several postings along the way warned of the trail's high degree of difficulty and potential dangers, and even suggested less-demanding detours for those wise enough to heed. More than a few game souls had dropped dead while tromping the rocky way, and any number of others had lost their footing at an inauspicious moment and fallen to the rocky coastline below. Sometimes their badly battered bodies were never found. But, as anyone who had completed the difficult trek would tell you, it could be well worth the effort. The incredible views of the Costa Smeralda were amazing, easily ranking with Europe's most spectacular.

"Sardinia is definitely not for the fainthearted," Darrin Greavey said, breathing heavily and trailing John Holloway by ten paces as they crested one particularly long pull. Up ahead, about two hundred yards, yet another climb began.

"You've got that right," Holloway agreed, stopping in his tracks, not nearly as winded. He turned to watch Greavey wring moisture from a kerchief, then give his damp brow a second wipe.

"I think maybe it's time for a rest," Greavey suggested, making a strained face.

"No," Holloway replied. "Not yet. Let's at least get to the base of the next upgrade." Without another word, he turned and pressed on.

Whenever burdened by a major problem, or needing to come to grips with a difficult decision, Holloway had always courted the physically demanding pastimes of hiking and rock climbing as his best allies. They helped him do his best thinking; the endorphins flowed then, the synapses fired then, the decisions came. And, for sure, he needed a damn decision now.

Charlie Janus was clearly in trouble—even if the man wouldn't recognize it. And now the cops were out looking for George Granger, so the jig was certainly up. If that was so, then the search for John Boyer Holloway was right around the corner, if not already begun. *Shit!*

"Hey, John," Greavey called out just as they neared the start of the next upgrade. "Cut me some slack, for God's sake, will you?"

Frustrated and angry, but trying not to show it, Holloway turned and nodded his agreement. "All right. If you're tired we'll sit for a while."

"Not tired as much as I need to get out of the sun," Greavey explained. "I'm roasting and dehydrating."

Holloway did a quick three-sixty and aimed a finger toward the only achievable spot of shade anywhere within sight. Appearing like a pockmark in the cliff face, the hole was accessible only by a short, narrow ledge. The dark recess was shaded by a gravity-defying outcropping of stratified rock that projected above it like an awning. The space was ample enough to accommodate them both. It would allow them to rest and recharge and, more importantly, get them out of the blazing sun for a half hour. Maybe Greavey was right, he thought. It *was* time for a brief rest.

"We have to do this ledge one at a time," Holloway announced at the threshold. "I'll go first. You come in behind me. You okay with this?" he asked.

Greavey nodded. "I'm okay with it. You just be careful, John."

Using his considerable rock-climbing skills, Holloway turned toward the cliff face and stepped boldly out onto the narrow ledge. Met by the steady blast of natural updrafts, he gripped the face with his strong fingers and inched steadily along the short distance to the mouth of the small refuge. Holloway slid into the hole and was immediately followed by Darrin Greavey, himself no stranger to the wall-hugging technique. Once inside, each quickly removed his backpack, took a short pull on his water bottle, and gazed straight down the cliff face to the disarray of ragged and alien-world-looking rock coastline seventy-five feet below.

"Isn't this wonderful?" Greavey said, his words filled with awe. "I feel like an eagle in an aerie."

"Well, don't forget, Mr. Eagle," Holloway reminded. "We've got to get back out of here too. So you get your strength up." Pressing Darrin Greavey's more pliable and softer backpack into service as a pillow, Holloway then reclined and resumed his deep thought.

"You know, the more I think about it, the more I think we should not do a round-trip hike," Greavey said. "When we get to Porto Cervo, I think we should consider taking the train back to Olbia."

"Generally speaking, public transportation in Sardinia is slow and unreliable at best," Holloway responded, speaking softly. The refreshing coolness of the spot, augmented greatly by the natural cliffside updraft, was delicious. He closed his eyes and sucked it in, wishing that Darrin would shut up. He had important matters to resolve in his head.

"Not the Trenino Verde," Greavey explained, sounding as if he were a tour guide. "It is the one delightful exception. That train runs on time."

"Let's see how we feel when we get to Porto Cervo," Holloway said, hoping for some quiet so he could order his thoughts. "Maybe we'll stay the night there."

"Now that's where we may have problems," Darrin responded. "Hotels and restaurants along the coast are either outrageously expensive or dismally primitive. I don't know if you're ready for either one."

"Unh. We'll see," Holloway muttered dismissively. When was this guy ever going to shut up?

"Were you aware that archaeological remains have been found in some of Sardinia's olive groves that date back to seventeen hundred B.C.?"

That was it, Holloway thought. It was time to bark. "Let me rest, Darrin, will you *please*?" He watched with one eye as a wounded Darrin Greavey grimaced in rejection, turned away, and faced out toward the Tyrrhenian.

Holloway's plans of a trip to New York with Darrin, and the making of a special and very profitable visit to Dr. Janus, were now entirely dashed. It was clear that ever returning to the United States—as John Boyer Holloway, at least—would probably be impossible. *Thank God for my new identity. How to get the cops off my back, though? How to get them to quit ever again looking for John Boyer Holloway? The only way those bastards would ever quit was if I were proven to be dead—and a staging of that could certainly no longer happen in New York City, or anywhere in the U.S., for that matter. Damn it all.*

"Are you angry with me?" Darrin asked sheepishly, still gazing out at the sea below.

"Oh, don't be silly," Holloway replied, lifting his head from the pillow and gazing warmly at the man. "After all, we have a future together, you and me."

"I truly hope so," Darrin said softly, turning to

make adoring eye contact with Holloway. "I guess I just needed you to reassure me."

"Let me assure you. We do have a future."

Darrin smiled and turned back to face the sea.

John Boyer Holloway, aka John Anson Conover, shifted his position. He brought his shoulders firmly up against the cool stone wall of the recess's shallow interior, quickly pressed his hiking boots against Darrin Greavey's narrow back, and thrust his strong legs forward. Greavey's scream lasted but a few seconds. When it stopped, all that remained was the rush of the windy cliffside updraft. The Sardinian cops will write this one off as just another idiot foreign hiker, he thought.

Holloway opened Greavey's backpack, removed the man's wallet, and pulled out any and all of Darrin Greavey's identification. He then opened his own backpack, dug past the ID packet for John Anson Conover, and pulled out several pieces of identification for John Boyer Holloway; he slipped them neatly into Greavey's Velcro-sealing wallet and placed the wallet back into Greavey's pack. He then closed the backpack and tossed it to the winds. He watched as it scuffed, bounced, and collided along the cliff face. Good shot, he thought. It landed right next to the smashed and mangled body of his ex-lover.

Tonight he would call Mother and advise her to stand very close to the phone and await the notification from the Sardinian police—whom he understood to be a bunch of bumbling bozos. Of course, Mother would then have to make the trip across the big pond in order to identify the remains and arrange for the immediate cremation. John Boyer Holloway's ashes would then be scattered in the blue Tyrrhenian. It was going to be so nice to see her. He strapped his backpack on, crept from the hole, and, energized, began the downhill trek back to Porto Rotondo.

He could no longer be John Boyer Holloway; he was now completely John Anson Conover. But, as an added bonus, in a pinch he could also be Darrin Greavey.

It seemed as if every gate along Concourse A at Hartsfield-Jackson Atlanta International Airport was mobbed with weekend travelers and the usual supply of business suits. There was not a vacant chair to be had anywhere. Waiting for their delayed connecting flight to begin boarding, Savage and Winona Escalante leaned against the corridor wall and sipped at containers of lava-hot coffee.

"How long do you think we'll actually be in Miami?" Escalante asked.

"Don't know. Not long, I hope. I think a lot will depend on what we find out about the Dr. Koremvokis business," Savage replied.

"Except for the few calls that he made to that doctor, most of the calls our boy made were to Realtors. It would appear that at the time he was in the market for new digs."

"Yeah," Savage acknowledged, "but the overwhelming majority of those calls went to Realtors all the way down in Key West."

"Think we'll wind up having to go there?"

"Unless Granger jumps right into our arms and surrenders when we get to Miami, I can't see how we can avoid it," Savage said. He sipped again at his coffee while allowing his eye to be momentarily taken by a pair of knockout flight attendants. The luscious redhead and the dynamite brunette strolled by in animated conversation, towing their wheeled luggage carts. He'd always thought if he had it all to do over again, he would give serious thought to becoming an airline pilot. Layovers, he was sure, were aptly named.

"But when we contacted them, not one of those Key West Realtors recognized either the name Von Deutsch *or* Granger," Escalante pointed out.

"True enough. But maybe one of them will recognize Mr. Granger's photograph."

"Good," Escalante said firmly. "I'm glad we're going to Key West."

"Why good?"

"I've heard that Key West is beautiful," she replied, making strong eye contact. "And . . ."

"And what?"

"And," she purred, "quite romantic."

The flight from Atlanta wasn't bad—a little bumpy in spots maybe—but, despite the brief delay, it arrived more or less on time at Miami International at 12:10. Traveling with only unchecked carry-on luggage, Savage and Escalante moved quickly through the bustling terminal, bypassed the crowded baggage carousels, and made straight for the Budget car rental counter. They were first on line.

"How do you want to handle this?" Winona Escalante asked while digging her Visa card and Budget confirmation information from her Tumi portfolio. "Do you want to go and check in at the hotel first, or would you rather we head right over to Dr. Koremvokis' office?"

"We'll do the doctor's office," Savage replied.

Winona Escalante put up her company Visa card, signed off on the rental agreement, and listed Savage as a co-driver. Twenty-five minutes later, they parked the Mustang convertible in the concrete-bunker lot that adjoined the South Beach Medical Arts Building. The Koremvokis office, on the second floor, was closed and locked, but a notice taped to the door gave a phone number for those seeking to obtain their medical records. Savage dialed the number on his cell phone. A woman answered; she identified herself as Ellen Plotski. Savage identified himself in return.

"I was the doctor's nurse and assistant for ten years," Ellen Plotski advised. "It's just been terrible. Everyone, his family . . . me, everybody is just so devastated by this whole thing."

"I can understand that," Savage said, truly sympathetic. "But since you worked so closely with the doctor, perhaps you can help us."

"I'll try."

"Do you recall the doctor having a patient by the name of George Granger?" Savage inquired. "He would have been a white man in his mid-forties."

"The name is not at all familiar," the woman immediately replied.

"Fine," Savage said. "Did the doctor happen to have a patient by the name of Eric Von Deutsch? He also would be a male in his mid-forties."

"Oh, yes," Ms. Plotski replied. "Funny you should ask; so happens that Mr. Von Deutsch was one of the patients that the doctor saw on the afternoon of the day he was killed."

"Is that a fact?" Savage said, raising his eyebrows and showing a thumbs-up to Winona Escalante.

"I remember Mr. Von Deutsch well," the woman went on. "He was a very strange man. Not that one doesn't come across plenty of very strange men down here in South Beach. Let me see, upper and lower blepharoplasties, tightening next to the eyes, some facial moles—"

"What, if anything, do you recall about his office visit that day?" Savage interrupted.

"Well, I'm fairly certain that the doctor and Mr. Von Deutsch had some words during the examination."

"How do you know they had words? Did you actually overhear them?"

"No, I didn't actually hear it," Ms. Plotski replied. "But I could tell. When Mr. Von Deutsch left, he almost bowled me over when he stormed from the office. And judging by the look on his face, he was very angry."

"Did you ask the doctor about the incident?" Savage pressed.

"No. Doctor didn't tell me. If he didn't volunteer it, I would never ask."

"Have you told the Miami police about that incident?"

"No," Plotski replied. "I never thought it relevant. Is it?"

"Possibly. Could you describe Mr. Von Deutsch for me?" Savage asked.

"I can do much better than that," Plotski replied. "If you'll meet me at the office in twenty minutes, I'll show you pictures of him. His before- and after-surgery shots."

True to her word, Ellen Plotski showed at the Medical Arts Building twenty minutes later. She led Savage and Escalante into the tomblike quiet and unlit offices of the late Dr. Herbert Koremvokis, went into the Von Deutsch medical file, and extracted a series of Polaroid photographs.

"These are the before shots," she said, handing Savage six photographs. There, in both full face and profile close-ups, was George Granger.

"Yes!" Winona Escalante murmured through clenched teeth.

"These are the after shots," Ms. Plotski advised, handing over another six photos. "You'll notice he does look somewhat different, doesn't he? Much younger looking."

"Yes, he does . . ." Savage murmured slowly. "Different hairstyle and hair color—no more gray. A pencil-thin mustache, no more hooded eyes or crow's-feet."

"And look at those moles," Ms. Plotski pointed out. "They're all gone in the 'after' shots."

Savage gazed intently, studying the after photographs in order to etch the man's updated look into his mind's eye. He handed Winona Escalante both the before and the after shots and turned toward the nurse. "It's clear that Dr. Koremvokis was a very skilled surgeon."

"Yes," Plotski replied sorrowfully, "he was."

A quick perusal of the records in the Von Deutsch medical file indicated that his initial office visit with Koremvokis was back in April. All of the surgical pro-

cedures and all subsequent follow-up examinations,
however, were performed by Koremvokis in the weeks
following Granger's supposed death in late May.

It was flat-out eureka.

"Would you mind if we were to keep several of
these photographs?" Savage asked. "Just one straight
on, and one profile shot from both the before and
after groups."

"I suppose that would be all right," Plotski replied.

"And would you be good enough to make us copies
of the entire medical file?" Winona Escalante asked.

"I'm really not supposed to do that," Plotski replied
with a pained look across her face. "It's a serious vio-
lation of patient privacy."

"If you won't tell, then we won't tell," Savage urged
in a conspiratorial murmur.

Plotski quickly gathered up the records. "Would
you prefer *me* to keep the copies and let you have the
originals?" she asked.

"No," Savage replied, grinning softly, grateful for
the woman's eagerness to help. "Thank you very
much, but we'll take the copies. Miami Homicide will
surely want those originals."

As Ellen Plotski fired up the office copy machine
and went to work, Savage dialed Detective Merle Fennimore of the Miami Homicide Division. Fennimore
was the detective who was holding the high-profile
Koremvokis murder case. The detective agreed to
come right over.

When Fennimore arrived at the Koremvokis medical office, Savage gave the Miami investigator a chronological overview, bringing him up to date on the
matters in both New York and Florida and how he
believed they were related.

Fennimore agreed that Granger/Von Deutsch would
now be a very viable suspect in his case, one that up
to that point had no suspects, viable or otherwise.
They had been working on the premise that the killing
was nothing more than the random act of a psycho-
path. Fennimore also stated that he would immedi-

ately put out a nationwide alarm for Granger/Von Deutsch, using both names.

Savage then excused himself and put in a call to Manhattan South. He broke the interesting news to Pete Pezzano.

"Dynamite!" Pezzano said. "The chief is gonna go wild. What's your next move?"

"A double martini, poolside at the Delano," Savage replied. "I'm taking the rest of the day off."

It seemed to Savage that lower Collins Avenue had changed quite a bit in the years since he'd last driven along it. The Miami Beach main drag had somehow become *tackier,* for want of a better word. Even the Jewish deli opposite Collins Park, where he'd once had probably the best corned-beef sandwich in his life, was gone, the building boarded up and haphazardly plastered with posters, handbills, and even some spray-painted graffiti.

"I've never been to Miami Beach before," Winona Escalante said, adjusting the AC vent on the passenger side. "Truth is, I've never even been to Florida before."

"What do you think of it?"

"I'll say this for it, it's hot," she said, sticking out her tongue and clutching dramatically at her slim neck. "Will we ever be able to put the top down?"

"In the South Florida sun, in August? Convertible tops only come down when it's dark."

Savage steered the Mustang into the winding driveway of the Delano Hotel and pulled it to a stop in the shade of the porte cochere. They turned the car over to a valet parker, grabbed their bags, and entered the pink-marble lobby. They went directly to the registration desk.

A semi-attractive older blonde, whose tan but heavily wrinkled flesh had seen far too much ultraviolet down through the years, greeted them. The name tag on her blouse identified her as Sylvia Diamond.

"Good afternoon and welcome to the Delano," Sylvia said. Savage could tell by the woman's central-casting Bronx accent that she was raised somewhere along the Grand Concourse. He could also tell she'd repeated that greeting countless times; it just rolled off her tongue as if prerecorded.

"We're here to see Daphne Dempsey," Savage said.

"I'm afraid Ms. Dempsey is unavailable at the moment. Can someone else be of service?"

"When will she be back?" Escalante inquired.

"I'm not sure," Sylvia replied. "Will you be staying with us?" she said, glancing first at the bags they carried, then back up at Savage.

"My name is Savage," he announced. "I'm with the New York City Police Department." Nodding then at Winona, he added, "Ms. Escalante and I are here in Miami on an investigation." He glanced at his watch. "Ms. Dempsey was supposed to be expecting us at about this time."

"Oh, yes," Sylvia said, nodding in recollection. "Ms. Dempsey told me to expect you both. She was called out suddenly about an hour ago. I'm not sure when she will be back. However, she has arranged accommodations for you both during your stay. Adjoining rooms, if that will be all right."

"That will be just fine," Winona Escalante assured her. She placed her Visa on the counter. "Both rooms are to be billed on that card."

"I'll have your bags brought up to your rooms," Sylvia said, motioning to a nearby bellman. She slid a pair of key cards across the counter. "Ms. Escalante is in room twelve twenty-one, and you, sir, are in twelve twenty-two. Rest assured that I will contact you at the very moment Ms. Dempsey returns."

Room 1222, as it turned out, did not face the ocean. Nor did it even look down on Collins Avenue. It faced instead the stucco beige walls and bronze-toned windows of the hotel next door. But, hey, Savage figured, the price was right.

He opened his bag and began to unpack. He removed the case folder with the Granger and Welch photographs and placed it on top of the dresser. He removed his dress slacks, and from beneath his tees and shorts he removed his holstered Smith & Wesson. He dropped the thirty-eight onto the bedspread alongside his socks. Then a knock came at the door. It was his traveling companion.

"How does your room smell?" Winona Escalante asked, barging in and sniffing around his room as soon as he opened the door.

"Smells okay," he said. "Why?"

"Mine smells like a goddamned ashtray, for crissakes," she complained. "The last guy in there must have smoked like a tire fire."

She sniffed around the room some more, even to the extent of pulling back the queen-size spread and lifting each of the two bed pillows up to her nose. "This room smells okay, though," she announced approvingly. "But they'll just have to give me another. I had asthma as a kid and have just never been able to deal with the odor of cigarette smoke. If I stay in there, I'm definitely going to get sick."

"Don't bother them," Savage said, not wanting to waste the time or bug the hotel staff. "We'll just switch rooms."

Not exactly enamored of the scent of ashtray himself, he quickly tossed his underwear and socks back into his softside.

"I didn't see you wearing a gun on the way down," Winona said, as he slipped the piece into his belt.

"Hey, even though I'm a cop, I'm not permitted to carry a loaded weapon aboard a commercial airliner," he advised. "It had to make the trip inside my checked luggage."

Winona nodded understanding.

Tailed by the insurance investigator, Savage gathered up the case folder and trudged next door to 1221. She was right, the room did have a mild odor, but he could live with it. After exchanging key cards, Escalante shouldered her bag and disappeared.

Savage again unpacked his socks and underwear

and laid them out evenly in the long dresser's top middle drawer. He then unpacked his shirts and slacks, placed them carefully on hangers, and hung them up. Along with a small refrigerator, coffeepot, and wide-screen TV, the room also provided a fold-down ironing board and a steam iron. He checked his three pairs of slacks; he hated seeing fold lines. Surprisingly, they had all survived wrinkle free. If they hadn't, he'd be road-testing the iron.

Thirty minutes later, after ten breaststroke laps in the hotel's Olympic-size swimming pool, Savage sat comfortably at the poolside tiki bar. Clad only in bathing trunks and sandals, and with a Delano towel draped casually around his neck, he ogled the incredibly small bikinis that barely covered the well-constructed young ladies who grooved with their boyfriends, husbands, or significant others on the adjacent sun-soaked dance floor. He marveled that they were doing everything they possibly could to someday wind up looking like the leathery Sylvia Diamond. He took another sip of the Belvedere martini. It was frosty cold, just the way he liked them.

This was all terrific, he thought, but he couldn't help wondering if the suddenly required Miami excursion was actually going to pay off. Would they be able to locate and collar George Granger while there? If not, would they be at least able to prove beyond a doubt that the man was still alive? Savage was still convinced of needing the latter in order to put Dr. Janus safely behind bars. These were problems, no question. But his real problem lay in how in hell he was going to patch up the Hampton beach house debacle with Maureen, if such was even possible. In this morning's conversation with her, Maureen had been barely civil.

"May I get you something, ma'am?" the bartender said as he carefully wiped the bar area immediately next to Savage. He set down a pink napkin bearing the Delano logo.

"I'll have whatever this good-looking gentleman is having," Savage heard Winona Escalante reply.

Turning to face her, his mouth nearly dropped. Though looking directly into her dark eyes, his secondary vision took in the complete package. Talk about a brief bikini. Winona Escalante was leaving very little to the imagination.

"I've always thought that Midwesterners were very conservative," Savage teased.

"Oh, we are," Escalante coyly responded. "But when we get away from the cornfields and pastures, we really like to let it all hang out." She looked toward the couples who were now dancing to something smooth and slow by Sinatra.

"You a good dancer?" she asked.

Pointing to his half-finished martini, Savage chuckled and said, "I don't even consider dancing until I've got at least a dozen of these aboard."

"Just as well," Winona replied, looking down at Savage's open sandals. "I'm hardly the Ginger Rogers type myself. Guess you could say I'm *rhythmically challenged*. Since I was a teenager, every time some poor guy has asked me to dance, I've wound up putting a high heel right through his damn instep."

"Thanks for the warning."

"Another one for you, sir?" the bartender asked as he placed a fresh martini before Winona.

"Yes," Savage replied. "Straight up with a twist . . . and merely *think* about the vermouth this time."

TWENTY-NINE

Born and raised in Brooklyn and educated in parochial elementary and high schools—and Long Island University—Carroll Xavier Henderson was all of twenty-two years of age when he became a New York City cop. Prior to entering the police academy for the one solid year of required training before being allowed to hit the streets, the son of poor Irish immigrants from County Clare had tried his hand at a number of other occupations: retail sales at Macy's, grounds-keeping assistant at Shea Stadium, and barkeep in a couple of the more popular Irish slop chutes over in Woodside, just to name a few.

Truth was, though, Carroll had wanted to be a New York City policeman ever since the day he stood on the rooftop of his Park Slope apartment building and looked on in horror as the Twin Towers of the World Trade Center burned, collapsed, and became the mass grave of three thousand people—two of whom resided in his same building. Besides, he was tough. It wasn't easy for a young man, especially a very good-looking young man, to grow up on the neighborhood streets of Kings County bearing the name Carroll. That burden, that plight, helped him develop an even demeanor, a laissez-faire acceptance of things over which he had little or no control . . . and an excellent left hook.

Carroll "Hollywood" Henderson let himself into the squad room of Manhattan South Homicide. Knowing whom to ask for, but unsure of whom to ask, he approached Eddie Brodigan at the wheel desk.

"Excuse me," he said in a low tone. "I'm Officer Henderson from Thirteenth Precinct."

"Well, of course you are," the wheelman acknowledged, not even bothering to look up. He shuffled papers seemingly needlessly around his desk.

"I was notified downstairs that I was not to get into uniform today, but to come right up here and report to a Detective Jack Lindstrom."

"Well, of course you were," the wheelman replied, his voice a blasé monotone, his expression deadpan.

"Well . . ." Henderson asked, "do you think you could point him out to me?"

"I could do that," Brodigan said, finally making real eye contact. "But first you must answer a question."

"Okay." Henderson didn't know what the hell was going on, but he decided that the wheelman was awfully strange.

Leaning across his desk and speaking in a whisper, Brodigan said, "Tell me, what is the square root of sixty-nine?"

Jesus, what's with this guy? Henderson thought. That's one of the oldest, most trite jokes in the world. Maybe he's one of those rubber gun guys they press into service to answer telephones.

"I'm not sure," Henderson murmured respectfully, willing, for the moment, to play along and wishing not to offend the veteran cop, lest he never locate Jack Lindstrom. "But I think maybe the answer is 'atc' something."

"You are exactly right," Brodigan announced with a flourish. Wide-eyed, he slammed his palm down on the desktop. "Therefore, you now get to move to the next plateau." He wheeled in his chair and called out across the squad room. "Hey, Jack," he said with a chuckle, "you got another mathematics major here to see you."

A tall man, gaunt, dressed in an ill-fitting gray suit, stood up at the center of the room. "C'mon over," the man said.

Henderson nodded queerly at Brodigan, crossed the

squad room, and shook Lindstrom's hand. The detective gestured to the chair alongside his desk.

"Brodigan hit you with the square root question?" Lindstrom said first thing as Henderson slowly sat.

"Yeah," Henderson replied. "What's with that guy, anyway?"

"Brodigan never had any toys as a kid," Lindstrom answered. "So now he sometimes gets off playing with rookies' minds."

"Jeez, am I that transparent?" Henderson asked quietly, raising his brow.

"Yep."

"That's bad, huh?" Henderson mumbled.

"No," Lindstrom replied, laughing softly. "As a matter of fact, that's good. And that's exactly why you're here."

"Oh?"

"Our team is going to do a little acting job early next week, maybe on Tuesday or Wednesday—whenever Sergeant Savage gets back from Florida." Lindstrom smiled ominously at the rookie. "And guess who's going to be the star of the show?"

"I'm Daphne Dempsey," the freckle-faced redhead said, extending her hand as she approached both Savage and Winona Escalante at the poolside tiki bar. "I'm terribly sorry that I was not here to meet you as promised. But we've had a terrible tragedy."

Unless Savage missed his guess, Daphne Dempsey, like Sylvia Diamond, was also raised in the Bronx. She had both the accent and the unmistakable New York attitude.

"Oh?" Savage said sympathetically.

"Yes," Dempsey went on. "One of my employees was killed several days ago. Poor man got run over; hit-and-run. The Highway Patrol notified me and asked if I would come over and identify his belongings."

"That's terrible," Winona Escalante said. "Did he leave a family?"

"No," Dempsey replied, exhaling hard. "He was a bachelor, but a very dear fellow. We're going to miss him."

"How sad," Escalante said.

"Since this whole thing has happened, though," Dempsey added, "I've been giving something I witnessed Ramon do last Tuesday a good deal of thought."

"Ramon?" Savage asked, sipping at his martini.

"Ramon Mendez. He worked at our reception desk, and I'm almost certain that he knew Mr. Von Deutsch. I think, in fact, he might have known him *very* well—if you get my drift. You see I happen to know that Ramon was . . ."

"Gay," Savage said, finishing the woman's sentence.

Daphne Dempsey nodded in assent. She then related the entire story of Ramon's odd behavior—and his immediate request for time off—upon seeing the Granger photograph coupled with the information from homicide detective Lindstrom. She knew he was off to Key West.

"Now, the Florida Highway Patrol informs me that Ramon's hit-and-run was absolutely intentional. They've even discovered that the tires on Ramon's car had been tampered with, causing him to get a flat with no spare. Do you think this could all be tied in?"

Savage and Winona Escalante exchanged millisecond glances. Savage drained his glass.

Up to that point, he had considered possibly having a third martini, but now he decided against it. The first two were kick-ass anyway, served in something the size of an aquarium. It would be early to bed tonight, no question, and up early in the morning. They would be heading for Key West. George Granger was going down.

With rubber gloves protecting his hands, George Granger squirted a generous amount of Palmolive dishwashing soap into the right basin of the double kitchen sink. He then ran the water on full hot until it was three-quarters filled with slick soapy suds. Methodically, one by one, he took down each and every dish from the kitchen cabinets, washed it, and set it in the dish drainer to dry. When every dish was thoroughly washed and dried, he carefully returned them all with gloved hands to their place in the wall cabinet. He repeated the process with every knife, spoon, and fork in the silverware drawer.

Although he'd used only a small portion of the provided utensils during his brief stay at the Lazy Parrot Cottages, he washed and carefully towel-dried every pot, every pan, every glass, cup, and saucer, until he was certain he'd left not one fingerprint on any of them. He then went to the bathroom and wiped down the hot and cold tap handles in both the vanity basin and the tub. He scrubbed the bathroom floor and toilet bowl with a Pine-Sol mixture and was proud of himself for also having the presence of mind to wipe down the toilet's brass-plated flush handle.

He had to get out of there. He had to leave the cottage residence, and Key West, immediately. Fact was he had to get the hell out of Florida entirely. He wasn't quite sure why, except that he was sensing the approach of trouble. He had always had an extremely keen instinct for survival. It was simply time to move on. For him, Florida had just become too damned hot.

Where to go? he pondered. Should he risk returning to San Francisco? Not wise, he quickly decided; he was too well-known there. It would be no fun anyway if he couldn't frequent his old haunts down in the Castro. Perhaps Seattle, he thought, or maybe Salem, Oregon. No matter, he would just pile his belongings into the car and head out for the West Coast. He'd pick up I-10 in Tallahassee and just keep on truckin'. He'd decide on his next destination as he drove cross-country.

The question then became who would he next be? Should he stay as Elvin Welch? Probably not, he decided. Go back to George Granger? Eric Von Deutsch?

"Shit!" he suddenly snarled, realizing that he couldn't leave Florida quite yet. There remained the question of all of his false-identity documents, as well as the hundred K and the Browning automatic he'd left in that safe-deposit box. He needed a plan.

He'd drive up to Marathon this evening, take a motel room for the weekend, and be at the Bank of America branch office there first thing on Monday morning. He would clean out the safe-deposit box and be free to leave for the coast.

THIRTY

To help ease the mild martini overhang, breakfast for Savage at the Delano was half a cheese Danish and two very dark coffees. Winona Escalante did orange juice, tea, cornflakes, and unbuttered wheat toast. To beat the morning rush-hour nonsense, they then made an early break from Miami Beach, leaving just before seven. With the ragtop folded down to take advantage of the not-so-nasty early a.m. Floridian sun, Savage steered southbound on U.S. 1, hoping to arrive at Key West—the last key in the long chain—sometime around ten, ten thirty. In order to do so, they could have no sightseeing stops along the way.

Aside from some light discussion of the phenomenal year-round weather in Florida, vis-à-vis the harsh winter climes of Auburn, Indiana, and New York City, the main topics of their sporadic talk during the early going centered on the George Granger matter, the cold-blooded butchering of Dr. Herbert Koremvokis, and the far too coincidental hit-and-run death of Ramon Mendez. However, Savage couldn't shake the sense that Winona had something else on her mind as well, something she was looking for an opening to bring up. Turned out that he was right on the money—the topic finally surfaced as Savage slowed the Mustang for a red light on the outskirts of Key Largo.

"Sorry I abandoned you last night," she said matter-of-factly. "Yesterday was a very long day for me. I was really beat. And I don't suppose those outrageous martinis you introduced me to at poolside helped

much either. I was in my room and zonked out by
nine thirty. What time did you finally turn in?"

" 'Bout a half hour after you," Savage replied.
"Went to my room around ten. I knocked right off
too."

He brought the convertible to a complete stop at
the light, behind a relic Winnebago. The tired motor
home had Land of Lincoln license plates, and the blue
vinyl cover of its side-mounted spare was lettered
DOT & AL, PEORIA. A faded and peeling sticker dangling from the misaligned and rust-spotted rear
bumper had once read GO BEARS.

"You didn't happen to try to call me last night, did
you?" she asked, seeming mildly ill at ease with the
query. "Like around nine forty-five, and then again at
ten thirty perhaps?"

"No," he replied, turning to look directly into her
eyes. "Why?"

"Got two phone calls," she said, shrugging slightly
and making a befuddled face. "Two hang-ups. Woke
me from a sound sleep both times. I was groggy, I
said hello, and then I heard, *click*."

"Wasn't me," he assured. The traffic light finally
broke green, and the eyesore Winnebago emitted a
sooty belch of gray-blue smoke as it struggled to break
inertia on its underinflated, balding tires.

"Hmm," she muttered. "I wonder who it might
have been. Truth is," she added coyly, "I was kinda
hoping that it *was* you."

He glanced at her again, only momentarily. She was
holding an undeniable sultry-eyed, it's-your-move
gaze. Not quite ready to go down *that* road yet, he
opted to say nothing and turned his eyes back to the
other road.

Trapped for the next several miles on the single
southbound lane by Dot and Al's mindless snail's
pace, Savage felt a sinking feeling slowly creep into
his chest. A troubling possibility, one that just might
explain the two hang-up phone calls Winona had received last night in her room at the Delano—a room

that in reality was assigned to him—dawned like an unwanted ominous epiphany.

"So, this other party never said a word?" he inquired. "You couldn't tell if it was a man or a woman, but whoever it was heard you say hello and immediately hung up?"

"Right," she replied, the sultry come-on in her voice, for the moment at least, discarded. "It was very weird. Must have been wrong numbers."

The first matter of business when they reached Key West would be to contact Maureen Gallo. He had a bad feeling—a *real* bad feeling—about those two damn calls, and he envisioned a probable scenario.

For whatever reason, either to soften the current tension existing between them because of the Hamptons debacle or to bring him news of Ray's status at the vet's, Maureen had telephoned the Delano at nine forty-five and asked to be connected to Mr. Savage's room. A woman answered—a woman who had been freshly awakened. Not knowing what to say, Maureen hung up. She pondered a myriad of possibilities for forty-five minutes, then decided that maybe she'd been put through to the wrong room by mistake. At ten thirty she again called the Delano, again specified Mr. Savage's room, and again . . .

Dammit!

As they passed through Tavernier, Savage finally saw an opening. He floorboarded the gas pedal, calling on all of the Mustang's eight cylinders, and roared past the dawdling Winnebago. In his rearview mirror, he saw Al flip him the finger. He and Winona spoke little for the remainder of the ride.

Critically checking the fit of her new Versace blouse at her ample bustline, and the drape of her Dior linen slacks at her tummy and butt, Hazel Holloway stood obliquely before the full-length dressing mirror attached to the back of her bedroom door. Both garments looked absolutely wonderful. It was amazing what expensive clothing could do to improve one's shape. She then ran a soft brush several times along the surface of her new do, lightly coaxing a few wayward hairs back into place. She smiled an exaggerated smile to check the line of her lipstick. It too was fine—perfect, in fact. Then, walking rapidly through the hall, she passed through the living room, grabbed up her snake-skin purse, and headed for the apartment door. It would be yet another morning of shopping at Neiman Marcus and Saks, then brunch at the Chin Chin Cafe at New York-New York. Today she would try their lemon chicken.

The doorbell rang just as she reached for the knob to let herself out; she checked through the peephole. Standing just outside the door was a uniformed Las Vegas police officer—a woman. Though near frozen with a dread that she was possibly about to be arrested, she cleared her throat and slowly opened the door.

"Mrs. Holloway?" the officer said, the accent of her medium-pitched voice as Western as that of any movie cowgirl. "Mrs. Hazel Holloway?"

"Yes," she replied, disconcerted. "I am Hazel Holloway."

"Do you have a son by the name of John Boyer Holloway?" the officer inquired, her mood plainly serious.

"Why, yes, I do," Hazel replied quickly and defensively, her mind spinning with all sorts of possibilities. "But he's not here. . . . I mean he's out of the country just now. I mean I don't even know where he is . . . actually."

"Yes, ma'am," the officer said soothingly. "I'm afraid I may be making a notification of some very bad news." She removed a letter-size document from her clipboard, unfolded it, and handed it across.

"What's this?" Holloway asked, her mind still in quizzical race.

"That is a communiqué from the United States State Department to the LVPD. They have requested us to make this notification."

"Well, what does it say . . . what does it mean?"

"It states that Mr. John Boyer Holloway met with a tragic rock-climbing accident on the island of Sardinia at one o'clock yesterday afternoon, their time. I'm sorry to inform you, but he is dead."

"Oh, my God!"

Hazel Holloway dropped to her knees. The officer let herself into the apartment and helped her to a nearby sofa.

"How can I find out just what happened?" Hazel asked.

"That information is contained right within the body of the communiqué," the officer said. Taking it in her hand, she read, " 'Please contact Captain Silvio Cosenza, Olbia Police, Sardinia, Italy.' It contains a telephone number if you wish to make an international call directly to him. Apparently they need to know your wishes as it pertains to the disposition of your son's body."

"Do you think I should call there now?" Hazel asked.

The police officer checked her watch. "I suppose there would be no harm in trying. It's a little after nine in the morning here, but who knows what time it is right now in Sardinia? Could be the middle of the night."

"No. It's just a little after six o'clock in the evening there," Hazel blurted and quickly realized that she should not have known that.

"Will you be all right now, Ms. Holloway?" the officer asked. When Hazel assured her that she was fine, the officer left.

Hazel Holloway brushed the dust from her knees, walked to the wall phone in her designer kitchen, and dialed the lengthy international number. After going through some language difficulties, she was finally connected to the English-speaking Captain Silvio Cosenza.

"Let me start by saying that you have my sincerest sympathy, Signora Holloway," he began.

"Thank you, Captain," she replied, "but are you absolutely certain that the person who was killed was in fact *my* son?"

"Quite certain, madam. He had in his possession several pieces of identification. Besides that, he was in the company of a companion at the time of the accident who has positively identified your son."

"What is the companion's name?"

"A Mr. John Anson Conover, a British citizen. I have a number here where he can be reached. He was eager to speak with you and answer any of your questions about what happened. He said that your son spoke frequently to him about you."

"I see."

"Madam, we can put you in touch with a local funeral service that has taken charge of your son's body. I am sure you wish to have him shipped back to the United States as quickly as possible."

"My son so loved your beautiful island," Hazel Holloway said wistfully. "I know that it would have been his wish to have his ashes spread across the waters there."

"I do understand."

"Do you think that could be arranged with the local funeral service? I mean, do you think that I could have his body cremated there and his ashes then spread?"

"I'm certain of it."

"Then that is what I will have done. But not until I have traveled to Sardinia and seen him for myself and made a positive identification."

"By all means."

After checking in at the Holiday Inn Beachside in Key West, securing two poolside rooms for a minimum of one night and leaving open the possibility of additional nights' stays, Savage and Escalante went to their respective rooms—again adjoining—to drop off their bags. Once he had unpacked, Savage sat down at the edge of his queen-size bed, lifted the telephone, and dialed Maureen's home number. It was nine thirty, and since Mo didn't open her gallery until ten, he thought he might still catch her there. There was no answer. He dialed her cell number; again no answer. Very odd. Maureen always answered on her cell. He opted not to leave a voice mail. He would try reaching her directly again later on in the day. The bad feeling was still there, only more so.

With the intense mid-August sun now higher in the sky, the first matter of business before leaving the Holiday Inn parking lot was to put the Mustang's convertible top back up and set the AC on max.

Their first stop was the Monroe County sheriff's office. There they met with Sergeant Jake Powers and informed him of their purpose in town. The sergeant said he would disseminate that information to his troops in the field, and he also gave Savage assurance of assistance should it become required. When asked for directions to the various Key West real estate companies that Von Deutsch had contacted by phone from Miami, Powers presented them with a detailed street map of the entire key, circled those business locations, and wished them luck. He also suggested they begin their interviews at Benjamin Brown Realty on Truman Street.

Benjamin Brown greeted Savage and Escalante on the neatly painted porch that wrapped the quaint Key West–style cottage that was his office. "Jake Powers called and told me you were heading over. Heck of a nice day, isn't it?" he said, shaking their hands.

Except for an almost imperceptible gimp—a souvenir of June 6, 1944—Ben Brown was in good physical tone considering he was well on the wrong side of seventy, and he emitted a very likable and charming youthful exuberance. He had a strange shock of white hair that plumed off the very top of his head like a pom-pom, an equally white fine mustache, and deep-set, very alert, steel gray eyes.

"I've been dealing in Key West properties since the

mid-fifties," he announced, gesturing them to sit in the soft chairs that faced the desk in his inner office.

"Sergeant Powers assured us that you were the first man to go see," Savage replied with a smile. For some reason he liked this guy. Brown offered coffee, which they both declined.

"I've heard it said that I must know every square inch of this eight-thousand-acre island," Brown said modestly. "I don't know if that's so true, but I do know just about every piece of property that's for sale here, and every efficiency that's for rent."

"Is that you?" Savage asked, pointing to a plainly framed black-and-white eight-by-ten hanging prominently on the office wall. In it, a very slender young man and a white-bearded Ernest Hemingway were posed together beside a huge hanging marlin being weighed in.

"That's me," Brown replied proudly. "In much better days," he added with a friendly laugh. "As a kid, I used to sometimes mate on Papa's boat."

Framed just to the left of the Hemingway photo was Brown's honorable discharge from the U.S. Army. Enclosed in a matching frame on the right side was a certificate honoring Brown's World War II service with the Eighty-second Airborne Division. It was no longer a mystery to Savage why he had instantly liked this man.

"Now, what can we do for you fine folks?" Brown asked.

Savage began. "Sometime within the last week, one of my detectives contacted this office."

"I recall that," Benjamin Brown replied. "A New York detective. I took that call."

"Then you recall him inquiring if you had had any dealings within the past few months with a client using either the name Eric Von Deutsch or George Granger."

"Yes," Brown said. "I told the detective that I had no recollection of either name."

"Fine," Savage went on. "We'd like very much if you would now look at some photographs we've brought along and see if you recall a face."

Winona Escalante removed the collection of photographs from her tote, stood, and placed them before Benjamin Brown. He looked them all over. Savage saw recognition flash in the man's very alert eyes.

"You recognize him, don't you?" Savage asked.

"Yes, I do," Brown replied. The former airborne trooper quickly stood and stepped to a file cabinet in the corner of the room. He pulled open the drawer marked RENTALS and thumbed through a row of folders. Extracting one, he returned to his desk and sat.

"Arranged for a short-term rental for that man about ten days ago," Brown informed. He licked the tips of his thumb and index finger and began flipping through dozens of sheets of paper, quickly scanning each one.

Savage and Escalante exchanged hopeful looks.

"I set him up on a month-to-month over at the Lazy Parrot," Brown said as he continued digging. "Gotta tell ya, I recall him as a real strange man—an oddball, know what I mean? Here it is," he finally said, pulling a sheet from the folder.

Brown's eyes quickly perused the information on the form. "Started him with a three-month stay at the Lazy Parrot; August, September, October. He provided the first month's rent, the last month's rent, and one month's security." Brown looked up. "That was on the seventh. Because only three weeks were left in August, we prorated and gave him credit for that week."

"So he should still be there at the Lazy Parrot," Savage said.

"Oh, yeah," Brown replied. "He's booked into cottage number twelve and still has about ten weeks left. The only thing is he didn't use either of those names that you've asked me about."

"What name did he use?" Winona Escalante asked.

"Welch. Mr. Elvin Welch."

"How did he pay you?" Savage inquired. "Cash . . . check . . . money order?"

"Gave me a check," Brown said. "Bank of America, Marathon branch. See for yourself; got a Xerox of it right here."

"Would you mind making another copy of that check for us?" Escalante asked, as Savage perused the rental agreement and check record.

After getting directions from Brown to the Lazy Parrot, Savage called Manhattan South Homicide. He was put through to Sergeant Billy Lakis, the Team One boss.

"I need a favor, Billy," Savage said.

"Shoot," Lakis replied.

"Could you have one of your people check with all the airlines that service the Miami–Fort Lauderdale area from any of the New York metro airports? See if they can get anything on an Elvin Welch flying from New York on or immediately after May twenty-eighth, this year."

"Anything else?" Lakis asked.

"Have someone get with Troop E of the Florida Highway Patrol out of Miami. Have them fax our office everything they've got on a hit-and-run of a pedestrian by the name of Ramon Mendez. Have them make it to the attention of Jack Lindstrom."

"You got a time and place of occurrence?"

"Three days ago. It went down along the Overseas Highway, somewhere above Key Largo."

THIRTY-ONE

Savage's instincts told him to bypass contacting the local sheriff's and police departments and requesting that they provide any sort of assistance in taking Granger down. He would prefer to simply drive right over to the Lazy Parrot and knock on Georgie Boy's cottage door as if he were a Jehovah's Witness looking to save a wayward soul. When the murderous bastard answered the door—no doubt to tell him to get lost—Savage would simply barge in and introduce Mr. Granger to Messrs. Smith & Wesson. Then, and only then, would he ring up the local sheriff's department and request that one unit swing by for transport.

Then, after an in-depth interrogation of Granger—with a view toward acquiring statements about the murder of Elvin Welch and information on the current whereabouts of John Boyer Holloway—Savage would turn Granger over to Miami Homicide to answer for Dr. Herbert Koremvokis and possibly Ramon Mendez. He could leave it up to the State of New York to haggle with the State of Florida on questions of jurisdiction, and any hope for Granger's eventual extradition. But then it would be end of story here; he and Winona Escalante would be on the next plane out to New York City. Once home, he could take care of his own damn business, like looking in on Ray and trying to straighten things out with Maureen . . . not necessarily in that order.

However, Savage realized that he was a stranger in a strange land and owed it to local law enforcement to apprise them of his plans to collar a deadly hump implicated in possibly three murders. The problem inherent there was that they would want to give more than assistance. Unless he missed his guess, they would completely take over and maybe turn a simple arrest into a three-ring made-for-TV cop circus. He could just see it all now: The call would go out, and all the local SWAT team members would have to run home and get into their G.I. Joe camouflage gear, take a half hour to lace up their jump boots and fully load their Uzis or MAC-10s and pull on their black ski masks—whatever the hell hiding their faces was over all about.

In a fraction of the time it would take to get all that bullshit even started, Savage figured he could already have Granger collared, cuffed, transported, and cooling nicely in a sheriff's holding cell, and himself off to Duval Street for a relaxing lunch and celebratory cocktail with Winona. Always an advocate of less is more, he would try to avoid "assistance" that he did not want.

With the top again down, radio tuned loudly to something by the Beach Boys, and Winona Escalante beside him smiling like a gaga trysting tourist, Savage pulled the Mustang right into the Lazy Parrot driveway and parked near cottage numbers 12 and 14. He saw peripherally that no one had peered out of 12; the place just had that quiet no-one-is-home look. He stepped out of the convertible and looked around as if surveying the cottages as a place to stay. He then ad-libbed some gobbledygook small talk with Escalante, who remained seated in the car. She kept smiling and nodding enthusiastically.

When certain that they had established themselves as a pair of out-of-town rubes to anyone who might be looking on, Savage made his move. Doing his best to appear nonthreatening, he schlepped up to the front door of cottage 12 and knocked three times. No one answered. He peeked through the front window. No one. Thinking perhaps that the man was relaxing near the pool, Savage followed the signs along a winding

flower-lined path to the back of the complex. There
were half a dozen people lounging poolside, four men
and two women. All were naked as jaybirds. One of
the chicks—a thirtyish bottle blonde—had a body
suited for a *Penthouse* centerfold but a face more
suited for *Popular Mechanics*. Poised at the tip of the
diving board, keeping absolutely no secrets from the
world, she was taking her time contemplating whether
to jump or dive. George Granger was not among the
group.

"Nice form," Winona Escalante murmured, having
sidled up to Savage just as Miss Hacksaw bounced
once and made a headfirst plunge into the inviting
blue water.

"Oh, yeah," he commented with a slight laugh.
"*Very* nice form. Wanna take a dip?"

Winona Escalante smiled too eagerly.

"Can I help you?" The question came from an older
man with a three-day growth of gray beard. He was
dressed in wrinkled khaki shorts and approached them
from one of the nearby outbuildings. His unlaced Top-
siders and scruffy T-shirt had paint speckles that
matched perfectly the pink shade of the cottage's
shutters.

"Hi, there," Savage said, casual and relaxed. "The
missus and I were just admiring the place. Do you
have any vacancies, and can we find out about your
rates?"

"I'm Jacob, the caretaker here," the man said. "You
need to speak with Mr. Hagerty. Please follow me."

Stopping every few feet to pluck a weed from the
flower beds that lined the winding path, Jacob slowly
led them to a small registration office at the front of
the complex and well within view of cottage 12. The
door to the office was locked. Jacob opened it with
a passkey.

"Oh, I guess Mr. Hagerty isn't here just now,"
Jacob advised. "He's probably gone downtown for
supplies or to the post office. You'll just have to wait,
or try calling back later in the day."

"Well, there would be no point in our calling back if there are no vacancies," Savage pointed out. "Can you at least tell us that much?"

"Only one vacancy," Jacob replied. He pointed across the driveway. "Unit twelve."

"How long has it been vacant?" Winona asked coyly.

"Since last night. But don't worry," Jacob quickly assured. "The place is absolutely spotless and ready to go. The man who had it must have been some sort of clean freak. He scrubbed down the entire place before he left. I'll tell you, in this business, you don't see that happen too damn often."

Thank God I didn't contact the locals, Savage thought. I'd have an army descending on a dry hole. Inexplicably, his thoughts slipped momentarily to Ray. He again wondered if Maureen's attempts at calling him at the Delano last night had anything to do with his ailing roommate.

"How about letting us in so that we could do a quick look around?" Savage suggested. "See if unit twelve will suit our needs."

"I suppose that'd be all right," Jacob replied. "Come, follow me."

As soon as Jacob pushed open the front door to the quaint cottage, a blast of Pine-Sol and other scouring-agent aromas assaulted them like a well-planted punch. Just as the handyman had said, unit 12 was spotless—scrubbed and scoured to a fare-thee-well.

George Granger was gone, and it was time to bring Jacob aboard. Savage and Escalante introduced themselves and announced their real reasons for being there. Jacob quickly identified the photographs of George Granger as the man who had lived there under the name of Elvin Welch.

"We were informed that Mr. Welch had a lease for this place and was paid up until October," Savage said, carefully swinging open the kitchen cabinets and drawers. Every glass and dish sparkled. Every knife and fork was wiped clean and neatly stacked. Clearly the man had fastidiously erased every possible fingerprint.

"That's true," Jacob replied. "Yesterday, when he suddenly announced that he was checking out, he tried getting some of his money back from Mr. Hagerty." The gritty-looking handyman laughed slightly. "But that's like getting blood from a stone."

"Did he say why he was leaving and where he was going?" Escalante asked.

"Nope. All the man said was that something had come up in his personal life and that he had to leave Florida. Then he borrowed my Pine-Sol, pulled on a pair of green rubber gloves, and spent the balance of the day scrubbing this whole unit down. Every glass, every dish, every doorknob . . . everything. The guy was like a dynamo. Mr. Hagerty wanted to hire him."

"Didn't you think that was a bit weird?" Winona asked, scrunching up her face. "A guest scouring the entire place like that before he leaves?"

Jacob looked mildly askance at the insurance investigator, then cracked an easy smile. "Ma'am, this is Key West," he said. "Weird was invented here."

"What kind of car did he have?" Savage asked, continuing to open every closet door and every drawer as he moved through the cottage.

"A Mercury," Jacob replied, tagging behind. "A big one, a Marquis. Tan. Don't know the year, but it looked pretty new."

"When he checked in, was his license plate number recorded anywhere?" Savage inquired.

"Mr. Hagerty generally makes it a point of getting plate numbers of guests. You'd have to ask him, though."

"Did this guy ever have any visitors?" Savage asked.

"One, that I recall," Jacob replied. "A Hispanic-lookin' fella. Stayed the night. Had him a real crappy car, an old Toyota; leaked oil all over the damn driveway. Took me an hour to clean it up the next day."

"Did you know the guy's name?" Escalante asked. "No."

"Was that Toyota a red Corolla?" Savage inquired.

"Yeah, a Corolla, that's it. And it *was* red, but it was badly faded. Needed a muffler too."

Savage and Escalante exchanged a knowing glance.

Jacob then peered out the front window as a purple vintage VW Bug pulled into the lot. A large man with big ears emerged and let himself into the registration office. "Looks like Mr. Hagerty is back," he said.

"Something is missing," Savage announced, throwing open his palms in question. "I've looked in every drawer and every cabinet. Can't find that bottle of Pine-Sol."

"It's out in the trash bin," Jacob said. "There wasn't that much left in the bottle when I gave it to him, and he used it all up."

"Did you put it in the trash bin?" Savage inquired.

"No. He did. I saw him do it just after he put his bags in his car and just before he drove off."

"When he put it in the trash, was he still wearing those green rubber gloves?"

"Matter of fact," Jacob replied, mildly straining his recollection, "I don't believe he was."

After leaving the Lazy Parrot Cottages with the discarded Pine-Sol bottle—and the license plate number of Granger's car, supplied by Bob Hagerty—Savage and Escalante spent the rest of Saturday afternoon into early evening at the Monroe County sheriff's office. There, Savage was able to institute a statewide alarm for the man and the tan Marquis he'd somehow managed to rent from Avis under the name Eric Von Deutsch.

In contact also with the Florida Highway Patrol, Savage learned that a green Lincoln with body damage to the right front had been found abandoned in a shopping center parking lot in Marathon, it had been stolen on Wednesday last, only hours before Ramon Mendez had been run down. Highway Patrol believed it to be the death car; they were still checking the vehicle for prints and awaiting blood-spot analysis. They had already pretty much confirmed a match of the tire tread marks left on the soft shoulder at the hit-and-run scene.

Monroe County sheriff Jake Powers informed Savage that his crime scene tech was away for the weekend at a "SWAT competition" up in Palm Beach, but he nonetheless arranged for Savage to borrow his department's fingerprint-dusting kit. With it, Savage was able to raise several prints on the plastic Pine-Sol container. By Saturday evening a number of things had been established. Although the Pine-Sol bottle bore a number of different prints, one matched perfectly the right index finger of George Granger. Now, beyond any shadow of legal doubt, it could be said that Granger was, in fact, very much still alive.

At ten after seven, Savage and Escalante left the sheriff's office. They drove to the heart of Key West's historic harbor district at Land's End, parked the Mustang, and decided to have dinner at Turtle Kraals waterfront place on Margaret Street. They were shown to a two-top right at water's edge that looked out across the Key West Bight.

"I'm Heather," the pretty, well-tanned young waitress said, "and I'll be your server. Cocktails?"

"I'll have a Rum Runner," Winona replied.

"Extra-dry Belvedere martini, up, with a twist," Savage said.

Heather returned in only moments with their drinks. "The sunset tonight is at seven fifty-five," she advised, glancing at the watch on her slender wrist. "Which is in twenty minutes. You've got the best seat in the house."

"Does everybody watch the sunset in Key West?" Winona asked.

"We don't watch sunsets here," Heather lightly replied. "We celebrate them. May I take your orders?"

Winona went with oysters on the half shell as an appetizer, followed with spicy jalapeño fritters, a TK house salad, and a six-ounce lobster tail as an entrée. Savage opted for clams on the half shell and flash-fried calamari; he took a pass on the salad and ordered the seafood platter entrée broiled in Key lime garlic butter.

After Heather turned toward the kitchen to place the orders, Savage and Winona clinked glasses.

"Cheers," they said simultaneously.

Savage's cell phone then rang out. The caller was Sergeant Billy Lakis, the Team One boss back at Manhattan South Homicide.

"What are you doing in the office?" Savage questioned. "I figured you'd gotten stuck with that detail up at Gracie Mansion or the Waldorf."

"Damn things got canceled, thank God," Lakis replied.

"Lucky you. What's up?"

"We got a call from Patti Capwell over at Telephone Security a few hours ago."

"Talk to me," Savage replied, taking a sip of the icy top-shelf vodka.

"Jack Lindstrom had requested a trace on a number that Janus had dialed from his office phone the other day. Apparently Janus had placed the call just a little while before you and your team actually collared him."

"Right. Marcus had picked it up on the wire. It was a call that went to an answering machine. We wanted to know the who and where."

"I thought you'd like to know that, according to Patti Capwell, that phone number comes back newly registered to one Hazel Holloway in Las Vegas, Nevada."

"Awright," Savage said, elated. He flashed his eyes toward Winona.

"That's not all," Lakis went on. "She then did a search of all the phone numbers that have been called from that new listing; came up with something really quite interesting."

"Okay."

"One of the last calls made from that number—shortly after nine o'clock this morning—went to an exchange in friggin' Sardinia."

"*Sardinia!* As in Europe . . . Sardinia?"

"You got it," Lakis replied. "Then right after the call to Sardinia, several calls were made to a Continental Airline eight-hundred number."

"Someone flying in from Sardinia?" Savage mused.

"Nope," Lakis said. "Apparently someone's flying out. I took the liberty of calling Continental Security. One Hazel Holloway is booked on flights from Vegas to Houston to London, and from there, a connecting flight straight into Sardinia. She's scheduled to arrive there tomorrow afternoon, four o'clock local time. I haven't the foggiest idea what that would be in our time."

"That's ten o'clock in the morning for us," Savage mumbled without hesitation. "Did Telephone Security say if they had any way of identifying who owned that number she called in Sardinia?"

"Oh, yeah!" Lakis replied. "Get this. She had a twenty-two minute connection with someone at police headquarters in the Sardinian town of Olbia."

"Jesus!" Savage replied, his mind suddenly racing. "Give me that number, Billy," he said. "Tomorrow's going to be a long day. Running down that call in Sardinia will give me something to do."

As Lakis read off the foreign telephone number, Savage scribbled the digits onto a paper napkin.

"The boss wants to know what's going on down there," Lakis said, "and when you'll be heading home."

"We're all the way down in Key West, and we missed Granger by only hours," Savage said. "The freakin' trail is ice cold now. Tell the boss I'll be back in New York by Monday evening."

"If Granger's long gone, Pete's gonna want to know why you're not coming back tomorrow, on Sunday?"

"Got one more piece of business while I'm down here," Savage responded. "Granger's been writing checks from an account he opened at a bank up on Marathon Key. I intend to be standing tall at that bank when they open their doors for business on Monday morning."

THIRTY-TWO

Brushed by a tropical depression spinning its way up the Gulf side of the Florida peninsula, Key West was battened down and covered up on Sunday morning. Savage had never seen it rain so hard. If Noah and his sons were alive, surely they'd already have a keel laid.

After a hot shower, a needed shave, and a cup of room-brewed coffee, Savage sat down at the desk in his Key West motel room and, with more than one attempt, succeeded in making the fifteen-digit overseas telephone connection. It then became a tedious process of explaining who he was, and his purpose, to three separate people, each speaking varying degrees of English. He was finally put through to the office of Silvio Cosenza, captain of the investigative wing at the Olbia, Sardinia, Police Agency. As it turned out, the man spoke almost flawless English. In short order, Savage brought the captain up to speed on the murder investigation he had been conducting, John Boyer Holloway's complicity therein, and his belief that the man might be somewhere there in Sardinia. Cosenza listened to the entire story without interrupting. When Savage was done, the Sardinian policeman explained that John Boyer Holloway was dead, killed in a fall there three days prior.

"Are you absolutely certain that the dead man is really John Boyer Holloway?" Savage asked, conflicted with relief and disbelief.

"As yet, I would have no reason to doubt," Cosenza replied. "The man was in possession of much identification."

"We've seen that act before," Savage remarked, then asked, "By any chance, was the dead man carrying any photographs of himself in that wallet?"

"None," Cosenza said. "Not that it would have made any difference. Mr. Holloway had fallen from a great distance. He must have struck his head and face several times against the ragged cliff wall while in free fall."

"Unrecognizable?" Savage inquired.

"Badly battered . . . totally unrecognizable. However, his height, weight, hair and eye color all conformed to the identification he was carrying. Beyond that, his body has been identified by a companion with whom he had been traveling."

"A *companion*?" Savage uttered. "What was the companion's name?"

"John Anson Conover," Cosenza replied. "A British national."

"Was this guy Conover with Holloway at the time he was killed?"

"Yes. They were hiking and rock climbing together."

"Was the fall witnessed by anyone other than this companion?"

"No. But fatalities up there are not uncommon. We drag bodies out of that region all too often."

"Let me ask you something, Captain," Savage said. "Just off the top of your head, how closely would you say that this guy Conover matches up against the ID that had been found on the body?"

"Very close," the Italian conceded. "Both men have blond hair, both have blue eyes. . . ."

"How about height and weight?"

"Quite similar."

"Shit," Savage growled, getting a bad feeling. "Does this guy Conover have *real* positive identification with him?"

"He carries a current British passport, and the photo inside of it is clearly him. Of that there is no doubt."

"Hmm," Savage mused, his mind in race. "We have information that Holloway's mother, Hazel Holloway, is en route to Olbia as we speak. She's due to arrive there from London around three p.m. your time, tomorrow. Which is in about twenty-five hours."

"I have myself spoken already to the woman," Cosenza said. "She declined to make arrangements to have her son's body shipped back to the United States. She instead insisted on coming here, making an official identification of her son's body, then arranging for it to be cremated."

"Cremated? *There* . . . in *Sardinia*?" Savage asked. The little hairs on the back of his neck had sprung to full attention.

"Yes. Then, Signora Holloway wishes to have the ashes strewn on the Tyrrhenian. Mr. Conover has offered the use of his boat."

"Jesus," Savage moaned. "Please don't let that happen."

"What is your problem, Sergeant?" Cosenza asked.

"My problem is that I believe that there is a body switch going on."

"À la the case in New York which you have described to me?" Cosenza inquired.

"Yes. À la *that* case, Captain Cosenza."

"Sergeant, if you are doubting that the body in our possession is truly that of John Boyer Holloway," Cosenza said, "then perhaps we can settle that question before we permit the mortician to cremate the body. Can you fax me Mr. Holloway's fingerprints? I will compare them to those of the dead man. If they do not match, I will even go so far as to compare them to his companion, Mr. Conover."

"That's very good of you, Captain," Savage replied, "but we have no fingerprints for John Boyer Holloway to send you. He was never in the military, nor has he ever been arrested here in the United States. His fingerprints are nowhere within our law enforcement files."

"Do you know if he has any scars or marks? Tattoos, perhaps? Something . . . *anything* to establish positive identity?"

"None that we are aware of."

"That is quite unfortunate," Cosenza said. "But if Signora Holloway identifies the body as her son, will that not satisfy you?"

"No," Savage replied. "She's the sole beneficiary of her son's million-and-a-half-dollar life insurance policy."

"I do not wish to sound naive, Sergeant, but do you actually think that a mother would intentionally misidentify her son as being dead?"

Savage had to roll his eyes, but he kept his tone even. "Captain, every nerve in my body is telling me that she is in league with her son. If I'm right, they get another million-five dropped into their laps, and with John Boyer Holloway officially declared dead in Sardinia and his body cremated, he ceases having to look over his shoulder as a fugitive from justice in the United States. It's a win-win. He starts off nice and clean with tons of found money."

"Ah, so," Cosenza commiserated. "But, Sergeant, in the absence of any proof that a crime has been committed here, I must accept a mother's word. I would be powerless to hold the body or stop the cremation."

"Please, Captain," Savage said, "stall it for as long as you can. Give me some time."

As soon as Savage hung up, he dialed the home phone number of Jack Lindstrom in New York. Just awakened, Lindstrom sounded groggy when he answered.

"How did the wedding go yesterday?" Savage inquired.

"It went terrific," Lindstrom replied. "Everything went like clockwork. Best wedding I've ever been to. My daughter was beautiful."

"That's great," Savage said.

"You back in New York?"

"Nope. Still in Florida," Savage responded. "Will be until tomorrow night. But I need you and the team to do that Harley Hopkins visit first thing tomorrow morning. It's imperative."

"We were scheduling that for when you got back."

"No time," Savage said flatly. He quickly related the conversation he'd just had with Captain Silvio Cosenza. "We need to know about any scars, marks, moles, or tattoos. Any damn thing that Hopkins may have seen on Holloway's body."

"Which could help truly determine if that DOA in Sardinia is, or is not, our boy, John Holloway," Lindstrom finished the thought.

"If Hopkins can give you anything at all," Savage directed, "you are to contact me immediately on my cell. That cremation is scheduled to take place at about noon, our time, tomorrow."

"And if it turns out that the DOA *is* Holloway?" Lindstrom asked.

"We close the case," Savage replied. "But if it's not him, we demand that Sardinia take a much closer look at his companion, Mr. John Anson Conover, before he can set sail."

THIRTY-THREE

Monday, August 19, 7:50 A.M.

With George Granger split from Key West without leaving any clue as to where he might be headed, Savage and Winona Escalante checked out of the Holiday Inn and began the hour-long drive up to the Bank of America on Marathon Key. There, they would make a brief stop and get whatever information they could on Granger's recent bank dealings, then continue on to Miami International. They were booked on an early-afternoon return flight to New York.

Although upset that they'd been a day late and a dollar short, and that the son of a bitch Granger was still out and about, Savage fully realized that the time spent in Florida had nonetheless been a success.

Maureen Gallo, however, was still not answering his calls—damned caller ID—either at home or on her cell phone. And only moments before driving away from the motel, Savage had placed a call to Dr. Jane Figueroa, but as expected, he reached only a recording; it was still early, and the vet's office up in New York was not open yet.

"Well, we're headed home," Winona, said, speaking over a Frankie Valli falsetto that was testing the Mustang's tweeters. "Bet you can't wait to get back to your desk at Manhattan South."

"Yeah, it'll be good," he replied. He wondered how his team would make out getting to Harley Hopkins this morning. If they came up with something—anything—he could recontact Sardinia and somehow try to stop that cremation—if it hadn't already taken place.

"It's going to be another hot one today," Winona opined.

"That's for sure," Savage agreed. "Why the hell are you wearing that business suit and those half-heels, for crissakes? You should be dressed a bit more casually, don't you think?"

"We're going up to a bank right now," she replied, "are we not? This is business, and I am representing my company."

"God bless you," he said, rolling his eyes. He'd opted for a light short-sleeved shirt and linen slacks.

"How did you sleep last night?" Winona asked, seemingly offhandedly. She reached to the dash and toned Frankie down a notch.

"Pretty good," Savage replied. "You?"

"Not so good."

"How come?"

"Did you ever ache for something," she said softly. "I mean really ache for something you wanted very much to have . . . and failed to get."

He didn't answer. He swirled the possibilities of where she was going with this around inside his head. He wasn't at all sure that he was going to enjoy the probable destination.

"I guess I have," he finally responded seriously, hoping it would end there.

"We've been in Florida for days," she said wistfully, clearly wanting to press the issue. "A thousand miles away from everyone we know. We've shared drinks and dinners together at perfectly romantic spots."

"Uh-huh."

"But we've been sleeping merely feet apart, separated only by thin walls and pass doors . . ."

"Yeah, I know," he murmured.

"I would have been very discreet, Thorn. If that's what was worrying you," she said outright.

"I know that," he said, his reply thoughtful and soft. He did not wish to hurt or in any way embarrass the woman, but right now he had more than enough lady problems on his hands.

"I like you very much," he went on, still softly. "What's not to like? And if things were different in my personal life, if I were not so involved in a long-time fairly committed relationship—despite its all too frequent goddamned ups and downs—I would have been the one to have made the moves on you, but . . ."

Winona Escalante exhaled hard, turned, and looked out the passenger window.

The car fell awkwardly silent for the next hour.

George Granger paid cash for his three-night stay at the run-down Sandrift Motel. Dressed in a loud and loose-fitting Hawaiian shirt, baggy shorts, and his favorite pair of two-strap Birkenstock sandals, he loaded his bags into the tan Marquis and made the short three-block drive to the Marathon Diner out on U.S. 1. He'd have some coffee, a light breakfast, and wait out the clock; it would be only another thirty-five minutes or so.

The weekend seemed to have taken a month. He'd arrived at the one-star motel on Friday night, and the next two days had seemed endless, as if they would go on forever. He'd spent most of the time smoking in bed and watching idiotic television. If only he hadn't needed to stick around Marathon until Monday morning, he'd have been halfway to the West Coast by now—probably in Texas already.

Granger pulled off the highway, parked the Mercury in front of the diner, locked the car's doors, and went inside. He sat at the middle of the short counter. Quickly scanning the whole place, he decided it could use a paint job, then, as he looked behind the counter, a little cleanser and some elbow grease, as well. He spotted a large roach darting behind some cups and saucers stacked beside the tall coffee urn. He glanced at the clock; only thirty more minutes to kill.

"It's not a roach," a waitress advised flatly, dropping a greasy breakfast menu on the equally greasy counter before him. "It was what we call a palmetto bug."

"Yeah, right," Granger mumbled. He thought he was going to puke.

The curt woman in the soiled waitress uniform was easily in her sixties. She wore way too much eye shadow and had way too little personality.

"Give me a coffee and an English muffin."

"Butter?" the hag asked.

"Yeah," he replied. "Butter."

A pretty redhead with a ponytail was visible in the entry foyer of the Bank of America. Dressed in a white blouse and tan skirt, she was unlocking the glass doors, opening the place for business just as Savage and Winona Escalante pulled into the strip mall parking lot.

"How's that for timing?" Savage asked. He whipped the Mustang into the nearest spot and shut down the motor.

They each gathered up their case folders and went immediately inside the bank. There, after identifying themselves to an older female teller, they were directed to the new accounts rep, Gloria Garibaldi. They walked to her desk on the opposite end of the building and sat, their backs to the teller stations.

At the very instant that the clock on the Marathon Diner wall read nine a.m., George Granger downed the last two gulps of his cold coffee. He left three singles and a dime on the counter to cover the three-dollar check, nodded in the direction of the snotty, overly made-up, and inattentive waitress, and left.

From the greasy spoon it was a mere few miles' drive up U.S. 1 to the bank. Once there, it would take him only minutes to take the hundred grand, the 9-millimeter, and his collection of identifications from the safe-deposit box. Then he'd be on his way out of Florida. Salem, in the beautiful state of Oregon, was beckoning. He slid back behind the wheel of the tan Mercury, lit up a Merit, and started the car's engine.

It was ten minutes after nine when he pulled into the strip mall. He parked nose in in front of Hanlon's Men's Store. Toting his large vinyl valise, he locked the Mercury's doors, quickly window-shopped the Tommy Bahama shirts in Hanlon's window, and strode directly into the Bank of America next door. After showing his Elvin Welch identification to a red-head with a ponytail, he was shown into the privacy of the safe-deposit room.

THIRTY-FOUR

It had been Continental Air from Las Vegas to Houston, then, with a change of planes, Continental to London Gatwick. From there, Hazel Holloway took a three-and-a-half-hour direct flight with easy-Jet into Olbia Sardinia Costa International Airport, arriving at three p.m. local time. The long trip had been uneventful but exhausting. Her son, John Boyer Holloway, awaited her at the gate. They embraced tightly.

"Darling," she whispered into his ear. "God, it is so good to see you. I've missed you so."

"Careful, Mother," he whispered back. "It's possible we're being watched. Remember, I'm John Anson Conover, your son's friend who has come here to meet you on this very sad occasion. Treat me accordingly from here on in."

They relaxed their embrace.

"Do you really think that we're being watched?" she asked quietly.

"You never know. I just don't want to take any chances."

"That's my boy," she ventriloquized. "Always thinking."

"Come," he said, extending his hand to take her carry-on bag. "I've hired a taxi."

"Where are we going from here . . . *Mr. Conover*?" Hazel Holloway inquired, handing over the bag.

"We are to meet with Captain Cosenza at a mortuary at four o'clock. I know where it is. He will be there to witness you making an official identification of your son's body."

"Other than what we discussed last night on the phone, is there anything else I need to remember?"

"Yes. Please remember to sob." He patted his pocket. "I've brought tissues along."

"And the cremation," she said. "When is that scheduled to take place?"

"If all goes well, ten o'clock tomorrow morning. Then we take the ashes for a nice boat ride and we are home free. I've even put some champagne aboard."

"I love you, darling," she whispered.

"Come, Mrs. Holloway," he said strongly. "We'll go collect your other bags. From here, it's only a ten-minute ride into downtown Olbia. Are you hungry, Mrs. Holloway? Would you like to freshen up at your hotel first?"

As they moved chatting through the small airport toward the baggage carousel, a balding man with a cherubic round face and dark glasses folded up his newspaper. He rose from the waiting-room seat and discreetly followed.

It was 9:05 A.M. when Jack Lindstrom pulled to the curb in front of the Connaught and parked. The staid apartment building's entrance was directly opposite Central Park at West Eighty-first Street. As he, Diane DeGennaro, and Richie Marcus all exited the car, a spit-and-polished Connaught doorman, Clifton, appeared on the sidewalk.

"May I help you?" Clifton inquired as Diane and Richie made a show of digging through camera equipment inside the vehicle's trunk. Clifton's query, though civil, came through with an unmistakably snooty I-beg-your-pardon-but-you-don't-belong-here ring.

Lindstrom discreetly opened his shield case and revealed his detective's gold. "We're with Special Investigations," he said in a muted tone. "We've got to use your rooftop to take some elevated photographs of this section of Central Park."

"Well, just whom have you cleared this all with?" the crisply efficient Clifton asked, frowning deeply. "No one has notified me to expect any—"

"What do you mean, who have we cleared this with?" Lindstrom said, irked, cutting the haughty man off in midsentence. "We don't need to clear it with anybody. This is a homeland security and police matter. You just show us to the elevators." He made sure his tone was firm and contained just the right amount of the *you*-are-*not*-in-charge-here dismissive.

"Do you think we should take both the Nikon and the Canon, boss?" Diane called out to Lindstrom, as if on cue.

"I don't think we'll need the Nikon," Lindstrom replied thoughtfully. "Just bring the Canon."

"Wait just a minute here," Clifton announced, raising his hands defensively and becoming visibly annoyed as the three detectives headed for the building's entry. "I know you're the police," he harrumphed, "but I just can't let you go browsing around our building—not without some kind of . . . approval."

"We ain't gonna be browsing around inside your building," Richie Marcus announced in his surliest growl. "We're going up to the roof to shoot some pictures, and then we're outta here. Got it . . . *Clifton*?"

As a humbled Clifton led the three through the lobby, Lindstrom thought that it was moments like this that made Richie Marcus priceless.

The three rode a polished-burl and beveled-mirror-lined elevator car to the building's twenty-second floor. There they exited and moved quickly along the wide and richly appointed hallway to the emergency stairwell. Bypassing floor twenty-three, they quickly climbed two flights of bare concrete steps to the heavy steel door that exited to the building's spacious gravel-covered rooftop.

"Nice ad-lib about the cameras," Lindstrom said to Diane, as they crossed to the roof's park side.

"Thanks," she replied, her soft blues spectacular in

the midmorning sunlight. "But it was a good thing you said bring the Canon—it's the only one we had."

They both laughed.

It was a beautiful summer day, and the three stood briefly in silent awe looking out at the phenomenal view. To the east lay the magnificent green of Central Park, the 843-acre oasis that ran from Fifty-ninth Street up to 110th Street smack-dab in the middle of Manhattan Island. From their height above the trees they could easily distinguish several park landmarks: the Delacorte Theatre at the foot of the Great Lawn, the Obelisk, the Shakespeare Garden and Belvedere Castle. Adjacent to the Connaught's south side, taking up two city blocks from West Seventy-ninth to West Eighty-first between Central Park West and Columbus Avenue, stood the imposing American Museum of Natural History. To say that this was a high-rent district, Lindstrom mused, was like saying that Bill Gates had a few bucks.

"You know," Marcus said, gazing out reflectively at the expansive park, "that place is what makes this city. New York wouldn't be shit without that park."

"Gee, I've never heard it put so succinctly or sagely, Rich," Diane responded.

Amused by Richie's crude observation and Diane's saccharine sarcasm, Lindstrom triggered the portable radio. "MS-One to MS-Two."

"MS-Two," Officer Carroll Henderson's voice replied. "Are you all in position?" he asked.

"That's affirmative," Lindstrom said. "We're on the roof. Subject's apartment is on the twenty-third floor immediately below us. We'll have access via the stairwell. Is our star all set?"

"I'm as ready as I'll ever be," Henderson replied.

"Roll 'em."

Jack Lindstrom looked over the edge of the roof and watched as the silver Taurus pulled to the curb on West Eighty-first Street near the entrance to the Hayden Planetarium. Seconds later, the temporarily borrowed rookie, Hollywood Henderson, emerged.

Henderson was wearing skintight jeans and a tan linen shirt open damn near to the navel; he wore an ersatz diamond stud in his right earlobe and carried a prissy shoulder bag. Diane had spent twenty minutes gelling and primping his short hair into the height of *GQ* chic. Before they left the office, Richie Marcus had slinked alongside Henderson and asked him what he was doing next Friday night. The rookie took it all in stride. He was a nice kid.

Lindstrom saw Henderson open the shoulder bag and discreetly extract a small portable radio. The bag also contained a mini tape recorder.

"Radio check." Henderson's voice crackled over Lindstrom's radio.

"You're coming in five-by-five," Lindstrom assured. "Break a leg."

The rookie slipped the radio back into the shoulder bag and continued moving along Eighty-first Street toward Central Park West.

Lindstrom didn't know if this gambit had even the slightest chance of working; he wondered if the soft-spoken rookie had the moxie to pull it off. He crossed his fingers. Too late to worry about it. Hell, it was showtime.

Gloria Garibaldi certainly was friendly enough, so much so that Savage wished he could start to do his banking there in Marathon, Florida.

"There is a problem, Sergeant," the new-accounts rep said. "Due to privacy laws, and strict bank policy, I am prevented from releasing any bank records whatsoever, absent a court order."

"I understand," Savage replied. "And I fully expected that. I will have those necessary orders in place within the next few days. May I forward them to your attention so that they can be expedited?"

"Absolutely," Garibaldi assured him with a big smile.

Savage opened his case folder and dropped the full-

face photo of Elvin Welch on the woman's desk.
"Have you ever seen this person before?"

"No," Garibaldi replied without hesitation.

"How about this fellow?" Savage asked, displaying
Granger's picture.

"That's the man whose account information you've
requested," she replied. "That is Mr. Elvin Welch."

"You're sure?" Winona Escalante pressed.

"Positive. I personally opened his account."

Savage and Winona Escalante were satisfied. They
had gotten most of what they had come for.

"Shall we?" Savage asked Winona, nodding toward
the bank's doors after shaking hands and thanking
Gloria Garibaldi for her time and help.

"I'm almost ready," she replied. "But it's going to
be a long ride to Miami." Turning then to Ms. Garibaldi, she asked, "Is there a ladies' room here?"

Garibaldi pointed to a door in the corner of the
room. "Through there," she said. "First door on
your left."

"I'll wait for you in the car," Savage advised. "I'll
get the AC cranked up."

"I'll be right out," she replied.

Although it was only fifteen minutes after nine in
the morning, he could already feel the South Florida
sun on his shoulders as he crossed the lot toward the
Mustang. He felt sorry for the overdressed Winona as
he unlocked the convertible's trunk and carefully
packed the case folder containing both the Granger
and the Welch photographs into his soft-sided bag.
Since the next stop would be the airport, and since he
could not board the plane wearing his weapon, he
pulled the holstered Smith & Wesson .38 Chief from
his belt and packed it inside the bag as well. The gun
would travel in the plane's belly with the checked luggage. He closed the trunk, unlocked the driver's door,
and climbed in behind the steering wheel. As he did,
something caught his eye.

It was a Mercury Marquis, a tan one, parked not

fifty feet away. To the best of Savage's recollection, the big sedan had not been there when he and Winona had arrived. He started the Mustang, backed it from its spot, and idled it slowly across the parking lot. When he got within twenty-five feet of the car, he was able to distinguish its Florida license plate number. It was a number that he now knew by heart. The Mercury also bore an Avis identifier decal on the rear window glass. He backed the Mustang up and parked it midway between the bank and the Mercury. He shut the engine off.

While in the bank, he hadn't seen anyone enter, and he didn't recall seeing anyone except female employees inside when he left—but he sensed that Granger somehow must be in there. But, then again, maybe he was in the card shop . . . or the men's store.

George Granger sat in a private cubicle inside the safe-deposit room. Though the teller with the ponytail was still in the room with him, tending to whatever, it was not possible for her to see him past the cubicle partition.

He had already packed the collection of identifications back into a side pocket of the valise and, one by one, carefully packed the stacks of hundred-dollar bills back into the more spacious center section. He pushed the holstered 9-millimeter into his waistband and covered it with his shirt. Suddenly another teller entered the room. He would wait until the two women finished before he got up and left.

"Myra," he heard one say to the other, "I want you to be on the lookout for a fax that should be arriving sometime within the next few days. As soon as it comes in, bring it right to me."

"Okay," Myra responded. "What will it be about?"

"It will be a court order from New York City. Those two New York detectives that were just at my desk want us to provide any and all records on the account recently opened by a Mr. Elvin Welch. And they want them ASAP."

"Oh my God," Myra whimpered in fear.

Granger quickly peeked around the partition to see that the woman with the ponytail was whispering frightened words to the older woman; she was also pointing in the direction of the cubicle within which he was seated. He zipped the valise closed and stood. Both women wore horrified looks at the sight of him. The older of the two turned, burst out of the safe-deposit room, and called out in desperation to a black-haired woman in a business suit who was walking through the bank. That bitch must be one of the New York detectives, he concluded. He pulled his gun and ordered the woman to stop.

Savage had no choice but to sit tight and wait. He would watch all three doors. When Granger popped out of wherever, that's when he'd drop the net on the rat bastard. He only hoped that Winona's timing was good, and that she would either well precede Granger's eventual exit or follow some time after. Realizing that his gun was packed in luggage deep inside the Mustang's trunk, Savage snatched the keys from the ignition and hopped quickly from behind the wheel to retrieve it. It was too late.

George Granger exited the bank, holding an automatic to the head of Winona Escalante, whom he was using as a shield.

"Stop right there, asshole," Granger barked, stopping Savage in his tracks. "You're the only son of a bitch out here," he went on, "so you must be the other cop."

"Give it up, George," Savage said evenly, car keys still in hand. "The game is over."

"The fuck it is," Granger replied angrily. "I'm getting into my car and I'm outta here. You make a move for a gun, and I'm going to blow your partner's pretty brains all over this fucking lot. *Understand?*"

"I hear you, George," Savage replied, again evenly, moving slowly and unthreateningly in the direction of the wild-eyed man. When he had gotten to within ten feet, he lifted his shirt. "Got no guns, George—see," he said. "We are not armed. She isn't even a police officer. If you hurt her, things will only go a lot worse for you."

"Toss the car keys to your girlfriend, asshole."

Savage carefully lobbed the keys to Winona. She caught them.

"Just drop them in my shirt pocket, sweetie pie," Granger ordered. She complied.

"No weapons?" he laughed evilly. "Gee, ain't that a fuckin' shame. Little old Georgie's got the drop on two New York City fuckin' hotshots." Granger motioned Savage back with the gun. "Get outta my way, motherfucker," he said.

"Can't do that, Georgie," Savage replied matter-of-factly, not moving, still blocking the man's path to the Mercury.

Holding the automatic in his right hand, Granger pressed its thick barrel tightly up under Winona's chin and advanced toward Savage. "I'm leaving here, cop, and you can't do a fucking thing about it."

"Oh, I think I can," Savage replied cockily. For only a millisecond, he made intense eye contact with Winona; she was staring intently back at him. The lady looked afraid, but she still looked savvy. He had no choice but to trust her overall smarts and instincts.

"What do you think *you're* gonna do?" Granger snarled. "Call out the fucking marines?"

"I'm gonna ask this lovely lady to dance," Savage replied, again exchanging intense eye contact with Winona Escalante. The message conveyed in his eyes was simply *do it*.

"How about it, ma'am?" Savage said, smiling artfully. "Would you care to dance?"

"Huh?" Granger grunted, almost amused.

The message had made it through. At that very instant Winona Escalante raised her right leg and stomped the heel of her black pump into Granger's unprotected right instep.

The man howled loudly and reared back, momentarily losing his grip on the woman, who broke entirely free. In that instant, Savage was on him.

George Granger was strong, Savage instantly realized, deceptively strong, and the bastard still controlled the goddamned gun, which he now held high above his head, clutched tightly in both hands. He wasn't going to go easy. Savage dug against the hot pavement with his sneakers to get as much leverage as he could and leaned heavily against Granger, reaching both of his hands up the man's long right arm to wrest the weapon away. Granger, meanwhile, repeatedly elbowed Savage in the face with strong downward blows of his bony right elbow. Blood flowed freely from Savage's nose; he knew it had been broken.

"I'll bite you, motherfucker," Granger threatened in a gasping spittle-spewing snarl. "I've got fucking AIDS, and I'll pass it right along to your ass." Savage knew that to be a fact . . . but it was too damn late to let go now. This was do or die—but he couldn't permit himself to be bitten.

Savage strained with every ounce of his power until he had wrestled Granger into a clockwise spin. They whirled like tightly coupled crazed dervishes, dancing right off the sidewalk edge onto the tarmac of the parking lot. Savage leaned into Granger's torso with his left shoulder and began to push against him with everything he had. Granger's momentary loss of balance was all Savage needed to get some momentum. He dug in, pushed, and shoved until the off balance Granger began reeling backwards like a sacked quarterback fighting for footing. Savage continued pushing the taller man, building greater and greater momentum. The movement ceased abruptly when he rammed the man against the front fender of the Avis Mercury, the sheet metal crumpling like Reynolds Wrap when impacted by their combined speed and mass.

Still clutched tightly together, the two men rolled off the car and fell to the pavement. Incredible pain raced through Savage's arm as he landed heavily on his left elbow. The gun, no longer held high above

Granger's head, was now at chest level, the property of both men, each with a frantic half share. Faces pressed together, Savage could smell the man's foul ashtray breath; it was assaulting him in the form of heavy and deep animal grunts and gasps.

Savage realized that the painful fall onto his elbow was taking its toll, greatly diminishing his combined arm strength. Fucking Granger, however, seemed to be getting stronger by the second. Savage had learned a long time ago that it was almost impossible to win a fight with a crazy man—he knew the balance of power was shifting in Granger's favor. It was then that he first felt the barrel tip of the automatic poking and twisting beneath his chin.

Knowing his resources were quickly waning—and that he had very little time left before a 9-millimeter round would go crashing through his brain—Savage made a decision. He would disregard all pain in his body and make a final all-out effort.

Suddenly, the brutal explosion of a single gunshot rang out from the automatic.

THIRTY-FIVE

Jesus. What am I doing here? Carroll Xavier Henderson thought as he strode across Eighty-first Street and focused ahead at the sidewalk awning lettered THE CONNAUGHT.

Dressing up like an off-duty ballet dancer is not at all what I thought police work would be like. I can't wait to get enough seniority to be assigned to a damn radio car.

"May I help you?" an unsmiling doorman asked tartly as Henderson swung into the building's Art Deco lobby.

"I am here to see Mr. Harley Hopkins," Henderson said in his softest voice. The doorman's name tag identified him as Clifton.

"And you are?" Clifton said.

"My name is Carroll Henderson." The rookie discerned the man's millisecond reaction to his first name; that invariably happened.

"And your business?" Clifton pressed, looking him up and down.

"I'm an actor." Why is this guy asking me my business? Henderson thought. He's got some friggin' nerve. He reminded himself to remain passive and go along with whatever.

"I see," Clifton replied, still looking him up and down. He eventually moved to a desk phone, picked up the receiver, and punched in a few digits. Apparently it rang many times before being answered.

"Good morning, sir. I trust I did not awaken you." Clifton finally said in a newfound subservient tone.

"There is somebody down here to see you . . . a young man." The doorman then turned his back and carried on a whispered conversation inaudible to Henderson's ears.

"Stand over there," Clifton directed, pointing to a spot near a center lobby sofa.

Henderson meekly complied.

"Now look up in the direction of that camera next to the wall clock."

Henderson again complied, noting that it was nine fifteen. Clifton turned and again spoke in inaudible whispers.

This was just what the detectives had predicted might happen, Henderson thought as he stood there trying his best to look savvy and, at the same time, vulnerable.

Suddenly the doorman held up the receiver. "Mr. Hopkins wishes to have a word with you."

Here goes, Henderson thought nervously as he moved toward the phone. He sensed the wall-mounted closed-circuit camera in the lobby following his every step; he was also aware that there were more of those cameras in the halls of the twenty-third floor should he ever get up there.

He took the receiver from Clifton's hand, cleared his throat, and said gently, "Good morning, Mr. Hopkins. I hope I haven't caught you at a bad time."

"Just what is it that you want?" a very polished voice responded directly.

"I wish to see *you,* sir."

"Make an appointment with the people at my agency. We're in the book."

"Yes, sir. I know that, sir. But I'm scheduled to catch a flight at JFK in a few hours. I'll be in Austria for the next three weeks."

"That's your problem. Call my agency when you return."

"I know that's my problem, Mr. Hopkins," Henderson said, feeling confidence grow with each exchange. He always could ad-lib very well. "But it would mean so much if you could spare me just a little of your time."

"How did you know to come here?"

"We have a mutual dear friend, who wishes me to bring along his warmest regards," Henderson replied.

"And who might that mutual friend be?"

"John Holloway."

There came a protracted silence.

"Just how well do you know John Boy?" Hopkins finally asked. Henderson sensed that the man was intrigued.

"Quite well, sir. We were once roommates." Henderson concentrated on keeping a passive voice level. "He often spoke of you—in glowing terms, I might add—and suggested that the three of us ought to get together sometime. He thought that we would very much like each other's style."

"Unh. Tell me about our mutual friend," Hopkins said, testing, clearly not entirely satisfied with the visitor's veracity. "Do you know where John Boy currently is?"

"John is out of the country. He left several weeks ago for Amsterdam."

"Unh," Hopkins grunted thoughtfully. "Tell me, young man, what is your name?"

"Carroll."

"No, I mean your first name."

"That is my first name," Henderson replied.

"You're a very good-looking young man . . . Carroll," Hopkins said.

"Thank you."

"Do you like older men?" Hopkins asked outright.

"I'm told that I'll like you."

"What time did you say your flight was?"

Henderson glanced at his watch. "One thirty, Mr. Hopkins. But I must be at the airport at least an hour before."

"Well, then, we don't have much time, do we?" Hopkins said.

"No, sir, we surely don't."

"Put Clifton back on the phone."

Henderson passed the receiver to the doorman, who had a brief exchange on the line. Seconds later, Henderson was escorted to the bank of elevators.

"Press for the twenty-third floor," Clifton said. "When you get off, turn to the right and go to number two-three-oh-one. Mr. Hopkins' apartment occupies the entire southeast corner of the floor. Rap twice and wait. Mr. Hopkins will buzz you in."

As the elevator made its smooth ascent, Henderson opened the shoulder bag and triggered the radio.

"He's home and he's letting me come up. He's got the entire southeast wing, apartment two-three-oh-one."

"Ten-four," came Jack Lindstrom's acknowledgment. "When you're ready for us, just trigger the portable twice. We'll be waiting in the stairwell."

Henderson slipped the radio back into the shoulder bag and switched on the recorder. At the twenty-third floor, he exited the elevator and followed the classically decorated and thickly carpeted hallway around to suite 2301. He rapped twice firmly on the black-lacquered door and waited. He could feel himself on camera. Suddenly, there came a buzzing sound and he heard a latch electronically disengage. Henderson pushed tentatively against the door, and it swung quietly on smooth hinges. He swallowed twice and slowly entered the suite.

The anteroom was large, probably bigger than his entire apartment, Henderson thought. The floor was an intricately grained and highly polished white marble that reflected the subtle glow of a dimmed-down crystal chandelier that hung above; the mushroom-shaped fixture provided the only light in the windowless room. An ancient tapestry, threadbare in spots from antiquity, covered one entire far wall. A variety of oils in many different periods decorated the remaining walls, and two tall Oriental urns framed the wide passage into the balance of the endless suite. The place felt eerily cold. Henderson caught a whiff of sweet aromatic incense and heard what sounded like sensuous human moans recorded over muted music, the melody and instruments unlike anything he'd ever heard before. He didn't know why, but for some reason he decided it was Egyptian.

"Do come in, Carroll."

Harley Hopkins' soft voice was emanating from somewhere beyond the next room. The man's tone, though loud enough to be heard, was gentle, breathy, and clearly meant to be seductive. Henderson swallowed nervously and, with his bag tucked tightly beneath his arm, slowly advanced.

"Keep coming, Carroll," the breathy voice urged. "Don't be afraid. I'm in the very next room . . . the parlor."

And was he ever . . .

Seated in an Indian squat—Pooh-Bah style—on a large circular cushion in the middle of the room, was the very naked Broadway impresario Harley Hopkins. Large round eyes bulged from his unusually large head as though he had some sort of terminal thyroid disorder. He was very nearly bald—and unbelievably fat. The loose, hanging blubber of his short arms melded into the thick rolls of blubber on his sweaty and hairless chest. The blubber collection burgeoned at his belly, each successive roll expanding, giving him the shape of a massive mutant pear—or the Michelin Man.

Hopkins was watching an all-male porno movie being projected on a large wall-mounted flat-screen monitor. In the flick, a pumped-up and pharaoh-bearded, well-hung white guy was having his way with several Nubian slaves. A half-assed rendering of the Great Pyramid of Giza provided the cheesy backdrop.

Carroll Xavier Henderson was speechless. The repeating thought *What the freak is a nice Irish boy like me doing here?* spun in his head like a mirrored ball on steroids.

Harley Hopkins finally pulled his eyes from the screen. He faced Henderson and smiled lasciviously while slowly stroking his very odd-looking erection. The thing was long and ugly, tapered to a point, like a damn carrot.

The mirrored ball in his head stopped spinning long enough for Henderson to think . . . Jabba the Hutt.

"Do make yourself at home, Carroll," Hopkins said. "Come in and get comfortable. Do you like this room?" he asked. "John Boy and I have partied here on so many wonderful occasions."

Henderson gulped. He reached into his bag, triggered the portable radio twice, and removed his police shield. After clearing his throat, he held out the shield in much the way one might hold out a crucifix to a vampire and announced, "I'm Police Officer Henderson. I'm here to ask you some questions."

Harley Hopkins' jaw dropped. He picked up a remote, aimed it at the wall screen, and clicked. Both the movie and the weird Egyptian music ceased. The room fell totally silent.

"What is this?" Hopkins finally said, a sly grin appearing on his fat face. "Is this some kind of a joke?" The man's smile grew wider, as if something had dawned. "You don't look like no damned cop. Did John Boy put you up to this?" he asked.

"This is no joke, Mr. Hopkins," Henderson assured him. "I am a policeman. Please wait right there."

Carroll Xavier Henderson quick-walked back through the apartment to the anteroom. He opened the apartment door and let the three detectives step in.

"This is an outrage," Hopkins snarled, pulling on a red satin robe as the detective team entered the parlor. "You can't come busting into my home like this. This has got to be unconstitutional."

"Mr. Hopkins, you invited this officer in. I'm Detective Jack Lindstrom from Manhattan South Homicide."

"Homicide?" Hopkins echoed, his bug eyes about to pop totally from his head.

"We are investigating a murder," Lindstrom went on. "And—"

"*And* you think that I might know anything about a damned fucking *murder.*" Hopkins' voice was rising. He was hot, and he was getting hotter.

Lindstrom nodded "get lost" to the others, who stepped out of the parlor.

"If we had come here and announced ourselves downstairs and requested to see you, you would have declined to see us," Lindstrom said. "However, this is an emergency."

"I would not decline to let you in," Hopkins objected.

"You screen everybody," Lindstrom declared. "You would have simply acted as if you were not at home."

Hopkins licked his lips nervously, but he did not deny the officer's statement.

"We need some information on John Boyer Holloway," Lindstrom said. "We've got to know if he had any scars, marks, or tattoos *anywhere* on his body."

"I don't know anybody by that name," Hopkins replied defiantly.

"We know that Holloway spent the night here with you before he left for Amsterdam."

"Bullshit."

"Officer Henderson had a recorder rolling minutes ago when you volunteered about all the good times you and John Boy Holloway had in this very room," Lindstrom advised.

His wide nostrils flaring in anger, Hopkins crossed his arms defensively and remained silent.

"Mr. Hopkins," Lindstrom said sincerely, "you help us, and we go away; it will be as if we were never ever here."

The fat man's bug eyes locked on Lindstrom.

"Never here?" Hopkins murmured.

"Never here," Lindstrom assured him.

"What about that fucking tape?"

Jack Lindstrom called out for Henderson. When the

rookie entered the room, Lindstrom held out his hand. "Give me the recorder," he said.

Henderson handed over the mini-Sony and again left the room. Lindstrom popped the tape from the recorder, dropped the recorder into his jacket pocket, and laid the tape down on a nearby cocktail table. "So, Mr. Hopkins, can we talk?"

Five minutes later, Detective Jack Lindstrom returned to the roof of the Connaught. He flipped open his cell phone, leaned against a parapet, and dialed the number of Thorn Savage's cell phone. He hoped to Christ they'd have a good connection.

Savage answered after five rings. In the background, Lindstrom could hear lots of commotion—sirens, loud voices, even some police radio chatter.

"What the hell's going on, boss?" Lindstrom inquired.

"We just caught up with George Granger," Savage replied, sounding out of breath, speaking loudly over the background din.

"Is he in custody?" Lindstrom said, excited.

"No," Savage replied flatly. "Right now, he's in a body bag."

"Jeez."

"Look, Jack. Don't want to rush you, but at the moment I'm up to my friggin' eyeballs in post-shots-fired bullshit. What have you got? Tell me you succeeded on that Harley Hopkins thing. According to my clock, that cremation is probably just about to begin."

"Oh, yeah. We succeeded, boss. But you just ain't gonna fuckin' believe what we found out."

"Try me," Savage replied curtly.

"Remember how Holloway had supposedly sometimes been referred to as the Visible Man?"

"Yeah."

"Have you ever heard of a skin condition known as vitiligo?"

"I know the word from crossword puzzles," Savage replied. "But . . ."

"It's an extremely rare skin disease characterized by smooth white patches on various parts of the body. It's caused by the loss of the natural pigment."

"Holloway has this condition?"

"Yep," Lindstrom replied. "But you'll never guess where."

"You're kidding?"

"Nope. Hopkins swears to it. If that cremation hasn't yet taken place, maybe Cosenza could have the DOA's penis examined. If it's spotted, bleached, appears stonewashed, or you can see through it . . . it's fuckin' Holloway."

THIRTY-SIX

The least Sardinian of all the island's towns, Olbia was plagued with traffic on its narrow streets, which traced through long blocks of ugly apartment houses. At the foot of San Simplicio, opposite the little basilica by the same name, was the nineteenth-century building that housed the Mortuary DiNatale.

Captain Silvio Cosenza, a balding, middle-aged man with a round cherubic face and a two-pack-a-day smoking habit, paced on the sidewalk in front of the mortuary; he'd arrived ten minutes earlier. At five minutes after four, a green Fiat taxicab carrying Mrs. Hazel Holloway and her son's traveling companion, John Anson Conover, arrived.

"Sorry that we are a few minutes late," Conover apologized. "We stopped at the hotel and arranged for Mrs. Holloway's lodging and left her bags."

Cosenza nodded, dropped the stub of an unfiltered cigarette to the pavement, and crushed it with his shoe. The three then entered the mortuary.

They trailed behind Arturo DiNatale, who led them to the back of his baroque and somber establishment into the preparation room. As they stood by, waiting in reverential silence, DiNatale then entered a smaller refrigerated room and rolled out a gurney on which lay a sheet-draped human body.

"Are you sure that you are up to this, Mrs. Holloway?" John Conover gently asked the woman, showing great concern.

Dabbing at her eyes with a tissue, she murmured simply, "Yes. After all, I've come all this way."

Captain Cosenza nodded, and Arturo DiNatale partially drew back the sheet, revealing the upper half of the battered body.

"Oh, my God," Hazel Holloway whimpered, extracting another tissue from her bag. Conover placed his arm around her and hugged her for support.

"Is that your son?" Cosenza inquired.

"Well . . ." the woman hedged, a sickened question mark forming across her drawn face. "It does . . . *sort of* look like him."

"But, Signora, are you not sure?" Cosenza asked, not really surprised at the woman's inability or reluctance to firmly state a positive. Was she just holding on to a shadow of a doubt as a mother might? Or was she putting on a good act?

"Well, it's his face," she murmured, her tone unsure. "It's just so hard to . . ."

"I understand, Mrs. Holloway," Cosenza gently assured her. "But nobody knows their children like a mother does. Perhaps you can tell us if your son had any birthmarks or scars, any tattoos maybe?"

"None . . . nothing."

"Are you certain, Signora?" Cosenza pressed, frowning. "Even a skin condition of some sort which could help us with this identification?"

"Well," Hazel Holloway said, wiping at a tear, "he had this port wine stain—it was in the shape of a small heart—up under his left armpit. It is not at all easy to see."

Cosenza again nodded to DiNatale. The solemn mortician carefully rolled the body and pulled back the left arm. The tiny heart-shaped port wine stain was there.

"That's him," Hazel Holloway cried, all emotion bursting forth. She turned to Conover, who gently embraced her.

Conover glanced at Cosenza. "Will that be all, Captain?" he asked. Cosenza again nodded, and Conover began to lead the bawling woman from the preparation room out toward the mortuary proper.

"Signora," Arturo DiNatale said, stopping them,

"do we have your permission to now proceed with the cremation?"

Hazel Holloway looked tearfully at John Conover, then faced the diminutive mortician. "Yes, you may." She glanced once more at the body and cried, "Goodbye, my darling."

DiNatale drew the sheet fully back over the body and rolled the gurney away.

Cosenza followed Hazel Holloway and John Conover out of the preparation room. In the mortuary proper he signaled to two plainclothes policemen who had been waiting there. They blocked the man and woman's path to the mortuary exit door.

"What's the meaning of this, Captain?" Conover asked.

"I'm afraid that I must ask you to come with me and one of these other officers into another room," Cosenza replied. "The other officer will wait here with Signora Holloway."

"For what reason?" Conover said guardedly.

"We will explain that to you in the next room," Cosenza said. "Please . . ." He motioned toward the men's room door.

A visibly rattled Conover, seeing no alternative, grudgingly complied with the request.

"What is it that you want?" he asked, once all three men were inside the bathroom.

"Remove your trousers, please," Cosenza directed.

"What?"

"Remove your trousers, sir."

"You can't make me do that," Conover protested. "I won't do that."

"You are in my country now," Cosenza said with no equivocation. "You will do as I say, or we will help you do it."

Two minutes later, Captain Silvio Cosenza poked his head from the men's room door and motioned to the plainclothesman who had waited outside with Mrs. Holloway. The officer produced a set of handcuffs and requested that Mrs. Holloway hold up her wrists.

THIRTY-SEVEN

After having been delayed for several hours before taking off from Miami, the flight back to New York City turned out also to be a bumpy one, arriving at LaGuardia shortly before one a.m. Tails dragging, Savage and Winona Escalante toted their bags to the unmarked he'd left in long-term parking. He drove her directly to her hotel on Forty-second Street.

"It's been a long, long day," she said, as he pulled up in front of the Grand Hyatt.

"Sure has," he replied.

"Will you be in the office tomorrow morning?" she asked.

"Oh, yeah," he replied. "I'll be there by eight thirty."

"Well, then . . . I guess I'll see you there."

Savage popped the trunk release, and they both climbed out of the car.

"Room eight-four-eight," she said to the blue-jacketed bellman who appeared on the sidewalk as if by magic. The man tipped his cap, lifted both her bags from the trunk, and disappeared into the lobby with them.

"Guess I can't talk you into coming upstairs to see my etchings," she said, playfully batting the lids of very tired eyes.

His decline was delivered with an I'm-sorry grimace.

"You're a good man, Charlie Brown," Winona Escalante said evenly. "I wish there was somebody like you waiting for me to get home to in Indiana."

He nodded, smiled, and gave her a gentle hug. She

turned and walked into the hotel without looking back over her shoulder. He closed the trunk, got back in the car, and drove slowly off.

By some miracle, probably because of the late hour, he discovered a parking spot directly in front of his apartment house. He grabbed his soft-sided from the backseat, climbed the stoop, and checked his mailbox in the outer entrance foyer—just a few ads. Letting himself into the building, he climbed the squeaky wooden staircase to the second floor, and unlocked the door of apartment 2. Once inside, he flipped on the living room lights and set his bag on top of the dinette table. He signed in contentment; it was good to be home.

He was stunned when he heard a faint, yet oh so familiar meow. He whirled to see Ray tucked comfortably in the meat-loaf position on the middle cushion of his sofa. The big tom stared back at him with huge golden eyes.

"How did you get here, big guy?" Savage said, elated, not believing what he saw. Crossing quickly toward the sofa, he was met halfway by a slower-moving-than-usual Ray, who had jumped down to the floor to greet him.

"I brought him," Maureen said, her voice a gentle whisper. She had appeared from the bedroom, dressed in a satin nightgown. "The vet said he could go home this afternoon. He still has some weakness, but he's ninety percent back to his old self. She said it was a miracle."

Savage picked up the cat, stroked his neck, and turned to gaze tightly into Maureen's eyes. He searched for the anger he expected to find. He did not see any.

"I hope you don't mind that I decided to stay and spend the night," she said.

"No, not at all," he declared, totally befuddled by the change in his fortune. "But I'm guessing that we've got something you want to talk about."

Maureen shrugged, and a single tear rolled down

her cheek. "After I tried reaching you on Friday night," she said, "I decided to go out to the Hamptons by myself first thing Saturday morning. I purposely left my cell phone home. I just wanted some time alone to do some real soul-searching."

"I can explain everything," he said, his tone low yet assured. "It's not at all what you might think."

"I believe that," Maureen said, wiping away the tear. "I had plenty of time to think about us—you and me—while I laid on the beach. I realized just how vital you are to my existence, Thornton Savage. I also realized that somehow maybe I'd forgotten that."

Savage didn't know what to say.

Maureen gently took his free hand. "We can talk in the morning," she said. "Right now, all I want to do is climb in bed and wrap my arms around the man I love."

She reached over and switched off the light.

JOHN MACKIE

Novels of the NYPD

MANHATTAN NORTH
0-451-41095-5

A vicious Harlem drug dealer has been killed and a
patron of the arts is the main suspect. For Detective
Sergeant Thornton Savage, Manhattan South
homicide, this case is going to take him to streets
meaner than ever before.

MANHATTAN SOUTH
0-451-41045-9

Welcome to the Manhattan South homicide squad.
Today's assignment: a triple murder in a
chic Midtown bistro. NYPD sergeant Thornton
Savage suspects a professional hit.
But the truth is far more complicated.

EAST SIDE
0-451-41141-2

With the New York Archdiocese, the mayor,
and the police commissioner all cranking up the
political heat, Thornton Savage and the Manhattan
South homicide team are in a race to catch a
priest-killer before he strikes again.

Available wherever books are sold or at penguin.com

Penguin Group (USA)
is proud to present
GREAT READS—GUARANTEED!

**We are so confident that you will love
this book that we are offering a
100% money-back guarantee!**

If you are not 100% satisfied with
this publication, Penguin Group (USA)
will refund your money!
Simply return the book before
December 1, 2005 for a full refund.

**With a guarantee like this one,
you have nothing to lose!**